I0573970

Brittle Systems

AN ICF STORY

Xander Franklin

Meddleworks Publishing

Previous Books From The ICF Universe:
Absolute Zeros

*For my wife Kati, the world's greatest
arm-chair detective.*

*And for all the support crews sweating it
out just to keep the mission running.*

BRITTLE SYSTEMS

Prologue:

The ICF freighter bounced and wove through empty space, out-flanking an enemy that could not pursue. Standard practice, all deep-jet runs concluded with a series of evasive maneuvers designed to max-imize survivability under fire. The fact that the *Hendrix* was not cur-rently under fire, and that its last mission had been to a mining colony under peaceful, albeit disgruntled, trade rule by the Coalition Republic, mattered very little to standard practice. It was written into the poli-cies of the Interstellar Coalition Force that all deep-jet runs were to be accompanied by the execution of one of the six proprietary maneuver sequences designed by a highly paid team of twelve experts, all care-fully versed in strategic survivability policy, but without a single logged flight hour among them. So it was written in ICF policy, so shall it be done.

The light within *Hendrix's* cargo module was dim and red. Reed-Sergeant Harbison bumped against his nylon harness, jostled by the freighter's maneuvers as it tumbled along, alone in the vast shipping lane. He ignored the turbulence, his grim stoicism betrayed only by the movement of his long hair as it flopped over his grey eyes. He ignored that too, waiting for the next bump to flip it back in place as he stared straight ahead across the cramped confines of the module. The rest of his platoon lined the wall on his left, quietly bouncing against the ny-lon straps of their jump seats. There was a cough from one of the men seated near the end, and Sergeant Harbison's flinty eyes shifted, momentarily honing in on the source of the sound. Another twist in the ship's trajectory brought the muffled clang of boots on alloy as their feet briefly lifted off the ground. A hush hung over the exhausted platoon, and Sergeant Harbison returned his gaze to the far wall, counting down to himself.

Eight...seven...six... His train of thought was interrupted by the firing of repulsors along the fore of the ship, slowing the *Hendrix* down and stabilizing it along its route. Sergeant Harbison frowned. They'd dropped out of maneuvers five seconds early, an unwelcome irregularity capping off what had already been a frustrating and erratic mission. The creases around his mouth deepened as he thought. It was possible that his count was off, but he banished that thought with a shake of his head. Reed-Sergeant Harbison held the entirety of the universe in suspicious contempt, but in himself he placed full trust.

The ship leveled off, and the silence in the cargo hold was broken by the clicks of harnesses being released. All along the left wall men stood, stretched, and shifted to a more comfortable spot in the module. Sergeant Harbison held still, ignoring the protests of his stiff limbs, suspicious as he was of outside forces like time and age acting against him. The frown held fast on his face as his eyes flitted around the module, finally fixing on a Trooper still seated near the far end, leaning forward with his head in his hands. The Reed-Sergeant studied the young man while a series of analyses and calculations ran through his mind. None of the outcomes sat well with him.

A scowl twitched through him, showing only in a slight hardening in the line of his mouth. He unclipped his harness and rose, feeling, rather than hearing, a series of pops from within as his back aligned itself. With swift, confident movements he made his way across the module, his gaze never wavering from Private Wurley's seated form. Sidestepping one Trooper and over the sprawled legs of another, Sergeant Harbison drew abreast of the young man. With an air of forced casualness, he dropped himself lightly in the seat next to the Trooper. If Wurley noticed, he didn't show it, still staring at the space between his boots, his elbows resting on his knees.

Sergeant Harbison studied him in silence, his face impassive as he forced himself into mindset of the younger Trooper. It had been sixteen years since he'd joined the Commando Raiders, stepping aboard the gangplank of a module much like this one, his boots still shiny and clean. He had forgotten what it was like in the long years since, to be unsure of the universe and your place in it. Sergeant Harbison raised a hand and patted it on the Private's shoulder.

"How's it, Wurley?" He flashed what was intended to be a fatherly smile, but his eyes were cold and searching.

Private Wurley said nothing, a small tremor ran through his body. Sergeant Harbison picked up his hand and patted the shoulder again.

"You all right, son?"

Silence again.

He cleared his throat, ready to try again when he was interrupted by a shake of Wurley's head.

"I...I'm fine, Sarge." The Private's voice was flat, quiet as he continued to stare at the floor.

"You sure, son?" The Reed-Sergeant's voice was level and firm. "Nerves can get the jump on any—

"S'not nerves, Sarge," Wurley interrupted, looking up suddenly. "I just didn't think..."

Sergeant Harbison held very still, giving the young man space to breathe. His hand was still on Wurley's shoulder when he spoke again.

"I just didn't think it'd go down like that."

The young private dropped his head, eyes on the floor.

The smile slipped off the Reed-Sergeant's face.

"Like what, son?" He feigned ignorance. "The egress? A little rough, sure. Truth be told you'll see a lot worse in time an' be whole about it."

Private Wurley shook his head. "No, Sarge, not the egress. The mission. All of it." He locked eyes with the Reed-Sergeant. "I just don't get it. You said we were there to retrieve some intel, collecting on the Kickerland Movement. We met our source six miles from the scheduled objective. It's just some guy driving a beat-up BredRan with a crate in the back. No tablets, no flashfiles, just a big crate. We secure the package, get ready to evac and then, boom, Corstley shoots him."

At the mention of the name, Sergeant Harbison flicked his eyes over to the bearded Buck-Sergeant. Sergeant Corstley's eyes narrowed, his hand twitching near his waistline, but the Reed-Sergeant waved him off with a slight shake of his head.

Private Wurley was still going, working himself up and oblivious to the exchange. "...I mean, maybe that guy had a weapon, maybe I just didn't see it. But I dunno, it just felt too...quick. We load the crate, then bang, that guy's down. One shot, dead. It felt off."

Sergeant Harbison tried once more for the fatherly smile, but the hard mouth merely twitched.

"Son, I think you're getting wrapped up on the wrong axle," the Reed-Sergeant soothed. He could feel the weight of the platoon's stares watching him and the young Private.

"Basentz reached for a weapon, you just didn't see it 'cause of the glare. An' Corstley's a quick shot. Damn well should be after all these years." Sergeant Harbison forced a laugh. "Spend enough time in the Raiders' an' you'll get there too."

He waved his left hand across the room, his right still on Wurley's shoulder.

"Takes time to get used to this unit. Sometimes I get surprised myself. Right, Zimmer?"

The broad Special-Trooper nodded, crossing the cargo module and settling in the seat on Wurley's other side.

"Right, Sarge," said Zimmer, his voice gravelly and slow. "Train hard, get harder."

Sergeant Harbison shifted his gaze from Zimmer back to Wurley's watery eyes. "See, son, it just takes some settling. Then you'll be right in the thick of it."

He moved his hand from the Private's shoulder to rub the back of his neck.

"I guess so Sarge." Wurley's shoulders slumped, giving in to the weight of the NCO's logic. The Reed-Sergeant relaxed slightly, letting a small breath escape as he swept his eyes around the room.

"Sarge, there's just one last thing that I don't get."

Sergeant Harbison felt, rather than saw, Wurley tense again.

"When we were loading on the module and got ambushed. We were taking fire and, God, they were so close. All around and right on us."

The Sergeant stared down at the young man, watching his hands shake.

"We were just getting the door closed when one of them called out to us, yelling something about 'Barrett Harbison.' I dunno, I just don't get it, Sarge."

Wurley locked eyes with the Reed-Sergeant, the shake in his hands had progressed to his shoulders.

"Your name, Sarge. How'd they know your name?"

The next moment was swift, its action marked only by its silence. Sergeant Harbison's right hand shifted, encircling his arm around Wurley's neck while his left pushed down on the back of his head. Special-Trooper Zimmer clamped down on the Private's hands, holding him down while the Sergeant squeezed. Wurley thrashed under their grasp, throwing his head back, trying to smash the bridge of the Sergeant's nose. Sergeant Harbison tucked his head into his shoulder, flexing his arm and cutting off the carotid. He held on long after the Private was still, counting down to himself.

Three...two...one. He lifted his head from his shoulder, nodding to Zimmer and releasing his grasp. Private Wurley slumped forward against the nylon restraints of his jump seat. Sergeant Harbison stood up, the frown etched deep in the creases of his face.

"Zimmer, Kantz!" he barked. "Clean this shit up. Bonsly, Huges, find his gear!"

He pointed to the bearded Buck-Sergeant. "Corstley, scrub his dossier when we dock. I want him de-indexed from this mission."

Sergeant Corstley nodded. "AWOL, suicide, or accident?"

The Reed-Sergeant thought for a moment before shaking his head. "Neither, he boarded with us right before the mission. Delete his whole file. Scrub him out entirely."

The bearded man nodded again, whistling softly as he checked his fingernails.

The Reed-Sergeant turned back to the rest of the platoon, supervising as the men loaded Wurley into the IncinUnit in the back of the module. He watched as they first dumped the body, then his weapon, then his two black gear bags, piling it up in the narrow stall. Zimmer and Huges struggled with the sliding door, kicking the young man's hand into the stall as they slammed it closed. Kantz pressed the orange button on the side, and for a moment the cargo module lit up with the flash of Private Wurley's de-atomization into component elements.

Designed for use in the wake of a total mission failure, the IncinUnit was a powerful tool for disposing of mission logs, classified gear, and intel—anything that might jeopardize the secrecy of the Commando Raiders. It fell in line with the first rule written in the *Raiders' Handbook*;

'I will let nothing compromise my mission, nor the security of the Raider unit!' Sergeant Harbison cracked a small smile as he watched the Troopers sweep up the ashen remains into a small grate in the stall's floor.

So it was written, so it shall be done...

Chapter 1:

Ian Bernard awoke to the soft sounds of a toddler vomiting. His eyes crept open, blearily making out the numerals illuminated above his bed. It was three a.m. and just for a moment, all was still. Silence pervaded the small apartment, the kind that hangs in the air in the early hours of the morning when the blankets are warm and the body is tired. Ian succeeded in convincing himself it was just his imagination, and the eyes crept closed again.

A low wail rolled out from the room down the hall. Soft at first, it lilted and rose like a siren in the distance before cutting off with a muted hiccup.

Ian's eyes snapped open. The floating blue numerals above him spelled out 03:02. He shut his eyes tight, and for a moment pretended that he was still asleep. Uncharitable prayers ran through his mind, all centering on what sound would come in the next few seconds.

From down the hall came a sniffle, and then a whisper. "Daaaaaabby."

His prayers ignored, Ian sighed and resigned himself to getting up. Eyes still shut, he dragged himself upright, jostling his wife's arm as much as possible along the way.

"He called for you," she muttered and defiantly turned deeper into the warm embrace of her pillow.

His bid for clemency ignored as well, Ian sighed again, dragging a hand across his face and rubbing his eyes open. He swung his legs over the edge of the bed, leaned forward, and grumbled in tones described during daylight hours as 'sullen,' but found to be perfectly acceptable after midnight. He bobbed his head, psyching himself for the task at hand, and pushed away from the bed.

The wail rose again as Ian shuffled down the hall, vividly imagining a time from before he was a parent. He flipped on every light as he passed, spitefully hoping the glare might reach his wife. Stopping at the threshold of his son's room, he peered into the warm gloom. His feet crushed into the thick pile carpeting, eyes still adjusting to the rosy glow from the *Whimsy Whale* nightlight humming in the corner. He padded over to the crib centered in the room, and the small, teary face hanging over its railing.

Little hands reached up for him. "Daaaaabby."

Ian reached down and scooped Taniel up by his armpits. At the sight of the large, brown stain obscuring the elephant on the front of his son's nightshirt, his nose crinkled. When the smell wafted over, he gagged, bile rising momentarily in the back of his throat. It had been over nine hours since he had last seen that chicken salad, and time had not been kind to his son's dinner. A quick grimace, along with a masterful gritting of teeth, and he succeeded in holding his own dinner down. A few short puffs of breath were enough to strengthen his resolve, and away they went.

Gingerly, Ian held out his son at arms' reach, waddling to the bathroom in the middle of the hall. He was joined along the way by a small, black tornado of fur swirling around his ankles. Having been disturbed from his slumber underneath the bedside table, his wife's middle-aged Scottish Terrier saw fit to investigate the source of this impertinence and vent its frustration with a few choice nips.

"Douglas, no! Go on, get out of here!" Ian hissed, stepping high to lift his feet out of range of the tiny, sharp teeth. Undeterred, the Scottie continued to visit his wrath upon the pale skin of his master's exposed ankles.

Ian plodded along, attempting to ignore the furry ball of fury with the same resolution by which Douglas ignored his muttered commands. He duck-walked his way to the bathroom, stepping across the threshold of the tiled sanctuary and slamming the door closed with his foot. Setting Taniel down, he breathed a sigh of relief as he sat on the closed lid of the toilet. Large brown eyes looked up at him out of tear-stained cheeks, overlooking a fat lip on the verge of quivering.

"Hey, hey, it's okay," Ian soothed, wiping a tear from his son's cheek as it started. "We'll get you cleaned up and back to bed."

Taniel nodded, screwing up a pudgy fist to wipe his other eye as Ian leaned over to activate the bath. Selecting the third preset button, he listened for a soft gong announcing the tub was filling. He undressed his son with quick, practiced movements, holding his breath as he folded the soiled garments into a neat square and placed them by the door. Back by the tub, Ian tested the water with the inside of his wrist. The tub had yet to fail in delivering water at exactly 96°, but he checked it anyway.

Ian lifted the toddler into the tub and gently bathed him, taking special care to wash out the chunks that had matted in his son's soft curls. Freshly clean, he lifted the boy out, dressed him in clothes pulled from the dispenser mounted on the wall, and carried him back off to bed. His son was half asleep by the time he set him down, and Ian tiptoed his way out of the room across the thick pile carpeting. Once in the hall, he turned to face the unwelcome sight of Douglas snuffling about in the pile of dirty clothes.

"Nooo, *don't!*" Ian warned, squeezing as much authority as he could out of the whispered syllables.

As usual, the terrier ignored him, digging deeper into the pile. Ian's heart sank as he watched the tell-tale gulping and shake of the dog's weak stomach play out as a tragedy across the hallway's new rug. As the smell washed over him, he felt a trembling churn rise through his body. This time, gritted teeth were not enough to save him.

It was a quarter to five by the time Ian crawled back into bed. As he sank into its warm confines, he pulled hard against the sheets tightly wound around his sleeping wife. A struggle ensued, ending when his hand slipped and punched himself square in the eye. He made do with a diagonal length of comforter just long enough to cover his right side up to the wrist, and fell into a dreamless sleep.

Three things occurred at exactly six o'clock that morning; the corrugated steel blinds encasing the windows ground open, flooding the small apartment with light; the floating numerals above Ian's bed transformed into a graphic of a rising sun accompanied by the soft tinkling of wind chimes; and in the kitchenette, the Bernards' venerable SimuCaff brewpot exploded.

Ian listened to the rusty squeal of the blinds, the alarm's gentle melody, and the sputter of the brewpot ejecting instant grounds and steaming water across the countertop. He took all of it in, accepted it, and clenched his eyes further shut. The mattress shifted beside him, Ian felt the light brush of lips on his cheek.

"I've got it, dear. Get ready for your trip."

Ian nodded, eyes still shut. The mattress creaked, and then he was alone, listening to the patter of slippers down the hall. He snapped his fingers twice and the wind chimes ceased—the room quiet save for the dulcet sounds of Suzette cursing under her breath as she cleaned up the mess on the counter. The weight of the day pressed upon him, and for a few moments he flirted with the idea of spending it in bed. Then the floating numerals above him changed to 06:05, his backup alarm began to sound, and Ian resigned himself to participating in his day.

For the second time that morning, Ian shuffled to the bathroom in the middle of the hall. He stepped around the new rug, still damp from his furious scrubbing, and shuffled past the stainless steel hatch to the laundry chute. He noted the smudge of soapy fingerprints on its handle, creating a new entry on his mental list of daily tasks. Ian liked lists; he liked creating them even more than finishing them. His current mental ledger boasted forty-seven entries, all slated to be accomplished before noon. He nestled this newest item at twenty-one, between the disposal of his dirty towel and retrieving his son for breakfast.

Ian stepped up to the speckled bathroom counter, aligning his tablet in its mentally marked space to the right of his toothbrush. The mirror in front of him lit up.

"Good morning, Ian," it chirped, the words dancing across his reflection in cheerful green letters. They faded away to display the date—20 August 2332.

Ian yawned and waved them away, allowing the inputs from his tablet to flow onto the mirror screen. His tailored newsfeed filled the edges of the glass, leaving a hollow spot in the center for him to use. A quick glance at the red-outlined box in the left corner and the *Republic News Network* began outlining the morning headlines.

"Interstellar Coalition Force ground troops report continued engagements on Karnassus, with the topic of sanctions once again raised on the floor of the Coalition Republic's Large Council," a stone-faced woman announced with the banal civility of someone who discusses genocide in between commercial breaks.

"Hmmm," Ian replied, bending over to retrieve his razor. A few of his classmates had deployed to Karnassus. To hear them tell it, the colonial separatists were deeply entrenched and well supplied. That close to the outer rim, a lot of planets chafed under colonial rule, generations of pioneer spirit pushing back against the warm, bureaucratic constraints of the Coalition Republic. Ian had never been to the outer rim. In fact, he had yet to leave Earth for any reason, but the stories of his classmates' deployments filled him with the creeping dread of someone who spent their whole life developing a healthy abhorrence for the entire concept of camping.

The newscaster changed topics to the category-six hurricane expected to make landfall in Richmond, and the preemptive shutdowns city officials were planning to the trio of reactors that surrounded the coastal city. Ian nodded along, presently engaged in chasing the last few hairs under his chin with his razor. He always shaved before he showered, ever since he read a lifestyle article declaring that shaving after a shower risked clogged pores and follicular splintering. He'd been horrified to learn he'd been shaving the wrong way his entire life. So consumed with worry, he wholly missed the final paragraph announcing the debut of the article's author's brand-new line of pre-wash, wet-or-dry men's razors, now open for delivery.

The steady drum of the news-speak filled the background of his morning ablutions as he went about completing lines thirteen (shower, test out new conditioner brand) through nineteen (brush teeth, order more toothpaste) off his mental list. Ian liked listening to the news. It gave him comfort to have the problems of the universe laid out for him each morning in cold, crisp diction. *'Forewarned is fore-armed,'* his father always said, and in that Ian took great comfort. Each day he armed himself by obsessively researching up-to-the-minute information for each item on his ever-growing list of worries. It allowed him to exert the smallest measure of control over the innumerable threats and inscrutable forces that shaped his world. And as a newly-minted Buck-Sergeant in the ICF, control over his world was in precious, short supply.

~~Ian strolled down the hall on his way to his son's room, pausing just a moment to clean the fingerprints from the stainless steel hatch (item twenty-one) off the laundry chute. The *Whimsy Whale* nightlight hummed faintly in the corner, Ian watched for a second as it reached its internal timer and quietly shut off. He nodded, satisfied, and turned around to an empty crib.~~

"*Already got him, dear,*" Suzette sang from the other room.

Ian nodded, crossing off another line. He smiled to himself, *ahead of schedule.*

The kitchenette was a scene of chaos, neatly contained into manageable boundaries by people who had spent the better part of fourteen months chasing the sticky whims of a small child. Butter and bits of pancake graced all four corners of the highchair where Taniel sat, presently attempting to lick syrup off his elbow. *None on the ceiling,* Ian mused after a quick inspection, *so at least we're making progress.* Suzette leaned against the sink, cleaning insta-grounds from under her fingernails.

Ian leaned in for a quick kiss. "Thanks for getting him, Sue. I appreciate it."

Suzette smiled a little, still examining her nails. "Got the pot going again—should have some fresh 'caff in a minute."

Ian bobbed his head, retrieving some mugs from the cabinet next to the sink. He felt a twinge of guilt as he placed them in front of the aging brewpot. She'd asked Ian for a new one years ago, but he kept deferring, the state of their finances remaining a top-list worry in his mind. A small gong rang from within the decrepit appliance, and he pulled the carafe, gently pouring a few draughts of the bitter, brown liquid into each mug. He handed a mug to Suzette, her soft thanks sending another pang of guilt through him. One of these days the SimuCaff brewpot would sputter its last, finally surpassing either of their mechanical expertise. On that day, Ian resolved himself to purchase the nice *Heuron Express* that Suzette had pointed out to him last year, the red deluxe model with the add-on frother for lattés. His guilt temporarily assuaged, he sipped a little from the mug before joining Suzette in extricating their son from the remains of breakfast.

A brief struggle ensued as they worked to separate child from chair and syrup from child. Ian dodged the swing of a sticky fist, wiping the corners of Taniel's mouth while Suzette concentrated on removing a wad of soggy paste from between his toes. Ian felt something soft and wet strike the back of his head.

"Oh dear, looks like he..."

"Yep, sure did..."

"Well, do you want me to..."

"No, no, I'll take care of it."

"Should you go now? What time do you need to be there?"

"Quarter to nine."

"It's half-past seven now."

Shit, Ian thought, glancing up to read the clock on the wall. He locked eyes with Suzette.

"Go. I've got it, dear."

Ian pecked her on the cheek and rose from the tangle of limbs and wipes. He rushed for the door, slipping on his uniform coat and boots as he passed, wallet clenched firmly between his teeth.

"Ian!"

He looked back to the kitchen, one hand on the door.

"Pancake."

He stared at her blankly. Suzette gestured to her head.

With a curse of recognition he stormed back to the bathroom in the hall, furiously dabbing the back of his head. He succeeded in removing the majority of it by the time he reached the tile floor, rinsing his hands and smoothing over his straight black hair. It, along with his tan skin and wide, dark brown eyes, were the legacy of an island-faring people whose ancestral lands disappeared beneath rising waters over two centuries ago.

Newly clean, he made his way down the hall again, intercepted along the way by Douglas' furious yapping around his heels. Staggering past the kitchenette, Ian waved goodbye to his family. He yanked the door open with both hands, made a half-hearted kick to throw the terrier off his trail, and stumbled through into the Manitoba sunshine.

It was a hot August day in Winnipeg, the air held the stifled, metallic tang common to most mega-cities. Ian filled his lungs as he leaned against the door, Douglas' muffled yips echoing faintly around the edges. He fished the tablet out of his pocket, unfolding the screen and pulling up his transport program with a flick of his thumb. A quick tap of his destination prompted a map highlighting the nearest access point and a small timer counting down to his ride. Ian snapped the tablet closed, stuffed it in a pocket, and strode off to meet his transport.

The sidewalks were packed; thick with pedestrians and delivery drones, dotted here and there with quick-serve stalls hawking wares as people passed. Ian hugged the line of apartments, weaving around doorsteps and stoops, keeping fair distance between himself and the whizzing thrum of the cyclist lane. A class of joggers mushed by, their leader running backwards to shout encouragement to his sweating charges.

Ian sidestepped a bulky delivery drone as it surged out from an alleyway, four treads reverberating on the concrete. He knocked into a *Heuron Brite-Bite* stall with his shoulder, offering a quick apology before remembering it was inanimate. The stall, recognizing a potential human customer through quick analysis of its four-panel, market-view lenses, began shouting at Ian about the substantial savings benefits of joining its breakfast rewards club. Ian declined, offering another apology before remembering again that the quick-serve stall was just a machine, and he was under no obligation to treat it politely. The stall offered him a complimentary NutriWafe, extending the wrapped biscuit from a small conveyor hatch. Again Ian declined, this time putting up his hands as he backed away. The stall's customer retention circuits fired to life, made a calculation based on trajectory and estimated market share, and chose to fire the biscuit to the spot it best perceived Ian's hands would be. That the biscuit sailed far left of where Ian's hands actually were and instead impacted an elderly woman on her morning constitutional is yet another testament to the fierce internal strife waged between Heuron's market physics team and their product delivery team.

A small chirrup sounded from the tablet in his pocket, announcing to Ian that he had two minutes to reach his transport and he had best hurry now. He took the tablet's advice, breaking into a run and placing distance between himself and the growing crowd of people stopping to assist the old lady. He wove through the throng, breathlessly apologizing to the angry bell-chirp of a cyclist he cut off and ducking under a pair of Ban-drones as they zipped overhead, a holographic advertisement for the newest season of *Delia* suspended between them. As he reached the transport access point, he snagged the rail-post, swinging around and stopping just short of the terminal edge. The clam-shell doors hissed open as the transport capsule leaned out of the clear, poly-plex tube. Ian stepped aboard, grabbing a space on the bench between a pregnant woman in purple spandex and a short, dark-haired man traveling with what appeared to be a small family's worth of luggage. The clam-shell doors hissed closed, and the capsule receding back into the transport tube before speeding off. Ian rested his head against the curved window of the capsule, his heart still pounding from the run. The city outside began to whip past as the capsule picked up speed, traveling along what used to be Highway 7.

Once hailed as "the first shining step forward in modern man's motion," the *Pliter Transport System* replaced the city's vast complex of surface roads, highways, and rails at the start of the twenty-third century. Built from an unprecedented partnership between *Focus Corp* and the city's municipal government, the vast system of automated, encapsulated transports indexed through a neural network to link citizens to destinations via convenient shuttles. Joston Pliter, city mayor and architect of the development agreement, described the project as the first of many, one that would begin in Winnipeg and soon spread to cities throughout the world. Critics at the time cited concerns over the project's over-reliance on proprietary *Focus Corp* products for all future upkeep and maintenance, the drain on the city's power grid, and system's use of clear poly-plex tubing in a city that receives over three-hundred days of sunshine per year. Mayor Pliter cited that critics at the time were often impediments to forward thinking, and if they were so knowledgeable about public transport then perhaps they should have been elected mayor instead. Critics at the time cited that electoral success was not a benchmark of sound infrastructure planning, to which Mayor Pliter cited that they would all be better served by shutting up. The fact that *Focus Corp* was the single largest donor to the Pliter re-election campaign fund was considered inconsequential at the time.

Ian dozed as the buildings began to blur outside, the soft purr of pneumatic pressure mingling with the muggy heat in the capsule. He double-checked the destination alarm set on his *Focus Corp Ride-A-Long* program and allowed himself a brief nap.

The capsule arrived at the access point for ICF Base Winnipeg at half-past eight. A small chirrup sound in Ian's pocket, waking him with enough time to step off before the capsule continued on. As the clam-shells hissed shut behind him, Ian took in the drab concrete gates of the military base. *Won't be seeing these for a while,* he mused, *maybe never.* He sucked in a breath, shook his head, and stepped forward under the flat, red roofline.

The air inside the gatehouse was cool and damp. Ian shuffled up to the inner doors, a series of hidden cameras matching his gait to recognition records deep within the ICF database. A quick scan from the retinal display and the doors swung open, Ian stepped through into the installation proper.

"You still here, Bernard?" asked the security Trooper seated at a desk without looking up from his tablet. "Thought you shipped out?"

"Last day!" Ian replied warmly, heading for the hallway to the installation interior. "Just gear issue and ticketing."

At his cheeriness the security Trooper merely grunted, his attention never wavering from the game displayed in his hand. Ian left him behind, his attention refocused to his list of pre-deployment tasks. Alone, the guard grunted again to the empty gate shack.

"Glad *someone's* getting out of here."

There was nearly a quarter mile of hallway between ICFB Winnipeg's main gate and 17th Logistics and Supply Depot. Ian crossed it with practiced ease, his heels faintly ringing off the dingy tile. He walked with brusque purpose, waving as he passed to people he knew, and occasionally, to those he didn't. It was his last day on the installation, and there was much to be done.

There was gear to checkout, out-processing paperwork to sign, and tickets aboard the deep-space carrier ship to reserve. He had a final meeting scheduled with his section lead followed by another with her supervisor. His desk needed to be cleaned out, his network storage profile had to be wiped clear, and he was still deliberating over the exact wording of his out-of-office message. He needed a flashfile copy of his personnel and medical records, one last comprehensive blood draw for the clinic, and to return the stapler and two styluses he had borrowed from coworkers over the last three months. Ian Bernard was a busy man, but, grouping his task list by location and priority, he was presently a happy one.

Ian turned the last corner of hallway, his feet making the transition from dingy tile to the well-worn concrete of the supply bay. So preoccupied with the content of his list, he completely failed to notice his platoon gathered around the bay in festive hats, the ornamental sheet-cake on the table, or the bright yellow banner with 'Farewell Bernard!' written in crimson letters across the doorway.

The men and women of the 17th Logistics and Supply Depot had waited in the bay for nearly an hour, quieting suddenly when they heard him coming. They had stood still, poised with party hats and noisemakers, only to watch as Ian entered the bay, strolled past the waiting festivities, and disappeared into the offices in the rear. A confused hush crept over the gathered crowd. Ian emerged from the offices after several minutes, SimuCaff mug in one hand, stapler and styluses in the other, and passed them by without noticing a second time. It was at this point the crowd erupted.

"Grab him!" cried Reed-Sergeant Humphries.

And so it was that Private Duch and Senior-Trooper Thorlick rushed into the hallway, seized Ian by the elbows, carried him bodily overhead, and deposited him roughly amid the celebration.

Ian had just started into his second piece of lemon sheet-cake when he was cornered by Lieutenant Krigil and Reed-Sergeant Humphries. Somewhere between being lifted off the ground and landing in a pile of confetti, Ian had deduced his meetings that morning were a ruse to cover his going-away party. Now, after a quick commencement speech and a shaky rendition of the 17th Battalion's fight song, it would appear that his section leadership was in the mood to talk.

"Bernard! How's Buck-Sergeant feel?" Reed-Sergeant Humphries asked, clapping him on the shoulder.

"Good, ma'am," he mumbled around a mouthful of cake.

"Newly promoted and they're already shipping you off. You excited for Anius?" asked Lieutenant Krigil, cutting off his escape.

"Yes ma'am," said Ian, turning abruptly to face the platoon commander.

"First deployment? And they're sending you to face the 'Dirt Star?'" Sergeant Humphries let out a low whistle.

Ian turned back sharply to the senior NCO.

"Is something wrong with Anius?" He tried to keep the worry out of his voice.

"Not wrong, per se," Lieutenant Krigil cut in. "Just *different*. It's not your usual deployment."

"And it's about as far as you can fuckin' get from this place," Sergeant Humphries laughed.

Lieutenant Krigil watched Ian's face fall. She snapped her fingers to break him out of it. "Hey, don't worry about it. It's nothing the second-in-class at the NCO academy can't handle."

"Yes'm," Ian mumbled, suddenly finding it difficult to swallow.

"Only second?! What, didja trip the commandant on the last formation?" The Reed-Sergeant laughed, tipping a wink to the Lieutenant.

"Bernard? Trip somebody?" laughed Lieutenant Krigil. "He'd *still* be apologizing."

A small smile crossed Ian's face. He renewed his focus on the cake in his hand.

"Never mind the laughs, Bernard," Sergeant Humphries said, settling back down. "Always knew you were a star—glad to see my eye was right."

"Always a star," echoed the Lieutenant with a wan smile. "And now you're rising on out of here."

A tinge of color began in Ian's cheeks.

"S'way it goes, LT," gruffed the Reed-Sergeant. "You can never tie the good ones down for long."

"You sure?" Lieutenant Krigil stroked her chin thoughtfully. "I hear the new fiber-cable's pretty strong. Might be worth a shot."

They shared a laugh before the two departed, leaving Ian alone with his crumpled cake and rosy cheeks.

The rest of the day passed in a flurry of appointments, forms, and goodbye handshakes. It was a quarter to eleven, and the sun had long since faded when he found himself traveling home in the capsule, encircled by four enormous gear bags. As he heaved the last of the luggage up the apartment stoop, he leaned against door for a moment, appreciating the stillness of the late hour. The bustling of the sidewalk had quieted, the pedestrians gone and the stalls shut-down. He stared up at the bright harvest moon. He couldn't remember the last time he'd really looked at it. Now he didn't know when he'd see it again. He marveled for a second at its pockmarked light, taking him back to the time before he was married, when Suzette had dragged him to a picnic in a moonlit park. It had been a harvest moon then too, orange and bright.

Ian sucked in a breath, shook his head, and pushed on through the door to the small apartment. Tomorrow he would board a great ship, blasting away from the only world he had ever known.

Chapter 2:

It was six o'clock the next day when Ian rose to the tinkling of wind chimes. The air was fraught as he made his way through his morning routine, heavy with the feeling of sullen inevitability. The apartment was quiet, muffled. The newscast playing on the mirror seemed distant and remote. Ian drifted through the start of his day, a man poised on the edge of an unknown future.

"Ian, dear? Are you alright?"

Suzette's voice cut through the fog. Ian was surprised to find himself standing by the counter of his kitchenette. He blinked at her, eyes resolving themselves to focus. He stalled for time while his brain caught up.

"Hmm? What, Sue?"

"I asked if you're alright," she answered slowly. She pointed at his hands. "You've been stirring your mug for over five minutes now."

Ian followed her gaze, discovering the full mug of SimuCaff in his left hand. There was a faint clink of steel on ceramic as he watched his right hand trace the inner edges with a steel spoon. The clinking stopped abruptly as he looked up, shaking his head to clear it.

"Sorry Sue. Just....thinking."

She smiled, reassuring him with a pinch on his arm. "We'll be fine. We knew this day would come. Two years..."

Twenty-one months, he corrected in his head.

"...isn't a terrible deployment. It's not like a remote tour on the outer rim."

He set the mug down on the counter, freeing up his hands to rub his chin.

"And we'll be able to vidchat. We'll still get to see you every day."

"Hopefully…" he replied, his eyes shifting over to his son, currently splashing in a syrup puddle in the highchair.

All of the information he'd scoured for Anius was perfunctory at best, just surface level facts about the planet's settlement in 2204 following the discovery of vast pockets of helium and heavy water, the establishment of the ICF's transitional supply hub in 2299, and a brief note about the Commando Raiders' compound expanding after the fall of

Avina. Apart from an extremely detailed review of the poor service in the Ansbrock hotel and a video of the provincial governor celebrating his fifty-ninth birthday by riding his pet Gluffant to the capital building, there was nothing posted to the LinkNet in the last two years. Nothing remotely up-to-the-minute for Ian to itemize and digest. He had no knowledge of the base's conditions, his duty schedule, or even the strength of their LinkNet connection.

Suzette read the worry on Ian's face.

She stroked his cheek. "Don't worry, dear. Whatever happens, we'll make the best of it."

He nodded, his eyes on the dining table and his empty spot at it. She turned his head, locking eyes with him.

"We. Will. Be. Fine." She said slowly, carefully enunciating each syllable. "It's an important job, that's why they're sending you."

The stroke on his cheek turned to a playful slap.

"So you better kick ass while you're there."

The ride to the launch station was long, but peaceful. The launch station was far enough outside the city that the capsule they rode in was empty. As the cityscape turned to countryside outside the tube, they passed the time singing along to the *Whimsy Whale* soundtrack. Ian lounged, resting his head on a stuffed grey duffel, an entire bench to himself.

Whimsy Whale / has a flimsy tail / but life is what you make it!

With a mile of smile / and a pile of style / you cannot mistake it!

Humming to the tune, surrounded by his family, the farmland outside a blur of yellow and green, it was easy to get lost in the simple tranquility of the moment. All too soon the moment passed, the gleaming white towers of the Sandy Bay launch station rising into view. Ian sighed as the capsule slowed to a stop. Rising from the bench and gathering his luggage, his attempted bravado in carrying the five bags himself was quickly thwarted, with Suzette slinging one over her shoulder and snatching another from his hands.

"Got to make sure I get my goodbye kiss," she said, tipping him a wink. Ian opened his mouth to respond but thought better of it, making use of his free hand to hold on to Taniel.

And with that they were off, shuffling across the concrete platform. They approached the vast, white, space terminal, lines forming outside the terminal entrance. Ian tried not to think about the deployment ahead, how very little he knew about Anius or the battalion he was joining. He winced a little as a heavy grey duffel knocked into the back of his knee. He tried not to think about the four large bags of mandatory gear stuffed with everything from solar chargers to ionic field hydration units, and the type of environment that would require him to use them. He felt Taniel's hand tighten its grip on his finger, and he tried not to think about how big he would be the next time Ian saw him. They slowed as they reached the nearest line, resting their bags on the concrete in the shade of the terminal overhang.

"Lot of people," Suzette said. "I didn't realize this many were headed to Anius."

"Some are," explained Ian. "But Anius is the staging point for ICF traffic to the outer rim. I'm sure most of them aren't staying there."

The line inched forward, and Suzette nudged her bag along with one foot. "I haven't seen this place since they started construction back in '27. I never thought it would be so big."

"Or so white," Suzette added after a moment, shielding her eyes against the glare.

Ian had listened to several newscasts regarding the Sandy Bay launch site over the last few years, paying careful note to the allegations of contractor fraud that arose while it was still under construction. He granted himself half a second to worry about the quality of the alloy struts supporting the latticework of the tower before shaking his head clear. *Must put on a strong face, Ian. For them...*

The line thinned, and then it was Ian's turn at the burnished turnstiles. He let go of Taniel's hand, crouching down and bringing him in for hug. He sniffed the top of his son's head, breathing in the faint smell of syrup and blueberry shampoo. He patted his son's back and released, his mouth a tight line.

"Be good, Tan. Listen to mom, and take care of Douglas."

"Okay, Dabby." The large brown eyes looked up at him, a wide smile on the freckled face. A small hand extended up.

Ian gently returned the high-five, clearing his throat hard and standing up. He turned to Suzette, focusing intently on the curly bangs hanging above the teary brown eyes.

"Sue, I—"

She cut him off with a quick, earnest kiss before drawing him into a tight embrace. He felt the light brush of her eyelashes against his neck. A few teardrops remained when they finally pulled apart.

"Remember, pinky swear," she said, wiping one eye with the back of her hand.

"Pinky swear," he echoed, his eyes beginning to well.

It was a promise they'd shared when he first joined the ICF, the first time he'd told her he loved her. *'Pinky swear?'* she'd said. He'd laughed, gripping her finger tight in his. *'Good. Now I know you're serious.'* They'd walked for a bit, enjoying the sunset city skyline when she'd turned to him sharply. *'Now promise me you won't get hurt.' 'What? How?'* he'd asked. *'Do it! Promise me you won't get hurt—that you won't do anything brave or stupid. Promise me you'll always come back.'* He took her gently by the hand, firmly wrapping his finger around hers. *'Pinky swear,'* he'd said, and kissed her against the orange sky. Two weeks later he bought a ring.

Ian cleared his throat again, swallowing hard on the sudden tide of memories. He blinked rapidly, holding back tears as he scooped up his bags. Pivoting away, he marched up to the counter by the turnstile.

"Orders," drawled the dour-faced man on the other side of the counter, extending a hand to receive Ian's tablet.

"Buck-Sergeant Bernard, reporting." Ian scrunched up his nose, hoping his watery eyes might be mistaken for allergies.

If the dour man noticed, he pretended not to, offering a derisive snort and stamping his thumbprint on the clear screen. He handed the tablet back to Ian, looking bored as he waved him on to the burnished turnstiles. Ian tossed his bags on the conveyor belt, turning back one last time to his furiously waving family, and stepped through the platform gate.

It took nearly forty-five minutes to cross the gate. Along the way he passed through seven pressure-sensitive stance-analysis pads, five carbon turnstiles, four infra-scanners, two ozone-detection panels, and past a suspiciously imposing and archaic-looking box that Ian was certain was an x-ray scanner, but was actually just an empty box made to look suspiciously imposing and archaic-looking for purposes of security deterrence. After nearly an hour, the most advanced security-scanning technology ever assembled successfully confirmed that the Ian Bernard that entered the gate matched the 'Buck-Sergeant Bernard, Ian' written on his orders. Ian stepped through the last turnstile, his index finger still smarting from the blood-composition analyzer, and out on to the shining white concourse of the Sandy Bay launch station.

First conceived in the summer of 2325 as a last-ditch effort by W.I. Bernstrop to save his failing architecture firm, the Sandy Bay Inter-Space Launching Platform (commonly referred to as 'Sandy Bay' or as the 'Sandy Bay Launch Station' by those with the good sense to know what 'inter-space' actually means) was designed over the course of two fruitless weeks of design-boarding and re-redesigning, and one very productive night of furious sketching inspired by hallucinogenic stimulants from a small red box marked 'Emergency' he kept in his desk. *I'll make it white!'* Bernstrop had roared to the empty office, his associate design team long-departed to scrounge for freelance work on a home makeover show. *'And shiny! The future is always shiny.'*

And so it came to pass that W.I. Bernstrop's design was presented before a board of governors, council staff-assistants, and ICF Colonels. The board was impressed, both by the state-of-the-art, gleaming white proposal and the passion of W.I.'s chemically-accelerated pitch. The site broke ground in late 2327. Though its construction was marred by controversy (and a local ecologist's discovery that the concentrated sunlight reflected from the tower's panels incinerated passing birds) the Sandy Bay station opened in early 2330 to brief fanfare. There was a ribbon-cutting ceremony led by a twitchy and distressingly thin W.I. Bernstrop, a short article on the *Republic News Network* page, and then it was off to work ferrying personnel to and from low orbit.

Ian stepped out into the morning sunlight, shielding his eyes from the glare as he gazed up. The passenger shuttle resembled a great, bloated grey tick clinging to the tower's side. Another line ringed the tower's base as people waited to board to the ship in ten-passenger groups. Ian fell in behind his fellow Troopers, his excitement at boarding quickly tempered by the stale monotony of queuing.

An hour later and he was aboard, his heart fluttering as he clicked his five-point harness into place. Gingerly, he rested his head back against the rough fabric of the teal seat. Safety instructions danced across the wall-length monitor screen ahead of him in worrying, bright red letters. Ian shifted in his seat, craning his neck to read around the heads of those in front of him. The final groups boarded, fifteen-hundred ICF Troopers bound for travel through the deep channels of space. The harness clasp auto-locked closed as a countdown appeared on the giant monitor screen. At five seconds to launch, Ian was possessed with the abrupt panic that he needed to use the restroom.

But there was no time left. The clock reached zero and the magnetic accelerators engaged, rocketing the fat grey shuttle to escape velocity. Ian was pressed down against the scratchy seat, gripping the hand rests tight as he fought the forces of gravity acting against him. As they approached the upper limits of the atmosphere he felt his stomach rise, drowning out his previous discomforts.

A chime sounded in the cabin and a pleasant voice called out, "Sickness bags are located in the seatback in front of you."

Ian availed himself of one as they broke through the stratosphere. The instructions on the monitor screen blinked out, replaced by an image of the planet receding below them. Ian looked out as his home shrank, and a small pang of loss ran through him. The image blinked again, replaced by an upward look of the ICF *Telmore* as the deep-space passenger ship grew in view.

Having slipped the surly bonds of gravity, the shuttle slowed, drifting into docking position with the *Telmore*. There was a thunderous click in the cabin as the transit locks engaged. Another countdown began on the main screen, disengaging their harnesses at its conclusion. Ian took a deep breath and pushed away from his seat, joining the line floating towards the exit. As he gripped the handles by the hatch, he gave a backwards look to the world he once knew, but the monitor screen was black and empty. He shook his head, sucked in another breath, and pushed himself through the hatch door.

The gravity aboard the *Telmore* was a welcome change after the weightlessness of the shuttle, even if it had the unsettling effect of being just a hair too weak. Ian stepped down the stairs to the main passenger bay, holding steady to the rails. He narrowly avoided bumping into the Trooper in front of him, a thick-set woman who exuded aggression and lacked a defined neck. Ian looked out over the crowded bay as men and women milled around, each searching for their hibernation capsule among the hundreds of rows. He parsed out a few apologies as he wobbled his way through the crowd, heading over to the row of pods marked with a glowing 'B' overhead.

He found his capsule, docking his tablet in the front slot to unlock it. He swiped a thumbprint on the handle and lifted up, the poly-plex canopy swinging open and admitting him inside. Ian settled down into the soft cushions of the pod, sliding a bit on the faux-satin sheets. The canopy closed overhead, and he inserted his arm into the receptacle on his right. Ian shut his eyes tight, trying to calm his pounding heart. His mind recalled half of an article he read about the dangers of long-term cryo-hibernation on people with peanut allergies. Then there was a slight pinch as the needle entered his wrist, and his world went black.

Faster-than-light interstellar travel was considered the greatest scientific achievement of the midpoint of the twenty-second century. Long thought to be functionally impossible, the breakthroughs in the experiments of Doctors Wung, Izell, and Al-Bakkal in 2145 allowed for the development of a device that allowed for solid matter to travel beyond the speed of light in a near-frictionless environment. This device, and its subsequent refinement into engines capable of propelling manned ships, was the principle development that finally allowed mankind to become an inter-galactic colonizer. The W.I.B. device also allowed Earth's Coalition Republic to transform almost overnight from an international, bureaucratic-governing hegemony into an interstellar one.

The subsequent discovery of faster-than-light particles opened the door to the creation of the new LinkNet, capable of transmitting information across galaxies in seconds. The miraculous nature of this technology, and its transformative effect on the Coalition Republic, was not lost on the more skeptical-minded members of the human race. Hundreds of years after the discovery of the W.I.B. device, rumors still persist denying the very existence of interstellar travel. That contact with these far-reaching planetary settlements is not only possible, but conducted nearly instantaneously thousands of times per day is labeled a hoax. That ships can be seen departing the Earth's orbit, reappearing years later, is rejected outright—clearly the work of insidious video editing. That millions of men and women can claim first-hand experience traveling across the universe is waved away—paid informants for the grand conspiracy. In spite of nearly two hundred years of use and acceptance, there are still some that crowd in dark corners of the LinkNet, eager and willing to overlook the truth in front of their faces.

Though the miracle of the W.I.B. device (and the family of engines developed using its principles) allowed for travel at greater-than-light speeds, the vast distances of space stretched even the most routine planet-hopping into multi-month excursions. Suspended animation assisted most passengers in enduring the long tedium of months in space, but interstellar law prohibited captains and crew from taking part. These crewmembers spent much of the time watching vidplays, gambling, fighting over gambling losses, and pursuing distance learning degrees. As such, the men and women of the ICF Space-Flight Corp often boasted the highest education rate of any population, averaging two MAs or a PhD apiece.

Ian awoke after fifty-nine days of sleep, in stable orbit over the planet Anius. As the canopy lifted overhead, he rose groggily, the effects of deep hibernation lingering in a stiffness in his joints and a ringing in his left ear. Ian shook his head, adding sudden dizziness to his list of symptoms. A glowing arrow illuminated on the floor and he stumbled after it, still teetering in the lighter gravity. He joined the other Troopers in line for the next shuttle, listening to the snorts and grumbles of people waking up.

The hatch door spun open and he stepped through, drifting across the shuttle to find a seat. *No screen this time*, he thought as he stared at the black wall ahead, ideas registering in slow motion as his brain readjusted to consciousness. The last Trooper drifted through the door and found his seat, clicking into place as the transit locks disengaged. There was a jolt, and a growing sensation of movement pressing down on him. A rattle shook through the cabin as the shuttle picked up speed, entering the planet's atmosphere. All around him people bumped and bounced, limbs jostling in the falling craft. The squinty-eyed Trooper next to Ian leaned over, dry-heaving into the seatback pocket. Ian's empty stomach joined his heart in his throat, competing for space as the shuttle shook in the turbulence. A roaring sound filled the cabin as the atmospheric friction built around the ship. Ian stared straight ahead to the discomforting blankness of the wall ahead. He felt, rather than heard, the firing of repulsors slowing them down to impact speeds. The roaring outside tapered off, the cabin quiet save for the retching of his neighbor.

A few moments passed as they descended, terminating in a thunderous bump that let them know they'd landed. Across the cabin harnesses clicked open, Troopers standing up and stretching in the new gravity. The hatch door spun open, filling the cabin with the smell of ozone and burning tires. Ian walked unsteadily towards the door, joining the other Troopers in their first steps on a new planet.

The sky was dark as he looked up, filled with unfamiliar stars. It was uncomfortably hot on the tarmac of the port, but Ian found himself able to breathe. Dimly, he recalled reading that Anius had been colonized early on because of its atmospheric similarities to earth, although it had a significantly higher oxygen content. The world spun for a moment, and Ian shut his eyes to keep steady. A Trooper knocked into him from behind, cursing as they both fought for balance.

"Arrivals over here!" a voice shouted in the distance. "Customs and arrivals here!"

Ian snapped his eyes open, an apology on his lips as he joined the jelly-legged crowd in stumbling towards the voice. A blurry figure waved them over, assembling the hung-over soldiers in lines feeding into a wide, domed hangar.

"Step inside, take a seat!" the figure commanded, the Troopers nodding along and obeying.

The air inside was pleasantly cool, Ian's eyes adjusting to the fluorescent light as he made his way over to the rows on rows of folding chairs. He collapsed into an alloy seat, head still reeling from the months of travel. All around him Troopers tripped their way to similar arrangements, the hangar filled with the groans and creaks of cheap, metal seats.

The figure piped up again, booming from the front of the hangar, "Settle in and shut up! Customs brief is starting!"

Ian blinked slowly as an image resolved itself on the front wall of the hangar, the words 'Welcome to Anius!' projected in bold blue letters. A thin Trooper ambled up to the wall, gesturing to the letters with a sweep of his hand.

"Welcome to Anius," he began, a noticeable lisp creeping into his voice. "I am Buck-Sergeant Johnson—

"No you're not, I am," whispered the blond Trooper on Ian's left. Ian read the name and rank on his uniform jacket, he wasn't lying.

...part of your Customs and Immigration Cell," continued the former Buck-Sergeant Johnson. "And here to guide you through your integration into the ICF mission here on Anius, and your interactions with the Anian people."

Sergeant Johnson paused, beaming a smile out to the rows of surly Troopers. A few squeaks and groans from chairs in the crowd let him know he was taking a bit too long. The smile dropped and he hurried back into his monologue.

"Here on Anius we have a number of rules." The image changed behind him, illuminating a dense wall of blue text. He rattled through the list of prohibitions and regulations, moving quickly through the ten-slide list. Ian's head spun again, the words blurring in front of him. He wondered how much of this he needed to know. He wondered if there was a test.

"Think there's a fucking pamphlet for all this shit?" his neighbor whispered.

Ian grunted back, struggling to read the words on the rapidly shifting
slides.

"...And no gambling," Buck-Sergeant Johnson concluded, beaming
his smile back at the dozing crowd. "Remember folks, 'With temerity and enthusiasm, we carry out this tour!' Now let's get you *in*-processed and *on*-mission!"

He paused again, awaiting applause. He was met with silence, broken only by the loud sneeze of a Trooper in the front. The smile dipped again, and Buck-Sergeant Johnson slunk off as quickly as he'd come.

In his place came the figure from before, introducing herself as Chief-Sergeant Hatoya, the installation's superintendent. She martialed the crowd to stand, directing them to file in rows through the processing line in the back. Ian joined the Troopers in his row, grabbing his bags from a pile in the corner and duck-walking over to another line. He passed a stout woman with short black hair engaged in tense discussion with an Anian customs official.

"No, no, no," the woman protested, holding a multi-colored set of polyhedral dice in her hand. "They're not for gambling, they're for a game!"

The customs official said nothing, suspicion emanating out from his starched white uniform. He pointed an imperious hand towards the incinerator in the corner, a stamp of his foot announcing that he considered the negotiation over.

Ian watched the woman scrunch her face and accept her loss, walking to the can with morose resignation.

"Cuttin' no slack, eh?" whispered Ian's neighbor from before. "My buddy said the Governor is cracking down after a shooting in the Ansbrock bar."

"Shooting?" Ian whispered back, pressing ahead in the line.

"Yeah, two Troopers and an Anian. Rumor is it was over some bad *Glib* they dealt him," the blond Sergeant replied, shuffling forward with his bags. "Guess the Governor is trying to stamp out any vices he can."

"*Glib*?" he asked. "Where'd they get it from?"

Sergeant Johnson shrugged. The potent narcotic was known for being extremely difficult to manufacture, requiring an advanced knowledge of chemistry and a carefully controlled crystallization environment. Ian had watched a documentary on *Glib* once, ICF officials believed that the majority of the drug was manufactured on special 'chem ships' before being offloaded by smugglers at major ports.

Ian nodded, cataloguing the information into a new list of worries. He stepped forward in line, dropping his bags onto the conveyor belt for the scanner. A sour-faced official waved him forward, brusquely ordering him to lift his arms and spread his legs. Ian complied as the customs official swiped a scatter-wand up and down, confirming the lack of vices present on his person. With a grunt the official waved him past.

Ian collected his bags from the conveyor, carefully avoiding the eye of another scowling official. He marched to the door, thankful to be done with lines for the immediate future. He stepped back out into the stifling

air, the stars fading above as the first light of dawn crept over the horizon. He looked out on the desert planet, the farthest from home he had ever been.

"Sergeant Bernard!" A voice called behind him. "Buck-Sergeant Ian Bernard!"

Ian snapped his head around. He searched for the source of the voice.

"I'm Sergeant Bernard!" he called back, pointing to himself.

A swarthy man stomped over, broad shoulders stretching the edges of his grey ICF uniform. He swiped the bags out of Ian's hand, slinging them on one arm.

"That's great," he huffed, heading back around the corner of the hangar.

"Now hurry up. We're fucking late."

Chapter 3:

Terrance Torres was not a man given to patience. He shrugged Bernard's bags higher on his shoulder, brown eyes squinting in the pre-sunrise gloom as he rounded the hangar corner. The LITCAT was still where he'd left it, the small utility truck double-parked in front of a pair of passenger buses. A quick scan confirmed that lot was still empty. Good. The last thing he needed was some slope-chinned Reed-Sergeant lurking around just to chew him out over a five-minute parking job. Buck-Sergeant Torres rarely had time to suffer the lectures of self-important middle management, and today was no exception.

Terrance picked up the pace, hurrying over to the truck. He didn't bother checking if Sergeant Bernard had followed. Bernard looked smart enough, albeit scrawny; Terrance was sure he'd catch up. He tossed the bags in the LITCAT's bed, continuing on to the square brown cab without breaking his stride. Hopping up onto the dusty running board, he pulled open the door and swung himself inside. It was refreshingly cold inside—he'd left the truck running to keep the air conditioning on full blast. The thought that it might get stolen had certainly crossed Terrance's mind, but he quickly dismissed it. Life was never without risk. Besides, it wasn't actually his truck.

A few minutes later and the passenger door opened up, a wave of heat accompanying a gasping Sergeant Bernard as he crawled inside. Terrance paid half a glance to his heavily sweating colleague as he dragged himself upright in the seat. The sun had yet to rise on the sand-swept desert planet, but the temperature outside was still an ex-cruciating one hundred and twenty degrees.

"Did...you...say...we...were late?" Sergeant Bernard panted, wiping away the river of sweat running into his eyes. "For...what?"

"A meeting," Terrance replied, throwing the truck abruptly in gear. "With Colonel Schwarz."

The sweaty brow furrowed. "Who?"

"Installation commander," said Terrance, stomping on the pedal and launching the truck forward.

"We're off to see the Baron."

The Baron? Ian wasn't sure he'd heard right, the cobwebs of cryostasis still hanging over his mind. He opened his mouth to ask more but was cut off as the LITCAT sped out of the parking lot. He scrambled for the straps to his seatbelt, fumbling over the five-point harness as the truck sped along. Sergeant Torres ignored him, eyes straight ahead.

At twenty miles per hour the seatbelt warning light came on, the squiggly icon flashing in the center of the truck's viewscreen. Sergeant Torres ignored that too.

A second later and an angry chime began to sound throughout the cab, momentarily drowning out the clatter of gravel rebounding in the alloy wheel wells. Sergeant Torres punched the radio on.

At forty miles per hour the angry chime grew deafening. The squiggly icon transformed into a full-screen message, warning in bold letters that continued non-compliance would result in engine shutdown. Sergeant Torres sighed, snatching both hands off the wheel. He pawed for the strap hanging behind him, never letting off the gas. His eyes were still straight ahead as he dragged the left strap down, slamming it closed in the central buckle. The bold letters vanished and the chime cut off. Sergeant Torres sighed again, returning his hands to the wheel.

Ian's mouth hung open. He watched the right seatbelt strap hang loose behind Torres' shoulder, swaying as the truck bounced along the road. The lap belts clattered idly against the base of the seat. Ian closed his mouth, double-checking his own harness was securely fastened before turning back to the front. He blinked slowly, his mind struggling to process the unbridled recklessness he'd just seen. He found his words and his mouth opened again.

"We're...going to meet the commander?"

"Yep."

"Why?"

"One of our Troopers was caught tripping on *Glib*. Stupid fuck was running through the dorms swinging a sword around yelling about fulfilling a prophecy. Naked."

A hundred questions blossomed in Ian's mind. He picked the most immediately relevant.

"So we're meeting with the commander to..."

"To witness the disciplinary action, yes."

"Oh."

A hundred more questions sprang up. Ian settled on the one most pertinent to his present anxiety.

"And we're late? How?"

The sigh that poured out of Sergeant Torres was long, stretching far past the simple term of 'heavy', and entering into the territory wherein it became a genuinely impressive feat of sustained exhalation. Ian waited, his hopes for receiving a more detailed explanation dwindling away as the sigh dragged on. As it faded away, the warbling of the radio filling the cabin once again. Ian shifted in his seat. 'Late' was not a state of being he was comfortable inhabiting.

It has long been observed that the term 'late' carries a significantly different connotation within the military than it does within civilian life. Whereas most members of society might attribute being 'on time' with arriving at or just before the specified arrangement, the default expectation within the military was to be at least fifteen minutes early. This then created a new spectrum along which the concepts of 'early,' 'late,' and 'on time' existed. If the expectation was to be fifteen minutes early, then 'early' becomes the new 'on time,' any time after becoming 'late.' This then means that to be 'early,' as all Troopers must strive to be, one must plan to arrive even more than fifteen minutes early, preferably by even a half-hour.

Buck-Sergeant Torres preferred to arrive in the sweet spot of ten minutes before the agreed time. Just late enough that he didn't feel rushed, but not so late that risked the ire and commentary of senior leadership. Sergeant Torres didn't like to waste time, his own most of all, and nothing wasted time like a briefing from a senior NCO.

By any metric though, they were late. Ian watched the dusty countryside whip by on the LITCAT's viewscreen. The four massive wheels of the *Light Individual Transport, Category: All Terrain* (a smaller, more streamlined cousin to the *Massive Modular Utility Transport* used commonly throughout the ICF) churning against the dry gravel road. He dozed, watching dunes pass and thinking about his family. A grey dome rose in view, capped here and there by clumps of sand deposited in the last storm.

The dunes outside slowed as Sergeant Torres eased off the pedal, guiding the truck over to an opening at the base of the dome. They reached the entrance and descended, riding the winding ramp into the garage below. Torres drove past several levels, finally settling on one half-way down. He slowed the truck to a crawl, creeping along in the dim light.

"Look for a sign," he grunted at Ian.

Ian shook his head, returning to the present. "Sorry, what?"

"A sign, a fucking sign," he snapped, gesturing towards the 're-served' markings lining a few of the available spaces. "Make sure I don't park in a spot with a sign."

Ian nodded, looking out on the rows of spaces. As they continued to creep by, he found his search was in vain, as space after space denoted its reservation for varying levels of rank. They completed their loop around the level, reaching the spiral ramp once again. Sergeant Torres eyed the ramp to the lower levels, weighing it against the time displayed in the corner of the viewscreen.

"Fuck it," he growled, and gunned the truck forward. "Look for one marked 'Command Staff Only.'"

Ian nodded, a slight grimace betraying his discomfort over his involvement in this decision. Nevertheless, he obeyed, spotting one off to the left, directing them over with a quick wave and a point. Sergeant Torres acknowledged with a grunt, whipping the truck into the space and cutting the engine. As they both stepped down, Ian noticed that they were crooked, the right two wheels hanging well over the yellow line into the next space. He opened his mouth to mention it, but thought better, the tension in his partner's shoulders reminding Ian that they lacked time. He settled instead for falling in behind Sergeant Torres as he pushed through the swinging doors at the end of the level and entered Command Central.

Terrance hurried down the dingy hallways of Command Central, heavy boot steps echoing quietly. Sergeant Bernard followed close behind, stepping quickly to keep up as they rolled along. They passed through cubicles and by offices, up three flights of stairs and down two ramps. They passed meeting rooms both empty and full, as serious people sat around SimuWood tables discussing serious things. They passed a locked blast door with 'Classified Actions Only' emblazoned on the front, the flashing red light overhead and grim-faced guard standing outside letting them know they had best not linger.

They marched along, until at last they reached their destination. There, at the end of a long hallway, glass doors stood, 'Colonel John Schwarz Jr., Installation Commander' engraved above them in thick, imposing letters. Terrance sucked in a breath as he reached them, grabbing hold of the steel handle and pushing his way in. The secretary eyed them from behind a row of monitors.

"You're *laaate*," he sang out to them as they passed.

"I know, Tim. I know," Terrance grumbled back. "I was stuck picking up the new guy."

Sergeant Bernard gave a small wave.

The secretary's eyes narrowed over the edge of his monitors. Mr. Timoson Freeman considered himself to be an excellent judge of the human condition.

"*Hmph,*" was his assessment of the new Buck-Sergeant. He turned back to Terrance. "He the new Polowski?"

Terrance nodded. "Yeah, Pol left on the rotator today."

Mr. Freeman frowned behind the screens. Sergeant Bernard was beginning to grow uncomfortable under the secretary's scrutiny. He looked around for something to focus on, settling for the diamond stud twinkling in Mr. Freeman's ebony ear. Mr. Freeman watched him closely.

"*Hmph,*" was all he said.

Terrance cut back in, "They start already?"

"*Mhmm,*" said Mr. Freeman. "You know he don't wait."

Terrance nodded, rubbing his chin. "Should I knock?"

Mr. Freeman shook his head. "No, just go in. He's expecting you anyway."

Terrance nodded again, walking up to the grey doors of the commander's office. He took a breath, waving Sergeant Bernard over before he pushed his way in.

"Nice to meet you," Bernard offered, rushing to join Terrance by the door.

They opened the door as quietly as they could, the low sounds of the Colonel speaking seeping out as they entered. Mr. Freeman returned to his monitors.

"*Hmph.*"

Colonel Schwarz loomed over Private Silman, frowning down at him with his thumbs hooked in his belt. Over six feet tall from polished boots to thick black hair, he stood like a man accustomed to wielding authority. He radiated magisterial calm from the very core of his being, projecting his disapproval through his whole body. He liked to think that he had seen just about everything in his eighteen years serving in the ICF. It was his fourth installation command, his second back-to-back, and, God willing, it might be his last.

Colonel Schwarz stared down at the young Private, the corners of his mouth drawing lower the longer he stared. Private Silman did his best to hold absolutely still, staring straight ahead past the Colonel to a painting of a ship on the wall.

"So," the Colonel began, his voice soft and low. People tended to listen when a Colonel spoke. Rare was the occasion he needed to yell. "You tested positive for the use of a banned substance."

"Yes, sir," Private Silman squeaked.

"You are aware that the use of '*Glib*' or any other class III stimulant is strictly prohibited by Republic law and ICF regulation."

"Yes, sir."

"Additionally, while under the influence of a class III stimulant, you were found to have engaged in behavior unsuitable for a member of the armed forces. Stripping naked in public, brandishing a three-foot scimitar, and declaring that you will 'ride the Gluffant King to fulfill the ancient prophecy,' are considered actions outside of the acceptable spectrum of behavior for ICF service members."

"Yes, sir."

"Do you understand that given the circumstances, in addition to facing a punishment under the military judicial system, you could also face civil claims for endangering the public?"

Private Silman's eyes began to water. "Yes, sir."

"You understand that at the very least, the consequences of your actions necessitate an immediate removal of rank and the brokering of orders for your return to your home station, to potentially include discharge from the ICF?"

"Yes, sir." A tear rolled down the Private's cheek. He kept his eyes on the painting straight ahead.

Colonel Schwarz looked over the ruddy young man. He was used to discipline, applying it with practiced ease. He was used to Privates fucking up, it had been a constant during his career and the careers of every officer before him. He was not used to using discipline this frequently, the rash of drug-related incidents spiking suddenly and without warning. And so he frowned.

The sound of the door opening drew his attention from Private Silman. He watched Sergeant Torres and another Buck-Sergeant sneak in, taking up a position on the back wall near Lieutenant Ligen and Reed-Sergeant Gherwiz. He nodded, returning his attention to Silman. It was time to wrap this up.

"Private Silman," the Colonel began again, his voice a little louder as he rendered his judgement. "Effective immediately, I do hereby strip you of your rank, reducing you to the rank of Null-Private with corresponding reduction in pay."

He looked up from the Private, locking eyes with the Lieutenant in the back. "I order you to thirty days of administrative punishment, or longer, concluding with your departure from this installation on the rotator ship."

Lieutenant Ligen nodded, her bushy brown hair bouncing a little with the shake of her head. Thirty days was a long time, but there were plenty of floors to sweep.

Colonel Schwarz turned his attention back to the demoted soldier. "Finally, I order you to write letters of apology to each of the two-hundred and thirty-one people who were exposed to your state of undress. Individualized and delivered in person. Do you understand?"

Null-Private Silman nodded, eyes still watering furiously.

"Dismissed."

Private Silman snapped a quick salute, marching out the door as fast as he could. Reed-Sergeant Gherwiz followed close behind, both to give counsel to the young man and to go through the mountain of paperwork needed to finalize the disciplinary action. Colonel Schwarz lumbered back to his SimuWood desk, falling wearily into the comfort of its luxuriously cushioned chair. He ran a hand through his hair, mussing it a little before dropping his hand to rub his eyes.

"Does anyone know where he got a fucking sword?"

The three on the back wall looked among themselves.

"No? Anyone?"

They shook their heads.

The Colonel sighed, a weary exhalation that threatened Sergeant Torres' previous record. He waved them over to sit on the couches across from his desk. Ian paused over his seat, not wanting to be the first to sit down. He relented when Lieutenant Ligen settled into an armchair

underneath the painting, propping her feet up on the stone coffee table.

"I mean, a fucking *sword?*" Colonel Schwarz dropped his hand from his eyes, staring straight up at the pock-marked ceiling. "I just...*how?*"

Murmurs came from the three in front of him.

Colonel Schwarz sighed again. "Was he at least a good Trooper?"

"No," Lieutenant Ligen answered. "But not terrible. He failed his first development volume and was late to work a few times. Nothing excessive—Sergeant Torres was working with him to get his studies on track."

The Colonel rolled his blue eyes over to Sergeant Torres. "And how were his studies going?"

"Shitty," grunted Sergeant Torres. "I almost think he couldn't read."

Ian's eyes went wide. He'd never heard someone curse in front of a Colonel before, but then again, he'd never heard a Colonel curse before either.

"Ah," Colonel Schwarz shrugged, placing his hands on his head and looking back up to the ceiling. "Then I guess it wasn't too much of a loss."

They sat in silence, the three waiting on the Colonel to speak. Ian sneezed, muffling the sound as much as he could. The sudden movement drew the Colonel's attention.

"Ah yes," he said. "Who's this?"

Ian sat up in his seat. "Buck-Sergeant Bernard, sir."

"And where is Sergeant Bernard from?"

"ICFB Winnipeg, the 17th Logistics and Supply Depot." Ian tried to sit up straighter.

The Colonel sized him up. "Manitoba, eh?"

"Yes, sir." Ian became acutely conscious of his appearance, lines of dried salt running down his neck, his uniform wrinkled from months in hibernation. He was pretty sure he smelled as well.

Colonel Schwarz turned his attention to Sergeant Torres and the Lieutenant. "He the new Polowski?"

"Yes, sir," Ian answered, cutting in ahead of the Lieutenant. If they were going to talk about him, he might as well lead the conversation. And he wasn't sure he wanted Torres speaking on his behalf. The blue eyes snapped back over to him. Ian began to regret speaking up.

"Ah, good," the Colonel announced after an interminable moment. "Sergeant Polowski was a good man. You've big shoes to fill."

Ian nodded. "Yes, sir. I gathered as mu—

"Although he did have that mustache," Colonel Schwarz interrupted, turning back to Lieutenant Ligen. He fixed an eye back on Ian. "You're not planning on growing a mustache?"

Ian blinked. "No, sir, I hadn't consid—

"Good!" boomed the Colonel. "Because it was terrible, just terrible. All bristly and long, like a blond walrus. Right, LT?"

Lieutenant Ligen nodded, a small smile on her face.

"It was awful, just awful," the Colonel echoed. He turned back to Ian. "I mean, can you even grow a mustache?"

Ian paused a moment. "Maybe? I've never tri—

"Well don't!" laughed Colonel Schwarz, interrupting again. "You'd look terrible. They're all terrible, the crusty soup strainers."

Ian began to feel that he was losing his grip on the conversation thread. "Yes, sir. I gue—

"Cookie dusters!" the Colonel laughed again.

"Yes, I—

"Crumb catchers!"

Ian's mouth flapped open and closed, he wasn't sure he was still a part of this conversation. Lieutenant Ligen started snickering in the corner. Colonel Schwarz took some getting used to. She watched the new Buck-Sergeant shift uncomfortably in his seat, clearing her throat loudly and interrupting the Colonel before he could embark on further mustache aphorisms.

"Well, sir, we really should be going," she said, drawing his attention back to the matters at hand.

"Really? So soon?" the Colonel asked, a smile lingering on his face.

"Yes, sir. Sergeant Gherwiz and I need to deal with Silman, and Sergeant Torres needs to take Bernard to his lodging. He just got off the rotator today and starts work tonight. He should get some rest."

"Ah, yes," the Colonel bobbed his head, running a hand through his hair. He fixed his eyes back on Ian. "I suppose you do need some sleep before you come on shift."

Ian nodded back, no longer sure that words were an appropriate response.

"Well, good! Get out of here then," he said, dismissing them with a wave of his hand. "Get on with the mission."

Ian rose and followed behind the Lieutenant and Sergeant Torres, still puzzled by the bizarre exchange.

"Oh, Sergeant Bernard," the Colonel called out.

Ian froze, his hand still on the door. "Yes, sir?"

"Sergeant Polowski did great things while in his tenure here. I've been a bit spoiled so far; I'll expect the same performance from the number-two graduate of the NCO academy."

Ian cracked a smile, his cheeks reddening slightly. "Yes, sir. I will."

"Good," the Colonel nodded, turning to the monitor on his desk. "Cause if you don't, I'll burn your ass quicker than Silman's."

Ian rode quietly in the front seat of the LITCAT, the radio host announcing in dull tones that something called the 'Sultan of Swing' would be playing next. Ian watched the dunes roll by, more thoroughly unsure than at any other point in his life. Sergeant Torres was fixated on

the front viewscreen, a single shoulder strap connected to preempt the alarm. It was lighter out now, fully dawn; another hour or so and the landscape would be bathed in scorching light.

Sergeant Torres said something, and Ian realized he'd been speaking this whole time.

"Wha-what?"

"I said, I got you in at the BPD. I pulled a favor so you wouldn't get stuck in the *Trash*."

"Oh, thanks," Ian said, not quite sure what any of that meant.

Sergeant Torres took one hand off the wheel to fish for something in his pocket. He pulled out a small token, handing it over for Ian to see. "There, now you can go straight to your dorm in the *Better People District*, no waitin' in the *Trash* until someone rotates home."

Ian took the key in his hand, still unsure of what it meant. *At least he's in a better mood now.* The tension in his partner had dissipated after leaving Command Central. He turned the token over, 'BPD 1356' stamped in blue on the back. *The Better People District, hmmmm.* "What's BPD actually mean?"

"'Built Permanent Dwellings,'" Torres answered, humming along with the radio. "Newer dorm buildings built in the last few decades. Most people have to wait awhile in the *Trash*, 'Transient Sustainment Housing'— the slum dorms over on the far east. Lodging folks owed me a favor after I fast-checked a shipment for them, so I cashed it in to get you in a good dorm from the start."

"Oh, thank you." Ian wasn't sure what else to say. He was unused to favors from strangers.

"Don't mention it, we're going to be running a crew together, you'll have plenty of opportunity to catch me back."

"Right," Ian said quietly, looking back out the viewscreen.

"Once you're dropped off, I'll swing by Transpo to see about your truck. Most Bucks don't get one, but Logistics supervisors do. Supply shipments are the main mission here, and they know we're on call in case they get a random drop in the middle of the day. It's not often, but it happens."

"I get a truck?"

"Yeah, it'll be a LITCAT like this one, maybe a little shittier 'cause you're new, and they don't know you. Hopefully it's not one of the ones they got back from the Security platoons. My first one was like that, there were teeth-marks in the fucking steering wheel."

"Huh," Ian said, a shadow crossing his face.

Sergeant Torres noted the shift in his partner's demeanor. "You can drive, right?"

Ian eyed the steering wheel with unease. Living in a city his whole life had allowed him to avoid *riding* in most wheeled vehicles, let alone operating one. His uncle had let him tool around on an old tractor on their

algae farm when he was fifteen, and he'd certified on a MMUT-CAT in basic training just like everyone else. Ian scrunched his nose, the code of man prohibited him from admitting weakness in front another man.

"Uh, yeah. Of course." Ian forced the confidence into his voice. "Just uh, where's the throttle sticks?"

Sergeant Torres eyed him critically, before shrugging. "It's an older LITCAT, it won't have throttle levers like the bigger MMUT-CATs do. It's a wheel to turn and pedals for gas and brakes."

"Yes, of course," Ian nodded. He had no idea what that meant.

The dunes outside gave way to domed huts, clustered around in groups of four. There were signs out front noting the platoons and missions for the units in each one. Ian noticed that the further in they drove, the shabbier the buildings seemed to become, the more faded the paint on the signs. He pointed this out to Sergeant Torres.

"The base got built outwards, newer complexes established as the mission grew here over time. A pilot told me it looks like a big star from overhead, radiating out from the old Command hub."

Makes sense, Ian thought. "Is that why they call it the 'Dirt Star?'"

"No, not at all," Sergeant Torres laughed, bouncing in his seat after hitting a pothole. They crested a small hill, looking out over a land dotted with huts, the sun finally risen in the north. They watched a dust storm building on the horizon, the sky to the east ominously orange.

"No," Sergeant Torres said, watching the sandy winds pick up. "It's because we're in the asshole of the universe."

Chapter 4:

Terrance sat in the front seat of the LITCAT, staring out at the empty expanse of sand and gravel. The dunes glowed orange with the light of a setting sun. An empty bag tumbled into view, traveling along the wind before catching on one of the squat, tubiform cactuses that dotted the Anian wastes. Terrance watched it flutter, billowing around the cactus branch. The wind picked up and the branch snapped off, dragged down the road by the entangled bag. Another man might have found the moment poignant, a noble metaphor for mankind's engulfing, destructive impact on the natural world. Terrance Torres ignored metaphors, just as he was generally indifferent to sentimentality, poignancy, or anything else that failed to add to his wallet, his spare time, or his benchpress. He was a man with few priorities, but he pursued them with zeal.

Terrance took a swig from the can of *Chargeit!,* ignoring the cloying, metallic tang of the yellow energy drink. The chill of the can had long since departed. Only a hint of condensation lingered on the side that faced the air conditioning blasting from the vent. Pan flute music warbled through the cab from speakers in the doors. He bobbed his head along with the tune, nursing the last dregs while he waited. The sands outside continued to glow, the planet's slow rotation drawing out the edges of twilight.

The passenger door opened, a blast of hot air searing through the cab. He finished his drink, tossing the empty can to join the pile of others in the seat behind him. Letting out an enormous belch, the cab momentarily filled with the distinct aromas of citrus, peppers, and eggs. He patted his chest with a closed fist, setting another two free in the process.

"Ready?" Terrance asked, sparing a glance to the seat behind him.

Sweat ran in rivers into Sergeant Bernard's wide eyes, momentarily obscuring the disgust on his face. He managed a nod, his mouth still slightly agape.

"Good," said Terrance, throwing the truck in gear. "We've got a long day ahead of us."

The stars were beginning to show on the horizon when they reached

the cargo port. Lights shone in patches around the vast, ringed building, the wide, open center scorched from decades of ships landing and launching. Sergeant Torres guided the truck to a spot in the overhang, ignoring the sign reading 'Reed-Sergeant Parking Only.'

Ian clung to the door handle as he stepped out of the cab, his head spinning when he leaned over. He'd slept eighteen hours when he'd finally gotten into his room, dropping his bags and slumping face-first onto the bare mattress. Only the discovery of a yellow stain a few inches from his face had jolted him back awake, his horror spurring him on in a furious search for some means of protection. A frantic search through his bags had ensued, clothes, webbing, and gear strewn around the room in his haste. An hour later and he had returned to sleep, nestled atop five layers of sheets, blankets, foam padding, and an inflated camping mattress.

He had awoken to a pair of alarms set on two different devices, with four hours to spare before he had agreed to meet Sergeant Torres. The plaster chunks dug out of the bare white walls of the room had given him little confidence, but he had been pleasantly surprised to find an access-mirror mounted over the alloy desk in the corner and a respectably strong LinkNet signal throughout the dorm. The attached bathroom had also been a nice revelation, with only a touch of black mold nestled in the corners of the shower. After a quick vidchat with Suzette letting her know he was okay, he had set out executing items three through forty-seven of his preparatory unpacking list. There was much to be done, but he was finally getting his life back in order.

Now if only I could get the rest of the world back in order. Ian shut his eyes tight to stop the spinning, the alloy door handle cool under his hands. He breathed slowly through his mouth as waves of nausea rolled through him. He could feel the heat rising off the sunbaked ground, beads of sweat beginning to roll down the small of his back.

Gravel crunched to his right.

"You okay?" Sergeant Torres' voice was tinged with something almost bordering on concern.

Ian swallowed hard, forcing his eyes back open.

"I'm…I'm fine," he said, pushing himself up. He shook his head to clear it, causing the world to lurch violently back and forth. *Shit.* He took a step back, teetering on the edge of being violently ill.

Sergeant Torres threw out his hand, snagging Ian by the wrist and pulling him steady. "Easy, buddy. It's gonna be a minute before you're used to the extra oxygen and added gravity. 'Specially with the post-cryo hangover."

Ian concentrated very hard on standing very still. His cerebellum waged a fierce and fiery debate with his stomach over the decision to expel his breakfast. He closed his eyes, freeing up some additional neurons to aid in the dispute. His brain won out, and he opened his eyes again.

Ian nodded slowly to Sergeant Torres. "Thanks, I think I've got it."

Sergeant Torres released his hand, watching him for a moment before turning and heading for the port's door.

"What about the heat?"

Torres stopped, turning back to his shaky compatriot. "What?"

"The heat," Ian coughed. He cleared his throat, a new bead of sweat forming on his temple. "You said it takes a minute getting used to the atmosphere and the gravity. What about the heat?"

"Heat?" Sergeant Torres laughed, making his way to the door.

"It's the coldest day of the year."

The *Orbit to Surface Port of Containerized Cargo Distribution and Supply Dispersal Network* (officially labeled the OSPCCDSDN by ICF doctrine, unofficially labeled 'the port' by the kind of people who viewed vowels and brevity as critical components of human speech) bustled with activity. All around Ian, Troopers hustled with scantools, crowbars, wrenches, and straps. A mountain of steel and alloy crates rose on the left, stretching up into the rafters of the high, domed ceiling. A yellow mechlift creaked by on the right, twin treads leaving a trail of rubber scuffs on the stained concrete floor. Ian stepped out of the way as it passed, hydraulic arms groaning as the Private inside clamped them around the nearest crate. Another Trooper hurried behind, rushing up to secure the safety lines from the crate to the loader. A sharp beeping cut over the noise of the port as the mechlift pulled back, emitting a mechanical whine of protest as the arms lifted up the dense black crate. The beeping stopped when the loader spun deftly in place, speeding off and heading around the building's curve with the other Trooper close behind.

The air inside was thick and humid; fumes, sweat, and exhaust swirling in a cloud around rafters of the port. Ian watched the action closely, looking for familiar patterns in the cacophony of work. In terms of scale, it was exponentially bigger than anything he had seen working in the 17th Depot, but the core principles remained the same. Ships came in to be loaded or unloaded. Containers waited to be sorted and unpacked. Unpacked supplies were further sorted for local distribution or repacked for continued transit. Outbound shipments were palletized and loaded. Mechanically, it was the same job he'd done back in Winnipeg, in much the same way that an aircraft carrier is mechanically the same as a canoe.

Ian swallowed hard, the quick beat of his heart letting him know he was very far from home and very close to being overwhelmed. *Focus. Find something small you can work with.* Ian looked around, honing in on a Trooper standing off to the side with a clipboard.

"Where's her vest?" he asked, tapping Sergeant Torres on the arm. He pointed to the Trooper with the clipboard, drawing an imaginary vest on himself at the same time. "Load supervisors are supposed to wear high-vis green vests."

Ian looked around, spotting another supervisor wearing only their uniform pants and grey undershirt. "Him too. No vest?"

"Not enough vests," Torres said with a shrug. "Gotta prioritize them for the Troopers working around the mechlifts. Plus it's hot as fuck in here."

Ian's brow furrowed. The air inside the port was only slightly cooler than outside, but he hardly saw that as sound reasoning. He looked around, spotting a lone Trooper ratcheting down on a pallet strap. He pointed him out to the other Buck-Sergeant

"What's he doing? Standard practice is to use two Troopers ratcheting on either side so the tension is even."

"Not enough manning," Sergeant Torres grunted.

Ian frowned, something wasn't adding up. "Manning? How? This is the biggest port in the ICF."

"Exactly," replied Torres. "We see seventy to a hundred ships a day. Even working eighteen hour shifts that's a thousand to fifteen-hundred tons of cargo every day, in and out. So we spread 'em out, one Trooper to a pallet."

Ian's frown deepened. He didn't like what he was hearing.

"But what about him?" he asked, pointing to a thick Trooper with no neck bending over a stack of boxes on a dolly. "Don't tell me you don't have enough back braces."

Sergeant Torres followed the line of Ian's finger.

"Him? That's just Bradshaw." He offered Ian another shrug. "Fucker's too big, can't find one that fits."

The frown on Ian's face dipped lower than he thought possible. He scratched his head. *What the hell is going on here?*

Torres read the consternation on the younger man's face.

"C'mon," he sighed turning his back on Ian. "There's a lot more we have to cover."

The rest of their tour proceeded much the same as the start.

Ian asked why the landing schedule wasn't displayed on the wall-mount vidscreens.

"Changes too often. We run a ship's order when it lands. Unload what we need, load what we gotta."

He asked about checking pallets into the BRT system.

"Can't, takes too long. We track locally with PZ."

He asked about matching load-sort instructions with the *Deepwater* database.

"We don't. We run them off the crate labels."

He asked about the maintenance schedule for the mechlifts.

"We fix 'em when they break."

He asked why the load assistants didn't have eye-protection.

"They ran out."

Ian asked about sonic plugs.

"Them too."

He asked why scantools weren't attached to Troopers' wrists.

"Straps broke."

He asked if they met with the ferry pilots to go over the load map.

"Nope."

He asked if they uploaded the load maps for use at the reception port.

"No."

He asked if they pulled previous load maps to cross-reference current orders.

"No."

He asked if they conducted quarterly training to optimize freight efficiency using previous load maps.

"No!"

He asked if they even stored previous load maps for later use.

"NO!"

Ian stopped, momentarily stunned into silence.

Sergeant Torres fumed, fists balled and nostrils flaring. His curly brown hair, normally kept in tight waves, was loose and disheveled from his hands running through it.

"C'mon!" he thundered, pivoting on a heel and walking out onto the landing dock. Ian followed close behind, a jet of air washing down on him as he stepped through the thermal curtain. Sergeant Torres grabbed him by the shoulder, turning him roughly to face a DC-242 coming in to land. He pointed to the ship, veins rising on the back of his hand.

"You see that!" he snapped, tracing his finger from the ship to the upper reaches of the sky. Ian followed the finger to the dozens of blinking lights arranged in a line. "There's almost thirty of 'em just like it, and another hundred more stacked in low orbit. We only get sixteen hours of nightfall here. That's just sixteen hours where the air is cool and dense enough to land a ship. We! Do not! Have *time!*"

Sergeant Torres spun Ian back to face him. He leaned in, his face inches away. "You have to forget whatever you think you know. You don't have time for any of that shit. There's the Academy way, and there's the Anius way. And you're not in the Academy anymore."

Ian nodded slowly, raising his hands to placate the agitated Buck-Sergeant. "Alright. Okay. I get it."

Sergeant Torres's brown eyes searched Ian's for understanding. After a moment, he relaxed and joined in Ian's nod.

"Okay, good." He released him, dropping his hands and walking back into the port. Ian watched him go, broad shoulders swinging stiffly as he stepped back through the air curtain. Ian let out a slow breath. He had played along, but internally he scoffed. Ian Bernard lived in a world of rules—rules created by people with experience and understanding. The

ICF Supply Corps operated with rules built off hundreds of years of tradition and experience. Rules that encompassed almost twelve-hundred planets, bases, and orbital ports. *What are the odds this place is the exception?*

The conclusion of the tour was much quieter. Ian nodded along as Sergeant Torres laid out the flow of work. The 379th ICF Supply Battalion ran in two, eighteen-hour shifts, with no work during the hottest portion of the planet's fifty-four hour day. Most of the planet kept the same schedule, he explained, so appointments and due-outs to the back office were only an option in the few hours before sunset or after sunrise. As Buck-Sergeants, they straddled both shifts, supervising the loading and unloading of the ships as they came in. Schedule was nine Anian days on, one day off, with two Buck-Sergeants on duty each day. Lieutenant Ligen and Reed-Sergeant Gherwiz's offices were on the second level with windows overlooking the loading bay. They traded off on the two shifts so one of them was always there to keep an eye on things.

"What about the office in between?" Ian asked.

Anian customs, Sergeant Torres explained. They were brought in after the governor's crackdown, but they never inspected shipments. The two officers rarely bothered with doing anything, usually hiding out in their office dicking around on their tablets all day.

"They're lazy shits," he added. "Mostly there for show."

Ian nodded, eyeing the empty office as he followed along. They passed by storage bays and sorting bays, past vast rooms filled with mazes of freight-laden shelves stacked to the rafters. They passed the landing control terminal, waving to the three Troopers directing ships in on headsets. All around them Troopers rushed, hurrying about with tools and clipboards. They finished the tour where they had started, having looped through the entire port. Sergeant Torres waved to another Trooper, a stocky woman with thick forearms, short, spiky black hair, and a chip on her shoulder from her days in Camden.

"Hey, Ishii, come meet the new Polowski."

Buck-Sergeant Ishii walked over to greet them, crescents of sweat showing below the chest of her grey undershirt.

"Oy, Torres, where the fuck you been, man? Sergeant Corstley's called twice with fast-track orders and the Baron popped by as well."

"I'm sorry," he said, slumping his shoulders. He jerked a thumb back at Ian. "I've been out dragging the new guy along. Gotta get him up to speed before my next day off."

Ian waved from the back.

Sergeant Ishii's eyes narrowed; she didn't return the wave. "Es a skinny one."

Sergeant Torres shrugged.

Sergeant Ishii looked Ian up and down. "'E looks like a nerd."

Torres rolled his eyes. "*I* didn't pick him, I'm just the one showin' him around."

Ian stared straight ahead, waiting for his inclusion in the conversation.

Sergeant Ishii snorted, her broad nose flaring slightly with disdain.

"Well if 'es a wank, then 'es with you," she said jabbing a finger in Torres' broad chest. "I had the last twat. You remember 'im— Sandoval? The git who got hisself run over by the mechlift?"

Sergeant Torres remembered. He assured her that to the best of his knowledge, Ian wasn't a twat, and if he was then Torres would take care of it.

Ian bristled at the implication. *Who the hell does this guy think he is?* He opened his mouth to respond but thought better of it.

"Why did the Baron stop by?" he asked, quietly changing the subject.

"Colonel Schwarz commissioned in the Supply Corps," said Torres. "He's been in command for a while, but he's still got a soft spot for loaders. Anius is the ICF's main supply point, so he checks in from time to time."

Ian nodded, grateful the discussion had shifted away from him. Sergeant Torres turned back to Sergeant Ishii.

"You get Corstley's orders in?" he asked, rubbing his chin. "We owe him for picking up the tab at Polowski's going away party."

Ishii shook her head. "Naw man, it's been all to pot aroun' here. Haven' had a chance to get my head straight."

The chin-rubbing grew more thoughtful. "Alright then, I'll handle it." He looked back at Ian, pensive resignation coloring his face. "Alright Bernard, come with me. We'll show you what makes the 'Dirt Star' go 'round."

It took three hours to locate the shipments for Buck-Sergeant Corstley, fast-tracking them ahead of fifteen others. Ian considered asking about unpacking and processing, but Sergeant Torres cut him off before he got the chance.

"Shipments for the Raiders don't get unpacked," he explained. "We log them coming off the ship, put them in PZ, and then dump them in a MMUTCAT to their compound in the West."

But how do they verify that the cargo matches the shipment order, Ian asked.

"We don't," Torres answered. "Raiders' shipments stay packed. If it's not right, they'll let us know."

They were better off not knowing, he explained. Anything deeper in dealing with the Raiders was asking for trouble.

Ian nodded, keeping his thoughts to himself as they loaded the last crates in the back of the blacked-out MMUTCAT. They shut the cargo hatch and waved the driver on, the red sigil of the Commando Raiders glinting in the soft light of the loading docks. A lightning bolt stabbing through a hissing snake-skull—the Raiders' publicity team said it represented the main mission and ethos of the ICF's most elite fighting forces, 'eradicating aggression with speed and violence.' Ian always thought it looked rather different, like a wrathful god lashing out, capricious and random. As with most people, his view of the Commando Raiders was shaped almost exclusively by vidplays, video games, and the best-selling tell-all books from some of their more literary-inclined, retired members. The stories they told painted the Raiders as specters, myths, hard men and women shaped by the most grueling selection process in history. Those who survived operated in realms of absolute secrecy on the knife-edge of the Coalition Republic's military actions. There were few with security clearances high enough to be privy to the details of their missions. Only the Small Council and the Raiders' direct chain of command could boast such privilege, and rumors said some missions were classified beyond those few as well.

Ian Bernard didn't put much stock in rumors. Like most boys, he'd grown up with a Raiders' poster on his wall, nestled between one for *Alto Deathtoe*, a punk band his friend played bass for, and another for Folsom Sieberman, the prominent astronomer. He did put stock in the hushed tones Sergeant Torres used to describe his dealings with them, filing the information away on his list of worries.

They spent the rest of the shift catching up on the other shipments, fast-tracking the unpacking and processing of a few others according to the direction of Sergeant Torres. To hear him tell it, the whole installation ran off favors; it was the *only* way to get things done and get what you needed. Ian nodded along. Time, it appeared to him, wasn't the only thing in short supply.

Sweating, their shift complete, they finished off the last shipping manifest and headed back towards the LITCAT. Sergeant Ishii met them on the way, offering a half-hearted wave, as they walked to the door.

"Long day?" Ian asked, his grey undershirt soaked with sweat.

Ishii answered with a loud crack of her neck.

"Long enough," she said, fishing around in her pocket. She pulled out a blue tin, flipping the lid up and offering it to Sergeant Torres. He accepted the tin gratefully, pulling out a clear tab and slapping it on his upper arm.

"Stip?" he asked, holding the tin out to Ian.

Although tobacco products had fallen completely out of use with the close of the twenty-first century, and most lab grade amphetamines were heavily banned by the Coalition government, nicotine remained quite popular. Evolving in its delivery throughout the preceeding centuries, nicotine joined caffeine in the pantheon of 'benign stimulants,' its use and abuse largely overlooked by the Republic's critical eye. *Stip*, short for 'stimulant patches,' was merely the latest iteration in man's thousand-year fascination with the drug. The long-term health effects of nausea, cardiac problems, and immune suppression were well known and generally ignored by its habitual users.

Ian declined with a shake of his head. Sergeant Torres shrugged, passing the tin back to Ishii. She slapped a patch on both arms, a shiver running through her as the dermal delivery unit took effect.

"*Ahhhh*, that's the stuff," she said, a twinge creeping into her voice. Excessive nasal drip was a well-known, short-term effect of *Stip*, with most users carrying a handkerchief or pack of tissues for discrete use in polite society. Torres and Ishii, it appeared, had declined their invitations to polite society.

Blrrrrrrrp. Ian looked on in horror as Sergeant Ishii put one finger to the side of her nose, leaned over, and blew a thick glob of snot out the other side. It landed with a foamy plop on the concrete floor. Sergeant Torres joined her shortly after, his own contribution mingling with an oil stain before running into an open grate. Ian choked a little as they stood back up, turning slightly green when they proceeded to wipe their hands on the side of their pants. He blinked hard on watery eyes, walking briskly to the door far ahead of the others.

The air outside was hot and stifling, the glow of sunrise threatening on the horizon. Ian sucked in a few breaths through his nose and out through his mouth, sweat starting again in rivers down his back. He made a mental note to track down some electrolyte powder. At this rate he'd have no salt left in him by the next shift. Resting for a moment against the wall, he looked north along the curved expanse of the port. To his surprise he saw figures in the distance, silhouetted against the sun as they clambered up and over the dunes.

"Fuckin' sol-chasers."

Ian looked back to see Sergeant Torres, shaking his head with contempt.

"Who?" he asked the stocky Buck-Sergeant.

"Sol-chasers, a bunch of rib-thin fuckwits that come out at sunrise to chase each other and 'work out.'"

The air quotes he placed around the last two words gave Ian the distinct impression that Sergeant Torres looked down on the committed cardiovascularists.

"It's like they're all in a race to see who's the skinniest," added Sergeant Ishii, joining them in leaning against the wall. "You see them over there squattin' with the poly-plex tubes? Takes the piss right out of proper lifting."

Sergeant Torres grunted in agreement.

"No form. No gains. I heard they don't even curl," he sniffed, shaking his head sadly. He stood up and flexed, contemplating his own arms and ruminating on the woeful priorities of other men.

"You in for deadlifts today?" she asked, smacking him on a flexed bicep.

Sergeant Torres replied with a belch that almost managed to sound like the words 'fuck yes.'

He turned back to Ian. "You?"

Ian shook his head, the rivers of sweat pooling in the small of his back and collecting in the waistband of his grey uniform pants. He looked out to the silhouettes, cavorting on the hot sands.

"Maybe another time."

Chapter 5:

Go.............

The LITCAT lurched forward, honeycombed wheels spinning on the gravel road.

Stop! Too fast!

The LITCAT slammed to a halt, momentum throwing Ian forward against the steering wheel. His right foot hovered over the throttle pedal, while his left pinned the brake to the floor. Try as he might, he could not seem to grasp the subtle nuance of the light-truck's archaic pedal system. He sighed, banging his head softly against the wheel. He rested his chin on his hands, looking out on the expanse of empty gravel road. The clock in the corner of the screen let him know he still had three hours before he was supposed to meet Sergeant Torres.

Only eleven miles to go...

It took the better part of three hours, but Ian guided the boxy truck to a stop outside Sergeant Torres' dorm, even managing a few extra laps of the BPD along the way. He set the LITCAT's brake, listening to the soft whoosh of the climate control systems as he waited. Ten minutes ahead of schedule, he crossed item twenty-six off his list. He relaxed a little in his seat, unclipping the buckle on his harness and leaning back. He had done it, he had mastered driving, and it had only taken three hours. Ian glanced back at the clock, it was now nine minutes before he was supposed to meet Sergeant Torres. He laced his fingers behind his head. *And now we wait...*

Nine minutes later and Ian sat back up in his seat, buckling his harness. He put a hand on the gear shift, mentally rehearsing putting it in drive and placing his foot on the gas. He felt good. He felt ready. He put his hands back on the wheel, preparing himself for the opening of the passenger door.

Two minutes later and Ian's face began to drop. He checked the clock on the front viewscreen, comparing it to the time displayed on his tablet. They matched, and as he watched the time change on both screens, they both informed him that Sergeant Torres was three minutes late. *No worries.* Ian fiddled with the knobs controlling the air in the cab. *Still plenty of time...*

Five minutes later and a frown stretched firmly across Ian's face. He began tapping his hands on the steering wheel, mentally reminding himself that they still had over an hour and a half to get breakfast and drive to the cargo port. *Be cool, Ian. His watch is probably slow.* Ian had never seen Sergeant Torres wear a watch, but it was the clearest explanation he could think of. He fired off a message letting Sergeant Torres know that he'd arrived and was waiting outside. *Still plenty of time...*

Ten minutes later and his teeth began to grind. His hands had stopped their tapping, and were now clenched on the knobby rubber of the wheel. As the seconds crept by he began to question the character and morals of the other Buck-Sergeant, mentally rehearsing the confrontation they would have when the passenger door opened and Torres stepped inside. *'I'm sorry your watch broke,'* he'd say, picturing the confusion on Sergeant Torres' face. *'But I don't have a watch,'* Sergeant Torres would say back, his dumb mouth flopping open, dumbly. *'Well then maybe you should spend less time in the gym, and more time in the watch store—BUYING A WATCH!'* Ian shouted in his head, further picturing the other Buck-Sergeant's face crumbling into apologies and abject shame. Ian rehearsed this scenario three more times, adding a higher pitch to Torres' voice with each one. The final one ended with tears, and Sergeant Torres' blubbering promise that he would never be late again. Ian looked back at the clock, reminding himself that they still had over an hour. *Still plenty of time...*

Twenty minutes later and doubt began to creep in. Ian pulled out his tablet, scrolling frantically through the messages Sergeant Torres had sent him the day before. He jumped past the agreed pickup time, confirming that he had arrived on time, now thirty minutes prior. He read through the address listed in the last message, matching it to the one painted on the domed huts outside. He double checked that his earlier message saying he was outside had gone through, sending another one just to be sure. Ian searched the huts for any sign of movement before slumping back in his chair, the tablet hanging loosely in his hands.

Forty minutes after their scheduled rendezvous and concern had replaced the doubt in Ian's mind. He envisioned a litany of scenarios in which Sergeant Torres had injured himself, becoming too incapacitated to keep their agreed appointment. *He's probably hurt. Or worse,* Ian thought, resolving himself to action. He unclipped his harness, throwing open the door and stepping out into the baking sun. He hurried over to the door labeled 'Hut 307, Side B,' running through all of the first-aid lessons he'd received back in basic training. He stepped into the brief shade of the hut's overhang, rapping two knuckles loudly on the metal door. He kept up his pounding for a full minute, the misfortunes befalling Sergeant Torres worsening in his mind as the seconds went by.

The door swung open just as the pain in Ian's knuckles was beginning to outweigh his concern. Sergeant Torres stood in the doorway, wearing only his boots and pants.

"What?" he asked, water dripping into his eyes from his sopping wet hair.

Ian faltered. "I, uh, was just checking if you...got my text." He searched around for something to focus on, settling on blank wall behind Torres' shoulder.

Sergeant Torres looked at him blankly, water tracing rivulets down his chest. After a moment, he shrugged. "Sorry man, must've had my tablet on silent."

He turned back to his dorm, motioning for Ian to either follow him or wait outside. Ian took a few hesitant steps across the threshold, a quick check of his watch telling him they were now forty-five minutes behind schedule. He took a deep breath as he shut the door, trying to think up a nonchalant way to bring up the time. He looked around the room, taking in the laundry strewn across the floor and desk, the nest of blankets wadded up on the bare mattress, and the poster of a kitten hanging from a branch taped to the wall. A tuneless whistle came from the bathroom as Sergeant Torres began drying his hair. Ian chewed his lower lip, crossing his arms and avoiding eye contact with his watch.

A few minutes later and the whistling stopped. Jaunty humming replaced it as Sergeant Torres stepped out of the bathroom to grab a shirt hanging on the back of a chair. Ian's lip-chewing had progressed to the point of grinding, his left arm going slightly numb from the tightness of his crossing. Torres turned towards Ian as he stepped past, and Ian caught sight of a pale pink scar curving under the line of his chest.

"Bypass?" he blurted out without thinking.

Sergeant Torres stopped mid-grab. "What?"

Ian's face grew warm as he was quickly reminded of his manners.

"Uh, your scar," he said, pointing it out as nonchalantly as he could. "I was, uh, just asking if it was from a cardiac bypass."

Sergeant Torres stared at him, the grey undershirt clenched tightly in his hands.

"No," he said sharply, tugging the shirt over his head.

"Oh, uh, good," Ian stammered, dropping his eyes to the floor. "Cause if it was, you know, the heat and your heart could..."

He trailed off under the intensity of Torres' stare.

"You know what?" he said, jerking his thumb back towards the door. "I'll just wait in the truck."

A few minutes later and the passenger door swung open, a wave of heat washing over him as Sergeant Torres flopped into the seat. They sat in silence for a few moments while Ian waited for him to buckle his harness. Another few moments and a loud cough let Ian know that vehicular safety wasn't high on Sergeant Torres' priorities. He tugged the shifter into gear, sucking in a deep breath as he pressed on the throttle. The LITCAT launched out of the parking lot, throwing them both back in their seats. Ian slammed on the brakes, jerking them forward as the truck stopped. A loud sigh filled the cabin as Sergeant Torres dragged a heavy hand down his face.

Ian eased his left foot off the brake, matching the movement with the pressure from his right. A horrendous grinding noise filled the cabin as the four wheel-mounted motors fought against the hydraulic brakes. Ian stopped, taking both feet off the pedals as prickly heat crept up his neck and stomped across his face. He turned towards Sergeant Torres.

"Would, uh, would you like to—

"I'll drive!"

They rode in silence to the chow hall in the old Command Central. Sergeant Bernard fiddled with the straps on his harness, the only sound in the cabin coming from the soft tap of Terrance's left shoulder strap dangling against the seat. Sergeant Bernard cast a sideways glance at his surly driver. He tested the waters by reaching for the radio, extending his hand slowly as he watched for a reaction. Bernard pressed the radio on, a twanging guitar and French horns filling the cab. He sat back in his seat, joining Terrance in looking straight ahead. They drove without speaking. The horns faded away and were replaced with what sounded like Gregorian chanting. He turned back to Terrance, face twinging into a forced smile.

"Weird channel, huh?" Bernard asked, straining for lightness.

Terrance stared straight ahead.

"Selection seems pretty eclectic."

Terrance sighed. He didn't know what eclectic meant, but he was pretty sure it meant their quiet time had ended.

"Yeah," he grumbled. "DJ's weird."

Sergeant Bernard bobbed his head, as if hoping for that answer. Chanting filled the cab once again.

"Well, are there any other channels?"

Terrance sighed. Bernard seemed bound and determined to hold a conversation.

"Three," he answered, a slight clench to his jaw. "Two ICF channels and a local. One ICF is for Command Access—it's just base updates, news, and coming events. The other plays music, but it's the same top one-hundred songs, and only the censored crap. So we stick with the local channel, it's weird, but at least it's something fucking different."

"Cool," Sergeant Bernard said, turning back to look out the viewscreen. "Cool, cool, cool."

The chow hall in the old Command Central was filled with the clatter of silverware on alloy trays and the dull roar of Troopers talking. Ian pushed his tray along in line, they were pressed for time but Sergeant Torres promised him it wouldn't take more than fifteen minutes. Ian counted thirty-five until their shift started, and he had his reservations about Torres' ability to keep on schedule.

Too bad he's still got my keys, Ian thought as the line shifted forward, the tray in his hand clinking on the railing. He watched from behind as Sergeant Torres cracked his neck, veins sticking out as he twisted. *What a goon,* Ian sighed to himself. *Still, he'd probably get us there faster than I could.* The line shuffled forward, bringing steaming trays in view. He was pleasantly surprised to see it was filled with real entrees, shaped and smelling like actual food. Most Troopers on deployments had to make do with the slop from RationVendors, mushy cubes of indiscriminate color and imperceptible taste. He mentioned it to Sergeant Torres.

"Yeah, perks of being the largest transit hub. They use full-on food printers back there, although there's only about twenty types of entrees."

Ian was elated, between the LinkNet access, the full dorm room, and this, he was beginning to think Anius wasn't as bad as he had heard. He stepped forward, reaching over the counter to get a scoopful of scrambled eggs and another of rice. A third tray had what appeared to be sausages, but a sharp look from Sergeant Torres convinced him to avoid them. He grabbed a cupful of 'orange electrolyte beverage' from the fountain dispensary and swung out of line, meeting up with Torres and Ishii at a table by the door.

"Oy Bernie, what's shaking?" Ishii waved him over to sit by her, a big smile on her face. She'd been genuinely pleasant to him ever since he'd shown her the picture of Suzette he used for the home screen on his tablet. "How's the missus?"

"She's good," Ian said, taking a sip of his drink. "A few complaints about her students. Apparently they're doing orthography now, and a lot of them are struggling with separating diphthongs from semivowels."

"Right, right." Sergeant Ishii nodded along, smile unwavering even though she was fairly certain he'd made all of those words up. "She's the history professor?"

"Dead languages," Ian replied. *Historic languages*, he corrected internally. As Suzette was always quick to point out, *'No language is dead so long as someone still speaks it.'* Ian had always contended that any language spoken exclusively by a collection of dusty academics cloistered in university halls hardly constituted a thriving means of expression. While Suzette usually responded by putting out her tongue and pointing to the hallway wall, where hung her three PhDs in neat black frames. Ian smiled a little at the memory. He missed them both terribly. Vidchatting every other day only really served to highlight how very far they were and how long it would be until he came home.

"Fascinatin,'" said Ishii, eyes bright as she worked her way through a stack of waffles. "How's your boy?"

Ian swallowed hard on a dry chunk of egg. "Tan's good," he coughed. "Not giving mom a hard time yet."

"Tan?" Sergeant Torres looked up from his plate. "Is that short for something?"

"Um, yeah," Ian said, shoveling in a spoonful of rice to buy time. He chased it down with a sip from his glass, adding softly, "It's short for...Taniel."

Sergeant Torres and Sergeant Ishii stared at each other for a moment before bursting into laughter.

"It was her grandfather's name!" Ian insisted, fighting to be heard over the rising laughter of the other Sergeants. "It means a lot to her, it's a strong, family name!"

But it was too late, they were too far gone, both NCOs were almost sideways with laughter. Ian wilted a little inside. Truth be told, he'd never liked the name either—it's why he always insisted on shortening it.

Ian cleared his throat loudly, succeeding in interrupting their giggling at last. Sergeant Torres caught sight of the hurt in Ian's eyes, composing himself with the reminder that the butt of their joke was still a small child. He kicked Ishii under the table, cutting off her cackling abruptly.

"Don't worry, man," Sergeant Torres said, holding back further jokes. "It's a good name. A tough, man's name."

"Unique!" Ishii added helpfully, wiping a tear from her eye.

Ian accepted their apologies with a gracious nod, changing the subject to the squad of rough-looking men that sauntered into the hall.

"Raiders?" he asked, pointing them out to the table.

"What gave it away?" Torres asked, stabbing at his tray with a fork. "The beards, or the attitude that everyone else in the world can all get fucked."

Ian watched the five men push their way to the middle of the line.

"Little rude, huh?" he asked, taking another drink from his cup.

"I dunno," Sergeant Ishii offered. "If I was in the top five percent of the ICF, I'd probably treat everyone like rubbish too."

"The big one is Zimmer," Sergeant Torres said, pointing out a broad Special-Trooper with severe high-and-tight. "He's a monster in the gym, I've seen him front-squat three-fifty."

"The two next to him are Kantz and Huges," he continued, pointing to a tall, reedy ginger and an equally tall, bull-necked blond. "They close down the bar every day—got a table off in the corner just to themselves."

Torres waved to a short, burly Buck-Sergeant with a woolly brown beard. The bearded man nodded back. "That's Corstley, he's decent, but

pushy. Always calls up with a short-notice ask or a shipment he needs fast-tracked. But he makes good on his favors. He's the one you'll talk to the most."

"And him?" Ian asked, looking over to the last man in the squad. Wiry, but unassuming, with long, salt-and-pepper hair swept back from a pair of piercing grey eyes. It was the eyes that drew Ian's attention, the way they swept around the room, as though in a constant search to size up each one of its occupants.

"That's Harbison," Sergeant Torres said quietly, taking a long pull from his cup. "He's their superintendent. Nobody knows fuck about him, and that's probably for the best."

They watched the commandos grab their food and head for the door, several to-go bags wrapped in each hand. Reed-Sergeant Harbison was the last man through, flinty eyes scanning the chow hall one last time before he stepped through the door. Briefly, he locked eyes with Ian. Ian felt a cold shiver run through him, he dropped his eyes quickly to his tray. When he looked up, they were gone.

Sergeant Ishii nudged him with her arm, breaking him out of his thoughts. "Oy Bernie, this is Torres' last day before break. You ready to fly solo wit' me tomorrow?"

He nodded, "Sure am. I'm excited."

"Good, good," she said throwing back the last of her SimuCaff. She set the cup down and belched. "You gonna lift with us after work? It's chest day."

Ian shook his head, "Maybe another time."

Sergeant Ishii shrugged. "S'okay, there's always tomorrow."

Ian smiled, swallowing his last bite of rice. He was well aware of what tomorrow was, and he had some ideas for it as well.

The next day Ian arrived at work an hour early, only two hours after he'd left his dorm. He summoned his crews for a meeting before the sun fully set and ships began lining up to land. There were to be some changes, he explained, some corrections were in order. There were a lot of blank stares when he finished that last part, and a few polite smiles faded away when he dove into detail about his expectations for the next shift. There were some whispers in the back when he had finished, and more than a few sideways glances. Undeterred, he ignored them. There were rules to this business, rules created for efficiency and designed to ensure safety. Rules he had spent the better part of five years inhabiting in every position he had every worked on the supply line, and while these Troopers worked for him, they would inhabit those rules too.

It took exactly two hours after nightfall for the entire operation to go tits up. Shuttles stacked in orbit as flustered ground crews explained load maps to a series of indifferent ferry pilots. Stacks of crates lined the floor of the landing dock, left there when the load supervisor was taken off the line and ordered to find a high-vis safety vest. Loose gear and bottles littered floor as Troopers worked in two-man teams to palletize items with half the crew they were used to. Stacks inside the sorting bay piled up, as Troopers sat on shipments while struggling to connect their tablets to the *Deepwater* database. Private Bradshaw stood dejectedly off to the side, trying to remember his passcode for the scantool after being pulled off of loading duty for missing his back brace.

All around Ian chaos reigned. As he looked out on the mess of Troopers, shipments, and shouting, Ian couldn't shake the nagging feeling that he might have made a mistake. He grabbed the nearest Special-Trooper, demanding to know why there were only two Troopers in the landing control terminal.

"Because, Sarge," the Trooper sputtered. "You said we needed sonic plugs, and D'hali said she knew where some were, so she left to dig them out of deep storage."

Ian scowled, releasing the young man to scramble away back to his crate. *When I gave the order, I didn't expect them to pull from the fucking LCT!* He looked around, heart pounding as he tried to sort out his next steps. Troopers rushed around him, some knocking into each other in their haste. He could feel himself losing his grip on the situation, panic rising in his chest with the rising din of the bay. *Focus, Ian! Find something small you can work with.* He cast his eyes around the bay, locking on to a mechlift creeping forward, a three-man crew gathered around it to guide it into place. *Idiots, you only need ground guides if there's limited visibility!* He opened his mouth to shout a correction, but he never got the chance.

"Oy, Bernie, what the bloody 'ell is going on?!"

Ian whirled around, catching sight of Sergeant Ishii barreling towards him, meaty hands in the air and murder in her eyes. He put his hands up, clipboard shielding his chest form the impending jab of her finger.

"What's happenin,' Bernie? Storage Bay B is all squiffy, and 'alf the landing dock is filled with crates. I got Corstley calling me up sayin' his order wasn't filled, and I only see one loadin' supe, an' she's workin' in the sortin' bay."

Ian took a step back, trying to put space between his thin body and her aggressive prodding. Sergeant Ishii pressed on, propelled by righteous fury.

"An' to cap it all off, I just got word one of my ferries had to make an emergency divert after one launched from your side ten minutes late, sayin' somefing about a fuckin' *load map?!*'

At the mention of the last two words, Ian's blood ran cold. Here at last was proof, incontrovertible and objective, that the reason for the day's pandemonium was not some errant twist of volatile fate, but was in fact him. The prickly heat crept up his neck again, spreading to his face. His

heart pounded in his chest as he looked around wildly for an answer. *Something, anything to make this right.* He opened his mouth to apologize but no words came out, his tongue dry and twice its usual size. A roaring sound rose in his ears, drowning out the noise of the bay. The last thing he heard was a voice in his ear, letting him know the Lieutenant was on her way. Then his vision tunneled, and his world went black.

Ian awoke on a scratchy green couch in a cool, quiet office. Lieutenant Ligen stood over him with her hands on her hips, the orange light from the desk lamp casting her face in hard lines. Her lips were tight and pursed. She stood back when she saw his eyes open, putting a safe distance between herself and the object of her anger. She leaned against the bare metal desk, crossing her arms and looking him over head-to-toe. Ian never felt smaller as he sat up, catching sight of Reed-Sergeant Gherwiz in a chair by the desk. Silence hung over the room—a poisonous, malignant silence.

Ian opened his mouth, breaking the quiet with a preemptive apology. "I'm, uh, I'm sorry, Ma'am, Sergeant."

At the sound of his words, Lieutenant Ligen's face twisted.

"You're sorry?!" she exploded, throwing her hands in the air. "I had to shut down half my port, reroute or reschedule dozens of shipments. I have pilots calling me up because they were held up on the ground and my LTC crew was out looking for earplugs. And you're *sorry?!*"

Ian stared down at his hands. "I'm, sor—

"It's a real mess down there, son," Sergeant Gherwiz said, interrupting. "A real mess."

Lieutenant Ligen shook her head, beating him down with each swing. "Just what the hell were you thinking, Buck-Sergeant?"

Ian's shoulders slumped. "I'm sorry, I—

Lieutenant Ligen cut him off with a wave of her hand. "You said you're sorry. What. Were. You. *Thinking?*"

Ian faltered. "I...I was just—

"*Yes?*"

"A real mess, son, a real mess."

"I was just—

"Spit it out!"

"Just a real mess, son."

"*I was trying to follow the rules!*"

Ian froze, eyes wide. He hadn't meant to shout that last part. Lieutenant Ligen and Sergeant Gherwiz shared a look.

"What do you *mean?*" she asked.

"The rules," he stammered. "From ICFOI 2397-42B: *Supply Port Operations and Maintenance.* I've been working here a week and there's about a hundred things we don't do right around here, rules we break that I was told were meant to keep us safe and keep things moving. I don't get it, I spent nine months in the Academy having all of them drilled into me. I get here and try to fix things like they taught me and in not even one day, it all fusses up." He dropped his head in his hands. "I just don't get it."

Lieutenant Ligen and Reed-Sergeant Gherwiz shared another look. Sergeant Gherwiz nodded and they both turned back to Ian. Lieutenant Ligen spoke again, her voice softer this time.

"Ian, look at me. It's okay. It's a busy port, and you're in a new job. There's going to be...growing pains."

Ian looked up at the sound of his name, a little unsure of this sudden change.

"Son, whatcha gotta know is that things aren't always as clear as they make it out in the regulation," Sergeant Gherwiz said, leaning back and steepling his fingers over his belly. "It ain't always black and white."

Ian's brow furrowed. "But, I thought..."

"He's right, Ian," Lieutenant Ligen added. "Sometimes certain things have to be adapted to fit the mission, modified for a new place."

Ian shut his mouth, his face a mask of confusion.

"You see, son," Sergeant Gherwiz offered, bristled mustache twitching. "The port here on Anius is like a big dance. And you know the thing about dances, right?"

Ian shook his head, at this point he didn't think he knew a single thing about dances.

"They require compromise," said Lieutenant Ligen, drawing his attention back to her.

Sergeant Gherwiz nodded. "One partner can't go left if the other's heading right."

"So can you do that for us, Ian?" Lieutenant Ligen asked, leaning in close.

"*Can you keep the dance moving?*"

Chapter 6:

"Push…good, use your lats…push…"

Slowly, shakily, the bar climbed through the air.

"That's three… keep pushing…tight grip on the bar."

The bar lowered, halting an inch above Ian's chest. He took a deep breath in, wrists quivering as he pushed again.

"Four…good, now breathe out… tuck your elbows in, shoulder blades squeezed, and keep your lats engaged."

Ian wasn't sure what his 'lats' were, or how to even approach 'engaging' them. He took another deep breath in.

"Keep going…gimme one more, *Number Two.*"

Ian rolled his eyes. He regretted mentioning his class rank when they were swapping stories about the Academy—he hadn't lived it down since. The shake in his wrists became more pronounced. *Don't think, push!* He pushed, forcing out the breath he'd been holding along the way. The bar moved up and out, reaching its peak by the sturdy metal hooks. Strong hands snatched ahold of it, pulling the knurled metal out of his fingers and racking the bar on the hooks.

"And that's five. Nice. Rest."

Ian pulled on the bar to sit up, his chest heaving as he leaned over on the cushioned bench. A towel was offered to him, and he used it to wipe away the sweat pooling in the corner of his eyes.

"Thanks," he said, turning back to Sergeant Torres. "How much was that?"

"One-fifty-five," Sergeant Torres replied, stalling for time as he sized up the two scant plates on each side of the bar. He offered an encouraging smile to soften the blow. "But that's still good! That's almost two hundred back on Earth."

Ian nodded, passing the towel across the back of his neck. *One hundred and fifty pounds, that's up ten from last week.* He appreciated his stocky friend's attempt at sympathy, but it wasn't necessary. He'd been making steady progress over the last three months with Torres and Ishii, and was pleasantly rewarded with an ever-so-slight crease separating his shoulder from his bicep. He eyed the twin plates, a small flicker of pride igniting inside him.

"'Nother round?" Sergeant Torres asked, walking back behind the metal frame.

Ian shook his head, tossing the towel over his shoulder as he stood up from the bench. "Not today, I've got some orders to fill before shift."

"Right, right." Torres nodded, slinging more weight on the bar and settling in under it. "Go on, get out of here, *Number Two.* Go make your power moves."

Ian rolled his eyes again, leaving behind the clang of metal and sharp grunts behind him. Heading for the door, he looked up at the maxim painted across the gym wall. 'Drop weakness,' it said, in bold, blue letters across a cartoon figure climbing a ladder, 'Seize your goals.' Ian smiled, his head high as he stepped out into the baking heat of the morning. It was good he was leaving a little early, he needed the rest. There was plenty to do in the evening to come.

He awoke a few hours before sunset, alarms ringing off two devices. He set about his routine with the usual efficiency, making sure to squeeze in a quick vidchat with Suzette as well. They talked a bit about school, the Winnipeg mayoral election, and Taniel's abrupt refusal to eat carrots. Ian even worked in a few deliberate flexes during the conversation, earning a whistle of appreciation for his efforts. He signed off with their usual exchange, catching Suzette's blown kiss and placing it on his heart, and then he was out the door.

It was 180 degrees outside, the dry heat sapping the moisture from his eyes in the twenty-foot walk from the hut to his truck. He pulled his sleeve over his hand to grip the blistering door handle, a lesson hard learned in the past, and swung it open. The air inside the insulated cab was blissfully cool, and he wiped away the sweat building on his temples. He'd hoped that he'd be used to the heat after a few months on Anius, but with midday temperatures over 200 degrees, there were limits to human adaptation. He prodded the ignition on the dash, spurring the LITCAT to life. A blast of cool air poured out of the vents as the radio kicked on, the DJ announcing that today was his birthday, and that he would be playing *Oi!* non-stop in his own honor. Ian smiled, he'd grown fond of Jerome's musical eccentricities over the past few months. He threw the truck in gear and sped off down the road, guitar wails and guttural punk shouting filling the cab as he went.

The dusty grey dome of Command Central rose into view, the dunes passing outside slowing down as Ian stepped off the throttle. He guided the truck over to the garage tunnel with practiced ease, riding the ramp down to the lower levels. He bypassed empty spots along the way; he still cringed whenever Sergeant Torres pulled into a reserved space. Ian had no idea what the consequences were for parking improperly on Anius, but he assumed them to be dire.

It took two laps around, but he found a spot marked 'Mid-level Supervisors' and pulled in, careful to keep the wide honey-combed wheels within the yellow lines. Ian killed the engines and stepped out, swinging around to the LITCAT's bed. A quick pound on the tailgate to knock the sand loose and he lifted the latch, dropping the heavy hatch down. Packages and parcels littered the truck's covered bed. Ian bent over and selected two, tucking one under each arm and closing the hatch. He walked through the swinging doors at the end of the level, humming along with a bounce in his step.

The hallways leading to the Baron's office were long and winding, but Ian navigated them with ease. He turned left at the locked blast-door with 'Classified Actions Only' emblazoned on the front, offering a friendly smile to the guard as he passed.

"Hey Richards, how's Theresa?" Ian asked without breaking his stride.

"Great, Bernard, thanks for asking," she called back to him, stern face breaking momentarily into a smile. "She loves that *Whimsy Whale* sweater."

"Glad we could find it." Ian offered her a thumbs-up, juggling the boxes under his arms. He turned his back to the guard and hurried off. Time, as always, was not his ally.

He took a right down the last hallway, passing through the glass doors marked 'Colonel John Schwarz Jr., Installation Commander' without a moment's hesitation. Mr. Freeman glared at his bank of monitors. The Colonel had recently decided that he would be returning to Earth to celebrate *Wan Songkran,* forcing Mr. Freeman to reconcile the two-month gap in his calendar. He looked up sharply as the glass doors opened, ready to lash out at the next irritant to slide across his desk. At the sight of Ian he brightened immediately.

"*Oooh,* is that for *moi?*" he squealed, leaping up from his chair.

Ian flipped a package out from under his arm, handing it over to the excited secretary. "Just came in last shift, I figured you didn't want to wait for mail processing."

"You figured *riiiight.*" Mr. Freeman snatched the box from Ian's hand, holding it overhead as he danced his way back to the desk. "Bernie, if only you knew how much I needed this today."

Ian cracked a smile. "What's up? Were the inspection results bad?"

Mr. Freeman frowned. "I wish. Inspection results are *his* problem. No, he got word that he getting another command assignment, maybe on Karnassus."

Ian winced. It was no secret that at this point in his career the Colonel considered himself done with commanding installations, and getting assigned to a combat theater tends to put a damper on anyone's day.

"It's official then?"

Mr. Freeman shook his head. "No, but it was enough to put him in a mood. He's decided he needs another vacation back to Thailand, and now I've got to clear his schedule for half the damn spring. So now it's *my* problem."

Ian smiled again. Mr. Freeman had the marvelous ability to never lose sight of the true tragedy in any situation. He pointed to the box in the secretary's hands, trying to lighten the mood.

"But that makes it better?" he offered hopefully.

It did.

"Oh, *yes!*" Mr. Freeman resumed his dancing in his chair, his calendar troubles momentarily forgotten. "And just in time for my lunch break."

Ian watched him tear into the package, gleefully pulling out a flashdrive wrapped in iridescent foil.

"Is that?" he asked, pointing to the drive.

"*Mhmm!*"

Mr. Freeman tore the foil off of Janessa T. Dashell's sophomore album '*I Ain't Prayin Again*,' admiring its purple sheen before sliding the thumbnail-sized drive into his tablet. He popped in a small white earpiece, Ian could hear a tinny bass line starting up from the other.

Mr. Freeman's happy shimmy grew with the music. "Mmm girl, preach!"

Ian glanced at the grey doors to the Colonel's office. He held up the other package in his hands, waving it to grab Mr. Freeman's attention. "Think this'll cheer him up?"

"Can't hurt," Mr. Freeman shrugged, bouncing his shoulders in time with the music.

"Should I just go in?" Ian asked, his eyes still on the formidable grey doors.

"I don't care, I'm on my *break*," Mr. Freeman sang, bending over to pull a salad out from a refrigerated desk drawer. "You do you, boo."

Ian nodded, taking a deep breath as he walked to the doors. He gave a look back to the dancing secretary. Mr. Freeman mouthed the word 'Go' and shooed him on. Ian took another deep breath as he pushed on the doors, preparing himself to face the surly Colonel on the other side.

The mood within the Colonel's office could best be described as grim. Colonel Schwarz hung his head in his hands, his thick black hair sticking up in all directions. He felt a shift in the air as the door opened, looking up with a glower. Ian was suddenly aware of how a mouse feels under the stare of a viper.

"*Yes?*" the Colonel asked, a trickle of menace in his voice.

"Package for you, sir." Ian proffered the box in front of him, shielding himself behind it.

The Colonel's eyes narrowed further, approaching the territory of 'dangerous slits.' He looked from the box back to Ian. A precarious moment passed between them before he returned his attention to the box, a slight nod of his head motioning for Ian to place it on the desk before him. Ian placed the package gently on the SimuWood grain, stepping back with his hands in the air. The Colonel stared him down, reaching into his desk and pulling out an ivory-handled stiletto. Ian felt an involuntary shiver pass over him as the blade snapped out, flashing dully under the fluorescent lighting. The Colonel continued to stare at him as he worked the knife blade under the lid of the box, severing its seals. He set the knife down on the desk without making a sound, point facing towards Ian. He opened the checkered white flaps, only then breaking eye contact and looking inside.

Ian watched the Colonel's eyes widen and a smile cross his face as he reached inside. The tension in the room disappeared like the flash of lightning, and Ian swore he smelled a faint whiff of ozone. He let out a breath he didn't remember holding. He weighed the merits of silently slipping back out the door before ultimately deciding he'd better capitalize on the Colonel's shift in mood.

"That's the one, right sir?" He blurted out, pointing to the box on the desk. "The one you were expecting last month?"

"Yes, my dear Buck-Sergeant," Colonel Schwarz answered, still looking into the box's contents. "It most certainly is."

Ian sighed with relief. There had always been the chance he'd guessed wrong. "Good, sir. I'm gla—

"What happened to it?" the Colonel interrupted, looking up sharply.

"Customs, sir. They held it up in their office."

The Colonel's eyes narrowed again. "So how did you come to retrieve it?"

Ian swallowed hard, the full details of the story skirted the edges of Anian law. "I talked it over with them, sir," he said flatly. "Once I explained who the package was for, they handed it over."

Colonel Schwarz frowned, Anian Customs Officials were not known for their generosity, or their respect for ICF chain of command. Still, Buck-Sergeant Bernard had managed to deliver him a package he'd spent a week mourning the loss of, he wasn't one to look too hard at a gift horse.

Colonel Schwarz shrugged, returning his attention back to the box. Ian breathed a little easier, suddenly reconsidering his decision to stay. He watched the Colonel reach into the box, pulling out a square, green bag.

"SimuCaff?" Ian asked, pointing to the bag.

"No, no," Colonel Schwarz chuckled, holding the bag up to the light. "This is real espresso, it is *far* more expensive."

Ian nodded appreciatively. There were only a few groves of coffee trees left, grown exclusively on heirloom farms. A pound of coffee cost more than a year of his salary.

Colonel Schwarz nuzzled the bag against his cheek before gingerly setting it down by the knife on the desk. He reached back inside the box.

"Ah-ha!" he exclaimed, pulling out a small jar, filled with what appeared to be orange paint. Colonel Schwarz watched a puzzled look cross over Ian's face.

"I paint," he explained dully. "Sometimes it's the only thing that keeps me sane around here."

Ian looked over to the painting of a ship on the wall. He jerked a thumb over and raised an eyebrow.

Colonel Schwarz rolled his eyes. "No, you Philistine. That's 'The Fighting Temeraire.'" He eyed the painting, running a bemused hand across his chin. "Although some have said our composition styles are similar."

An abrupt '*Ha!* erupted from outside the room.

Colonel Schwarz glared at the door.

"Tim thinks he's an art critic," he sniffed to Ian. Shouting through the door, he added, "Tim, grab my easel so I can show Sergeant Bernard!"

His demand was met with silence. Ian stifled a cough with his hand.

"Mr. Freeman!" the Colonel shouted again. "Bring me my easel!"

Another silence stretched in the room. Ian dutifully avoided the Colonel's eye, staring intently at his boots.

"Mister! Timoson! Freeman!" the Colonel thundered, his voice reverberating throughout the office.

"Mr. Freeman is on *break*," Timoson called back. "*Leave a message!*"

Colonel Schwarz glared once again at the door before turning his attention back to Ian.

"Civilians," he answered apologetically. "It seems you can't buy good help."

Having fulfilled his obligation at Command Central, Ian rushed back out to the parking garage. The LITCAT roared out of the tunnel, turning sharply and heading west to the cargo port. Over a dozen packages rattled around in the bed of the truck, but those errands would have to wait. The sun was beginning its slow descent over the southern horizon. Night was coming, and another long shift lay ahead.

He pulled the truck into a spot beneath the overhang. Stepping out once again into the baking waves of desert heat, he looked over and spotted Sergeant Torres' LITCAT parked a few spaces down, instantly recognizable by the wheels overhanging the faded yellow lines and by the crude vagina drawn in the dust on the door. Ian shook his head, sweat spilling down his back as he stepped through the doors of the busy space port.

He assembled his team, gathering them together for his pre-shift inspection and briefing. He ran through the agenda for the day, highlighting the four dozen ships his half of the port was expected to unload. He divvied up work assignments, congratulated a Private on making Special-Trooper, and even worked in a brief summary of current events. No one else seemed to share his affinity for greedily consuming the minutiae of inter-galactic news, but he felt it was a moral obligation to keep them informed about the worlds outside their own. He noted with a twinge of satisfaction that the vidscreens on the wall had finally been configured properly, and would now display the landing schedule with any and all up-to-the-minute changes. Ian broke his crew after answering a few questions, sending them off to their assigned duties. He grabbed a cup of SimuCaff from the brewpot on the wall and waded into the work at hand.

The DC-242 drifted down to the scorched landing pad, six repulsors firing bright blue to slow the dumpling-shaped craft's descent. They winked out as the ship touched down, rocking heavily on its squat, hydraulic legs. Just inside the bay, Ian stood with his clipboard, checking the ship in with the Landing Control Terminal. There was a hiss as the ship's cargo doors unsealed, cueing Ian to ready his crew to unload. Groans and pops filled the air as the door opened up, half the ship unfolding like the petals of a flower. Ian marshaled his crews up the ramp to begin unloading—he was short one Loading Supervisor after an unexpected death in the family—and was making do.

He linked his clipboard with the DC-242's cargo database, scrolling through the item inventory. He stopped by an item highlighted in red, double-tapping it to bring up its information. *'Ground-Based Autonomous Sentry,'* it read, *'Technician unload only.' Another kill-bot,* Ian frowned, *but where's its handler?* He looked up and down the ship's hold, seeing no trace of the contractually-mandated, certified company mechanic. Ian walked around to the cockpit, tapping on the door to get the pilot's attention. The door unsealed, spinning open as a bored looking man with a tightly curled mustache stepped out.

"Hello?" asked the copilot.

"Technician?" replied Ian, pointing to the GBAS entry on his clipboard.

The bored man nodded, the ends of his mustache quivering as he did. "He's inside. Said he gets sick riding in the hold, so he rode with us instead. I'll get him," he added, before ducking back in the cockpit.

The door spun shut on Ian's face. He looked at his watch, tapping his foot as he waited. According to the vidscreens there were still forty more ships stacked in orbit, and he did not have time to waste. Ian looked back at his watch, noting a minute's passage with some dismay. He busied himself by directing the unloading of the rest of the shipment, his crew working quickly around the static kill-bot.

A full fifteen minutes passed before the technician arrived, looking decidedly green as he stumbled forward on shaky legs. Ian sighed and waved him over, explaining in a clipped tone exactly where the eight-foot tall, armored killing machine needed to be parked within his bay. The mechanic nodded, stepping over to the GBAS and linking in his proprietary, company-produced controller. The kill-bot fired up almost immediately, stepping down the ramp with uncanny speed on six, double-jointed limbs. Ian stepped out of its way as it passed, ducking to avoid being clipped by the twin tempered-beam cannons mounted on its right arm. A chill ran down his spine. He'd never seen a GBAS in person before—the ones in vidplays having utterly failed to capture the inhuman, clinking dread of seeing one skitter towards you.

Ian watched the kill-bot step through the air curtain and into the bay, the mechanic following close behind. He offered up a quick prayer of thanks that he worked in logistics instead of combat arms, and would never have to see one of Dr. Hammet's whirring, alloy monstrosities in action. Ian shook his head, scrolling back through his clipboard and back to work.

The next fifteen hours passed by relatively uneventfully, another thirty ships coming and going in the bustling port. Ian stood back along the bay's wall, observing the activity around him. His crew was tired, but performing well, the second-shift crew picking up right at the midpoint of his day. He allowed himself a yawn, blinking his eyes wide to force them back open. *Easy Ian, almost done.* He looked down at his watch; only two more hours left in the day and the last few ships were coming along nicely.

Another yawn slipped out, this time against his will, and he looked around for his SimuCaff mug. Ian filled it from the brewpot on the wall, downing a few quaffs of the bitter, brown liquid. He sighed, feeling the caffeinated warmth spreading in his belly. His pocket chirped. Ian set his mug and his clipboard down on a tool cart nearby, pulling his personal tablet out with his hand.

Swiping across the screen, he pulled up a message from Buck-Sergeant Corstley. *Probably another shipment they need fast-tracked.* The Raiders never messaged his personal tablet for anything else.

'Ian,' the message read, in block letters over a small blue bubble. 'Got a crate coming in tonight, need it ASAP.'

What else is new? he mused. *It's not like they ever message me telling me to take my time.* The tablet chirped again, with another blue bubble filling in below the first.

'It's on a DC-229, tail no. 762437.'

Ian's brow furrowed, DC-229s were smaller cargo craft, usually used for ship-to-ship transfers. He wandered over to check the vidscreen on the wall, searching for the serial number from the message. He blinked and

the screen flashed, a new ship order appearing near the bottom; number 762437. He turned back to his tablet.

'No problem, we've got it.' he typed, firing the message off as he walked back to his clipboard.

The response was almost immediate.

'Thanks,' the bubble read. 'I'll owe you one.'

You owe me two already, Ian thought. Still, he had to admit that the Raiders always made good on their promises. He'd called in favors only twice before; once for a bottle of real French champagne given to Special-Trooper Banscom to celebrate the delivery of his second child, and most recently to arrange passage on a deep-jet run to Tamarin so Senior-Trooper Khumalo could attend his father's funeral. Ian sighed, taking another swig from his mug. On a base that runs off favors, it never hurt to have a few tucked away.

He checked the vidscreen again, number 762437 had skipped ahead in line. It was now the next ship in, touching down in the next few minutes. He looked around the bustling bay, searching for a few Troopers he could pull off the line to help unload.

"Bradshaw! T'Wallen!" he barked. The Troopers froze mid-step, turning around to face him. He waved them over with a sweep of his mug. "We've got a fast-track touching down in the next few minutes. T'Wallen, I need you to grab a mechlift and unload with Bradshaw."

Special-Trooper T'Wallen's dark eyes went wide.

"But, Sarge," she stammered. "I'm not licensed yet, I haven't passed the written test."

Ian considered this, looking around for a suitable replacement. Seeing none, he weighed his options. A chime sounded on his clipboard, letting him know the ship had touched down. Ian looked out on the Troopers hustling around them. He looked back at T'Wallen, then to his clipboard, and then to his watch.

"Screw it," he said, shaking his head. "It's just the written test. Drive safe."

T'Wallen nodded, rushing off to grab a mechlift, bushy black curls bouncing behind her. Ian turned to Private Bradshaw, but he was already heading off to the landing zone. *He may be dumb, but at least he's earnest.*

Ian met him by the base of the DC-229, the octagonal gangplank already opened up and ready for delivery. He linked his clipboard with the ship's cargo database, frowning when only one item popped up on screen. Ian rubbed his eyes, but he was seeing clearly. He manually re-linked the clipboard to double-check, but it was still there, just one crate earmarked for the Raiders. Stepping on board, he located the box in question and scanned its label. 'Carbon-nano Plates,' his screen read, '140 lbs.' Ian stared at the crate; it was half the size of usual ICF shipments. He looked back at his clipboard, frown deepening as he reread the text.

A chirp sounded from his pocket. He pulled out his tablet, putting it back when he read the name. He didn't need to read the message, it was Corstley again, probably just reminding him that they needed the shipment today. Ian looked back one last time at the unusually small crate before shrugging. *At least it'll be an easy load.*

The mechlift jerked forward, hydraulic arms creaking up and down as Special-Trooper T'Wallen worked frantically at the controls. Ian offered her a thumbs up for encouragement. He saw her nod from behind the poly-plex cockpit, furiously chewing on her lower lip as she concentrated on navigating the power loader forward. A trickle of doubt started down his back. *At least it's just one crate.* He shook his head, offering her another smile of encouragement as he pulled Private Bradshaw out of her way. T'Wallen swept the loader arms down, extending them forward to grasp the small grey crate. The arms clamped, locking into the crate's lugs. Ian breathed a sigh of relief, pushing Bradshaw forward to assist. He looked down at his watch, only an hour left and then this day was done.

"Sarge, problem."

Ian looked up sharply, Private Bradshaw was waving him over.

"What is it?" he asked, joining the thick Trooper by the crate.

"No cables, Sarge," Bradshaw grunted, showing Ian his empty hands.

Ian swore. They still had six ships left to go after this one. Another chirp sounded from his pocket—he didn't bother checking who'd sent it. He looked around, frantically searching for another option. The trickle of doubt crept down again. He shook his head. *Fuck it, it's just one little crate.*

"Forget the cables," he said, patting Bradshaw on the shoulder. "Just guide her on the way out so she keeps the arms locked."

Bradshaw nodded, explaining the plan to T'Wallen through the poly-plex cockpit. Ian stepped away, rubbing the bridge of his nose, head pounding in the stale heat of the loading dock. The mechlift rolled by, Bradshaw following dutifully in tow. Ian ducked in past the air curtain, leaning up against the wall to catch his breath. He allowed his eyes to close, resting for a moment against the cool alloy.

A sharp creak cut through the noise of the bay. Over the din, he heard someone shout 'Look out!' Ian's eyes snapped open, searching for the source in the crowded space port. He locked on to Private Bradshaw, standing under the mechlift, his hands raised up as if to catch it. Ian rubbed his eyes to clear them. He blinked his eyes wide to force them back open.

Just in time to see Private Bradshaw crushed beneath the falling crate.

Chapter 7:

The MMUTCAT wheel turned slowly in the gentle sunlight filtering through the trees. A light breeze picked up, whispering through the long silver branches and scattering light through rustling leaves. Shadows danced across the painted green side of the massive utility truck. A chirping cry rang out from deep within the forest.

The wheel continued its slow revolution, a lump of red loam caught in its tread tracing a path around and around. The air was warm, with a hint of something that smelled like cinnamon. It was another perfect summer day on Cerulia. Or else it would have been, if the MMUTCAT in question wasn't laying on its side, with two of its eight great wheels torn off and a thin trail of smoke winding its way up from the smashed front end, losing itself among the long silver branches.

Reed-Sergeant O'Neil stood in the shade of those long silver branches, staring hard at the wreckage of the big work truck. A frown draped itself across his pink face, drawing down the corners of his thin mouth and losing itself in the folds of his two chins. A wispy mustache twitched under a button nose, grown in response to an ex-girlfriend's assertion that when he tucked his chin, he looked like a thumb. He had hoped the thin blond hairs would eventually resolve themselves into a distinguished, respectable line.

They had not.

He scratched the back of his head, thick fingers raking short grey stubble. Something buzzed by his ear, and he swatted it away. Sergeant O'Neil resumed his staring, as if trying to assemble a jigsaw puzzle with his eyes. He tried to put the pieces together, the totaled MMUTCAT on its side, the clear, sunny day, and the long tire gouges through the red dirt on the side of the road. He turned the pieces over in his mind, but they only came together to say one thing—trouble. He sighed, reaching deep into his pocket for a tin of *Stip*.

A soft voice spoke behind him.

"Nice enough day," it said.

Sergeant O'Neil jumped halfway out of his skin, though to the outward observer this manifested itself as a violent twitch through his fleshy body and an involuntary emission of '*Gah!* The bright blue tin

slipped from his fingers, landing on its side in the red dirt road. A woman stood quietly behind him, a woman with light skin and curly brown hair pulled straight back. Kind brown eyes looked out over a long, straight nose. The kind brown eyes searched Sergeant O'Neil up and down, but he had the sneaking suspicion they were looking through him instead of at him.

The woman smiled, bending down at her thin waist and retrieving the blue tin from the dust. She wiped it off with her sleeve before offering it back to him. Sergeant O'Neil wasn't sure what to make of this, but he took the *Stip* can anyway. Cerulia had recently levied a thirty-percent tax on all *Stip* sales, and it was already shaping up to be a hell of a day. He stared down at the can, weighing out the best question in his mind.

He settled on one. "What?"

"I said, it's a nice enough day." The woman cocked her head to one side. Sergeant O'Neil was convinced more than ever that she was looking straight through him.

"Yes," he grunted, scratching his head again. *Where the hell did she come from?* He hadn't heard anyone pull up, and the road they were on was pretty far off of the main installation traffic. She was wearing the grey fatigues of an ICF uniform, but he couldn't spot a rank on her shoulders. The nametape on her chest read 'Levi.' No career insignia either. His pink brow furrowed.

The woman put out a hand. "Inspector Levi," she said.

Sergeant O'Neil went pale. "What does Military Police want with this?"

Inspector Levi took her hand back. "I'm not with MP."

Sergeant O'Neil went paler, beads of sweat forming on his brow. "OI?" he whispered.

She shook her head. "Nope, ISC."

The color returned to O'Neil's face with startling speed. He let out an audible '*whew*,' dabbing the beads of sweat with the kerchief he kept in his pocket for *Stip*. For a moment there he really thought the Office of Insight had shown up on his door to take him away in the back of a blacked out LITCAT. The ICF Safety Commission he could handle.

Sarah Levi watched the tension melt away out of the portly Reed-Sergeant. Good, she needed him calm. It was her experience that the calmest folks talked the most. And what she needed now, standing in the middle of a red dirt road on a nice Cerulian summer day, was a look at that truck and for him to keep talking.

Sergeant O'Neil fiddled with the tin in his hands, thinking through his circumstances now that the blood was flowing back to his head. It made sense that ISC was here to investigate the crash. He should have expected them really. He just didn't expect them to get there that fast. It was his Trooper, and he didn't even hear about it until an hour ago. He looked up from the *Stip* tin to Inspector Levi. The kind eyes stared back, still smiling. He remembered his manners.

"Uh, thanks for coming out so fast. Appreciate the help."

She nodded, extending her hand once again. "Of course, our pleasure."

Sergeant O'Neil turned back to the ruined MMUTCAT. "I suppose you want to take a look at the wreck."

"Ideally." Her voice lilted a little at the end. Sergeant O'Neil liked that; it put him at ease. She was a far cry from the hard-nosed investigators he'd met working with the MPs. He shook her hand; it was soft and warm. He liked that too.

"By all means then," he said, sweeping a hand towards the crash site and stepping out of her way. "Mind if I *Stip?*"

"Not at all," she said, stepping past him.

A thought ran through his mind as he pulled a patch from the tin. "You want one too?" he asked, the mustache twisting over a lopsided smile.

"No thanks," she replied, walking up to the front of the smashed cab. "Quit last month."

This was not true. Reed-Sergeant Sarah Levi, inspector for the Interstellar Coalition Force Safety Commission, had never used nicotine in her life. She found the nasal drip to be fairly revolting, but casting judgement wasn't useful in her line of work. People tended to clam up when they felt judged. And no one casts more judgement than the abstinent.

"Ah, good for you," O'Neil said, smiling as he pocketed the little blue tin. "Been meanin' to quit myself. Bad habit, wife hates it."

Sarah nodded along, taking pictures of the front end with her tablet and jotting down notes. She panned the camera around the wreck, stepping lightly to avoid disturbing the marks in the bright red soil. She took a long shot of the gouge, cutting deep through the grass on the side of the road and stretching back almost five hundred meters. She walked over the space where the rear tires used to be, pulling a small probe from her pocket and dropping it at the start of the trench.

"You dropped something," Sergeant O'Neil said helpfully.

"I know," Sarah called back. She followed the red trench cut by the MMUTCAT's skid, snapping pictures of the mark and the surroundings the whole way. She found the back wheels about a hundred meters away, where the wide skid broke into two narrower ones. She dropped another probe in the trench, marking the point where the truck tipped over. She traced the two lines back down the road, their winding path cutting an 'S' around both sides of the road. They ended at a sharp bend in the road, a ninety-degree turn around a clump of sandstone. Sarah dropped a final probe, syncing the measurements with her tablet and snapping a few pictures of the bend.

"Find anything?" Sergeant O'Neil shouted from crash site.

Plenty, she thought, picking up the probe from the road. She gave a friendly wave. The walk back to the ruined truck was quick, a small chirrup from the tablet letting her know the modeling software had finished its analysis. She scrolled through the data report, reading the program's computation for the likely speed and path of travel for the damaged MMUTCAT. It painted a picture of a speeding truck losing control at the start of the bend. Sarah closed the tablet and tucked it away. She'd figured as much already. A careless driver saw the bend too late and reacted too slow, overcorrecting and skidding out in the process. She'd known the how by the time she reached the bend in the road. The software was just there for the hard numbers she needed in the report. What she didn't know was the why.

Sergeant O'Neil broke into a smile as she walked up.

"Get some good pictures?" he asked, a nasal twinge to his voice.

"Some," she said, smiling back. An ex-wife had once told her she had a disarming smile. She used it as often as she could.

She turned back to the wreckage, the passenger side wheel had stopped turning. She crossed her arms, putting on her best impression of nonchalance. "What do you think happened?"

Sergeant O'Neil stroked his weak chins. "I dunno, probably took the curve too fast."

"Too fast? Do you think they didn't see the turn?" she prodded gently.

"Hard to tell." The chin stroking grew more thoughtful. "It's plenty bright out, and you can usually see that curve coming almost a quarter mile."

Sarah nodded along, agreeing with him about the nice day.

She pushed a little further. "Do you think they were distracted?"

"Maybe," he said, tilting his head, mustache scrunching up in an attempt at pensiveness. "Wouldn't be the first time."

"Oh?" she asked innocently, eyebrows arching as she matched his tilt.

"Nah," he said, the wispy ends bouncing as he laughed. "Not the first time Alicia's done this to me."

Sarah said nothing at the mention of the driver's first name. She waited quietly to see if he'd go on, still flashing a winning smile.

Not winning enough though. She watched O'Neil's face droop as the realization of his slip caught up with him. His shoulders stiffened, a little color rising in his cheeks as he whipped out his kerchief to blow his nose. She knew in that moment she'd lost the levity of the interrogation. It was time to be direct.

"Tell me, Sergeant O'Neil," she said, looking straight into his watery eyes. "How many accidents has Private Baker gotten herself into?"

It was chilly inside the conference room, the air conditioning set a hair too cold for the balmy day outside. Sergeant O'Neil sat on one side of a long table, his pink face a little green under the flickering, fluorescent lights. He leaned forward in the cushioned black chair, swinging his feet as he waited. It had been three days since the accident, three days since he'd last seen Inspector Levi. He'd heard she talked with some others in the platoons, requesting some records, going over logs and figures. Just the same, he'd hoped he'd seen the last of her.

Until this morning, when an email popped in his inbox with a signature block from the ISC—an email requesting his presence in the conference room of the 955th Orbital Fueling Squadron. Sergeant O'Neil knew then this ordeal was far from over.

He looked up as the door opened. Inspector Levi stepped in, thanking him for his time as she found a seat on the other side of the table. She smiled at him as she pulled her seat closer, offering him a cup of SimuCaff from the shop in the lobby. He accepted, feeling a little more at ease in spite of himself. Besides, he reasoned, how much trouble could he be in sitting here instead of in the interrogation cell of the 945th Military Police Precinct?

Sarah made herself comfortable in the cushioned black chair, pulling out her tablet and syncing it with the display embedded in the conference table. She tapped the tablet screen, pulling up a few programs to run in the background. Flicking the camera with her thumbnail, she angled it up to face her subject.

"Okay, Sergeant O'Neil," she said, enunciating clearly for the microphone. "This interview will be recorded. Do you understand?"

Sergeant O'Neil nodded, chins folding into each other with each shake.

"Good, this is an interview for ISC Investigation #2333-14587, conducted on January 24th, 2333."

She paused for a moment. The next part was always touch and go.

"This is an investigation into an incident occurring on January 21st, 2333 involving a MMUTCAT crash. This is a safety investigation, not a criminal one. Although, any evidence of a crime will be included in this report and referred to criminal authorities. At any time, you may abstain from answering a question or request the presence of legal counsel. Do you understand?"

Sergeant O'Neil set the cup back down on the table, the creeping unease was back. His mustache twitched.

"Should I request counsel?" he asked her.

"Perhaps," she answered. "Do you feel you need it?"

He squirmed a little in his seat.

"Do other people have counsel?"

"Some do, others don't." She shrugged. "I've seen it both ways."

He swallowed hard, the gulp rolling down his ruddy neck.

"Will I look guilty if I do?" he asked, his eyes pleading with her to give him direction.

She offered him a half smile. "It might."

A long pause stretched between them. Sergeant O'Neil shivered, the room feeling a little colder than it had before. He looked from Sarah, to the camera, to the cup, to the ceiling, to the table, and back to Sarah.

"I think I'll answer the questions," he said quietly, as though regretting his decision as he said it.

"Great," said Sarah, bobbing her head. "Then let's get started."

She tapped the tablet again, pulling up a blank page for notes.

"Please state your name, occupation, and unit."

"Reed-Sergeant Steven O'Neil, Fleet Supervisor, 922nd Transportation Battalion."

"And were you present for the incident occurring on January 21st, 2333?"

"No."

"How were you made aware of the incident occurring on January 21st, 2333?"

"I got a text from my day shift supervisor—

"Buck-Sergeant Gonzalez?"

"Yes, Sergeant Gonzalez. I got a text saying that there was a crash."

"Do you know how Sergeant Gonzalez became aware of the crash?"

"Yeah, he got the distress message through the FMS."

"FMS?"

"Fleet Management Software."

"Thank you."

Sergeant O'Neil picked the cup up from the table and drank deep. His nerves were rattling in spite of the easy questions. He set the cup back down, another silence stretching between them. Sarah coughed to bring his attention back.

"Do you know the driver of MMUTCAT involved in the incident?"

He nodded. "Private Alicia Baker."

"I have in my records that Private Baker's supervisor is Buck-Sergeant Gonzalez. Who is Sergeant Gonzalez's supervisor?"

"I am."

"To the best of your knowledge, was Private Baker trained to operate the vehicle in question."

He leaned back in his chair, crossing his arms over his chest.

"Yes, she certified in basic training like anyone else and then again when she arrived on station."

"To the best of your knowledge, was anyone else in the vehicle with Private Baker at the time of the crash?"

"No, she was alone."

"Can you confirm that she was alone and that she was the sole operator of the vehicle at the time of the crash?"

"Yes."

"Okay then," Sarah said cheerfully, double tapping her note page to close it. "That clears that up."

Sergeant O'Neil blinked slowly. He looked around the room, searching for a trick.

"Is that all?" he asked, his voice skittish and low.

Sarah shrugged again, favoring him with another smile. "Well, yes. The vehicle crash was caused by the driver's failure to slow down in preparation for a turn. Private Baker was confirmed as the sole operator of the vehicle. Records from her tablet show a text message exchange between herself and a Private Alexandria Spinoza occurring just before the time of the accident. Driver distraction and operator negligence are currently found as the root causes of the accident."

He put his hands out slowly, as though backing away from an angry bull. "So, that's it?" he asked again.

She nodded. "Sure is—that pretty well covers the incident, don't you think?"

He searched left and right again. Nothing sprung out at him, so he relaxed.

"So, I'm good to go?" he asked, mustache turning up in a smile.

Sarah shook her head. "Well, not exactly."

She tapped a fresh note page on the tablet, swiping past it to the previous programs left running in the background.

"You see, after reviewing Private Baker's records, I noticed a few discrepancies." She swiped up on the programs, casting the files onto the table's display directly in front of O'Neil. "This is her fifth accident in two years, Sergeant O'Neil. And even taking into consideration a few instances of retraining and counseling, I feel that this may point to a separate problem within your section."

The Reed-Sergeant froze, his face growing paler under the fluorescent lights.

Inspector Levi continued, "The first two incidents go as expected, with full documentation of the incident, root cause review from her supervisor, and a memorandum signed by Private Baker documenting her retraining and disciplinary counseling."

She swiped across the table, pushing aside the first two files and dragging the next two in front of him.

"And then there's these incidents, one in April 2332 and another in July 2332. Both of these crashes list the root-cause as 'equipment malfunction,' and neither has review from her supervisor. Additionally, the memorandums of counseling for both of these incidents aren't signed by her supervisor, Sergeant Gonzalez."

"Instead..." She paused, letting him sit for a moment in his discomfort. "They're both signed by *you*."

Sergeant O'Neil stared down at the files in front of him.

Sarah watched a bead of sweat bubble up on the pink brow.

"Well, I, uh," he stammered. "I took it into my own hands after the second incident, escalating the level of counseling to the next chain of command. Gonzalez wasn't getting through to her, so I was next in line to set her straight."

Sarah stared him down, her voice level and calm. "Sergeant O'Neil, she wrecked four MMUTCATs in two years. Why was she driving around in a *fifth?*"

"Well," Sergeant O'Neil said, clearing his throat. He met her gaze, watery eyes blinking slowly. "Well, because she's a good Trooper."

Inspector Levi bobbed her head, she was getting tired of playing this game. *Time to flip the board...*

"A good Trooper who let you sleep with her?" she asked quietly.

Sergeant O'Neil's eyes bugged out his head. He swallowed hard, emitting a sputtering cough as his face turned red. "I, uh, don't know wha—

Sarah stood up, cutting him off with a wave of her hand. She swiped across the tablet, sending a new file sliding across the table and pushing the others out of the way. Sergeant O'Neil pulled his hands back from the table as if he were burned.

"This is a message log taken from Private Baker's personal tablet," she announced matter-of-factly, "in which you are both a recipient and a sender. The messages in this log contain material of an explicit nature. Both in text, and," she eyed him carefully, "a few pictures. It describes a relationship between yourself and Private Baker, which you initiated on April 13th 2332 in exchange for overlooking certain *irregularities* on the part of Private Baker's conduct."

Sarah sat back down, folding her arms and watching him closely. Sergeant O'Neil's watery eyes closed, reality crashing down on his shoulders. Quiet filled the conference room once again.

"I think," he said, breaking the silence at last. "I think I would like that counsel now."

Sarah Levi stood on the balcony of her second floor room at the Hotel Astaria, watching the twin suns setting over Cerulia. She swirled a glass of *Stepdad's Choice* in her hand, savoring the caramel notes of the synthetic bourbon. She took a long sip, relishing the light burn down her throat as she stared out on the amber skies. It had been a long few days, but she was finally done, the last of her case notes compiled neatly in a report and delivered to her ISC home office, carbon-copied to the Commander of the 922nd Transportation Battalion as well. She took another drink, turning back to her room before the light faded and a chill set in. Night set in early on Cerulia, the warmth of the twin suns dissipating under a blanket of stars.

Sarah poured herself another drink as she sat down on the edge of the bed. She reflected on her time on Cerulia, the last three weeks on the sparkling, temperate planet had been pleasantly busy. It was soothing here, idyllic even. But she knew it couldn't last. She was starting to get the itching feeling in her bones, the prickly sensation on the back of her neck telling her it was time to move on.

She glanced over to the letter folded neatly on the bedside nightstand. The creased edges were worn and rubbed from hundreds of times of folding and unfolding. When she closed her eyes she could picture the letters, written out in neatly looping ink.

Sarah,

The time we spent together was some of the sweetest I have ever known. I know that when you read this, you will tuck it safely away. Just as you know that as I write this, I am tucking my heart away. I have loved you deeply, as we danced along the stars. But I know that when we danced together, you were never truly near. Even in my arms, you were never truly here. I leave you now in sadness, you are a love I cannot hold. Like chasing after the wind, it is I who grows too cold.

I hoped that you will find your way, in the work that sets you free. I hope one day you'll find yourself, and then come back to me.

Love,

Iris

She opened her eyes, watching the whiskey rolling in her glass. Sarah knew it was a foolish hope, carrying a torch for someone who left years ago. Iris had always been a free spirit, beholden to no one and as temperate as the seas. It had been a foolish hope to think she could be held down, penned in by the rules and decorum of life as a military wife. Sarah stared down at the glass in her hand, the roiling amber currents tumbling over the remaining ice cubes. Someday, she told herself, she would leave all of this behind. Someday, she told herself, she would dance under the stars again.

Her tablet chirruped from its charging port on the desk stand. *Until that time,* she thought, *there's always another case.* She walked across the thick pile carpeting, knocking back the last of her bourbon along the way. She double tapped the tablet screen, bringing up the message. To her surprise it wasn't an announcement from ISC headquarters. The address at the top told her it was from an old commander of hers, now enjoying the benefits of Colonel. She read through the details of the request. It appeared there'd been an accident involving a logistics Trooper, a loader, and a crate. She was being requested by name, at once, to run the investigation. Sarah picked up the tablet in her hands, tapping out a quick reply. She sat back down on the edge of the bed, emptying the bottle in one last drink. There was no need to save it, she couldn't bring it where she was going.

Tomorrow she would board a ship for Anius.

Chapter 8:

Daniel Carvman cut left, feet pounding turf, heart thudding in his chest. His breath escaped in short puffs, clouding his visor a split-second faster than the defoggers could keep up. He snapped his head left and right, searching for an opening. A window opened up ten yards away on the right. Daniel pivoted, driving hard as the seconds closed in. His vision blurred, sweat and tears running together as he ran as hard as he could, the roar of his rushing blood drowning out everything around him.

Only to feel crushing despair as he was tackled from the side and his legs swept out from under him.

"*Boom!* That's all she wrote!" Terrance crowed, turning his back on the viewscreen.

Sergeant Ishii continued to look past him, disbelief resolving into crushed resignation as she watched the last of the *Lions'* forward momentum crushed beneath the *All Blacks'* defense. She shook her head, a host of four-letter words disparaging the conduct and parentage of the English team slipping out under her breath. The clock onscreen ticked away the last of the half, and the match closed with the *Lions* down by two to the *All Blacks*.

"Stupid bastard," she muttered, avoiding eye contact with Terrance as he stood up to applaud the screen. She stabbed a fork into the last of her scrambled eggs. "Should've gone for the drop, 'stead of the try."

"Sucks to suck," gloated Terrance, sitting back down to bask in his victory. "But these are the breaks. And that means—

"Yeah, yeah," Ishii said. "I'll cover you two shifts next week. Don't be such a tosser about it."

Terrance beamed at her. He wasn't a Rugby fan, but he liked to win. And winning always felt better in close proximity to the loser. Sergeant Ishii got up, storming off to drown her sorrows in another tray of 3D-printed eggs. A quiet sniff drew Terrance's attention to the third party at their table. *Speaking of losing…*

Sergeant Bernard sullenly picked at the remains of his waffle, idly pushing the evenly cut squares around his tray. Terrance's smile faded by half; he clapped a hand on Bernard's shoulder.

"What's up little buddy? The waffles aren't that bad, or did you see another roach in the tray line?"

Sergeant Bernard shook his head, still tracing figure eights with his fork. Terrance sighed. He should've known better. The last time Bernard saw a cockroach, he had refused to enter the chow hall entirely, only returning when the survival rations he'd brought with had run out. No, he'd been in a funk ever since the accident last week.

"Hey buddy, it'll be alright," he said, patting Bernard's shoulder in what he hoped was a sympathetic manner. "I heard Bradshaw'll be out in a week. Docs are getting him patched up just fine."

"Three weeks," Sergeant Bernard corrected. "And they're having difficulty knitting the fractures in his lumbar vertebrae." Adding morosely, "He might need a brace for the rest of his life."

Terrance winced. He should've known better about that too. Bernard had stopped by the clinic after every shift this week—of course he'd have the updated report on Bradshaw's recovery.

Switching tactics, he tried again. "Three weeks ain't bad, and he needed a brace anyway. You were gettin' on him about that already."

Sergeant Bernard sniffled, pushing the tray away entirely and resting his head in his hands. Terrance sighed again. Sensitivity was never his strong suit. He grit his teeth for one last go.

"I mean, it's his own fault really. What was that dumbass even do-ing standing under it? Was he gonna catch the fucking mechlift too?"

Sergeant Bernard said something muffled and dropped his head to the table, hiding under his crossed arms. Terrance kicked himself for skipping out on last quarter's annual *Compassionate Understanding Training*, asking Ishii to check his name off on the sign-in roster. He scowled and turned back to watch the post-game highlights, one hand still patting Bernard's shoulder.

Ishii returned with a new tray of eggs, granting him temporary re-prieve. They shared a look as she sat back down. Without a word she dropped her tray on the table, startling Sergeant Bernard upright with the clatter.

"Didja get that packet to LT yet?" she asked, changing the subject. "Annual awards due next week, yeah?"

Terrance shook his head. "Nah, and I don't think I'm gonna. I was pushing Berkeley for 'Trooper of the Year,' but after he dropped that diss track about Sergeant Gherwiz I've got no fuckin' leg to stand on."

"I heard that, his flow was shite too," Sergeant Ishii commiserated. "I was pushin for Sanchez, but 'e skipped out on his final and failed the calc class I put 'im in. Dumbass."

Terrance grunted in agreement. "Lotta that goin' around."

A quiet stretched over the table, punctuated periodically by the scrape of Ishii's fork on the alloy tray.

"Did we get Menandez her new mattresses yet?" Ishii asked, breaking the silence at last.

"Not yet," Terrance popped off without thinking. "We put Brad-shaw on that, remember?"

Sergeant Ishii kicked him hard under the table. Terrance bit off a curse as he rubbed his bruised kneecap. Out of the corner of his eye he saw Bernard's shoulders slump as he began sliding down in his chair. Ishii shot Terrance another look

"I mean," Terrance corrected loudly, forcing a smile as he resumed his patting of Bernard's shoulder. "Not yet, but I'd be *happy* to tackle it before shift."

They drove without speaking to the shipping port, the cactus-marked dunes rolling by as Sergeant Bernard moped out the side viewscreen. They'd wasted a half hour waiting for Reed-Sergeant Menandez at the central lodging building. Thirty minutes Terrance spent loitering in the main lobby while Bernard sulked off to the side, only to be told it was her day off by a passing Private. He could think of a thousand ways he could have better used that time instead of hanging around, avoiding Bernard's moody looks. Terrance dragged a heavy hand across his face. Sedate guitar strings played from the radio, overlaid with the singer's melancholy drawl.

Organ music replaced the guitar. Terrance punched the radio off. The silence in the cab was filled with the scrape and ping of gravel on the underside of the truck. Off in the passenger seat, sorrow escaped Sergeant Bernard as one long, drawn-out exhalation. Terrance grit his teeth as the sigh filled the cabin over the clanging rocks and wormed its way into his head. He punched the radio back on.

The LITCAT drove, weaving around the shadows of dunes lit by the setting sun. It bumped along on the winding road, the radio turned just loud enough to drown out the sadness radiating from the passenger seat.

They arrived late for shift, the last of the sun's light slipping away behind the edge of the horizon. The terminal bay was already in full swing, Troopers rushing about to sort orders, tighten down pallets, or prep the loading dock for the first shuttle's arrival. Terrance looked around for Ishii, finding her standing atop an orange ReadyPallet, finishing up on her crew's briefing. He caught her eye and she waved him over, dismissing her crew off to the sorting bay.

"Thanks for covering. We got held up at housing."

"No worries," she said, passing her clipboard off to her loading supervisor. "Your crew's off palletizing,' and I got Bernie's working the LCT and preppin' the loadin' dock."

Terrance nodded, picking his crew out amid of the tumult of the bay. "How many comin' in?"

"Forty," she said, signing off on a clipboard thrust in her hands by a passing Trooper.

Terrance raised an eyebrow. "Each?"

Ishii shook her head as she handed the tablet back. "Total."

Good, a nice, easy day.

"Any rush jobs?" he asked.

Ishii shook her head again, walking off to supervise two Troopers guiding a mechlift through the doorway to the loading dock. A new policy in the wake of the incident required mechlifts to have two ground-guides whenever they were driven through the bay. Immediate, reactionary changes were the ICF's customary response to any incident. *Gotta show leadership 'fixing' a situation.* Terrance had seen enough of them over the last seven years of his career—it usually took two months before everything settled back to normal.

"Anything else?" he called after Ishii.

She thought for a moment before yelling back. "Actually, yeah, hold on a min." She finished up with the mechlift by the door and hurried over. "Some chick is askin' questions around about our loadin' procedures. I think it's about last week."

Terrance's heart sank. "MP?"

Ishii shrugged. "Dunno, probably not though, right? S'not like Bernie's a criminal or anythin.' Can't be too bad."

Terrance rubbed the back of his neck, his face scrunching up with doubt. Most of the incidents he'd seen had been resolved with a few, perfunctory procedural changes by leadership, a minor inconvenience at most. There'd only been one other time when they'd seen fit to follow it up with an investigation, after a Special-Trooper had accidentally set fire to half a dry-goods warehouse with an arc-welder.

This didn't bode well. If the powers that be thought the incident was serious enough for outside review, then they were looking for a root cause. He looked over to Sergeant Bernard, watching him tighten down on a pallet with another Trooper. Terrance's jaw clenched. That last investigation had concluded that their superintendent, Reed-Sergeant Gao, had created a 'culture of negligence.' In the court-martial that followed, they'd stripped him of his rank, fined him thirty thousand credits, and booted him out with a less-than-honorable discharge. Terrance could still see the stoic look on Gao's face, a small tear building in the corner of his eye as they tore the ranks off his shoulders. If they did that to a senior NCO, he could only imagine what they'd do to a young Buck-Sergeant.

He turned back to Sergeant Ishii, his tone level and firm.

"Where is she now?"

He found her on the south side of the bay, talking to a Trooper midway through climbing into a mechlift. He caught snippets of their conversation as he drew closer.

"So you use guides around the heavy machinery? How many?" He could hear her asking.

The Trooper nodded.

"Two usually. Well, recently. You know, after the accident and all."

Terrance picked up the pace. At the mention of the accident, he saw a gleam in the woman's eyes.

"Ah yes," she was saying as he closed the gap between them. "And what can you tell me about the incident last week?"

The Trooper thought for a moment. "Well..."

Terrance was almost running now, hurrying as fast as he could without drawing attention to himself. *Gotta get there before he says anything fucking stupid.* The woman's smile seemed hungry now, almost predatory in its intent.

"...I wasn't really there for that. Can't say much for sure, just that a crate dropped on a guy on the other crew." The Trooper shrugged. "Dunno much else. Maybe it...slipped?"

The woman's smile faded a little, a flicker of disappointment flashing behind her brown eyes. Terrance slowed just as he reached them. *Can't seem too eager...*

"I see," the woman said flatly, pulling out her tablet. She jotted down a few notes. "You say you think the crate slipped?"

"Oh, yeah. Slipped for sure." The Trooper nodded enthusiastically. "That's probably why it fell, it slipped out."

Terrance breathed a little easier.

The woman nodded along, pretending to write down the Trooper's suggestion. "Well, thank you for your time and your...help."

The Trooper smiled broadly. "Happy to, anytime!"

The woman looked around. "Didn't you say you use ground-guides?"

"Sure did," the Trooper laughed, buckling his harness in the cockpit. "Two of 'em."

The woman's eyes narrowed. "Then where are yours?"

Terrance watched the Trooper pause, his mouth flapping open.

"They're on the way," he said quickly, cutting the Trooper off before anything half-baked slipped out. "New policy, ma'am. Everyone is still adjusting."

"I see," the woman said again. Her eyes looked Terrance up and down, and he had the brief sensation of being judged and found wanting. He didn't like that feeling at all. He returned the stare.

"Inspector Levi," she said after a moment, all smiles as she put out her hand.

"Buck-Sergeant Torres," he offered reluctantly, taking her hand in his. *Hell of a grip*, he admitted in spite of himself, *I wonder if she lifts*. A quick look at the slack in her sleeves said otherwise, no way a real lifter would wear their jacket that baggy. She was thin, and no doubt fit as well. *Probably another sol-chaser*, he thought with a derisive snort.

"Well, Inspector Levi," he said brusquely, "I'm gonna need to see some ID. It's a closed bay, authorized personnel only."

To his surprise, her smile only broadened.

"Certainly," she said, fishing in her pocket for a small wallet and handing it over. Terrance took the creased leather in his hands, the front was imprinted with lettering worn away by time. He squinted hard, just making out the letters 'AD' with 'OTHERFU' below it. She flipped it open quickly, revealing a few social memberships on one side and a large, white credential on the other. 'Inspector Sarah Levi' it read in bold black letters, with no rank noted. The blue insignia of the ICF Safety Commission badge was stamped on the left, a magnifying glass emblazoned over a clipboard. He closed the wallet and handed it back, noting that she kept a tight grip on it the whole time.

"How can I help you?" he asked in a tone that implied the opposite.

The smile waivered but remained intact. She put the wallet away and returned to her tablet, pulling up a fresh page for notes.

"I'm investigating the incident that occurred on January 23rd, involving a Trooper impacted by a falling crate," she said, settling into the business at hand. "I was invited here by direct request of Colonel Schwarz."

Shit, thought Terrance. The accident must have a lot more scrutiny than he'd previously thought if the Baron was getting involved.

"I'm here to investigate what happened," she continued, typing his name at the top of her page, "to see where we can improve, and find the root cause of the issue."

Double shit. The 'root cause' was what they were looking for when they wasted Sergeant Gao. Terrance fought to keep his face neutral and blank.

"Ah, yes," he said, trying his best at keeping his tone airy and light. "The incident. On January 23rd. With Private Bradshaw."

She looked up sharply from her tablet. "So you're familiar with the case?"

He kicked himself. *She hadn't said his name yet.* He sucked in a quick breath, cheeks puffing out a little as he exhaled.

"*Sure*," he said, stretching the word out as casually as he could.

She stared at him, waiting for him to finish. He stared at her, hoping she would quit. A few seconds of silence crawled by, at the end of which Inspector Levi gave a small cough and motioned with her stylus that he should continue.

He paused for another second. Terrance Torres continues on his own say so.

"Bradshaw used to be on my crew," he added, doling the words out like a miser counting change. "And I was on shift at the time of the accident."

Inspector Levi nodded, a few more notes were added to her page. "And did you see what happened?"

"No," he answered truthfully. "I turned the corner after I heard the crash."

"So you didn't see the crate impact Private Bradshaw, but you were on scene for the immediate aftermath?"

An uncomfortable grimace flashed across his face. "Yeah, I was there. I helped Ranges and Smith lift the crate off of him."

She nodded as more notes appeared on the page.

"Did anyone else assist you in aiding Private Bradshaw?"

Terrance thought for a moment.

"Yeah, Bernard helped lift, and Isbil jumped in near the end. He used to be an EMT or something, so he was helping us get Bradshaw stable."

Inspector Levi looked up again, stylus frozen in her hand. "And who was operating the mechlift at the time?"

"Special-Trooper T'Wallen."

More notes on the page.

"Are licensing records kept for the mechlift operators?"

"Yeah, we upload them with the rest of the Trooper records and keep a backup list on the PZL."

"Can I get access to that list?"

He struggled for a moment.

"I guess, but you'll need to request it from Lieutenant Ligen."

She stared at him for a moment while he kept his face as blank as possible. It wasn't technically a lie—Lieutenant Ligen was the approving authority for PZL access—but so was Sergeant Gherwiz, and Sergeant Ishii. And him.

After a moment she spoke again.

"Great, then I'll get started on that right away." She cracked a half-smile, her first since the questioning began. Terrance stifled a sigh of relief. "I'll add that to my OI and reg requests. Is that where I'll find the shipping manifest for the crate as well?"

Terrance grunted in affirmation. *Maybe this won't be so bad after all.*

"Is that it?" he asked, hoping against hope.

"Not quite, just one more question."

He deflated a little. Mentally he'd been preparing to bolt.

"Go ahead," he grumbled. "Shoot."

"You said that Private Bradshaw used to be on your crew, but you were both on shift at the time, which I take to mean he was working under another loadmaster."

He nodded.

The note taking stopped. She looked up from her tablet, stylus frozen in her hand. Brown eyes bored through him.

"Who was Private Bradshaw's loadmaster during the incident?"

Ian sat at the desk in his dorm room, resting his chin on his hands.

Taniel and Suzette were up on the access-mirror, presently updating him on their first success in using a toilet.

"...and you would be so proud of him, dad." Suzette added, balancing Taniel on her lap so he could see the screen. "Tell him, Taniel. Tell daddy what you did today."

"I poo-pooed!" Taniel shouted at the top of his lungs.

"I told you not to yell in mommy's ear," Suzette scolded. "Daddy can hear you just fine."

Ian cracked a smile. Taniel responded with something incoherent before attempting to climb from his mother and onto the bathroom counter.

"No, honey. You're fine where you were," Suzette carped, wrestling the child back into her lap. "For the last time, you can't crawl through the mirror."

The screen on Ian's side went suddenly black, Taniel having managed to swipe a sticky hand across the mirror on his end. A minute passed before the image returned, with Suzette panting a little and looking flushed.

"Everything alright over there?" he asked.

"Your son," she asserted forcefully, stressing the possessive. "Is taking a break. In his room. With the door shut."

A loud wail echoed across the chat.

Ian tried not to laugh. "He seems to be taking it well."

Suzette nodded, wiping a hand across her forehead.

"How's class going?" he asked.

"Good," she answered, grateful for the chance to discuss her professional life for a change. "They're still struggling with convergent etymologies in central-Semitic languages. I legitimately had one student translate 'houris' as 'white grapes' and spend her entire paper arguing that fruit was the central promise of Islamic paradise."

Ian nodded along. After seven years together, he knew enough linguistic terms to laugh and shake his head at the appropriate parts. Suzette wrapped up her story with a dramatic reenactment of the student's tearful pleading after receiving her grade.

"So anyway, how was your day?"

Ian took a deep breath and sighed. It had been five whole minutes since he'd thought about Inspector Levi and the investigation. He knew a reprieve was temporary at best.

"Fine, I guess. I stopped by the clinic to see Bradshaw again."

Suzette eyes were full of sympathy. "Is that the guy? How's he doing?"

Ian slumped forward again, propping his head up with one hand. "Better, the ribs are healing fine. He's awake now, making a few jokes."

"Well, that's good," Suzette said, trying her best at a cheerful smile. "And he's happy to see you, I bet."

Ian shrugged, another heavy sigh slipping out of him.

Suzette's smile fell a little at the edges. She hated to see him like this, hated it more that he was too far away for her to wrap him in her arms and make him feel better. She bit back on her own sigh. *Brave face, Sue,* she thought to herself, *be strong for him.*

She tried once more for the cheerful smile. "Well, maybe your command will learn a little from this investigation. Put some changes in place to make it better for everyone."

"Maybe," Ian grumbled, his mind on Inspector Levi and the questions he'd heard her asking. Torres and Ishii had looked her up with a buddy they had on the installation safety council. She had a long reputation as a sharp investigator, with a savvy mind and an eye for minutiae that other investigators had missed. Her case log stretched back almost ten years, and every case concluded with a known culprit and punitive action by their chain of command.

Ian knew it was only a matter of time before she called him in for questioning. He was the loadmaster supervising the crew, it'd been his call that caused the accident. His call that put Bradshaw in the hospital. *If only I had waited, listened instead of rushing them. Maybe if I hadn't been so tired.* But he knew such thoughts were pointless. He didn't make the call because he was tired, he made it because he was so damn focused on getting that crate for Corstley. *You wanted it quick instead of done right. You wanted that damn favor. That's why Bradshaw's in a spinal cast right now. Because of you.*

Suzette watched her husband stew in silence, knowing there was little she could do to break him out of his own thoughts. She reached a hand out, placing it flat against the screen on her side and waiting patiently. A minute passed before Ian noticed, dejectedly pressing his hand up to hers. Her eyes searched his face in earnest, but he couldn't bring himself to meet her gaze.

"I miss you," she said, a tidal wave of affection and support pouring out in those three words.

"Yeah," Ian said, pulling his hand back and severing the call. He looked back up at the black screen, with only himself enshrined in its reflection.

"I miss me, too."

Chapter 9:

"Please state your name, occupation, and unit."

"Buck-Sergeant Terrance Torres, Loadmaster, 379th Logistics and Supply."

Inspector Levi frowned, looking down at the tablet on the conference table. She scrolled up on the file on screen, kind brown eyes searching quickly under a furrowed brow.

"I'm sorry, there must be some mistake. I have here that you enlisted as *Tonya* Torres?"

Terrance crossed his arms over his broad chest, an aggressive jut to his chin. "Sure did."

Inspector Levi looked up across the table, her eyes searching him over once again. Allowing Troopers to transition while in service predated the ICF by almost a hundred years, as it was widely understood that happy soldiers are effective soldiers. The practice also dovetailed nicely with the concept of a 'gender-neutral fighting force' so widely espoused in discussions of military leadership. The ICF had long maintained a specialized line of funding just for the various therapies and macrosurgeries required for transitioning Troopers, adding it as a Stipulated perk when they signed their six-year enlistment contract. It was an incentive rarely used, but not unheard of. The ICF needed every able body it could get.

"Is there a problem?" Terrance asked, a slight edge to his voice. Inspector Levi realized she'd been staring a fraction too long.

"Not at all," she said quickly, backpedaling over her lapsed social grace. She spared a moment to curse the back-logged ineptitude of the ICF Personnelist Corps. *Primary Career Files* were supposed to be updated as soon as the Trooper began their transition, precisely to avoid awkward moments like this. "I'll make a note to have the PCF updated."

"Good," Terrance said, leaning back in his chair. "Then let's get this fucking over with."

Inspector Levi paused for a moment to collect her thoughts, swiping past the personnel file and bringing up a fresh note page. She shook her head to clear it and began again.

"This is an investigation into an incident occurring on January 23rd,

2333 involving a Trooper impacted by a falling supply crate. This is a safety investigation, not a criminal one. Although any evidence of a crime will be included in this report and referred to criminal authorities. At any time, you may abstain from answering a question or request the presence of legal counsel. Do you understand?"

"Yes."

Inspector Levi eyed Ian from across the table. He avoided her gaze, staring down at the mug of SimuCaff clenched tight in his hands. His stomach roiled and churned. He was beginning to think accepting the coffee substitute had been a bad choice.

"And do you request counsel at this time?"

He looked up from the mug, trying hard not to focus on the button-sized camera attached to her tablet. He shook his head.

"No."

Inspector Levi nodded, checking a box on her note page. Her eyes were kind when they looked back at him, her tone gentle, but precise, as she spoke.

"Alright Sergeant Bernard, why don't you tell me about your day on January 23rd, 2333?"

"Woke up. Went to work. Did my job."

Sarah bit back on a sigh. "Care to add to that?"

"Sure," Sergeant Torres said, rubbing his chin thoughtfully.

"I also worked out."

Sarah stared at him, waiting a moment before motioning with her stylus for him to go on.

"It was chest day."

This time the sigh slipped out before she could catch it.

"I will remind you, that this interview is being recorded. And that it will be included, *in its entirety*, within the final report submitted."

Sergeant Torres' eyes narrowed. He crossed his arms tighter across his chest. A full minute crawled by while they stared each other down.

"Fine," he grumbled, breaking the silence at last. "It started when I woke up that evening."

Her jaw tightened. "*What. Time?*"

"Late."

She stared him down, but held firm. She had all day for this.

He rolled his eyes. "Fine. I stopped hitting snooze at 45:00."

"Then what?"

"Drove to work."

"Any Passengers? Anything unusual along the way?"

"No."

"To which?"

"Both."

"What time did you get to the port?"

"Around 45:50."

"And what time does your shift start?"

"46:00."

Finally getting somewhere. Sarah sat back in her chair.

"And what was the port like when you got there?"

"Busy," Ian said. "Really busy."

Inspector Levi nodded, jotting a few notes on her tablet. "And what did you do when you arrived on duty?"

"Got my agenda together for the day. Recognized Jackson's promotion to Special-Trooper, and split the loading assignments for the crew."

"Anything unusual about the briefing?"

"I don't think they were paying attention to the bit about the impact sanctions were having on the Karnassus' mineral economy, but I suppose that's not unusual."

Inspector Levi cracked a small smile as she added a few more notes. "No, I don't believe that's unusual either." The smile faded, all business once again. "What else?"

Ian took another sip from the mug in his hands. "Like I was saying, we were busy that day."

"Slammed. Packed. Ninety-six ships in eighteen hours."

Inspector Levi jotted down a few notes. "Busier than usual?"

Terrance nodded. "Not the worst day I've seen. But still fucking busy."

"And how do you manage? When it's busy like that?"

He shrugged. "Put your head down and grind through it. Mission comes first. That was the first thing they told me on day-fucking-one. People come in and people go out, but the cargo keeps moving."

"Sounds like an awful lot of pressure."

"It's like a dance," Ian explained. "There's so many moving pieces whirling all around you. One wrong step and the whole dance stops."

"Sounds like a lot to take in," Inspector Levi offered.

Ian nodded, setting the mug on the table to free up his hands. "At first it's overwhelming. I...found it overwhelming. Luckily most people already know their parts. You just have to stay out of their way until you find out where you fit in."

"And did you find out where you fit in?"

"Mostly," Ian said, a faraway look in his eyes. "It just took a little compromising."

"Of course there's compromises in this position," Terrance said brusquely. "You couldn't do the job without it. The third thing they told me about this place was that nothing's black and white. The 'Dirt

Star' is *weird*. Come in here trying to force everything to fit neatly inside the lines and you find out everything goes to shit real fuckin' quick."

"And is that what Sergeant Bernard did? Tried to force things inside the lines?"

He hesitated a moment before answering.

"Bernard...learned. It took a while, but he figured it out. It's not like the training problems in the developmental volumes. No X car going to Y station with four-hundred tons loaded on a three-fifty capacity. Nothing straightforward and simple here. It took some work, but Bernie learned quick. He's got arms like noodles and somedays I swear he's carrying a fucking redwood up his ass, but he's smart. He figured out what kind of place this is. Like I said, first thing they told me was 'keep the cargo moving.'"

"And the second?"

"*Nothing moves for free.*"

"Tell me more about these 'fast-tracks.'"

Ian sucked in a breath, cheeks puffing out a little as he thought through his response.

"They're little things," he said, carefully balancing his tone. "Here and there. Odd jobs and rush orders. Sometimes we move a shipment a little higher on the priority list, process it ahead of some others that have been waiting. Other times we set aside some items out of the main inventory for personal deliveries, you know, if someone asks for them later."

"In return for favors from the deliveries' recipients."

Ian winced, he knew he was skirting a fine line in this discussion. *Still, it's for the official record.*

"Yes, but only little things. Getting a Trooper moved into the BPD early because of her mold allergy. Or getting our viewscreens networked quicker so we can get our landing manifests on display."

"Anything illegal? Are you aware of any of these favors or fast-tracks violating ICF regulations or Republic law?"

"No, never!" Ian shook his head forcefully. "We would never!"

"What about Anian laws?"

"What the fuck do those have to do with anything?"

Sarah blinked at him from across the table.

"You're on Anian soil," she explained slowly. "Operating under a charter agreement between the ICF and the Anian governorship."

"And last time I checked, I'm Cuban. Which is on *Earth*." Sergeant Torres cocked an eyebrow as he leaned forward, tapping the table to punctuate his point. "And I joined the ICF, which means I work for the Coalition, not some dipshit governor."

Sarah opened her mouth to educate him on the finer points of intergalactic colonial sovereignty, but he waved her off.

"You think this base gives a damn about customs laws? Let one mattress order, or one pallet of *Chargeit!*, or *what-the-fuck-ever* get delayed by customs, and I'm buried up to *my* neck in calls and complaints."

He paused to let his point sink in. Sarah could see the gears grinding as he switched tactics.

"Besides, if customs laws were so damn important to them, they wouldn't put 'Heckle and Jeckle' in charge doing fuck-all in their office all day long, now would they?"

He leaned back in his chair, throwing his hands up in triumph. Sarah opened her mouth to speak, but for once she had no words.

"So the crate in question was fast-tracked."

Ian nodded, taking another sip from his mug.

"On behalf of the Commando Raider unit operating out of Anius."

"That's right." Ian set the mug down on the table, the cold Simu-Caff doing little to settle his stomach. "I got the word Corstley—Buck-Sergeant Corstley."

"And Sergeant Corstley told you in person about the shipment?"

He shook his head. "No, it was a surprise. The shuttle wasn't even on our initial manifests. First I got the text—

"Text? What text?" She looked up sharply from her notes. "You mean a message to your ICF address?"

He shook his head again. "No, my personal tablet. Corstley's messages—sorry, Sergeant Corstley—are always sent to my personal. They said it's faster that way."

Inspector Levi looked him over, a strange look on her face.

His brow furrowed with concern. "Something wrong?"

"Nothing, it's fine." She shook her head, wiping her expression away with it. "Can I get a copy of those messages?"

"Of course." Ian's brow wrinkled further. "Are you sure nothing's wrong?"

"How do you normally get notified to perform one of these 'favors'?"

"I dunno. I get messaged. Sometimes emails." Terrance shrugged. "Sometimes people just ask."

"What about the Raiders?"

"Text straight to my personal tablet."

"Always?"

"Always."

"First you got the text, then what?"

"I checked the tail number he sent against the landing manifests. Like I said earlier, it wasn't originally on our list. Literally popped up right as I was looking. I don't know how he knew about it before we did, but that's the Raiders I guess. It was weird though."

"Weird how?"

Ian tilted his head, half a frown on his face. "It was a DC-229."

Inspector Levi's brow wrinkled. "I'm not familiar. What's odd about that?"

"Two-two-nines are for ship-to-ship transfers," he explained. "Light cargo and passengers."

"You said it was just one crate. Doesn't that check out?"

He scratched the back of his head. "I guess. But orbit-to-surface deliveries cost a ton in fuel. You'd think a shipment that small would just get transferred mid-orbit to another shuttle and get rolled in with a preexisting landing."

"You said it was a rush order, maybe it was too important to wait."

"I guess," he admitted after a moment. The wheels turned in his head and his frown deepened. "But it was just a bunch of carbon plates."

"Tell me more about the mechlifts."

Sergeant Torres snorted. "They're big, and yellow, and they help you lift heavy things."

Sarah could feel her teeth grinding. "I meant their use and operation. What's the licensing process like to drive one?"

"Eight hours of classroom instruction, eight hours of hands-on familiarization, twenty hours of supervised practice driving, twenty hours supervision in a work environment, a practical test, and a written test," Sergeant Torres listed dully, counting off with his fingers.

"And where is this documented?"

His tone was bored. "In the Trooper's master training record and locally in the PZ."

"And to the best of your knowledge, was Special-Trooper T'Wallen trained to operate a mechlift?"

"I saw her driving one once or twice."

Sarah pressed the issue. "But was she licensed?"

"Fuck if I know."

He laced his fingers on top of his head, his face a mask of boredom and contempt. "You're the one with the access requests, why don't you tell me?"

Ian shook his head. "No she wasn't licensed. She hadn't finished the written test yet."

"And you were aware she wasn't certified to operate the vehicle?"

He winced. "Yes, she reminded me right beforehand."

"And you still directed her to drive the mechlift?"

"Yes."

"What does ICFOI 2397-42B say about safety cables during mechlift operations?"

"Use 'em."

She closed her eyes. A small vein began throbbing in her neck.

Terrance shrugged. "Ask a dumb question. Get a dumb answer."

"Were safety cables used to secure the crate to the mechlift during unloading?"

"No."

"Are you aware of their requirement under ICFOI 2397-42B?"

"*Supply Port Operations and Maintenance.*" He nodded. "Yes."

"Why didn't you use them?"

Ian looked off into the distance, the investigation was settling on him with terrible finality.

"They weren't on hand when we were loading," he said flatly.

"Why didn't you send someone to get some?"

"How the fuck would I know why he didn't send someone? What kind of fucking question is that?" Sergeant Torres' nostrils were wide and flaring.

Sarah knew she shouldn't enjoy setting him off like this, but she felt a small kernel of satisfaction just the same. *Lord knows he's been working my patience for the last hour.* She kept her face perfectly neutral as she spoke.

"I'm just asking for your experienced opinion," she said innocently. "I want you to postulate for me why he might have ignored established safety protocol regarding the use of safety cables."

Sergeant Torres' jaw clenched. He opened his mouth and shut it again without saying a word.

"I just asked your opinion," she wheedled.

He threw himself backwards in his chair, clapping a hand to his forehead and kicking back from the conference table.

"Fuckin-A lady, I don't fuckin' know." His tone was weary now, the fight draining out of him like air from a balloon.

"Maybe he was rushed. Maybe he had three shuttles stacked in low-orbit and *couldn't* wait for someone to grab them. Maybe another crew was already using them and we didn't have any to spare. Those titano-alloy cables snap every fucking shift, and we only get new ones once a quarter. People always assume that just 'cause we're supply corps we always have more in the back. Sometimes there just aren't any fuckin' more, and you have to push what's left to the shipments that really need them. 'Cause God forbid we ever slow-roll anything around here. Or maybe, just maybe, he was fucking tired."

He sat back up in his seat, lashing out with an accusatory finger. "*You* try working eighteen fucking hours each shift, day in and day fucking out. Try keeping *your* head on straight."

"So what time did you get up that evening?"

"40:00."

"Why so early?"

"I had errands to run."

"Errands?"

"Favors," Sergeant Bernard corrected, his tone flat and spent.

Sarah nodded, checking back over her notes.

"The incident occurred at 08:05 on January 23rd, 2332. At the time of the incident, how long had you been awake?"

He looked up at the ceiling, mouthing the numbers as he counted on his fingers. Hollow eyes met hers when he finished.

"Twenty-two hours."

"Are you suggesting that long working hours might have contributed to the accident?"

"I think it's pretty fucking likely."

"Are you aware that ICFOI 2397-42B forbids loading crews from working in excess of thirteen hours, especially when working around heavy machinery?"

Sergeant Torres threw his hands in the air, his eyes flashing with righteous anger. "*Welcome to fucking Anius.*"

"Do you feel that personal exhaustion might have affected your decisions during the incident?"

"No." Sergeant Bernard shook his head, his arms crossed tight against his chest. "I made the call. I was rushing. I wanted to get the crate out quick."

Sarah looked out across the vast gulf of the conference table. She felt a twinge of sympathy for the young Buck-Sergeant.

"Are you sure?" she asked again. "Are you absolutely sure that being tired had no bearing on your decision?"

"Yes," he said quietly, his eyes cast on the floor. "The decision was mine alone."

"I mean," Terrance continued, indignant rage boiling forth as he spoke, "why the fuck are you even asking *us*? Why don't you go ask the dumbass that was walking directly under a mechlift under load? Where's *his* interview?"

Inspector Levi opened her mouth to speak. "This isn't the only—"

"Or the Baron? Or fuckin' ICF command? Where's the interview for the fat Reed-Sergeant fuck that spun me around on tour for this place, looked me dead in the eye, and said if anything stops moving around here that me—*a fucking Buck-Sergeant*— would be held personally responsible. Where's *his* interview?"

Inspector Levi kept quiet, she knew he wasn't looking for answers at this point.

"Talk about personal responsibility, I mean for fuck's sake, what was Bradshaw even doing standing under there?" Terrance sputtered, a fleck of spit sailing across the room. "It took four of us just to lift it off him. Was he trying to fucking *catch* it?"

Sarah scrolled down to the last spot on her note sheet, double-checking her questions as she went. Sergeant Bernard said nothing, continuing to stare at the floor.

"Okay Sergeant Bernard," she said, adopting a cheerful tone. "Last question."

Sergeant Bernard nodded slowly, his face impassive. Sarah's brow began to knit with concern, but she shook it off. She had a job to do.

"After the crate impacted Private Bradshaw, what did you do next?"

"Helped lift the crate. Worked with Senior-Trooper Isbil to keep his spine straight while we called for medical support."

Sarah nodded, jotting down the last lines in her notes. "How long until medical arrived?"

"About fifteen minutes. They were already on the way to pick up an order of nu-gauze."

Sarah's tongue found a comfortable groove on the inside of her cheek. She drew a line at the bottom of the page, jotting down the remainder of her thoughts. Sergeant Bernard kept silent vigil, as if waiting for the world to open up beneath him. Sarah tapped the last note sheet, saving it and closing up. She moved to switch off the camera, but found her hand hesitating just above the lens.

"Okay Sergeant Bernard," she sighed, her hand still above the switch. "Now's your last chance. Is there anything else you would like to add to the record?"

"I just don't get it," he said quietly.

Sarah froze. "Pardon?"

"I just don't get it," he repeated, a little louder this time.

"Get what?" she asked, but he continued on as if he hadn't heard her.

"It was supposed to be simple. Just one crate. A light crate. I just don't understand." He uncrossed one arm, nervously running a hand through and pulling on his straight black hair. He looked up, weary brown eyes meeting hers for the first time that hour.

"I just don't understand," he repeated, his face wrought with confusion. "How did a hundred and forty pounds go so wrong?"

Chapter 10:

Sarah Levi tore across the gravel road, a trail of dust kicked up in her wake. Her arms pumped furiously, heart thudding in her chest. A dune rose ahead of her, bathed in the blue light of Anius' enormous full moon. Janessa T. Dashell's synthetic baseline and swooping vocals blared from her black sport earpieces. It was a song about redemption, about finding your way when no one was watching. It was Ms. Dashell's twenty-third most popular single, recorded just after her widely publicized falling out with her chef and bodyguard, Stavrom Bearsur. The doleful chorus cut in, carrying Sarah to the foot of the dune, spurring her further and faster.

She dug her toes into the soft sand, pushing hard as she climbed. The installation spiraled out before her as she reached the summit. A bright voice in her ear reminded Sarah that she was doing an excellent job, and that her heartrate was well within the acceptable fat-burning range for a woman her age. She ignored the voice, a factory pre-install that came with the earbuds. They were a gift from a well-meaning great-aunt, and they managed the tricky feat of perfectly tracking her mileage and pace while also reminding her that a woman's metabolism slows by five percent each decade.

She skidded down the dune, heels digging in to slow her descent. At the bottom, her earpiece cheerily informed her that she had completed two miles, burning the equivalent of one dark chocolate bar, or two glasses of wine. Sarah hated wine. She wasn't partial to chocolate either, but the caloric equivalency presets were hard-coded within her

126

Heuron Fitpiece for WOMEN! (winner of 2025's *Tamlin Excellence in Inclusive Design* award—men's category). She took off again, cutting left, past the first spiral of the BPD dorms.

The first line of huts slipped by her, the windowless domes sprouting out of the bare desert like great, grey mushrooms. She washed the dust from her mouth, swigging from the bottle in her hand. Sweat ran in rivers down the side of her face, a trail of salt drops dotting the sands behind her. She sucked in another lungful of the hot, dry air, head swimming a little from the extra oxygen. The burning in her legs chastising her for fighting against the planet's higher gravity. The ICF Physician's Corps maintained that it took forty-two days for a Trooper to fully adjust the environmental conditions of a new planet. Sarah took their word for it—she'd never had the opportunity to see for herself.

Some movement drew her attention out of the corner of her eye. Another runner approached on the left. She hugged the shoulder of the road, giving them ample room to pass. She wasn't opposed to a partner, not on principle at least. Most often they'd join her for just a few miles before splitting off. Their routes may intersect, but they rarely shared the same destination.

The runner drew alongside her, she acknowledged him with a wave and faced the front; the road was narrowing up ahead. The tap on her shoulder surprised her. She was further surprised as she turned to see Sergeant Torres, puffing hard and face flushed. He was saying something around the gasping breaths. Sarah tapped her earpiece, momentarily pausing Janessa T. Dashell's seventeenth most popular single.

"Yes?"

"Can...I...talk...to you?" Torres panted. His face was a shade between a faded barnside and a plum tomato, his breathing carrying the labored quality generally reserved for large, hooved mammals. She took pity on him and slowed her pace, but did not stop.

"What?" she asked coolly.

His breathing lost its rattling wheeze as they slowed down. "It's about...Bernard."

"I gathered as much. What specifically?"

He opened his mouth to answer, but choked when his body instead seized the air for something more vital. Sarah slowed down further, plodding along so he could keep up. She waited for the coughing fit to subside as he caught his breath.

Torres wiped the sweat collecting in his eyes. "Fuck's sake. Can we stop running?"

She thought for a moment. "No. If it's important, you'll keep up."

She took some pleasure in the muttered string of curses that followed. They passed three huts while he reached the limits of his four-letter vocabulary.

"Fine," he said, spitting out the last word. "I talked with Bernard. I think you should reconsider."

"Reconsider what exactly?"

"Him. The accident. This whole case." He waved his arms to add emphasis, slowing down even further. "I know how this goes, but you can't throw the book at him like this."

You killed my pace for this?

Her eyes narrowed, the usual kindness evaporating behind a wintery chill. "Even supposing that I took suggestions during a case—*which I do not.* And even supposing that I have the authority to recommend leniency—*which I also do not.* What *else* would you have me do? I find the facts, I report the facts, that's it. And the facts are that he bypassed customs laws to fast-track a shipment in return for favors. He let an unlicensed driver operate a mechlift. He ignored *all* regulations regarding safety cables. And he confessed to everything *in a recorded interview.*"

Her words hung in the air as they jogged. She watched gears turning in his head as he looked for a loophole. *You've got ten seconds to say something worth my time.* She raised a hand up to her ear, ready to press play once again.

Sergeant Torres saw her hand raise. He knew what it meant. The road ahead of them forked, he was running out of time.

"He's a good guy!" he blurted out at last. "The kind of guy that cleans his house before the maid comes over. Don't do this to him."

Her eyes narrowed further. "*I'm* not doing anything to him. *I* don't deliver sentences. *I* don't serve judgements. That's your leadership's call. Not. *Me*." She jerked a thumb towards her chest. "*I* deliver facts. Once I send in my case, I'm gone. That's what *I* do."

Nothing personal, it's just a job, she added to herself.

His mouth hung a little open, wide eyes crusted on the edges with dried sweat. "But...he's a good Trooper."

Funny how many saints I end up investigating in this job.

"That may be," she replied, turning her back on him, "but good troops still screw up. He sent a Trooper to the hospital. There are always consequences."

She double-tapped her ear and the music started up again. Torres looked around, scrambling for a lifeline. He dragged a heavy hand across his face, wiping his grimy eyes before it hit him in a flash.

"Wait!" he shouted, sprinting to catch up with her again. "What about the weight?"

Sarah blinked at him, tapping her earpiece again. "What about what wait?"

"The weight," he gasped, chest heaving as he drew alongside her. "The crate was too heavy. It took four guys to lift it off Bradshaw. I was there, it was heavy as *fuck*. I talked it over with Bernard, there's no way it was a hundred and forty pounds."

She slowed down, letting him catch his breath while she thought it over. She watched him closely, looking for a hidden motive. *Are you really trying to help him? Or just trying to cover your own ass?* Her brow wrinkled as she watched him pant. He'd been named in the report as well; she listed him as a 'secondary contributor,' a key player in the 'culture of negligence' surrounding the busy space port. He didn't make the call that caused the accident, but his attitude and contempt for procedure told Sarah he just as easily could have. She shook her head. No, there was no way he knew the extent of her conclusions, but he probably had suspicions.

The gravel road split before them, one lane leading towards her room in the *Transient Sustainment Housing*, the other winding back through the BPD. She jogged in place while she made up her mind.

"Well, Buck-Sergeant, this is my turn." She shrugged. "You can join me, but this conversation is done."

Sergeant Torres rubbed his eyes again, his chest still heaving. "How much farther?" he croaked.

She pinched her earpiece, the cheery voice informing her she'd completed three miles in twenty-nine minutes, and was halfway through her workout. She eyed Torres carefully for a moment, watching him cough as he swallowed hard on a mouthful of dust.

"Ten more miles," she said flatly.

He gawped at her, sucking in more dust and coughing into his hand. His hacking subsided, and he shook his head.

"Then I believe this is goodbye, Sergeant Torres." She turned away, pressing play as she took off to the right. She left him standing at the crossroads, watching the trail of dust clouds fade away as she receded into the distance.

"Fuck me," he said to the empty road.

The clatter of trays mingled with the dull roar of the dining facility. Sarah picked idly at her second tray of rice pilaf, chasing the last of the dry grains with a fork. She bumped elbows with the Trooper next to her, apologizing quickly as she drew back her arm. If he heard her, he took no notice, continuing on in a lively discussion with his friends about last night's *Delia* broadcast. Sarah sighed, setting her elbow back down on the table, tucking it in a little more than before.

She looked up from the alloy tray, eyes wandering over to a poster tacked on the wall. A cartoon Trooper crouched down on one panel, reaching a hand out to pet an alien-looking worm. The next panel showed the same worm, now grown to enormous size, swallowing up the cartoon Trooper. The caption below read 'Mannered? Or *MON-STER?*' She tapped the shoulder of the Trooper next to her, catching him mid-bite as she pointed to the poster.

"What? That?" Sergeant Johnson chewed over his chicken alfredo as he followed her finger. "Some idiot got his finger bitten off playing with the Dune Worms. They put that up for the rest of the slow learners."

She arched a brow. "Dune Worms?"

"'Bout a foot long, squirmy," Johnson explained, shoveling in another bite. "Them and the cactus are the only things actually from here."

She looked back at the poster. "And they get that big?"

"No," he snorted. "But the Bio-Environmental folks want to make sure the point gets across. They don't want anybody keeping pets."

This was not true. Unknown to Sergeant Johnson, Anius boasted a rather rich ecosystem, the sparse desert biome was home to nearly a thousand different species of cactus, scrub brush, and invertebrates.

Equally unknown to Sergeant Johnson, *Xenoannelida aphroditois* (commonly referred to as 'Dune Worms' after their passing resemblance to creatures from a popular series of science-fiction vidplays) did indeed grow to massive size. While the majority of their life was spent in a diminutive larval stage, those that survived to adulthood went on to undergo a series of rapid molts around their thirty-year mark, growing to nearly sixty feet in length. This late-stage nymph would then burrow deep underground, often for miles, before locating a pocket of heavy water and spinning a cocoon. It then pupated into its final stage as a eusocial queen, producing generations of servile offspring through parthenogenesis. This last stage was unknown even to xenobiologists, as any grant application furthering research into the Dune Worms' lifecycle tended to stall out while awaiting approval of the Anian governor. The fact that Governor Armao owned stock in JBS Ingc., the leading miner and exporter of heavy water throughout Coalition space, was surely unrelated.

Sarah thanked Sergeant Johnson and turned back to her tray, her thoughts drifted back once again to the case. The file was still open on the tablet in her dorm room, small black cursor blinking on the final line. She'd written the last few paragraphs when she got back from her run, composing her closing thoughts while she ignored the sweeping patches of multicolored mold threatening to engulf the shower's ceiling. After typing out the last line she'd hesitated, finger hovering over the send button. She knew it was silly to wait. She had more than enough to close the case out. After a week of investigation she was confident she'd found the root cause and that her findings might prevent a future tragedy. *But still...*

Something nagged at her, inchworms of doubt boring through her mind, holding her finger hostage as she tried to push send. It wasn't just what Sergeant Torres had said, although she had spent the better part of an hour reviewing the transcripts of their testimonies and checking them against the shipping label she'd included in the report. There was something else, something fishy about the irregular delivery ship, and its timing at the end of the shift.

And then there were the texts. Sarah had reviewed the messages from Bernard's tablet, a conversation covering months of deliveries and requests. There were nine messages from Buck-Sergeant Corstley during the time of the incident, escalating in tone and language far beyond what she considered normal urgency.

She frowned down at the smattering of beans and rice on her tray. Her head told her she was being ridiculous, that she should close the case out and move on to the next planet. But her gut told her there was something more. She might have pinned down the most obvious cause for the accident, but she had the strong suspicion that it wasn't the root.

Her nose crinkled as she pushed the tray away. She needed a walk and some answers, and she'd get neither in the chowhall. *No,* she thought as she walked her dirty tray to the conveyor by the door, *I need to look at this case with a new perspective.* And she knew just where to start.

The sandy slopes rolled by as she drove to the port, a chaotic synthbeat skittering out of the LITCAT's speakers inside the cab. A dull-voiced DJ announced the song's title to be '*Hunter's Keep*' from the band *SplinterKit,* and that he would be playing the remainder of their discography over the next hour while he enjoyed his lunch. Sarah lunged over to switch it off only to find the power button missing. The tuner and volume knobs were similarly absent, snapped off by the vehicle's previous owner. 'Sec Troops Fro Life' was carved in the dash above it, alongside an extremely detailed rendering of an erect penis, and the inscription 'Wagner Loves Cock,'—more gifts from the previous occupants. Sarah sighed, returning her hand to the wheel, carefully avoiding the suspicious sticky spots on its back.

She arrived at the port just after midnight, the loading bay awash with activity. Troopers rushed around her as she walked through the terminal. It should have bothered her when no one asked her for credentials or a reason for being there, but she knew better by now. Access control was the least of their problems here.

She wandered around, tracing the curve of the bay. She caught sight of Ishii shouting to a Trooper in a mechlift and pointing out a series of crates she needed loaded. Sarah kept walking, she had all she needed from the stocky Buck-Sergeant. She found herself ducking by Sergeant Bernard, huddled with two Senior-Troopers as they reviewed the landing manifests on the viewscreen. Sarah considered stopping him to talk, but waved the thought away. She knew where to find him if she needed more.

She passed a few more doors, watching a DC-242 coming in to land from the corner of her eye. Blue repulsors fired on the underside of the great, grey dumpling, touching down lightly on the scorched concrete pad. Sarah ignored it and kept moving, turning the corner to her destination at last.

She read the number '12' painted in bold letters over the door. This was her fifth walkthrough of the accident scene, running the last one just after the testimonies from Bernard and Torres. She knew the timeline of events by heart; she could have walked the path of the incident with her eyes closed if she wanted to. But she kept her eyes open, stepping lightly from the door to the center of the bay. A rubber scuff and a small bloodstain on the concrete floor were all that remained of the accident. She stopped by the scuff, careful not to touch it as she examined it once more for some semblance of a hidden secret.

But the scuff was just a scuff, a partial transfer from the mechlift's tread when T'Wallen stopped too quickly. *This is stupid. You've been through this already.* She stood back from the scuff, casting her eyes around the bay as she wracked her brain.

Not for the first time, she found herself cursing the lack of cameras in the bay, another standard practice noticeably absent on Anius. *If only I had a true witness,* she thought, eyes zig-zagging around the open room, *someone impartial, observant, who saw the whole thing go down.* She caught sight of burnished stripes over something silver in the corner of the bay, tucked away under a flight of stairs. *Could it be?*

She grabbed a Private by the arm as she walked over to the stairs. "How long has that been here?"

The Private followed her eye to the GBAS in the corner. "The killbot? About two weeks, ma'am."

Sarah studied the deadly robot, walking around its six folded legs to confirm the lit red light on the back of its targeting unit. She turned back to the Private. "I need you to tell me exactly when it got here."

Private Lidwell scanned the barcode on the back of one leg. "Looks like they unloaded it on January 22nd."

Pieces clicked into place behind Sarah's eyes.

"Get me the mechanic."

Ian had just finished checking the last shuttle, clipboard in hand as he synced its launch data with the Troopers in the control terminal. It had been a long day, his eyes a little bleary as he initialed off on the tablet screen. He rubbed his eyes with the back of one hand, careful to use the one clear spot around the dirt and smudges. He sighed as he saw the oil steeped around his fingernails. *A shower sounds mighty nice right now...*

He looked up from his tablet to see Sergeant Torres speeding towards him. *That's odd*, he thought, rubbing his eyes again. *He's off today.* Torres stopped in front of him, face flushed from hurrying in the stale heat of the bay. *Looks like he got his cardio today*, Ian chuckled to himself. His eyes drew closed for a moment while Torres caught his breath.

Torres' hand on his arm startled him back awake.

"C'mon," Torres said, yanking on his arm. "She's waiting in the spare office."

Ian's brow wrinkled as he felt himself pulled forward. "Who?"

"Levi," Torres called back, leading him out of the bay to the office at the end of the hall. "She says she's found something good."

"I was able to pull video from the GBAS in the corner," Inspector Levi explained, swiping up on the video on her tablet and casting it to the screen on the wall. "I had a hunch it caught a good view angle, and it paid off."

Ian blinked slowly, forcing his eyes into focus on the screen. Thoughts turned slowly in his mind. *GBAS? Is that kill-bot still there from last week?*

"They unloaded it on the 22nd," she continued, scrolling through the video to find the right part. "So it caught the whole thing."

Sergeant Torres leaned over the table beside her. "How? It's been off the whole time."

Levi paused a moment to check her spot in the video. "The main unit, sure. That got switched off as soon as they moved it into place. But the targeting reticle is on as long as there's still power, it auto-records anytime it detects movement and archives the footage for liability purposes."

"I don't understand." Ian rubbed his eyes again, his brain felt like it was soaking in molasses. "I thought the kill-bot was scheduled to leave on February 2nd?"

Inspector Levi's eyes flashed with excitement. "That's what I was told too, but apparently the mechanic from Austin-Brackard broke his toe playing racquetball last week, so they delayed the departure while he recovers. That's how I was able to snag the video today."

She scrolled across the tablet again, fast forwarding through the video. Ian watched dimly as a figure he recognized as himself chased across the screen, gesturing wildly as he directed the flow in the bay. Seeing himself rush about, swigging from his mug and barking orders at ninety frames-per-second, he could feel the weight of that day settling down on his shoulders. He took a seat at the table, dreading the part coming next.

"There," she said, pausing the video with a tap. The image froze on the wall, a suspended tableau of the tragedy to follow. He could see the mechlift, leaning backwards slightly as it rocked from T'Wallen's sudden stop. Bradshaw was poised underneath, arms raised up as if to brace it, tongue sticking out from concentration. Ian looked past it to the wall, seeing himself leaning against it, his expression serene with his eyes closed. Levi tapped the screen again. "And now, watch."

They watched the video play out at normal speed. The mechlift rocked forward, crate shifting out of the hydraulic arms. They watched Private Bradshaw disappear underneath the crate, the lack of sound blessedly obscuring the thundering crash. They watched as Troopers ran over, struggling to lift the crate. Ian felt a wave of guilt wash over him. *This was all your fault.* They watched the crate lift off of Bradshaw. Ian recognized himself kneeling beside the crushed Private. Any moment now Senior-Trooper Isbil would be rushing on screen, working with him to stabilize Bradshaw's shattered spine.

But to his surprise the video stopped as Levi quickly swiped backwards to rewind the footage. They watched the Troopers struggle to place the crate back on top of Bradshaw, dancing backwards until it lifted off of him again and sailed back into the mechlift's arms. She pressed play on the video, and they watched it fall again, smashing Bradshaw to the ground. Ian winced, it was even worse a second time.

Levi stopped the video again, drawing it back a few frames until the

crate was once again in the mechlift's grasp. She pressed play, the crate fell. She paused again, rewound it back until it was in the air. She pressed play again, and they watched Bradshaw get pulverized for a fourth time. She paused and rewound the video, tapping it a fifth time before Sergeant Torres interrupted.

"As fun as this is," he muttered, crossing his arms over his chest, "what the fuck are we doing here?"

Levi tilted her head. "You don't see it?"

"What? Bradshaw getting pile-drived through the fuckin' floor?"

Her brow wrinkled as she stared at him. "No, the crate. Look at the crate."

She rewound the video for a sixth time. Ian watched the tragedy play out, guilt stabbing through his gut at the impact. He rubbed the back of his neck, exhaustion weighing down his hands.

"I don't see anything eith—

She cut him off with a wave of her hand, freezing the video with a tap from the other.

"There," she said, pointing once again to the crate. She drew a circle on the tablet, highlighting one side on the wall.

He rubbed his eyes again. Try as he might, he just wasn't seeing it. "What? The crack on the side? I don't understa—

"What color are barbon-nano plates?" she said quickly. Ian blinked at her. She looked over to Sergeant Torres. "What about you? Do you know?"

"Purple? Gold?" Torres grunted, scratching the back of his head. "Fucking chartreuse? I don't know."

"Green," she said quietly. "Green, with black striations."

She walked over to the screen on the wall, drawing her finger around the crack. "Now what color is that?"

Ian squinted at the wall. The image turned slowly in his mind until suddenly, it clicked.

"Orange," he exclaimed, a flicker of excitement running through him. "But what does that mean?"

"It means," Inspector Levi said, turning back towards the screen, "we need to find that crate."

The walk back to door twelve was brief, but emotional. Ian couldn't help but feel himself buoyed by the briefest of hopes. *Easy Ian*, he thought as he tamped down on his excitement, *this doesn't mean anything yet.* They stopped at the scuff on the floor, Ian forcing himself still while he waited for Levi to speak.

"So where's the crate now?" she asked after a moment.

Torres sighed. "That's what I was trying to tell you, it's gone. Long gone. I'm sure they picked it up as soon as we cleaned Bradshaw off the floor."

The excited feeling drained out of Ian as quickly as it came. "So that's it then," he said, trying and failing to keep the dejection from his voice. "That's all there is to it."

Levi's eyes narrowed, her mouth drawing a thin line as she searched around the room. "Not quite, there's always something else."

She locked eyes with Sergeant Torres. "Where did you put the crate after you pulled it off Private Bradshaw?"

He thought for a moment, rubbing a hand across his chin. "We lugged it over to the side, by the hallway." He turned and pointed towards the door. "Right about there."

Levi took off in the same direction, stopping once she reached the door.

"Here?" she shouted back, pointing to a spot on the floor.

"Yeah," Torres nodded, trailing off as he joined her by the door. "Pretty much there."

Ian followed in behind, finding Levi on her hands and knees, furiously searching the ground. He joined her on the floor, still unsure what they were doing there.

"What are we looking f—

She cut him off and pointed to a nearby grate. "Get that open!"

Ian joined Torres at the side of the grate, grimacing slightly as his hands gripped the slimy metal. Together they pulled, heaving the grate up on creaking hinges. The three looked down the hole, an abysmal foulness clinging to the sides of the drain. Without a word Levi stuck her hand in, reaching around the bend in the pipe. Ian gagged as a waft of something corrupt and indescribable floated up, his shoulders beginning to burn from holding the grate open. He opened his mouth to say something but shut it when he saw her eyes go wide. She sat back from the grate, something clenched in her sludge covered hand. Ian started to reach for the kerchief in his pocket but stopped short as she wiped her hand on her pants.

They dropped the grate and gathered around her. She was muttering something as she looked at the prize in her hands. She held it up for them to see, a small vial of orange powder glittered in the fluorescent light.

"What is it?" Ian asked quietly, staring at the vial.

"What does it mean?" Torres asked behind him.

"It means, gentlemen," she said dryly, the vial casting an orange shadow across her face, "that Sergeant Corstley was right to be anxious about receiving that crate."

She turned it over in her hand, the tiny grains tinkling inside. "I hate it when my narcotics get held up too."

Chapter 11:

"I KNEW IT!"

Sergeant Torres' voice echoed across the open bay. He shook a triumphant finger under Sarah's nose. "I knew those elitist fucks were up to something!"

"Not so loud!" She shushed him, pocketing the glass vial. "You want the whole base to know?"

Quieted but undeterred, he threw a few jabs into Sergeant Bernard's shoulder. "I told you Bernie, didn't I? I told you that crate was too heavy. Hundred and forty pounds, my *ass!*"

"You did, you called it." A wan smile crossed Bernard's face as he rubbed his shoulder. "I suppose this takes some of the mystery out of how they got that bottle of champagne."

Torres nodded, all but crowing as he took a victory lap around the sewer grate. Sergeant Bernard looked back at Sarah, thin smile fading into something more thoughtful. "So where do we go from here?"

"We go straight to their secret-squirrel compound and kick in the fuckin' door!" Sergeant Torres said as he looped back into the conversation, jogging past the two of them with his fists in the air. "I can't wait to see his face. Corstley is gonna shit a brick!"

They watched as Torres stopped in place and dramatically pantomimed Sergeant Corstley's future look of shock and dismay, accompanied by his own impression of their smug looks of triumph. Bernard turned back to Sarah, questioning their plan with the raise of an eyebrow. She shook her head.

"As much as I'm enjoying the enthusiasm, we need to get some things straight," she said, her voice calm and clear. Sergeant Torres dropped his acting, her level tone grounding everyone once again. Sarah looked from Bernard to Torres, she needed them on one page for this. "Right now we have next to nothing linking Sergeant Corstley or the Commando Raiders to anything remotely illicit. Connecting the dots between them is going to require diligence, patience, and a lot of things going right. With a case like this, we have to be smart. *Subtle.*" Sarah looked directly at Torres on that last point.

"We will *not* go charging off half-cocked. The Raiders are well-known, respected, and protected. We need an iron-clad case, built out of irrefutable evidence—anything less and they'll slip away entirely." She emphasized these ground rules hard, punctuating each with a pounded fist into her open hand. "We will *not* mention the case to anyone—anyone with ears has a mouth. And we will *not* antagonize the Raiders in the slightest. If they catch wind of it, they'll go to ground and leave us with nothing."

She watched them closely, satisfied that they seemed suitably impressed by the gravity of the situation. "And it bears mentioning that none of this changes the existing facts of this case. No matter what we find here, the decisions that were made and the circumstances that drew me here still apply."

Sarah locked eyes with Sergeant Bernard, pausing for a breath before continuing. She knew this next part was going to sting. "At the end of all this, there will likely still be consequences. I do not have the ability, nor the authority, to alter the facts uncovered by this investigation."

She stopped and watched her words sink in. Sergeant Bernard's smile faded completely, the somber realization of what she'd said settling over him like a heavy cloak. Sergeant Torres rubbed his chin, his only acknowledgement was a muttered "Fuck."

Bernard's eyes searched the floor, his arms hugged tight to his chest. Sarah let out a slow breath, she knew it wasn't what they wanted to hear, but it was the truth she had, and the truth they deserved. A few moments of silence passed between the three sergeants.

"Well," Sergeant Bernard said at last, lifting his eyes to meet hers. "It's not much, but it's more than we had this morning." He shrugged, a thin smile returning to his face. "Maybe if we arrest all the Raiders, they'll run out of handcuffs by the time they get back to me."

In spite of herself, Sarah felt a small smile creeping over as well. "One can only hope."

Sergeant Torres let out a low whistle, fishing a blue tin out of a pocket. "I guess if we're riding shit creek, we might as well paddle."

He slapped a *Stip* on one shoulder, sighing as the dermal nicotine began to set in. He thought for a moment then offered the blue tin as an olive branch to Sarah.

She shook her head. "No thanks, quit last month."

"Shame." He shrugged, tucking the tin back in his pocket. "I was just beginning to like you."

They spared a few minutes more to discuss the parameters of the case, with Sarah outlining the broad strokes for investigative procedure. They needed to establish a firm connection between Sergeant Corstley, the crate, and a pattern of smuggling, as well as tie in any additional Raiders implicated in the operation. It was going to be difficult, she explained, Raiders are used to covert work and likely covered their tracks well. Their one hope so far was that Sergeant Corstley had been foolish enough to use the official ICF cargo port to bring in the shipment, and that meant there was a trail they could follow.

They cut the conversation short when Sergeant Bernard's yawning became a continual source of punctuation. Though he apologized for it profusely, they agreed that twenty-two hours of being awake was counter-productive to analytical thought. They broke for the day, agreeing to meet up the following night to lay out the information they already had and plan their next moves in detail. In spite of his protests, Sergeant Torres insisted on driving Bernard home, saying the last thing they needed was another accident. Sarah thanked them both for their help so far, heading out in her own LITCAT to get some rest. She would need it. She was going to attempt something unprecedented in her twelve years as an investigator—ask a commander for an extension.

Sarah paused for a moment outside the etched glass doors. In the eight years she'd known him, Colonel Schwarz had always been fair. Moody, dramatic, at times temperamental, but fair nonetheless. And though he was loath to admit it, he had a soft spot for anyone in whom he saw reflections of himself. Colonel Schwarz trusted himself more than anyone else, and by extension, trusted those he felt shared his better instincts.

Sarah took a deep breath. She prided herself in delivering ahead of schedule and had built a sizeable reputation for solving cases weeks ahead of commander expectations. Safety investigations were often seen as damaging, nocuous affairs, exposing the corruptions and failures within an organization. Most commanders were just happy to get them over with, anxiously awaiting her findings so they could administer punishments, declare a few immediate changes, and move on with their day. She'd never known a commander to like delays, least of all when waiting to see if *they* would be the ones implicated in her findings.

Sarah let the breath out slowly, pushing through the glass doors. She approached Colonel Schwarz's office, projecting her trademark calm as she walked by Mr. Freeman's desk.

"Does he have a minute?" she asked, floating the question out as casually as she could.

"Mhmm," Mr. Freeman nodded, pulling out an earpiece as he looked up from the bank of monitors. "You're good, he's doing 'commander time' right now."

She paused for another moment at the grey door handles, looking back to the secretary. "How's the mood?"

"Good," he said, eyeing her carefully as he replaced the earpiece. "For *now*."

Sarah nodded, steeling herself for the difficult conversation. She took

another deep breath, let it out, and pushed her way in.

She found Colonel Schwarz leaning back in his chair, applying a few choice brushstrokes of orange to what appeared to be the snarling face of a tiger mid-leap. The heavy baseline of east coast rap hummed softly from a speaker embedded in the vast SimuWood desk. He didn't look up as she approached the desk, only acknowledging her presence with a snap of his fingers to pause the music.

"Well, Inspector," he said absently, trailing the orange-tipped brush across the canvas. "I see you have come to join me in my 'commander time.'"

She stood rigidly, clasping her hands behind her back. "Yes, sir. It's about the case."

"Ah, yes. I assumed as much." The strokes continued at their languid pace.

She pursed her lips, thinking through her next words carefully. Timoson had told her the Colonel had taken up painting shortly after assuming command on Anius. She'd been told his mood drastically improved with each canvas he finished. Sarah hoped that was the case now.

She opened her mouth to speak, but he cut her off.

"You told me when you first arrived that the case would take you no more than seven days. Today marks one week exactly. I didn't see a report inside my inbox this evening, and now you are here in person." He paused, dabbing the brush on his palette. "This tells me that either you have failed to complete your task, something unheard of in your twelve years of service, or else that you have found something so terrible that you felt it could not safely be delivered by email."

Sarah said nothing, she knew him well enough to wait for him to finish.

He brought the brush back to the canvas, adding a trailing line to the tiger's chin. "So tell me, Inspector, what great malfeasance have you uncovered among my ranks?"

Sarah waited, mulling over her response. Silence stretched between them, broken only by the soft scraping of the brush.

She broke the quiet with a cough, choosing brevity as the best course of action. "I'm afraid, sir, that this is closer to the former than the latter."

The brush strokes stopped, Colonel Schwarz looked up at her for the first time.

She gave him no room to interject, pushing ahead on a single breath. "I've uncovered some items that bear further inquiry, sir. There are...*extenuating* circumstances at play that I did not initially anticipate. I suspect the problem runs much deeper than we previously discussed, and so I need to request—respectfully request—an extension on the existing timeline."

Colonel Schwarz eyed her carefully, setting the brush down to rest on the palette. He leaned back in his chair, folding his hands across his chest.

"Inspector Levi," he began gravely, "in all my years as a commander, I have *never* granted an extension on a deadline. A deadline is set for a reason, it's a promise of trust between the commander and the Trooper. To allow you more time would be...unprecedented."

Sarah kept her face impassive, clenching her hands tightly behind her back. Across the desk, Colonel Schwarz looked out over steepled fingers.

"Still," he said quietly, drawing the syllable out like a lofty stroke of his brush, "precedents should be broken for the right reasons."

Sarah let out a small breath. Colonel Schwarz continued to watch her, searching for some reaction as she stared straight ahead. He leaned forward in his chair, resting his elbows on the desk. "I accept your proposal, Inspector, and grant your extension. I trust you. After all, you're a seeker of truth—as am I."

He leaned back in his chair, inviting her to sit with a wave of his hand. She shook her head, politely declining in the interest of time. He shrugged, drawing a steaming cup from somewhere under the desk.

"So how much time do you need?" he asked, pressing the espresso mug to his lips.

"Three weeks, sir."

The brow wrinkled below the thick black hair. "It's that serious?"

She nodded.

"This must be some extenuating circumstances indeed," the Colonel mused, sipping thoughtfully from the tiny mug. He let out an appreciative sigh as he set it back under the desk. "You know, this reminds me of a similar inquiry I worked, back in the Eisenhower school."

"Ha! *Five!*" erupted from the other room.

The Colonel's eyes narrowed, boring a hole through the doors to his office. He returned his attention to Sarah with an indignant sniff, his voice droll and tired. "Mr. Freeman believes that I mention my time at the war academy...*often*. He doesn't seem to consider how the lessons learned at a war college might tend to apply to running an intergalactic military operation. But perhaps he's never had a commander before that attended Eisenhow—

"That's six!"

Sarah stepped out of the way of the Colonel's glare.

"Perhaps your time would be better spent counting the positions available *on the job boards!*" he roared back.

Silence returned to the office. Sarah coughed politely into her hand.

"Well then," Colonel Schwarz said at last. "As I was say—

"Ninety-seven, sir," Mr. Freeman interrupted from outside.

The Colonel looked from Sarah to the door. "What was that, Mr. Freeman?"

"Ninety-seven positions open in my field. Six on planet."

Colonel Schwarz rolled his eyes hard enough to shake the world. "And how many, pray tell, offer six-figure salaries?"

"*Three, sir,*" he sang back.

Sarah watched as the commander for the complete ICF component stationed on Anius, over ten-thousand Troopers in all, slump back in his chair and draw a hand over his eyes.

"You know, I used to lead troops in combat, dodging shrapnel EMP and kinetic rounds on the backroads of Avina. Now look at me, taking attitude from a gawddamn *civilian*." He sighed. "Inspector Levi, your three weeks are granted. I trust that you can see yourself out?"

A thin smile crossed her face. "Of course, sir."

He waved her off, pressing hard against his eyes with his other hand. Sarah turned and walked to the door, just reaching the handles when he spoke to her again.

"I also trust, Inspector, that these extenuating circumstances are not criminal in nature? Nothing outside the jurisdiction of a *safety* investigation?"

Sarah stared at the door ahead, her voice stony as she replied. "Nothing definitive, sir. But if something comes up, I'll be sure to pass it along to the MPs."

"Good, leave the heavy-lifting to the agencies best equipped for it," he said, nodding as he returned to his brush and paints. "It's always good to have an understanding of one's limits."

Sarah tucked her tongue into her cheek, biting off her first two replies.

"Of course, sir," she said, pushing through the doors. "You'll be the first to know when I reach them."

Sarah met Torres and Bernard at the spaceport in the hours just before sunset. The waning glow on the horizon lit up the dunes for miles as she pulled in under the overhang. They were waiting for her by the door, leaning against a dusty LITCAT with what appeared to be genitals drawn on the sand-caked door. Sarah shook her head as they ducked inside the port. She was going to have to let some things slide if they were going to get anywhere in this case. They found an empty office and slipped inside, closing the door behind them so they wouldn't be overheard while they discussed the case. Earlier that morning, she'd tasked them with putting together everything they knew about Sergeant Corstley and the Commando Raiders.

It turned out to be very little.

"How many Raiders are stationed on Anius?"

"We don't know."

"Who heads the Raider detachment?"

"We don't know."

"Do all their supplies come through this port?"

"We don't know."

"What kinds of missions do they run?"

"*Nobody* knows."

"How long has Sergeant Corstley been stationed here?"

"We don't know."

"How many Troopers work for Sergeant Corstley?"

"We don't know."

"Who does Sergeant Corstley work for?"

"We don't—wait I know this one!" Sergeant Torres sat up straight in his chair, uncrossing his arms to raise a hand. "Harbison, they all work for Sergeant Harbison."

"Good," Sarah said, jotting the name down on her tablet. "What's his rank and first name?"

Torres slumped back in his chair, arms folded once again. "I don't know."

Sarah sighed, they were getting nowhere fast. She pinched the bridge of her nose with her fingers. "How often do their shipments come in?"

"About twice a month," Bernard answered, speaking up for the first time from across the table.

That's something at least, she thought. "And how long have you been doing favors for Sergeant Corstley?"

"About nine months," Torres said.

"And is Sergeant Corstley the only one to ask you about receiving shipments?"

"Yes."

"Just you two?"

Torres nodded. "Usually, he doesn't like Ishii so he never bothers with her."

Sarah jotted down a few more notes. "Could there be any other Raiders working shipments with Logistics and Supply?"

"I have no fucking idea."

Sarah set the tablet down on the table. "Alright, gents, work with me here. We're investigating the most elite, secretive, special operations unit in military history. They have over a hundred years of experience infiltrating planets and conducting operations completely unknown to the public for decades afterwards. If we want even a *chance* of catching them, we're going to need to get smarter and stay one step ahead. So I need you, both of you, to get your heads together and help me work through this."

The room lapsed into silence as Sarah looked across the table to the two men. Bernard busied himself with his hands while Torres stared resolutely at the floor. Sarah scowled at both of them, leaning back in her chair to massage her temples.

It was Bernard who spoke up at last. "How about the video?"

Sarah looked up from her hands. "What about it?"

"Well, we got the accident on video," he said slowly, as if unsure of the words coming out of his mouth. "What about afterwards? Did we catch Sergeant Corstley picking the crate up?"

Sarah considered this for a moment. "That's not a bad idea. I didn't even look." She connected the tablet to the screen on the wall, rummaging through file names to pull up the video. Torres shot Bernard a reassuring thumbs up. She pulled the video up on-screen, tapping the red marker indexing the time of the accident. She pressed play and then began fast-forwarding through the three-hundred hours of footage remaining.

"So describe Sergeant Corstley to me," she said, watching the video blur.

Torres grunted. "He's a prick."

Sarah managed to roll her eyes without taking them off the screen. Figures rushed across the bay in the sped-up footage, darting around with clipboards, tools, and boxes. "Any other helpful descriptors?"

"He's shorter than the other Raiders, maybe five-eight," Bernard offered helpfully. "Stocky. Oh, and bearded. He's got a thick, curly beard."

"Lucky bastard," Torres muttered, feeling his own smooth jaw. Though ICF grooming regulations strictly forbid facial hair among its Troopers, with mustaches allowed only within strict confines of the upper lip, the Commando Raiders had long maintained an exception to policy. Carried over as a legacy from the insurgent wars of the twenty-first century, beards were seen as a mark of distinction among the crack corps of the Raiders. Though initially implemented to allow special operations forces to blend in with a surrounding population, Raider beards quickly took on a life of their own, with some units even hosting photoshoots for the more illustrious examples of imperial hirsuteness. What began as a means of urban camouflage quickly grew to distinguish and separate, marking their owners as members of the elite Commando community. Raiders wore their beards as a badge of honor, inspiring awe and attracting the envy of all Troopers living within the confines of rank-and-file regulations.

Sarah nodded, parsing through the video as it rushed past on screen. Twenty hours of footage rushed by in just over an hour, but they were beginning to get bored. Nobody matching Sergeant Corstley's description appeared in any part of the accelerated chaos of the spaceport. They watched the corner of the screen, eyes on the small, grey crate in the bottom left. Another minute past with no change. Sarah rubbed her eyes, blinking back the grit accumulating at their edges.

"Wait, just wait!" Sergeant Bernard yelped, jumping up from his chair. "The crate's gone."

Sarah snapped her eyes open, searching around the corners of the screen. "What, where? Did you see Sergeant Corstley?"

She paused the video with a quick double-tap. The video froze, the

bottom left corner empty on the screen.

"Fuck, man," Torres exclaimed. "We missed it."

Sarah calmed him down with a raised finger, reversing the video frame by frame. They watched as the crate reappeared, carried in hand by the hydraulic arms of a yellow mechlift. He knew it shouldn't, but Sergeant Bernard couldn't help but feel a pang of guilt when he saw the safety lines connected to the crate. The mechlift set the crate down and backed up, speeding away to another task. Sarah played the video forward a bit and then paused, freezing the image on the Trooper behind the mechlift's poly-plex cockpit.

"Alright gents, I trust you know who *this* is?"

They found Special-Trooper Johnston standing on the loading dock of the port. If he was surprised to be pulled aside by two loadmasters and a nice lady wearing a uniform without a rank, he didn't show it.

"Hello, ma'am," he said cheerfully, offering a wave to Inspector Levi. "Did you find out more about the crate? Did it slip like I thought?"

Of course, of all the fucking morons here, it had to be THIS fucking moron, Terrance thought bitterly to himself. He grabbed Johnston by the shoulders, squaring up and looking him straight in the eye. "Focus, Johnston, focus. The crate, the small grey one delivered two weeks ago with tag number 157-Bravo. The one with the big crack in it that was sitting by the door. Where did it go?"

Terrance's heart sank as he watched the vacant smile on Johnston's face. It took a few moments, but something clicked behind the dull, blue eyes. Recognition slowly crept across Johnston's freckled face. "Crate? You mean the one that squished Bradshaw?"

Terrance closed his eyes slowly, broad shoulders slumping.

"Yes," he sighed. "The one that squished Bradshaw."

"Oh, that one," Johnston said brightly. "I loaded it up for the Raiders."

Maybe he's not such a dead end after all. Terrance looked up, a small sprout of hope beginning to take root in his chest. "Okay, Johnston, who accepted the delivery?"

A confused look passed over Johnston's face. "Well, no one, Sarge. I just loaded it on the truck and it left."

Terrance felt the hope get plucked out of his chest, root and stem. He took one hand off the Special-Trooper's shoulder, freeing it up to drag across his face. He turned back to Bernard and Levi. "Well, I fucking tried. Your turn."

Sergeant Bernard nodded, stepping forward to take Terrance's place. Terrance watched a big, fake smile stretch across the Buck-Sergeant's face, dimly masking the crinkles of desperation around his eyes.

"Okay, Johnston," Bernard said slowly, practicing the same measured cadence he used on his toddler. "Who told you to load the crate on the truck?"

Johnston scratched the top of his sandy-brown hair. He thought for a moment, then shrugged. "I dunno, Sarge, some Raider I guess."

Terrance saw the tightness set in Bernard's jaw. The desperate crinkling around his eyes deepened. An idea came to him suddenly, and he stepped in between them, intervening before Bernard fully snapped and choked the kid out.

"Johnston, buddy," he said slowly, aping the same tone Bernard had used before. "Can you describe the Raider that talked to you? Did he have a big beard?"

The confusion deepened on the Trooper's face. "Beard? No, Sarge. It was a lady. She had a mean face and shaved head."

Now it was Terrance's turn to be confused. He looked back at Bernard. "Shaved head? You know any bald Raiders?"

Bernard shook his head. "I've only met two women Raiders, neither of them bald."

"No, not bald, Sarge," Johnston said, somehow possessing the gall to express exasperation at their lack of understanding. "She had a shaved head, like the sides. But she had a ponytail up top."

Recognition washed over Terrance. He locked eyes with Bernard and Levi. "I know her, that's Bonsly. I see her sometimes at the *PCCR* bar."

Inspector Levi nodded, jotting the name down on her tablet. "Then that's our first lead."

Chapter 12:

Ian stared down across the desk to the hissing viper coiled on the other side of the mirror. Thousands of lightyears separated the two, so Ian could only watch helplessly as the serpent turned on his wife. His eyes were wide as the viper's tongue flicked out, caressing Suzette's cheek with the sensuous contempt of a jilted lover. The snake drew back, bunched and ready to strike at her vulnerable neck.

"Not right now honey, we're talking with daddy."

"*Sssssssssss*," Taniel hissed, threatening her again with the plush boa constrictor. "*Sssssssssss.*"

On the other side of the mirror, Ian smiled through his hands. "I see the zoo was a hit."

"Oh yes," Suzette said, lifting Taniel into her lap. "He loved the—*no honey not in the face, mommy's talking.*" She put a hand up to catch the snake before it smacked her in the eye again, wrapping Taniel in her other hand to hold him still. She puffed her cheeks out as she looked back at Ian, a shock of curly red hair slipping out of her loose bun. "As you can see, the reptile house was the highlight of the trip."

"*Sssssssssss*," Taniel hissed again, smacking the snake against the screen. "Sssnake, Daddy. Snake! Snake! Snake!"

"Yes, honey, daddy sees the snake. Gentle with the screen." She pulled back on the plush tail, wrestling the snake and the tiny fist controlling it away from the mirror. "Why don't you tell him what else you saw at the Zoo?"

Ian stifled a laugh as Suzette struggled to contain the excited boy. "Go on, Tan. What other animals did you see?"

"Enephant!" Taniel shrieked.

The smile on Ian's face widened. "Elephants? Those are daddy's favorite. Were they really big?"

"Enephant! Big poop!"

"Big poop, huh?" Ian chuckled, raising an eyebrow at Suzette.

"Oh yes, the *other* highlight of the day," she sighed. "Couldn't leave the zoo 'till we saw that. Okay honey, why don't we go play with our trains?" Suzette lifted the wriggling child out of her lap, setting him back on the floor. He took off as soon as his feet hit the hardwood, darting away to his tracks and cars. She let out another small sigh as she turned back to Ian. "They're smaller than I remember."

"Which? The elephants or the poops?"

"Both," she snorted. "I always thought of them being much bigger. They always seemed enormous when I was a kid."

"You were smaller then too," Ian noted, scratching the underside of his chin. "They say the wild ones were much bigger."

"Oh yeah, for sure," Suzette said. "But no one's seen a wild elephant in two hundred years." She cracked a wan smile.

"That's the problem with the past though, everything was always bigger and greater back then."

Ian grunted in agreement. "How's class going?"

"Good, they're all anxious about their midterm grades." She stifled a yawn with her hand, bags trailing under her eyes as she looked back at Ian. "How's work? Is that guy doing better?"

Ian shifted in his chair. "Bradshaw's...better. He starts physical therapy this week. They won't know until then if he'll need a permanent StimBrace."

Suzette nodded. She read the guilt and worry in his tone. "And the investigator? Did she look at the heavy crate again?"

Ian hesitated a moment before responding, Levi's words of caution against discussing the case echoing in his mind. "She...did. She found some more things to look into."

Suzette smiled, relieved to hear some good news. "Great! Maybe they'll realize they shouldn't be pushing you so hard."

Ian shook his head. Suzette was many things—thoughtful, smart, caring—but she had very little patience for the intricate demands of military work. He watched her yawn across the screen, this time too slow to catch it with her hand. "Why don't I go, Sue? Let you get some rest?"

She nodded, another yawn cutting off her reply. "Sounds great dear. Love you."

He caught her blown kiss and placed it over his heart.

"Love you too."

Senior-Trooper Morgan Bonsly lounged in the chair across the SimuWood table, one arm hooked on the chair back and leg draped over the armrest. Her feet kicked idly as she waited, while her free hand tapped on the other armrest. The ICF had spent years and millions of credits training her, honing her instincts to meet the cutting edge of precision engagements, and right now her instincts were telling her that her time was being wasted.

Sarah watched her from the other side of the table. She double-checked the camera on her tablet, making sure the recording was live before they started. She pulled up a fresh note page, titling it with the interview subject and date. She broke the silence of the room with a small cough to clear her throat.

"Senior-Trooper Bonsly, I want to thank you for meeting with me." Sarah paused to look up from her notes, offering a warm smile to the Senior-Trooper. "I am Inspector Lev—

"I can read," interrupted Bonsly, staring down as her fingers continued their staccato beat. "Now what the fuck is this about, Levi?"

Sarah dropped the smile. "*Inspector* Levi. And this is in regards to an investigation into an incident on January 23rd, 2333."

The tapping continued. "You MP?"

Sarah tightened her grip on the stylus. "No, ISC."

"*Hmph*," said Bonsly, finally looking up from her hand. Her eyes cut across Sarah, up and down, left and right. She finished her assessment with another 'hmph,' running her tongue over her teeth. She lifted her chin and cocked an eyebrow back at Sarah. "And what can I do for you?"

You can cut your bullshit attitude and tell me about the drugs you picked up, Sarah thought, forcing a thin smile back on her face. What she said was, "What can you tell me about the crate delivered on January 24th?"

Cold blue eyes looked back at Sarah for a moment before she shrugged. "Probably nothing. We get a lot of deliveries. Care to be more specific, *Inspector?*"

Sarah tucked her tongue into her cheek. *Play it slow, play it smart.* She forced her voice to sound casual. "Small grey crate, number 157-Bravo, came in on the back of DC-229."

She watched Bonsly for a reaction. The blue eyes narrowed, but nothing more.

Bonsly shrugged again, returning her attention to her hands. "Doesn't ring a bell."

"Are you sure?" Sarah wrinkled her brow, pretending to check through her notes. "Because I have here that you entered the port on January 24th, made contact with a logistics Trooper, and specifically requested delivery of that crate."

She looked back at the sullen Commando. "Do you make a habit of showing up to personally accept delivery of a supply shipment?"

"Can't say that I do."

Sarah pulled up a file on her tablet, casting it on to the table in front of Bonsly. "But that's your signature, correct? On the request for crate 157-Bravo?"

The tapping stopped.

Sarah eyed her carefully. She fought to keep the triumph out of her voice. "Does it ring a bell now?"

A silence stretched between them. Sarah crossed her arms as she waited. *I've got all day for this.*

Bonsly took her leg off the armrest and sat up. She looked Sarah straight in the eye before leaning over and spitting on the floor. "I guess I

picked that one up. Next question?"

Good, now we're getting somewhere. Sarah dropped her eyes to her notes, buying some time to keep the smile off her face. "Do you know the contents of the crate?"

The blue eyes narrowed further. Another moment of silence passed.

"No," she said at last.

Sarah pretended to add a note to her page. "Do you often accept shipments without verifying their contents?"

The corners of the blue eyes tightened. "Sure do."

"What happens if it's the wrong shipment?"

"Not my problem," she grunted. *Or yours,* was the unspoken implication.

Sarah decided to press the issue. "Whose problem is it?"

"Probably the fuckin' pilot's."

Interesting, she thought. *Not Supply's problem? Not the loadmasters?* Sarah nodded as she jotted down the answer. *Time to switch tactics.* She looked up from her notes. "How did you find out the shipment came in?"

"Pilot told us."

"And do you normally speak directly with pilots bringing in a shipment?"

"Not me."

"But someone in the Raiders does? Who is that?"

Silence again. Sarah watched the young Raider shift in her seat.

Bonsly's eyes searched the floor for a moment before meeting Sarah's again. Her face was flat and impassive. "They talk to Sergeant Jass."

Sarah stared her down from across the table. "Sergeant...Jess?"

"Jass," the Senior-Trooper corrected, running her tongue across her teeth again.

Sarah nodded. "And what does Sergeant Jass do in the Raiders?"

"Public relations."

"Your PR section also communicates directly with pilots about logistics shipments?"

"Yep," Bonsly smirked. "We wear a lot of hats in the Raiders. Mission comes first, everyone pulls their weight."

"And what weight do *you* pull, Senior-Trooper?"

Bonsly said nothing. A vein began to rise on the side of her neck. Sarah shrugged and changed the subject.

"And does Sergeant Jass have a first name?"

"Yeah," Bonsly smirked again. "Hugh."

Sarah got halfway through jotting that down before it clicked.

"I will remind you," she said tautly, "that this is interview is part of an official investigation, and that everything you say is being recorded for its inclusion within the final report."

"I fuckin' hope so," Bonsly said, putting her feet up on the table. "I hate repeating myself."

Ian watched the interview on the wall screen of the next room.

"This is exciting," he said to Sergeant Torres. "Like an episode of *CrimCourt*."

Sergeant Torres shrugged, examining some dirt crusted under his fingernails. "I'd rather just get the cliff notes from Levi when she's done."

"Not me," Ian said, turning back to watch the drama unfold. "My dad always said '*forewarned is fore-armed.*'"

Ian left out the part where his father always followed that line with '*good thing I've got plenty already,*' and would flex his muscular forearms. He usually left that part out. It tended to undermine the gravity of the mantra.

"That's nice," Torres said switching his attention to the other hand. "My dad only said that '*redheads taste funny.*'"

He looked up to see Ian's look of dismay. "What? Not everyone's dad's a nice baker with a little shop downtown."

Ian shook his head and pulled his seat closer to the screen, staring hard as Senior-Trooper Bonsly yawned and scratched her crotch. He looked back at Torres, raising an eyebrow.

"You know, I don't think Sergeant Jass works in PR at all."

Back in the interview room, Sarah was putting the finishing touches on her notes.

"That it?" Bonsly asked, leaning back in her seat. "I've got appointments to keep."

I bet you do. Sarah saved her page and closed out the tablet.

"That should do it." She offered another fake smile to the Raider across the table. "Thanks for all your help."

"Happy to." Bonsly dropped her feet from the table and stood up. She rolled her broad shoulders back, cracking her neck with her hands before she turned towards the door.

Sarah waited until her hand was on the knob before she spoke again. "One last thing. Since this investigation is still open, we might have additional questions in the future. I'm going to have to ask that you stay local and keep yourself available for future questioning."

Sarah watched a ripple of muscle tighten on the back of the shaved head. She felt for the doorknob trapped beneath the Commando's vise-like grip.

"Of course, Inspector," Bonsly said at last. "If I have any travel plans, you'll be the first to know."

She met up with them in the other room, the empty office in the cargo port serving as a base of operations for their fledgling investigation. Bernard and Terrance had a few minutes to discuss the interview after the camera feed cut out. They put their heads together and arrived at the same conclusion.

"Well, that was a fucking bust," Terrance announced as Inspector Levi walked through the door. "She was about as clear as a cadaver's colonoscopy."

Bernard looked over to Levi, raising an eyebrow as he mouthed the words 'cadaver colonoscopy?'

"Dark, pointless, and full of shit," she muttered back. Terrance flashed a grin to Bernard from across the room. He'd heard that particular turn of phrase on a documentary of famed boxer Don Yolman and had waited for the right opportunity to use it. Sarah turned back to Terrance as she pulled up a seat at the table. "And for the record, it wasn't a bust. She was actually very helpful."

She pulled her tablet out of her pocket, syncing it up with the table and the screen on the wall.

Terrance rubbed his broad chin. "Did you watch a different video than we did? All I saw was a dipshit attitude and a bullshit pun."

Bernard looked from Terrance to Levi. "Pun? What pun?"

Levi opened her mouth to answer, but Terrance cut her off. "So what part of that sad Raider reach-around was helpful?"

Levi sighed, motioning for them both to join her at the table. "Sometimes it's not about what's said, it's about what's *not* said."

Terrance pulled up a chair, wiping the grimy dust off with a sleeve. "Okay, Confucius, there was a whole lot *not* said in there. What part exactly are we supposed to run with?"

Bernard voiced his agreement from across the table, stopping to wipe his chair down with the handkerchief from his pocket.

Levi sighed again, pulling up the note page on her tablet. "The part where we found out that they're in direct communication with the pilots when they're bringing in a shipment."

Terrance scratched the back of his head. "Which means?"

"Which means we have another lead to follow up on. Raiders are trained to dodge interrogations."

"Yeah, she looked real trained," Terrance muttered."

Sarah glared at him, clearing her throat loudly before continuing. "*Raiders* are trained for interrogations. Pilots, not so much. If we can track down the pilot we might get more out of them, something else we can use to map out their operation here on Anius."

"The tail number." Sergeant Bernard sat up straight in his chair. "I still have it on my tablet. We can use the number to track down the pilot!"

Levi nodded. "Exactly. Find the pilot, cross-reference their shuttle against the delivery dates we know of—

Terrance's forehead wrinkled. "Which dates are those? We have no idea when they were bringing this stuff in."

Levi and Bernard blinked at him.

"The fast-tracks," she said slowly. "The favors you've been doing for Corstley over the last nine months. We have to assume there's a reason they didn't want customs to look at them."

The wrinkles deepened. "I guess, but that could've been anything. Where's the proof?"

"We don't have any," Levi said, ponytail bouncing behind her. "But it's as good a starting point as any. We should also cross-reference those delivery dates with any drug-related incidents to see if they line up. I'll run a check through the MP's crime blotter to see what turns up. We may be able to tie their drug busts to Corstley's deliveries."

Now it was Bernard's turn to act surprised. "You have access to the blotters?"

She laughed, dropping her voice low. "You don't know the *power* of the ISC."

Fuckin' nerds, Terrance thought as he scratched a stubbly cheek. "Alright, so the pilot thing. Fine. Anything else you divined from your mystical ISC powers?"

"Yes," she said, scrolling through the remainder of her notes. "That this goes much deeper than Bonsly and Corstley, and that she's pretty damn removed from the head of this operation."

Terrance shared a look with Bernard to see if he was following. Bernard shook his head.

"Because it takes someone with brains to lead an operation like this," she said quietly, a smile breaking out across her face. "And the ones with brains ask for a lawyer."

It took them three hours to track through the database, cross referencing manifests, flight orders, and tail numbers for each of Corstley's special requests over the last nine months.

"That's odd," Ian said, combing through the last of the lists.

"What is?" Levi asked, as she and Torres looked up from their tablets.

Ian swiped up on his tablet, casting his tracker onto the larger screen on the wall. "So each of the deliveries over the last nine months are tagged to tail number 762437."

Levi nodded. "Right, the DC-229. Makes sense that they'd use the same shuttle for the same mission."

Ian shook his head. "No, that's the odd thing. I dug through the ICF ship registry and there's only one tail number 762437—and it's not a DC-229." He double-tapped the tail number on his screen, pulling up the ship's information and casting onto the screen. "That tail number's assigned to a freighter, Heron class, the ICF *Hendrix*."

Levi tilted her head, she shared a side look of confusion with Sergeant Torres. "Could it be a mistake? Or a shuttle assigned to the *Hendrix*?"

Ian shook his head. "No, every shuttle carries their own tail number, even if it's derivative of a primary ship."

They looked out at the ship on screen. Like most Heron class transports its main body consisted of a central, tubular fuselage, surrounded by a hodgepodge of ports and attachment points for cargo-hold canisters and instrument modules. The central tube ended in a bell-shaped command module flanked on either side by a pair of solar sails, stretching out into space like the gills of a great salamander. It was an ugly ship, built for the utilitarian practicalities of carrying ICF assets across vast gulfs of frictionless, empty space.

Levi searched the picture on screen for deeper meaning, but found none. She scratched her head, careful not to disturb the tightly wound bun. "Is the *Hendrix* even in service around Anius?"

Ian looked through the orbital manifests from the Landing Control Terminal. "Looks like it is, it's on track for delivery of two orbital satellites a few days."

Levi looked over to Sergeant Torres. "Think the pilot will stop in on surface?"

Torres nodded. "They usually do; spend a couple months drifting through space and you'll want to stop off on dry land too. Even if it's a shithole like here."

The three sergeants returned their attention to the ship on screen. Levi took a screenshot to add to her notes.

"Looks like we found our second lead."

Sergeant Harbison hunched over the faux-cherrywood desk of his office, scratching out the last few lines of his condolence letter to the Widow Murdoch. Long, greying hair flopped forward over his eyes as he scribbled the final words on the paper, shaking his pen to get the last remnants of the ink out. Standard procedure in ICF death notifications was to use a holovid message, relayed via robotic courier to ensure maximum speed in delivering the message. Sergeant Harbison didn't put much stock in standard procedure. He believed in the spirit, not the letter, of the law. Besides, the late Special-Trooper Murdoch had given his life in the service of ICF, taking a face-full of shrapnel after stepping on a kinetic mine during yet another ambush on Karnassus. The least Harbison could do was give his widow something personal in exchange for that sacrifice.

The desk around him was covered in a neatly controlled rat's nest of topographical maps, cultural ethnographies, operation orders, and weapon loadout sheets. A single screen played the muted broadcast of the *Republic News Network* alongside a throwing hatchet embedded in a bold yellow target. Sergeant Harbison believed in staying abreast of emergent situations, regardless of the details the *RNN* anchors omitted for the

public's ears. Information was power, he always maintained, and for everything else there was the hatchet.

The brash knock of Sergeant Corstley broke his concentration for a moment. He knew all of his NCOs by their knock, and he'd listened to Sergeant Corstley's stubby knuckles for the last five years.

"Enter," he said, finding his spot on the page once again. He finished the closing of the letter as the bearded Buck-Sergeant walked in, signing off with a promise to visit the Widow Murdoch in person within the month. He looked up as he dotted the last period, smoothing his hair back with a sweep of his hand. He locked eyes with Sergeant Corstley and nodded for him to speak.

"Sarge," the burly Sergeant began, "I just got done talking to Bonsly. An issue's come up about the last shipment."

Sergeant Harbison's grey eyes narrowed. "Go on."

"Apparently there was an accident during the delivery off the shuttle, some logistics Trooper got crushed unloading our shipment."

A frown crept across Sergeant Harbison's face. The shipment had come in over two weeks ago. He didn't like being blindsided with information he should have already heard about by now.

"Anyway," Sergeant Corstley continued, "an investigation's been launched into the accident. Some Inspector was pumping Bonsly for information about the crate."

The creases around Harbison's mouth deepened. "OI?"

Corstley shook his head. "No, Sarge, ISC."

Harbison nodded, a safety investigation made sense given what he'd just heard. He felt his shoulders unwind by a hair. It was still a threat to him and his operation, but the ISC had considerably fewer resources than the Office of Insight. "Did she let anything slip?"

Corstley shook his head again. "No, Sarge, she did good. Gave them bullshit or silence. That's all."

Sergeant Harbison mulled this over for moment. "Just as well, remove her."

Sergeant Corstley raised a thick eyebrow. "Permanently?"

Harbison weighed his options, a series of analyses and calculations running through his mind. He shook his head after a moment. "No, she's not close enough to this. Just transfer her out for a while."

Corstley ran a hand through his beard. "There's an advisor role open on Ataxia right now. She won't be happy, but it'll keep her busy for about a month and a half."

Sergeant Harbison nodded. "Make it happen."

"Roger, Sarge." He turned to make his way to the door. He stopped with one hand on the knob. "And the investigation?"

The Reed-Sergeant thought for another moment, then shrugged. "I can't work without intel. Find out what they know."

A shadow passed over Corstley's face. "And if they're close?"

Harbison studied him in silence. He'd started his career in the Raiders as a sniper. Observing a target for days, ignoring fatigue, hunger, and all distractions before the taking the long shot. He knew a thing or two about waiting for the right moment. Flinty grey eyes looked from Sergeant Corstley to the hatchet on the wall.

"Then we remove them too."

Chapter 13:

Serena Daniels looked out from the balcony bar on the second floor of the Ansbrock hotel, enjoying the view of the glittering city stretched before her. The steady bassline of the bar's speakers thrummed behind her, matching the pulsing hues of the neon lights. She took a sip of her drink—a martini of some sort— that she'd ordered blind off the specialty menu. It was nice; there was a crisp hint of cucumber under the synthetic vodka blend. There was risk in ordering something called the 'Midnight Chancellor,' but Serena didn't mind. Chances always seemed to turn up in her favor, no matter how low the stakes. Serena sighed as she set the glass down on the balcony railing. She'd almost hoped it'd been terrible, at least bad drinks had a peculiar sort of interest to them.

A man cleared his throat behind her. Serena turned back from the city skyline, collecting her glass as she leaned back against the rail. A tall, blond man in an expensive-cut shirt stood before her, the glow from the bar's backlight playing across his fair skin.

"Enjoying the night?" he asked, offering a wag of his eyebrows that someone must have told him looked charming.

"I was," she said coolly, looking down at the swirling martini in her hand. She looked up to see him staring, blue eyes intent on tracing her figure up and down. He took a long pull on the straw in his drink, his eyes never leaving her in what he must have thought was a look of roguish enticement. Then his straw slipped on an ice cube, throwing him off his game as he slurped up a bubble of carbonation. Serena watched him sputter as she took a sip of her own drink, the acrid notes of the vodka seeming a little clearer now.

He recovered himself and his dignity as he set the drink down on the table, wiping the corners of his mouth with a spotted yellow kerchief that matched the lapels of his shirt. He flashed her a practiced smile. "First time at the Ansbrock?"

"Sure," she said, cupping the stem of her glass. It was as good an answer as any.

"Beautiful, isn't it?" he remarked, the lofty sweep of his hand including her in the glittering scene as well. "The truest beauty always comes out when it's *dark*."

He lingered a little on the word, a none-too-subtle reminder of her Sudanese heritage. She closed her eyes very slowly. Bad *drinks* may be interesting, but at least they have the courtesy not to loiter. She opened them again to see the blond man still in front of her, her wish for the power to incinerate with her mind continuing to go unanswered.

"It's so nice to see the stars come out," he began again, picking up his drink and joining her by the rail. "They're a reminder of the universe beyond this place, and the smallness of ourselves inside it."

Serena ignored the vista behind her, watching the crowd inside the bar. She didn't need to be reminded how big the universe was. She'd been hurtling across it for the last eight months. She felt the brush of his arm against hers and drew back, making the mistake of meeting his eyes when she did. A sly grin spread across his face. She said nothing, but it didn't matter, her silence was all the encouragement he needed.

"You know a night on Anius is only eighteen hours long," he said leaning in, his arm brushing hers again. She could feel a hand on the small of her back sliding lower. He whispered in her ear, "Just enough time to watch the sun rise when we're done."

Serena kept her eyes locked on his as she set her glass down on the railing beside her. She crooked a finger and invited him closer, entwining her other hand around his glass. His grin stretched ear to ear as her fingers danced lightly over his. She flashed a smile to match, leaned in closer, and dumped his drink down the front of the expensive-cut shirt.

"You bitch!" he sputtered, staggering back from her and wiping frantically at the spreading stain on his shirt.

"Say it louder for the folks in the back," she called after him, smiling sweetly. He glared at her as he stormed off, furiously dabbing his ruined shirt.

Serena took a sniff of the glass in her hand. *For a dick, he had good taste.* She muttered an apology to the gods of alcohol for wasting it before finishing the rest and returning to her martini. She leaned over the railing, watching the traffic trickling by below her, the city lights ahead having lost a little of their luster. *Fifty-three populated planets, and they all manage to feel the same.* She sighed a little into the glass rim as she polished off the 'Midnight Chancellor,' playing with the empty glass on the tips of her fingers.

"Have a moment to talk?" a quiet voice asked behind her.

And here comes the next contestant. She sighed as she turned around, momentarily surprised to see a woman instead. Kind brown eyes looked out from under a tangle of curly brown hair drawn straight back. The woman smiled at her; it was a nice smile. Serena felt herself relax.

"I hope I'm not interrupting," the woman said, brown eyes searching Serena's. "I thought I'd ask to borrow a moment of your time."

Serena considered the woman with a quick look. A little older than her tastes sure, but she had the poise and quiet confidence of a life-long

athlete. Serena smiled back.

"Serena," she replied, holding out a hand. "And at the moment I wouldn't mind an interruption."

The woman accepted the handshake, her hand was warm to match her smile. *Hell of a grip,* Serena thought. The woman opened her mouth to introduce herself but was interrupted by the arrival of a short, Polynesian man with neatly combed black hair. The woman didn't seem surprised to see him, and he stood next to her at a familiar distance. Serena quickly put two and two together.

"Sorry folks," she said, putting up her hands and backing away from the couple. "I'm flattered, but I don't do tricycles. Company policy."

Not after that disaster of the last one, she thought to herself. She turned to head for the exit, the glowing neon bar having lost all its appeal. She was beginning to regret taking her shore leave off-base at the hotel. *Still, it beats everyone standing at attention every time I walk through the door. And at least they offer room service.*

She heard the man call after her. "Captain Daniels, wait!"

Serena stopped cold. *How did he know my name?* She turned back towards the couple. The woman was still smiling.

"As I was saying, ma'am," she said. "We'd like to ask a moment of your time.

"Like I told you already, I run the *Hendrix*, not some pissant 229."

Ian nodded, taking a moment to scratch out some notes on Inspector Levi's tablet. "I know, I'm sorry. But can you think of any reason why a shuttle would have your tail number?"

Captain Daniels shrugged. "Chance? Happy accident? Aren't you the fucking detectives here?"

I'm not, he opened his mouth to correct her but stopped short. At least regarding this case, she wasn't wrong.

Captain Daniels continued, wiping her mouth as she finished her drink. "Maybe they heard the *Hendrix* was the best freighter in the ICF and decided to pay her tribute."

"I wasn't aware they ranked freighters."

They both looked up as Inspector Levi returned to the table with another round of drinks. She passed the larger one to Daniels, per their agreement she kept talking as long as they kept buying. Levi took her seat next to Ian, passing him one of the smaller glasses before sliding in behind hers. He picked up the glass apprehensively, watching the brown liquid washing over the ice cubes in the tumbler. He raised a questioning eyebrow at Levi.

"*Stepdad's Choice*," she answered back. "My favorite bourbon."

Ian sniffed the glass in his hand, smoky notes and wheatgrass singeing his nostrils. He gave Levi a dubious look.

"I put extra ice in yours," she offered encouragingly.

"Don't be such a scrotum—take the drink," Daniels called out from across the table. She raised her glass appreciatively to Levi. "*Le'chaim.*"

Levi passed the Captain another glass as she drained the double bourbon. After the first round, she knew to bring extras.

Ian cast another sideways glance at Levi before tipping the tumbler up. He coughed and sputtered as the liquor ignited the back of his throat, liquid bog-smoke barreling down to his stomach. He set the glass on the table and pushed it away, trying his best to keep the redness out of his face as his eyes teared up. He avoided looking at the other two as Levi and Daniels shared a laugh at his expense.

"So anyway," Levi said, returning to the business at hand, "you have no idea why someone might use your tail number for their shuttle?"

Captain Daniels stifled a belch with the back of her hand. "Nope, no clue."

"And you don't have any connections to the Raiders?"

A thoughtful look crossed the Captain's face.

"Well, I didn't say that," she admitted. "I've done a few deep-jet runs for them." She contemplated the roiling bourbon in her glass. "Come to think of it, there's been an awful lot of requests for deep-jets over the last six months."

Levi watched the glass in the officer's hand. "I've heard it enough times, but what is a 'deep-jet' exactly?"

Seeing his chance to reestablish his position in the conversation, Ian jumped in ahead of the officer. "Twice operational speed, strict trips, no stops along the way."

Captain Daniels focused her eyes enough to glare at the young Buck-Sergeant. "You gonna explain any more of my missions for me?"

Ian felt the color rising in his cheeks and busied himself organizing the notes on the tablet.

Captain Daniels gave a derisive sniff before turning back to Levi. "As I was sayin', it's a top-speed mission. We run the engines hot so it's always a short trip. With the Raiders' runs that also means we don't slow as we reach the destination. We jettison their capsule at full speed as soon as we're in targeting range. Their dropship takes them into orbit and we keep on keepin' on, still runnin' hot. We'll snag an orbital track a few star systems over and sling back, picking their drop ship up again in high orbit over the target planet. That's the only time we slow down, just long enough to snag them and make sure the coupling is complete, then it's back to top speed."

She set her glass down on the table, offering Ian a scornful look as she crossed her arms over her chest. "And *that's* how we run a deep-jet."

Suitably chastised, Ian worked to jot the rest down. "And how long is that usually? How long are they on the surface?"

Captain Daniels scratched the underside of her pointed chin. "No more than forty-eight hours for them. It's a bit different for us since we're going thirty lightyears a second." She shrugged. "S'all relative."

"Can you give us any more information?" Levi asked, bourbon sloshing in her glass as she leaned intently across the table. "Destinations? Manifests? Timelines?"

Daniels shook her head, keeping her eyes closed to banish the dizzy spell that immediately followed. "Destinations are wiped as soon as the mission's complete. Manifests I've got no fucking idea. I can give you timelines but only as the gaps in my ship log memories. Beyond that, best I can do is give you the overall weights for the mission since that gets logged in with my fuel 'spenditure."

She held out an empty hand when she finished, which Levi filled with another bourbon. She drained the glass in one long gulp, setting the tumbler down with a bang on the table. Bleary eyes looked over at the two NCOs. "Anythin' else?"

Levi leaned over to double check Ian's notes on her tablet. "No ma'am, I think that covers it." She looked over at the swaying officer. "You're sure you can get us those logs?"

"It'll be the highlight of my day," she promised them, stumbling upright. She gave them a lopsided smile and bid them adieu. "There's a bathtub in *moi* room," she explained slowly, drawing out each word. "I must find it and crawl inside."

Ian watched the Captain stagger away from the table. "Does every officer drink like that?"

Inspector Levi smiled as she finished his glass of whiskey as well. "Only the commanders."

Sarah leaned out against the balcony railing, enjoying the ebbing burn from the whiskey down her throat. A few fading cubes clinked in the tumbler in her hand. She held it up to her eyes, watching the city lights refracted through the curved glass. Cranes towered among the distant skyline, whirring to and fro as they assembled the half-built skyscrapers along the city's edge. To Sarah it looked like a jagged crown jutting out against the star-filled night sky.

"Pretty, isn't it?" Sergeant Bernard asked on her right, taking a swig from his bottle of hard cider. "I never realized how large the city was."

"Mhmm," she murmured, still watching the glittering cranes through the winding glass. "Or how much of it was new construction."

Bernard nodded behind his bottle. "Forty new towers, or so I'm told. I read that they can't use extruders though because of all the dust. They have to print and mold the buildings in sections and then lift them into place."

Sarah mulled this over as she chewed the ice left in her glass, savoring the final remnants of bourbon that clung to them. She was content to sit and watch the city hum, but she knew Bernard liked to talk.

"I wonder how they afford all this?" she asked, indulging him in his

penchant for conversation. "How do you justify spending millions of credits building up a desert like this?"

Bernard set his bottle on the railing. "Must be all the mining they do Anius is supposedly the biggest supplier of helium and heavy water in the Coalition Republic. Guess that covers the bill for all this."

"Fifty years!" laughed a raucous voice behind them. They both turned to face its source, a bearded, elderly gentleman seated at a table behind them. He shook his glass at them and laughed again, a thin straw teetering on the edge of the rim. "They got fifty more years of good money before it all runs dry!" He chased the straw around with his mouth unsuccessfully for several seconds, taking a long, satisfied pull when he finally caught it.

Bernard gave Sarah a sideways glance. She shrugged, *might as well take the bait.* She turned back to the old man. "Fifty years until all what runs dry?"

This was clearly the opportunity he'd been looking for, a chance to engage with a captive, enraptured audience.

"*This!* All of *this!*" he cried, sweeping his hands to encompass the world, and sloshing his drink in the process. "They've got about fifty more years before their mineral deposits run dry. That's why they're building all of it! That governor thinks he can turn this heap into the next Banzir; he's countin' on tourists to keep this place afloat!" He paused in his address to slurp a droplet of gin off the back of his hand. "And keep his family in office."

Sarah nodded along with the old gentleman's speech. She read the stitched in red lettering on the breast of his shirt—'JBS Ingc. Engineering Dept.' She saluted him with a raise of her glass. "Thanks for the insider tip."

"Of course, of course," he said, sweeping his arms out in facsimile of a bow. "I've been in this sand pit for forty years, might as well bestow my knowledge where I can."

She turned back to watch the city. Bernard, ever curious, pressed ahead with some of the more tantalizing rumors he had heard.

"Is it true the Governor has a pet Gluffant?" he asked, taking another sip of his cider.

"Sure is!" the old man thundered back, slapping the wrought alloy table with the palm of his hand. "He's all black with magnificent horns. They keep him over yonder in that great clear dome—lets the sunlight in but keeps it ice-cold for the hairy beast."

Clears that up at least, Sarah chuckled to herself as she clinked her glass on the railing. The last true livestock, developed and raised to be served to the ultra-rich, Gluffants were bred huge and hardy for arctic weather. When she'd heard about one living among the blistering sands of Anius, she'd dismissed it outright as pure imagination.

"We gave it to him," the old man continued, spitting words around

slurping pulls at the straw. "It was a gift from our CEO thirty years ago." He dropped his voice in a conspiratorial whisper. "Helped us clinch the exclusive mineral rights in this place."

Sergeant Bernard nodded, eyes wide as he fired off another half dozen questions. Colorful though he was, the old man seemed continuously game to answer them. Sarah brought the glass to her lips, forgetting for a moment that it was long empty. She set it back down on the railing, a light breeze picking up and whistling past her ears. The city before her continued to thrum, the cranes twisting and turning, and the traffic churning down below. She found herself tuning out of the boys' conversation, her mind returning once again to the facts of the case. It was precious little so far, only the barest scraps of circumstantial evidence. She'd hoped they'd get more out of the commander of the *Hendrix,* but that had proven almost fruitless. Shipping weights by themselves held little context for proving a smuggling operation. She sighed. Bernard and Torres placed all their faith in her intuition and investigative skills. Not for the first time, she worried she might have allowed them too high of expectations.

"It's a waste!" the old man shouted, dragging Sarah's attention back into the moment. "An absolute, criminal, waste!"

Bernard's eyes nearly bugged out of his head. "So you don't think the ICF should keep investing in the port here on Anius?"

"Hell no!" the old man cried, the tip of his beard dipping momentarily into his drink. "Like I said, it's damn near a criminal waste!"

Criminal waste, Sarah mused, *now there's a phrase.* The words turned slowly in her mind. *I wonder if that's the next thing the ISC will dig into having me investigate, illicit garbage.* She laughed quietly at her own joke, conjuring up the image of bags of trash in old-fashioned robbers' masks. The words 'criminal waste' floated by again, buoyed up on the low tide of alcohol in her system. She looked down in the alley below, a soft beeping drifting up as the rusty, green dumpster began its slow compaction routine. Suddenly it clicked.

She whirled around to face Bernard. "What does Anius do with its trash?"

"I, I don't know," he sputtered, the question clearly caught him off guard. "Burn it?"

Sarah shook her head, the planet boasted close to fifty thousand people, incinerators on that scale would light up the horizon. She turned back to the old man. "Do you know? What does Anius do with its trash?"

"Do?" The old man chuckled, swilling the last of his drink. "Why, the same thing anyone does with a big problem and a bigger swathe of empty space: leave it out for someone else to deal."

Sarah locked eyes with Sergeant Bernard, an idea forming in her head.

"Still got the keys?" she asked, a smile flashing across her face.

His brow knit in puzzlement. "Of course, we took my truck..."

"Good," she said, tossing the empty glass on the table. "Because I'm in no condition to drive."

The Anian dump stretched before them, a jagged range of heaped hills over five miles long and four miles across. Ian pulled the LITCAT slowly towards the gate, the motion of the truck triggering a light on inside the small, rectangular shack. They drew alongside it, the dim light revealing the frantic movements of a silhouette inside. Ian put the truck in park and got out with Levi, allowing her a moment to steady herself on the door handle. He walked slowly towards the gate shack, utterly lost to the proper customs and procedures covering the situation at hand.

A suspicious-looking man with dark, greasy hair and broken teeth stepped out of the shack, snapping a crisp salute as he stood by the rusty door. Ian and Levi froze, returning the salute in the awkward surprise. They stood facing each other in silence, each unsure who should be the first to drop their hands. Ian's shoulder began to burn. Cautiously, he lowered his hand first, just to see if the others followed. Inspector Levi lowered hers next, then the greasy man. The man squinted hard at the two Troopers, straining for recognition before his face broke open in a scowl. It wasn't often that he received visitors at the dump, and he'd initially mistaken them for officials from the Ministry of Civil Care there to inspect him.

Inspector Levi smoothed over this initial misjudgment with a small transfer of credits to the dump guard's personal account. When an explanation of their reason for being there failed to engender any sort of understanding in the mind of the guard, another small donation served to enhance his comprehension. They quickly discussed the layout of the vast dump, the guard even furnishing them with a crude map highlighting the salient features of the junkyard hillscape. A final donation served to pin down the precise location of their target, narrowing down the parameters of their search to a single heap in the far southwest corner of the map. They thanked the greasy man and got back in the truck, returning his salute as they drove through the heavy alloy gates.

Ian guided the truck along the narrow path, weaving around the towering heaps of trash and refuse that comprised the closest vision he had of Hell. The air inside the LITCAT was stifling and hot. He'd switched the air conditioning off as soon as they'd crossed the gates, it becoming readily apparent that the noxious smell of the dump was fully capable of overwhelming the truck's cabin filtration systems. They drove along, the mournful tune of a dour country ballad drifting out of the speakers. Ian took a left at the southern shoreline of a vast brown lake, the contents of which he readily guessed, but refused to confirm with a second look.

After half an hour, they'd found their spot at the base of a small trash hill. The guard had sworn that this was the spot that all the trash from the Raiders' compound was dumped. It was kept separate from the other heaps from the base out of fear for what it might contain. Although, that fear was clearly balanced with a healthy dose of greed, Ian noted, taking stock of the torn bags strewn around the heap. Some scavengers had clearly targeted the hill in the hopes it might contain some secret, classified treasures.

Ian and Levi dismounted the truck, their filtered survival masks clamped firmly across their faces.

"Well," Ian said, surveying the mound before them. "I suppose now is the time that we start digging?"

Levi grunted behind her mask, spinning the ring on the folding survival shovel to lock the head in place. She started in on the nearest bag, stabbing into it with the shovel and pulling back to drag open its contents. Ian sighed as he bent down to rummage through another bag. *Maybe ICF prison isn't such a bad alternative after all...*

They dug for hours, sifting through the rotting waste, pausing only twice. Once for Sarah to dodge out of the path of a particularly aggressive Dune Worm that decided to claim the northeastern corner of the heap, and another time after Sergeant Bernard pulled on a degrading trash bag only to fall back when it split, disappearing momentarily into a hollow pocket in the trash pile and on top of a particularly robust hibernaculum of a few thousand cockroaches. Though muffled behind the survival mask, his screams were prodigious enough and numerous enough that he temporarily overwhelmed the air flow mechanisms of his mask. As he ran back to the truck shedding layers of clothing and arthropods alike, Sarah determined that it was an opportune time to take a brief hiatus. They took a few moments to clean up and regroup, beginning again once his full-body quivering had stopped.

They dug, and sifted, and mined, and searched. They rooted through the disgusting, disintegrating refuse of the Interstellar Coalition Force's most elite soldiers. They tunneled through the mound of trash, until the first rays of sun began to show on the horizon. Five hours in, and Sarah's shovel clinked against something solid. She turned the shovel head slowly, sweat running down her aching arms as she uncovered a pair of horizontal slats.

"Success!" she cried, throwing her arms up in triumph.

"You find it?" Bernard asked, a cloud of sweat fogging up the left half of his mask.

Sarah dug with renewed determination, throwing up handfuls of trash and revealing the disassembled crate beneath. Bernard joined her as she reached down amid the pile of trash, helping her to lift the top side of the crate. He read the smudged label printed on the edge, confirming the string of numbers with the copy of the label on his tablet. They carried the crate side over to the truck, returning to the site and digging once again. Sarah thrust the shovel deeper, further, clinking along the edges of the other sides. She dropped down to her hands and knees, pawing frantically at the sand and trash. Bernard followed suit, and after a few minutes they succeeded in uncovering the other five sides. They carried them over to the truck, leaning them up against the honey-combed wheels.

"So," Ian said, stripping off his stained cold-weather gloves. "We found them, now what?"

Sarah climbed back into the LITCAT cab, returning with her purse in hand. She crouched alongside the nearest piece, rifling through the contents of her red canvas bag. She found it in a few moments, drawing out the electronic swabs and syncing them with the tablet in her other hand.

"What are those?" Bernard asked, but she ignored him, swiping the sensors along the inner wall of the crate. She gave the sensors a few minutes to upload the findings to the tablet, waiting on the chemical analysis program to spit out the results. A small chime sounded from the tablet, displaying the various chemical compositions recorded along the composite frame. There were your expected outcomes: organic matter, alloy shavings, blood. But there at the bottom, on the very last line, plain black letters spelled out the chemical name of a very particular, crystalline-structured, synthetic narcotic.

Sarah pumped her fist in the air. At long last, they'd found their hard evidence linking the Raiders to the drugs they'd found. A wide smile beamed out from behind the clear mask.

"I take it you found what you're looking for?" Bernard asked slowly, not willing to jump to any optimistic conclusions.

"We did," she answered joyfully. "And then some."

"Good," he said, throwing a finger behind his mask to wipe the sweat running into his eye. "Now what about those?"

She followed his point to the crate side furthest to the right, what she quickly determined was the bottom when it had been assembled. Her eyes narrowed as she took in the red letters painted inside in connected, looping script.

"I'm not sure," she said quietly, taking a quick snapshot of the writing. "But I think our next step is to find their source."

Chapter 14:

"You dug through trash with your bare hands?"

Sergeant Bernard nodded, eyes on the dunes rolling by outside the LITCAT viewscreen.

"Fuck man, that must've been torture for you." Terrance laughed and shook his head. "I still can't believe you did it."

Bernard gripped the steering wheel, knuckles whitening at his memories of two nights ago. He forced a shrug. "I mean, I had gloves. Snagged them and the breather masks out of the emergency kit from the back."

Terrance let out a low whistle. He'd seen Bernard wash his hands three times in a row just to get the mechlift grease out from under his fingernails. He could barely imagine the sheer force of will it must have taken for him to dig through garbage. He watched as Bernard guided the light truck smoothly around a steep pothole in the gravel road. *He's come a long way in the last six months.* Terrance stroked his chin thoughtfully, he felt burgeoning respect for the young Buck-Sergeant.

The dunes outside transitioned to domed huts as they made their way along the winding road. The radio in the truck began playing a funeral dirge. Terrance tapped his fingers to the mournful tune as they passed the dorms of the BPD. At the conclusion of the song the DJ announced that it was played to honor the death of political decency, in the wake of the Coalition Republic's continued sanctioning of the people on Karnassus. The DJ then announced that the station would play a moment of silence, to share in the suffering of the Karnassian people.

"Did you hear they're planning a drawdown for the ground troops?"

Terrance had not heard. He tended to ignore political coverage and most other things that didn't occur within a fifty-mile radius of his present location. He figured any shitstorm further than fifty miles away was raining down on someone else, and if it turned in his direction, he had ample time to step out of its way. Besides, there was always a Bernard or two around to catch him up on what he missed.

He shook his head. "Must've missed that one."

Bernard looked at him with wide eyes, mouth dropping open in his usual mix of shock tinged with disdain. "Missed it? *RNN's* only had wall-

to-wall coverage all week. The Large Council's vote was almost unanimous in favor of halving the forces on Karnassus." He dropped his voice from edifying sermon to conspiratorial whisper. "I think they're diverting forces in preparation for more action on Ataxia."

"Could be," Terrance mused, turning to look out the side viewscreen. It was no secret that the Council's patience for the occupation of Karnassus was growing thin. The eight-year counterinsurgency against the secessionist rebels had cost the Republic trillions, and despite a succession of troop surges, pivots to ground troops in place of using GBAS's, pivots to orbital bombardments in place of ground troops, and six months of sanctions hamstringing the colonist's economy, peaceful resolution was still nowhere in sight. There had been seven total-force commanders for the Karnassus theater, each younger than the last, and each promising a new era of innovative, 'smart' strategy to outmaneuver and pacify the insurgent elements.

Terrance had orders to Karnassus five years prior, back when he was still a Special-Trooper. He'd been excited then, ready and willing to do his part in the fight for republican democracy. His orders were cut short in favor of keeping him in place on his home station, when his load-supervisor suffered a brain hemorrhage after slipping on a patch of oily concrete. Since then Terrance had watched the conflict unfold with a certain air of detachment, receiving updates here and there by Troopers like Bernard, those with a prying sense of political engagement.

Terrance's thoughts drifted back to the here and now, just as Bernard was finishing up on his blow-by-blow recap of the growing unrest on Ataxia and the predicted impact that could have on the Republic's titanium market. Terrance interjected a few 'huhs' and 'ahs' amid Bernard's lecture to keep the conversation going. Internally, he shrugged. Karnassus, Ataxia, Herzakhy, he just didn't have the will or the energy to keep abreast of every twist and turn in the story of the Coalition Republic's galactic reign. *God bless those that do*, he thought, watching Bernard throw his hands in the air in a moment of passion. Until he was on a ship heading in that direction, everything outside Anius was firmly in the category of 'someone else's problem.' *Besides*, he thought to himself, *it's always on the shithole planets. You never see anyone on Tamarin or Cerulia starting an insurgency.*

They pulled to a stop outside a dismal looking hexagonal building, the roof pockmarked and worn by decades of sandstorms and neglect. Decrepit even by the usual standards of the *Transient Sustainment Housing*, it appeared that Inspector Levi had few friends in the lodging section. Ian and Torres walked to the hut, announcing their arrival with a quick rap on the scratched and dented door.

The inside of the dorm looked little better. The grey carpet was scuffed and worn, thin enough in spots to see the concrete underneath. There were chunks of plaster missing from the walls, several in neat fist-sized circles. The glossy white of the ceiling panels above had long since faded to yellow, and there was a dinner-plate sized patch of black mold in the corner, having spread from the bathroom on the other side.

"How do you live like this?" Ian asked, shaking his head ruefully.

"Temporarily," muttered Inspector Levi, digging through the pockets of a red suitcase. In contrast with the shabbiness of the room, her three suitcases were arranged with practiced care ascending in size atop a folding metal armature. Ian had seen models just like it on a flight to Quebec. They were coated in proprietary non-slip resin to keep pests from climbing up and into your bags. Levi's appeared to be the deluxe version, with a folding flattop desk and integrated stool. A few more minutes of digging and she removed her prize, pulling out the wireless projector with a loud 'ah-ha!' She synced the projector with her tablet, spinning it around and focusing the image on the wall with the fewest holes.

"So, I finally got ahold of the *Hendrix's* log data," Levi said, pulling up a spreadsheet of numbers and dates. "If we cross-reference those entries with the ship logs that are missing destinations, we can confirm which trips were for Raider missions."

Torres crossed his arms as he leaned against the corner of the narrow room. "So, what's that get us then?"

"I'm glad you asked." Levi tapped a column on the spreadsheet, highlighting one of the numbered lists. "These are the cargo weights." She tapped another part of the screen, drawing their attention to a third column. "And these are the fuel expenditures. We can use the expenditures to work out the distance traveled for each trip, then make a rough estimate to where their destination was for each mission."

Ian nodded. "And the cargo weights?"

Levi scrolled back to the first tab. "If we compare the outgoing weight with the incoming weight, we should be able to put together a picture for the size and scope of the shipments they're bringing in. That, plus their destination data, will help us pin down their supplier locations."

Ian's brow furrowed. "I don't follow, I thought they were having the drugs delivered by the shuttles? All the fast-tracks and whatnot?"

Levi nodded, pulling up another index with the swipe of her hand. "They are, and that's definitely an avenue we need to examine further. But I've been doing some digging in the MP blotters from the last few years, there's a correlated spike in drug-related incidents in the weeks following each of Corstley's request for a fast-track." She swiped again, pulling up an orange line graph showing the number of incidents marked by time. "The incidents rise on a semi-regular inter-

val, mostly matched to the two-week period following each delivery."
She drew her fingers together, shrinking the graph to a mountainous
range of spikes and valleys. She tapped it again, and several of the peaks
turned green. "But then there's this, these are spikes that *aren't* correlated with a delivery. They're irregular and don't match the dates on
Corstley's texts. What's more, they're usually a different drug trend."

She walked over to the wall and traced her finger around the orange peaks. "These are all incidents with *Glib*. They match Corstley's
deliveries, and that's what we found in the crate so we can be pretty
sure that they're connected."

Ian looked over to the disassembled crate sides leaned against the
wall. Tying the incident trends to the deliveries made sense. *So far, so
good.* "But what about the green spikes?"

A smile broke across the inspector's face. "That's where it gets *really* interesting. Those spikes don't involve *Glib* at all. They're all *Nor-
Can*, or *KX*, or *LiScan*, or *2BFree*."

Sergeant Torres grunted from the corner of the room. "You made
some of those up."

Levi shook her head. "The point is that they're irregular drugs
on an irregular pattern. A pattern I think correlates with the Raiders'
deep-jet runs."

Torres shrugged. "Maybe they're from other suppliers."

"I doubt it," she said. "These incidents all involve members of the
ICF, and they come in waves, with a local supplier you'd expect to see
a continuous string of incidents with a few peaks at the start and end
of the deployment windows. I haven't gotten incident trends on the
Anian side to rule it out, but given what we know, I sincerely doubt
that these specific peaks will match anything comparable to a local supplier."

She paused to let her words sink in.

"Okay," Torres said, walking over to examine the graph closer.
"So, we match the incidents to the deep-jet runs, and tie those to their
most likely origins. But that just shows a pattern, right? A pattern ain't

the cause. We already have Corstley's crate tied to the *Glib*. Why not just stop there?"

"Because it's not just Corstley," Ian said quietly. He stepped forward to join the other two by the wall. "This many shipments, with this much variety, means the operation stretches way beyond one Buck-Sergeant and his Trooper. This is too big for them to handle alone, especially if they're using deep-jet runs as cover." He traced his finger along the path of the projected graph. "This could involve the entire Raider unit, maybe more. If it's this big, affecting this many people, then we have to keep digging. Right now, we're the only ones who know about it, which means we're the only ones in a position to do something about it."

He turned back to face the other two. "We have to make this right."

Silence followed his address. Inspector Levi positively beamed at him while Sergeant Torres frowned and stroked his chin.

"Fine," he grunted after a moment spent considering their position. "Then what's the next fucking step?"

The next step, they agreed, was to crunch the numbers. Bernard and Torres couldn't that night, they were already pressed for time and needed to get back to the port for their shift. They also needed to get ahold of the local crime trends for the Anians, both to rule out a local supplier and to see if the Raiders' distribution stretched beyond the installation. Sergeant Torres agreed to head that one up, citing a favored owed to him by Sergeant Johnson in the Customs and Immigration Cell. Bernard's next night off wasn't for another few days, but he volunteered to match the fuel expenditures to the planetary destinations within each radius. That left Sarah with three days to run down any other leads they could think up. Some brainstorming over the course of a productive, warm shower led her to the conclusion that it was time to approach the problem directly. She'd spied the Raiders' compound when she'd crested a hill during her morning run a few nights back. The dun-colored walls flanked by squat guard shacks encircled a perimeter around a dozen or so prefabricated domed buildings. She'd read once that good fences make good neighbors—now was as good a time as any to put that to the test.

The LITCAT rolled across the gravel road, winding past dunes dotted with scrub-brush as the sun glowed orange on the horizon. The air inside the cabin was pleasantly cool. Sarah had finally managed to switch it on after jamming a screwdriver into the empty slot where the control knob used to be and wriggling it around just enough to initiate the truck's climate systems. *Now if only I could do something about the damn radio,* she mused, listening to the dying embers of a Dutch reggae song. The DJ cut in as the song faded out, announcing in his usual listless tone that the next song came courtesy of K-pop supergroup *BTZ-13*, so chosen because he admired the singer's haircut. He did not specify which singer in particular among the band's current roster of three-hundred and twenty-three, but he did highlight his enjoyment of its 'bouncy style' and 'defiant panache.' Sarah shook her head as the pinging beat erupted out of the LITCAT's dusty speakers, a smile creeping over her face despite herself. Vaguely defined genre tastes aside, she had to admit that the station at least offered something different than the usual ICF regulated playlist. She felt the glimmers of a growing affection for the droll, eccentric station spokesman.

She bounced along the dusty road, bobbing her head to match the operatic Korean belted out of the speakers. On the horizon, the compound for the Commando Raiders drifted into view. The corrugated tan walls stretched out in an oval almost a mile across, small guard tower outcroppings dotting its expanse every few hundred feet. As she crested a hill overlooking the encampment, she confirmed her early count of a dozen buildings, including one towering structure that clearly served as an exclusive launch platform of some sort.

She drove the light truck to what she assumed was the front gate, flanked on either side by the squat shacks she'd observed earlier on her run. The gate itself was black and imposing, with a crimson sigil of a lightning bolt stabbing through a hissing snake-skull painted across an alloy plate bolted to the front. Short, thick poles jutted in a line from the ground in front of the gate. To Sarah it looked like the bottom jaw of a hungry giant.

She pulled over next to a curved pole jutting out of the side of the driveway. Leaving the engines running, she swung open the truck's door and stepped outside in the sweltering heat. She approached the pole cautiously, a rounded speaker capped it off on the end with a silver button just below it. She pushed the silver button.

"Scan now," the speaker said, a thin red line emanating out from its bottom.

Sarah frowned. She didn't have anything to scan. She leaned down to speak into it.

"Hello? This is Inspector Levi."

"Scan now," the speaker repeated. Sarah might have been imagining it, but there appeared to be a harsher edge to the pole's command. *Maybe I have to hold it down to transmit.* She pushed the button again

"This is Inspector Levi, with the ICF Safety Commission. I'm here to speak to Senior-Trooper Bonsly."

She released the button and stood back.

The red line beneath the speaker flashed twice. "Scan *now*."

Definitely harsher that time. Sarah looked around for a camera or a window to speak to instead. She waved at a flat, reflective panel midway up the side of the guard shack.

"I'm Inspector Levi, ISC. Here to meet Senior-Trooper Bonsly."

"*Scan now,*" the speaker repeated behind her, its voice soft and tinged with menace. The panels on the guard shacks retracted down, revealing a pair of automated beam turrets that slid out on articulated arms.

Okay, time to go. Sarah put her arms up and side-stepped slowly back to the LITCAT cab. The turrets tracked her every move, right up until the moment when she slipped behind the open door. She gripped the steering wheel and let out a sigh of relief. She wasn't an expert on beam cannons, but she guessed correctly that they were MLW-51s, antipersonnel weapons not calibrated to penetrate the thick alloy of a vehicle. She reached over to pull the door closed when the speaker on the pole emitted a crack of static.

"State your name and business," the speaker said, the clipped tone revealing its origin to be human, rather than artificial.

Sarah leaned out of the cab, making sure to keep behind the cover of the door. "Inspector Sarah Levi, ISC. I'm here to speak with Senior-Trooper Bonsly."

Silence followed. Sarah wondered again if she was supposed push the button, but she dared not leave the safety of the truck to find out. She opened her mouth to repeat herself when the speaker crackled again.

"She's gone," the voice said.

Sarah wasn't sure she'd heard right. "What?"

"I said she's gone," the speaker said tersely. "She transferred."

Sarah's brow wrinkled. Bonsly had told her in their interview that she'd arrived on Anius only nine months prior. Most assignments were two years, so it was far too early for her to be transferred out. *Something isn't adding up.*

"Well, is there anyone else I can speak to?"

"*No*," the speaker snapped back.

Sarah frowned. *There's at least one fucking Raider in there, and I'm not leaving until I get a peek behind those walls.* "I am here investigating an incident on behalf of the installation commander. I can call him to confirm my entry authorization if need be."

Silence followed. Sarah sat back in her chair, pulling out her tablet and thumbing to Colonel Schwarz's name. She preferred finesse to get herself in, but she wasn't above brute force either. She waited in the truck's cab with the door open, her finger poised over the call button.

Sergeant Harbison sat alone in his office, craned over the aged yellow paper of an ore deposit map. He traced his fingers along the concentric circles used to mark elevation, trying to get a feel for the terrain for the landing site in advance of their next mission. It was a scouting mission on the presently named planet UDR, an uninhabited rock orbiting the outer rim that the ICF hoped would prove a fruitful location for a new ion cannon array. Normally a siting mission would be far below the scope and capabilities of the Commando Raiders, but there'd apparently been some trouble at a security outpost near the system and ICF command wasn't taking any chances.

Or rather 'they' won't be taking any chances, the Reed-Sergeant thought bitterly, *that's what the Raiders are for.* Stubby fingers rapped at the door for his office, drawing him out of his thoughts.

"Enter."

Sergeant Corstley stepped through the door, hugging the wall and taking up a spot directly across from the faux-cherrywood desk.

"Got a problem Sarge," the gruff man said. "That investigation's on our doorstep."

"What is it?"

"Inspector here, the one heading the case. She's wants to speak to Bonsly."

Sergeant Harbison shrugged. "Tell her she transferred."

"We did, Sarge. She isn't budging. She's at the gate now threatening to call Colonel Schwarz if we don't let her in."

Sergeant Harbison sighed, pushing the old mining survey map away and leaning back in his chair. He fixed his flinty grey eyes on the bearded Buck-Sergeant. "What does she know?"

Sergeant Corstley thought a moment, running a hand through his thick beard. "Not much, I cased her dorm myself last week. They've got a dose of *Glib* that they found somewhere—probably ours from the busted crate—and not much else, just some shipping entry logs, my texts back and forth with Bernard and Torres, and the interview with Bonsly. Oh, and a video recording of the Trooper that got crushed."

"How is he?" the Reed-Sergeant asked quickly. "Recovery still on track?"

"Sure," the burly Sergeant grunted. "As of yesterday. He's walking now, still with the brace. They'll trial him without it in a few weeks."

Sergeant Harbison nodded. He hated the thought of a good Trooper wasted by an injury incurred in the line of duty. "An' the other two, the loadmasters, are they outside too?"

Sergeant Corstley shook his head. "No, she's alone."

Sergeant Harbison tapped his fingers on the desk's integrated keypad. A thin screen rose on the edge of the desk, displaying the twin video feeds from the MLWs out front. He stared at the LITCAT cab, trying to discern the thoughts of the woman inside. He chewed his options over for a few minutes as he watched the feed, calculating the risks involved before he made his decision.

"Let her in," he said after a moment.

Sergeant Corstley raised a thick eyebrow. "You sure, Sarge? Sounds like this case is heating up a little, you really want to bring her in here?"

"Yes," Sergeant Harbison said sharply. He tamped down on the wave of anger that flared up inside him at the Buck-Sergeant's questioning. *Corstley's a good Sergeant,* he reasoned, *just trying to keep me thinking down both sides of the road.* "She's more heat if we keep her out, and getting installation leadership involved will definitely make it worse."

The Buck-Sergeant nodded, the reasoning was sound. Besides, he trusted Sergeant Harbison with his life. "Anything else, Sarge?"

"I want *you* to give her the tour," the Reed-Sergeant said, leveling a hand at Sergeant Corstley. "I don't want anyone else turning this into a goat-fuck. Take her around just like we do with leadership. Let her poke around, answer her questions. Show her just enough so that she leaves happy." The flinty grey eyes shifted back towards the screens.

"But not enough that we can't let her leave."

Sarah had just made up her mind to call when the pole speaker crackled to life.

"Sorry about the wait, ma'am," the speaker said, the voice this time was much more cordial, colored with a hint of frontier roughness.

"This is Buck-Sergeant Corstley. We'll get the gate down in a second, and I'll be there to answer your questions."

Finally. Sarah shut the door on the LITCAT cab, buckling her harness and putting the truck back in gear. Ahead of her, the line of short poles retracted into the ground. The black gate swung open, hinges silent under the weight of tons of alloy armor. Sarah drove cautiously through the gate, sparing a moment to marvel at the coincidence of Sergeant Corstley being the one to show her around. It occurred to her that maybe he knew he was the subject of her investigation and was trying to throw her off. But no, she thought as she shook her head, if he knew then he wouldn't have let her in at all.

She met the bearded Buck-Sergeant on the other side of the gate, parking the light truck alongside the inner wall and dismounting the cab. She introduced herself as Inspector Levi, and they exchanged pleasantries, with Sergeant Corstley apologizing for Bonsly's absence. She was on a critical advisory mission, he explained, and would likely be gone for several months fulfilling that role. Sarah accepted this answer, in part because she had no choice. There were few people that could verify the facts of a Raider mission and fewer still with the authority to alter its directives and recall someone home early.

Briefly, Sarah outlined the objectives of her investigation into the unfortunate crushing incident of January 23rd. She omitted any aspect of the narcotics and described her interest in the Raiders purely as the tying-up of loose ends. There were allegations, she explained, that the crate had been improperly labeled with the wrong weight class and that had contributed to accident. She was there to clear up that matter in order to finalize her report. She requested an inspection of their headquarters and their supply facilities, in order to better understand the Raider mission on Anius and to more accurately capture their supply procedures in her report.

Sergeant Corstley nodded, thanking the kind Inspector for her care and diligence in conducting a thorough investigation. It was a rare trait, he noted, finding someone dedicated to pursuing the fullest responsibilities of their office. As to her request to inspect their supply facilities, that was beyond his ability. Their materials were coded to those with Delta-Level clearance. Sarah remarked that it was unusual that a supply warehouse would be classified so strongly, to which Sergeant Corstley merely smiled. Those decisions occurred well above him, and as a fellow NCO, surely she understood the necessity of following instructions, even when their logic was mysterious. In lieu of taking her directly to their unit headquarters, he offered her a tour of the compound, sans any areas restricted by classification. He was a visual person, he explained, not gifted with words, and the complexity of the Raider mission was best viewed in person. Sarah considered this arrangement for a moment before agreeing, deciding that at this point it was her best chance to snoop around.

And with the small talk done, they were off, walking clockwise along the length of the compound's wall. Sarah asked about the turrets posted at the gate, questioning the necessity of mounted anti-personnel weaponry on Anius.

"Standard procedure, ma'am," Sergeant Corstley replied with a smile. "All Raider compounds employ them at the gate and every one-hundred meters along the wall. They're primarily intended to repel an invading force, but they do a number on the local thieves." He chuckled. Sarah didn't.

They reached the first of the domed structures, a tri-level, hexagonal building with a triangular pattern of clear skylights on the roof. Sergeant Corstley held the door for her and followed her in. The air inside the lobby was blissfully cool, a welcome change from the sapping heat outside. A sign by the door revealed it to be the Raiders' private gym, dedicated to a Special-Trooper Norman in 2305. Sarah walked along the hallway stretching the length of the first floor, passing a basketball court and Olympic-sized pool. Another room held free weights, machines, and a half-dozen Commandos hard at work. She didn't pause to watch the show, the grunting and clanging echoing out of the room informing her that all was in order. The track on the level above them was occupied by a single runner, making his way around the oval loop. The third floor, Sergeant Corstley explained, was filled

with spare equipment and specialty environmental rooms, for training under the precise atmospheric conditions a Raider might face on
a given mission. Sarah didn't take his word for it, but appreciated the
gracious patience he displayed when she insisted she be shown those
rooms as well.

They returned to the heat outside and continued their tour, making their way past four tri-level, rhombic structures clustered together.
A quick pass through the hallways and common areas confirmed they
were dorms, although Sarah noted with no small envy that the rooms
they passed were twice the size of her own, without a speck of mold in
sight.

Their tour took them past a pair of high-domed buildings, the one
on the left marked with a wide antennae dish array mounted on the
roof while the one on the right was outfitted with thick blast doors.
The communications hub and armory, Sergeant Corstley explained,
gesturing from left to right. He politely declined Sarah's request to take
a tour inside, citing her lack of Golf-Level clearance access.

Continuing on, they reached the launch pad, the towering structure Sarah had observed from outside the gates. While all Raider personnel officially immigrated and emigrated through the primary
personnel hub near the southern spiral of the installation, this tower
was used exclusively for Raider missions.

"What about Anian customs?" she asked. "Do you check in with
them?"

Sergeant Corstley chuckled again. Missions often dropped with
little more than forty-eight hours' notice, he explained, and their
movements required a certain degree of discretion. Thus, the tower
was built, allowing the Raiders to launch their mission capsules into
deep orbit for their collection by a freighter on a deep-jet run. It
had been a sore spot with the Anian provincial government when it
was first installed—the governor in particular disliked the idea of the
Raiders coming and going without his people's observation. But in the
end, no man stood in the path of the Raiders' mission. The governor
found himself quite obliged to permit their plans for installation after

being summoned for an in-person meeting with the Coalition Republic's Small Council.

Sarah nodded along to the Buck-Sergeant's story, offering a warm smile at the parts he clearly thought were jokes. They walked further along the compound wall, stopping to discuss an enormous storage warehouse (which Sarah was again informed she did not hold the clearance to tour) and an equally large vehicle hangar (which Sarah was permitted to enter, so long as she stayed further than two-hundred feet from any vehicle and refrained from taking pictures). Sarah walked quietly through the wide hangar, catching sight of vehicles she'd only heard of in the wildest discussions of the ICF's skunkworks division. The next buildings they passed were a long quonset hut housing the Raiders' firing range (touring restricted owing to the red sign displaying that shooting was in progress) and a fortified rectangular bunker used for testing the Commandos' heavy weapons.

They ended their tour at the foot of a small, domed hut, just barely bigger than the dorm building Sarah inhabited at the TSH.

"And this?" Sarah asked.

"Leadership cell," Sergeant Corstley replied. "Our last stop on our happy tour."

"So, we are stopping in then?" Sarah stepped quickly towards the door.

The burly Buck-Sergeant moved fast, cutting her off with speed unnerving in a stout man. "I'm afraid not, ma'am. Even barring the classified info we have in every room and every wall there, our chain is hard at work planning missions. Can't have Sarge getting disturbed while he's keeping us safe." He offered her a lopsided smile.

Sarah frowned. "I appreciate your concern, Buck-Sergeant. But I was granted full authority in this investigation. I'll need to clear some things up with your leadership. I promise I won't disturb them."

Sergeant Corstley just smiled broader, one arm still barring her progress through the door. "Can't allow that, ma'am."

Sarah's frown deepened, she decided to dig in. "Then invite them out. I can get my answers just as well out here."

Sergeant Corstley shook his head, the smile on his face undercut by a flicker of anger in his eyes. "Sorry, ma'am. No one disrupts Sergeant Harbison when he's planning. No one."

Interesting. "Is Sergeant Harbison in charge here? How long is his tour on Anius? Is there a better time I can arrange to speak with him or is he going to transfer as well?"

Sarah saw the wheels turning in Sergeant Corstley's head as he contemplated just how much to let on. After a moment, he spoke. "He's our superintendent, and he's been keeping our operation running for the last ten years. Not much is gonna change that. He's always busy—busiest man I know. Not much is gonna change that either." He smiled again, nothing behind his eyes this time. "But if you leave me your info, I'd be happy to set up an appointment at a later date."

"That would be splendid."

Sarah thanked him for his time and showing her around. As she hopped inside the LITCAT and fired up the engines, she turned over everything she'd learned. She was convinced now, more than ever, that the drug operation stretched well beyond the actions of an errant Buck-Sergeant. *In fact,* Sarah thought as she drove the light truck through the heavy, black gate, *I'm willing to bet it stretches back the last ten years.*

Chapter 15:

Ian hunched over the tablet on the desk in the dark dorm room, his face a mask of concentration backlit by the soft glow of the screen. He studied the numbers on the spreadsheet, jotting notes occasionally with his other hand on the tablet cradled in his lap. The silence in the room was heavy, the tangible sort that hangs over university libraries during finals week. It was broken only by the stirring and clearing of throats from the other two occupants, punctuated by the muted pops and buzzes of the screens' interactive features.

He juggled back and forth between the two devices, brow furrowing as he squinted hard at the tiny numbers in their neat lines. Scroll down, find the appropriate entry, mark the date and weight on the tablet in his lap. Scroll up, find the fuel expenditure, jot that down too. His eyes watered from staring too long, the numbers blurring as his vision swam. Ian sighed, cursing the infirmity of the human form as he wiped his eyes. Not for the first time that day, he longed for a program to do the analysis for him. But it was not to be—fuel expenditure logs were tallied in a proprietary software, and only able to be read on the *Hendrix's* primary operating system. The spreadsheet in front of him was an image file taken of the log's printout, and so it fell to the human eye to sift through page after page of data.

Ian blinked back tears and accumulating dust, realizing with a muttered curse that he had lost his spot on the page. It took him a full minute to find his place again, grumbling the whole time until he found the entry marked for September twenty seventh. With a jolt, he recognized that date as his first arrival on the woeful desert planet. He drifted back to the hazy memories of the landing shuttle and the barking direction of Chief-Sergeant Hatoya. He snapped back into the present only to realize he had lost his place once again. His mouth opened to mumble a curse when he was cut off by a series of louder swearing from across the room.

"Gawd-*damn*, monkey-*fucking*, ass-*sucking*, *tit*-slapping. Piece. Of. SHIT!" Inspector Levi bellowed from across the room, throwing her hands in the air as she jumped up from the articulated luggage stand.

"Trouble, officer?" Sergeant Torres asked serenely from the far corner of the room.

"This!" Levi shouted, tossing her tablet on the neatly made bed. "And THAT!"

She jabbed an angry finger at the crate side leaned against the wall. She drew a circle in the air with the shaking finger, highlighting the looping red symbols scrawled on the slat. "I've run that through every translator I can download, backtracked it through every reverse-image search engine I can find. I even matched it against OI's database of all known sigils for terror groups and organized crime. I've been staring at this damn crate for hours, and I've. Found. *Nothing!*"

She flopped backwards on the bed, staring up at the ceiling in defeat. Ian locked eyes with Torres from across the room. Up till now they'd never heard her so much as raise her voice. Ian mouthed the words, 'What should we do?' to Torres while Levi continued to stare at the faded yellowing tiles. They both watched as she began humming an off-key tune to herself. It took Ian a few moments to recognize it as '*I'll Climb Mountains*,' the soundtrack to a series of ICF recruitment videos aimed specifically at women from a few years back. Sergeant Torres looked back at Ian and shrugged, turning back to his work in the corner. She had just started on the second verse when Ian cleared his throat, interrupting her.

"Maybe, uh," he said, setting his tablets down on the desk and standing up. "Maybe I should take a look at it."

"By all means," she replied, in a voice utterly devoid of emotion. "Perhaps a *man* can solve it."

She resumed her humming as Ian walked over to the battered crate side. He scratched his head as he surveyed the looping inscription.

"You know," he said after a moment, "it looks like writing of some sort."

"Really?" Levi said airily from her place amid the rumpled covers. "I hadn't noticed..."

Ian crouched down to get a closer look. "I definitely think it's writing. Just no language I've ever seen before."

"How peculiar..." Levi mumbled from the bed.

Ian walked back across the room as the humming grew louder, passing Sergeant Torres as he pretended to busy himself with his work in the corner. Ian retrieved his tablet from the desk, striding back to the crate with tremendous purpose. He crouched down and snapped some pictures, sending them off in a message with a few taps of his finger.

"There, that should do it," he announced loudly, breaking in over Levi's third rendition. "Should have our answer in a few moments."

The humming stopped as Inspector Levi sat straight up on the bed. Her eyes narrowed suspiciously. "What do you *mean?*"

"My wife," Ian said proudly. "She's a professor of historic languages at the University of Manitoba."

Levi's eyes drifted as she processed what he'd said. She mouthed the words 'historic languages' and looked over to Sergeant Torres in the corner. Torres shrugged and looked back to Ian.

"Ah," Ian said as the tablet chirped in his hand. "It's Sanskrit."

"I thought it was Suzette?" Torres grunted from the corner.

Ian blinked in confusion. "What? No. I mean the writing, Suzette says it's Sanskrit." He chuckled as he looked over to Inspector Levi's shocked expression. "I'm not surprised you couldn't find it. Sue says nobody's used it in three hundred years."

Levi rose from the bed and joined him by the crate, her mouth still slightly agape. "But, you... you said she can read it?"

"Well," Ian replied, bobbing his head equivocally. "It'll take her a bit to translate. Her specialty is Semitic, and she says this is more Indo-Aryan." He brightened. "But she says she can work with a colleague in her department and get back to us in a few days."

Inspector Levi closed her mouth, offering Ian a grateful pat on the shoulder.

"Well...done," she said, turning back to face the crate. "We may make a detective out of you yet."

"What about me?" griped Sergeant Torres from the corner. "*I'm* doing important work here too."

Levi rolled her eyes. "What work? We already input the Anian crime trends and matched them against the MP blotters. That was almost three hours ago."

Sergeant Torres rose indignantly from his corner to defend himself.

"One," he said, counting off huffily on his fingers. "Without that info, we never would have known that the local cops had drug trends that matched ours, just a week or two later. Two, you don't know how difficult it was to get those stats. I had to go all the way down to the CI Cell and convince Sergeant Johnson to talk to the Anians into helping us out. You have *no* idea what that cost me."

This was true, Ian and Inspector Levi had no way of knowing how difficult it had been for Sergeant Torres to persuade Sergeant Johnson. He had barely gotten the words out of his mouth when the excitable Buck-Sergeant leapt up from his desk, rushing down the hall to his Anian counterpart. Eager to demonstrate the utility of the Customs and Immigration Cell, Sergeant Johnson had all but dragged the surly, white-dressed official back to his desk to answer Torres' questions and gather the requested information. Working through the excitable go-between had been excruciating for Sergeant Torres, who tallied it as the second-worst thirty minutes of his life, just after the time he mistook a Swedish taxidermist for a rideshare service.

"And three," he continued, voice rising with moral gravitas, "that's not the work I was referring to. *This* is."

He stepped back, revealing the corner behind him with a showman's flourish of his arms. Behind him a series of names were tacked to the wall on roughly torn scraps of cardstock. They were the names of everyone connected to the case arranged in a hierarchy and connected by bits of crimson string. The cards appeared to be held up by a motley collection of screws and bolts pushed through the crumbling plaster. Ian was impressed. Not only was this the biggest demonstration of personal organization he had ever witnessed in Sergeant Torres, but he had no idea where he was even able to *find* string.

"You like it?" Sergeant Torres asked, running an apprehensive hand through his impeccably brushed hair. "I tried to show the whole scale of the operation."

"Looks great," Ian said. He followed the scraps of cardstock, beginning with a crudely drawn image of Private Bradshaw crushed beneath a falling crate labeled 'Subject #1.' A line of string followed from the crate to a card marked 'Bonsly' and another crude illustration of the named member. A list below it detailed everything they knew about her in bulleted points, spelling out such things as 'Picked up Crate,' 'Shitty Haircut,' 'Bitchy Attitude,' 'Transferred Out,' and 'Nice Delts.' Other cards were similarly arranged in a line on this second level, spelling out the names Zimmer ('Gym Monster,' 'Shitty Attitude/ Haircut,' and 'Good Form'), Kantz ('Ginger,' 'Bad Breath,' 'Drinks at PCCR'), and Huges ('Ditto but Blond'), each with Torres' signature artistic interpretation of the Commando beneath. These lines were connected upward to a single card marked 'Corstley' ('Called in Favors,' 'Nice Hair,' 'Pushy') with a rather loving depiction of a bushy brown beard. Corstley's card flowed into another labeled with 'Sergeant Harbison,' underneath which read 'Ringleader?' and 'Murder Eyes.' A thin red string flowed further upwards from Harbison's card to another marked 'Satan?' with the words 'ULTIMATE BOSS???' scrawled below it in bold, black letters.

Sergeant Torres stood back, reveling in the triumph of his own creation. "Isn't it great? It's just like they do it in the vidplays."

Inspector Levi's mouth hung open. "You...put holes. In *my* wall. For *this?*"

Ian watched the smile slide right off Torres' face. He hid his own grin behind his hands while he watched the Buck-Sergeant backpedal.

"I thought that's how it's done," he sputtered, jumping in to protect his labor of paper and thread. "What do you care? There was plenty of holes already. *It's just like the vidplays.*"

"I put my *name* on this room," she snarled back. "They'll bill me for *any* additional damages!"

Sergeant Torres looked around the shabby dorm. "Yeah, maybe. But that's like twenty credits, tops."

Ian saw the throbbing vein rising in Levi's neck. Her fists clenched, nostrils flaring. She looked ready to slug him.

Ian stepped him between them, palms raised high to placate the fuming Reed-Sergeant.

"Let's just agree that it was an admirable effort," he said, nodding back to Sergeant Torres. "But perhaps the *execution* was a bit, uh, misplaced."

He looked back at Inspector Levi, the kindness in her eyes evaporating behind righteous fury. "I think we can all agree, that if there are any damages assessed, that Torres would be *happy* to cover them."

"What? Fuck no, man—

Ian silenced him with a backwards look. He turned once again to Inspector Levi. "Agreed?"

She stood quiet for a moment, vein pulsing in her neck as she thought it over. At long last she shouted, "Fine!" and stormed off to the bathroom, slamming the door behind her.

Sergeant Torres shared a look with Ian. He shrugged. "Maybe she hasn't seen the vidplays?"

Thirty minutes later and Sarah joined them once again, her hair wet and wrapped in a towel from her shower. She seemed refreshed, a little more at ease after taking the time to 'wash away the idiocy.' She met the two men as they crowded around Ian's tablet.

"So good of you to join us," Sergeant Torres remarked. "You missed out on all the exciting work we've been doing."

"Without that shower," she responded dryly, "things would have been quite a bit more *exciting* around here."

She pulled the towel off her head, fluffing her curly hair with her hands. "So, what've you got, boys?"

"Well," Bernard said, syncing the projector with the tablet on the desk. He swiped up on the screen, casting his note sheet on the wall. "I found thirteen deep-jet runs over the last three years."

Sarah's brow furrowed. "Thirteen? That's not nearly enough to match the crime trends."

Bernard assuaged her with a wave of his hand. "That's thirteen just for the *Hendrix*. Captain Daniels said there's forty-six other freighters that run Raider missions, so thirteen missions is still an awful lot. Most occurred in the last six months. Like the Captain said, they've been ramping up."

He swiped across on the screen, bringing up the line graph of drug trends. He tapped it again, and several of the peaks turned green. "Like before, these are the peaks for drugs other than *Glib*. I was able to match five of these peaks to the dates for the deep-jet runs." Another tap on the screen, and red circles surrounded five separate peaks along the graphs.

The Inspector nodded. "Makes sense, I should've guessed that they weren't bringing in shipments on every mission."

"Course not," Torres grunted. "Gotta spend *some* time playing hero."

Sarah walked over to the projection on the wall, tracing a hand along the green peaks of the graph. "Did we figure out locations to match the missions?"

"Uhhh...some, yes," said Sergeant Bernard, waffling a bit with his hands. He tapped two of the circled peaks on screen. "Based on the distance traveled we figured these two, in March of '31 and January of '32 were to Ataxia."

"Makes sense," she said. "Those peaks are for LiScan and 2BFree, designer dissociatives are all the rage on the agri-planets."

"The one in last April we pinned to New Wilstown," Sergeant Torres said, highlighting a green peak near the end of the graph. "But we're stuck on the last two, the one from June of '30 and the one from last September."

Sergeant Bernard spoke up from the desk. "Based on the distance it's either Faris or Lexell, they're both about a hundred-and-thirty-thousand lightyears from here, which matches the range estimated from the fuel expenditures. But we don't have any sort of heading data to go off of."

Sarah thought for a moment, mulling over what they'd said as she pulled her hair back into a tight bun. "Which drug is associated with the time?"

Torres consulted the spreadsheet, thick finger tracing down the lines of notes. "NorCan."

"Ah," Sarah said, looking back over the graph. "That's Faris then. All my NorCan cases started on Faris."

She turned back to the two Buck-Sergeants. "This is solid detective work; that's a positive link then between the deep-jet runs and the irregular drug trends. You've matched opportunity, to timeline, to crime. You're just short a motive."

"So, it's settled then?" Bernard asked, looking from Sarah to Sergeant Torres. "We're sure that the other Raiders were involved?"

Torres locked eyes with her and shrugged, offering the Inspector the chance to answer.

Sarah looked back at Bernard and nodded. "One hundred percent. Using official ICF missions to smuggle in additional shipments smacks of a larger organization, one that reaches higher up in the chain of command."

Sergeant Torres slugged Bernard on the arm, gesturing back to his scrap-paper hierarchy. "Told you. You gotta trust the vidplays."

"Ow," Bernard said, rubbing his arm. "*I* wasn't the one in question."

Sarah sighed, rubbing her temples with her hands. She took a deep breath before continuing. "As much as it pains me to say it, you are correct. Reed-Sergeant Harbison is the most likely ringleader. He has the authority, the organization, the training, and the skills to keep an operation like this secret over the last nine years."

Sergeant Torres took a second opportunity to point triumphantly at his craftsmanship. Sarah rolled her eyes hard enough to register on the Richter scale. "Like I said, from what I saw, this case involves most of the Raider unit and most especially their superintendent."

Bernard's forehead crinkled. "Because of the supply warehouse?"

"Precisely." Sarah tapped her finger to her nose. "I've dug through every operating instruction and regulation that even *mentions* supply storage. None of them say anything about a Delta-level classification."

Torres crossed his arms, unconvinced. "So, maybe the reg was classified too."

Sarah shook her head. "It still doesn't make sense. Their communications array was only Golf-level clearance. Show me where it makes sense that a storage container rates a higher classification than a critical telecom node they use to discuss their ultra-secretive missions?"

Bernard and Torres looked at each other, Torres offered a shrug and turned back. "It...doesn't?"

"Exactly," Sarah quipped. "The only way I can reconcile it is if they're using it to store their product. Not everyone that works in the compound is a part of the operation. I'm sure there's an inner circle and those on the outside looking in. That's why they added security, to keep the inner loop tight. Based on what I saw in their compound, it's the answer that makes the most sense."

Quiet followed her address as the two Buck-Sergeants digested the information.

"Now about that tour," Sergeant Torres said, scratching the underside of his chin. "Let's talk about that for a moment. I don't like it—doesn't sit right with me that you went in alone."

"Concerned about little old me? How *chivalrous* of you," she mocked. "But I can take care of myself. Been doing this job for over a decade, don't you worry about me."

"I'm not," Sergeant Torres snorted. "But if you die before this case is finished that still leaves *us* on the hook."

A dozen angry retorts scrambled through Sarah's mind, wrestling with each other over the rights to her tongue. Sergeant Bernard put up his hands between them to cut her off.

"I think that we can *all* agree," he said calmly and slowly, making deliberate eye contact with the two NCOs, "that this case is *bigger* than when we started. And that the *most* important thing is to catch these guys before something worse happens to someone else down the line."

Sarah tucked her tongue into her cheek, stifling the last of her snippy remarks. She wasn't used to being reminded of the priorities in her own case. She frowned, unsure of when the roles had shifted. *You've been running non-stop, twenty-hours a day, every day, for the last four weeks. Maybe, just maybe,* she admitted to herself, *you're a little tired and a little on edge.* She looked past Bernard to Sergeant Torres, who offered her a reconciliatory raise of his eyebrows. She sighed and nodded.

"Okay," Bernard concluded, lowering his hands. "Now Levi, ma'am, you're the expert. We've got the data, we've got our analysis. Now what's our next move?"

Sarah thought long and hard over the next few moments. Her eyes drifted over to the corner of the room, traveling up the patchwork hierarchy.

"Have you ever been fishing?" she asked. Bernard and Torres shared a look, they both shook their head. She ignored their confusion, staring off into the distance. She thought about a trip she'd been on as a little girl when her uncle had taken her fishing on the Mediterranean. They'd traveled far out on his creaking wooden sailboat, the harbor disappearing on the horizon before they set their anchor. They were looking for big fish, her uncle explained, in the deepest waters.

She could still smell the salt of the air, and the cloying, rotten smell of the bucket as he dumped it over the side into the waters.

"If you want a big fish," she said, her gaze lingering on the cards tacked to the wall. "You need to chum the waters."

Sergeant Corstley sat alone at wide table in the empty conference room. He knew he was at the right place at the right time for his appointment. He'd even arrived fifteen minutes early, just to maintain the thin veneer of military protocol the Raiders espoused adherence to. He braced himself in his chair and leaned back, the creaking metal hinges echoing in the long room. He lifted his hands and leaned forward, sighing as he dropped his elbows on the table. Waiting was never his strong suit.

There was a knock at the door. He cleared his throat, unsure for a moment as to the protocol in this situation. Inspector Levi let herself in, walking briskly to the table and sitting down across from him.

"I'm glad you could make it," she said, pulling a tablet out of her pocket and setting it on the table. "I have a few questions to get on record so we can close this out."

He nodded, Sergeant Harbison had prepped him to expect as much.

"Do you mind if I record?" she asked, flipping a camera up with her thumbnail. "Standard procedure for all case-related interviews."

Sergeant Harbison hadn't prepped him for *that*. Still, he nodded. He knew to expect everything he said would join the official record.

"Great," she said, flashing him a warm smile. "Can you state your name, occupation, and unit for me?"

Sergeant Corstley leaned into the camera. "Buck-Sergeant Hermes Corstley, Platoon Sergeant, 4th Commando Raider Group."

Her warm smile broadened. "Excellent, now that we have that out the way. Really quickly, I want to reiterate that this is a safety inquest, not a criminal one, but your full testimony here will be included in the final report and may be referred to criminal authorities. At any time, you may abstain from answering a question or request legal counsel. Do you understand?"

"Certainly," he answered, shifting his focus back to her. He relaxed a little. Everything was happening the way Sergeant Harbison had said it would.

"Excellent," she said again, the warmth disappearing around the edges of her smile. Her eyes narrowed sharply, honing in on him. "Now what can you tell me about the contents of the crate you requested on January 23rd 2333?"

"Well," Sergeant Corstley said, taking a deep breath. "What I can tell you is..." He paused to look directly into the camera, "that I request a lawyer present."

As the final word left his mouth, he sat back, crossing his arms and offering her a smug smile. He expected her to look disappointed. He expected her to yell or throw a chair across the room. Sergeant Harbison had told him to expect a lot of things when he pulled out the lawyer trump card. What he got was nothing of the sort.

Instead, her smile grew wider. "You do? Well, great. I'll leave the room so you can get in contact with them. You can even use your own phone."

And with that, she left him, walking briskly back through the door. He stared dumbly after her as the hinges swung softly shut, before quietly pulling out his tablet and dialing his emergency contact.

"What was that?" Terrance asked, watching the projection on the wall as Sergeant Corstley idly scratched his nose. He turned to Sergeant Bernard, dumbfounded. "He says one thing, and then we're done? Just like that?"

Sergeant Bernard frowned. "I'm sure she has a plan."

They both turned as Inspector Levi walked through the door.

"What the hell was that?" Terrance demanded. "I thought you were going to throw the book at him."

She shrugged. "He requested counsel."

Terrance shared a look with Sergeant Bernard. "So? Where's the yelling? Where's the chair-throwing?" He dropped his voice low in an imploring whisper. "I thought you cops were all about getting the confession."

Inspector Levi rolled her eyes. "This isn't the vidplays—

"That's for sure," Terrance snorted. "I thought you were gonna beat it out of him."

"There are *rules*," she insisted, brown eyes urging them to understand. "If we don't follow them, then none of this helps, because none of it will count in court."

"Is that why the audio feed is cut?" Bernard asked, pointing to the screen.

Levi nodded. "Until he has representation, nothing he says is admissible."

"Then remind me why we brought him in for questioning?" Terrance asked, throwing his hands in the air. "Was all of this just to piss him off? I thought we weren't supposed to antagonize them during the investigation?"

"We're not antagonizing, we're agitating," Inspector Levi corrected, watching the Buck-Sergeant rock back and forth in the camera feed. "There's a small, but distinct difference."

Terrance folded his arms over his chest. "And that is?"

Levi's eyes never left the screen. "That it's not about *him*."

They watched in silence as the door to the conference room opened. Reed-Sergeant Harbison entered the room purposefully, grey eyes constantly shifting to assess for any potential threats. He strode over to the sitting Buck-Sergeant, clasping a paternal hand on his shoulder as he took up a chair next to him. They exchanged a few words before the Reed-Sergeant's flinty eyes noticed the tablet sitting on the table. With a calm, almost gentle movement, he pulled a kerchief from his pocket. He tossed it over the camera in the tablet.

"Well," Sarah said, as the live feed on the wall cut to black. "That's my cue."

And she stepped out into the hallway to wait.

Sarah was accustomed to waiting. Patience, along with listening skills were chief among the talents she viewed as critical to the role of Inspector. Luckily enough, she did not have long to wait.

A commanding-looking man in the mottled grey of the ICF duty uniform strode down the hallway. Tall, square-jawed, and broad-shouldered, he walked with the confidence only a lifetime of good looks, wealth, or both, afforded. His swept blond hair framed piercing green eyes.

"Major Chadwick Hudson," he announced, thrusting out his ICF ID card. "Commanding officer for the 4th Raider Group."

The third, she noted reading the name of the card. *How distinguished*. She moved her eyes off the card and onto the Major.

"And how can I help the commanding officer of the 4th Raider Group?" she asked sweetly.

In a move that was clearly practiced, Major Hudson flipped the card back into his pocket with one hand. "You can start my releasing my client. Any further questioning can be submitted to myself for his later perusal."

A number of options spread themselves before her. She chose to feign ignorance. "Your client? I thought you were his CO?"

"I'm bar-licensed and certified," he assured her, the haughty blond curl bouncing a little as he spoke. "Standard practice in Raider units. Keeps away the distractions and inconveniences, and it frees up our brave Troopers to focus on the mission that *matters*."

Sarah watched as the door to the conference room opened behind the Major, with Sergeant Harbison leading a silent Corstley back down the hall.

"Ah yes," she replied dryly, her eyes still on the retreating NCOs. "I wouldn't want any inconveniences distracting them from their gravely important *mission*."

She looked back at Major Hudson. "Don't worry, sir. I'll be in touch. We'll get this whole matter cleared up for you and your client."

And with that, she turned her back on him to walk away.

"Wait! Sergeant Levi!" he called after her. "What organization did you say this investigation is a part of?"

Sarah stopped herself mid-step, a half-smile crossing her face. As an Inspector she didn't wear a rank on her uniform, it helped ensure impartiality in the pursuit of justice. He must have just assumed she was an NCO because she was polite and treated him with respect. *That, or he's just used to being the big dick in any conversation.*

"Actually, Major, it's *Inspector* Levi," she said, walking away. "And I didn't."

She met the boys back in the other room, the smile still on her face as she shut the door behind her.

"Alright," Torres said, rocking back and forth on his heels. "You want to share with the class what that was supposed to prove? Besides whipping your dick out hard enough to poke the Raiders in the eye."

"Certainly," Inspector Levi said, plunking herself down in a chair. She leaned it back on its legs, resting her head against the wall. "But before I explain, I want to know what you saw. Bernard, did you catch it?"

Ian shifted a little where he stood. He didn't like being put on the spot. "We saw the interview, then Sergeant Harbison came in and cut the feed."

"Right," she said, tilting her head. "And?"

"And nothing, nada, zilch," Torres said, scowling. He hated riddles. "Harbison came in, cut the feed, and the Major met you outside. That's it."

"Is it?" she asked innocently. "And was there anything else significant in that interaction? Anything significant about the room or who was in it? What do you think, Bernard?"

Ian thought for a moment, dragging a hand down his face. Levi watched the wheels turning before it clicked.

"The Major," he remarked suddenly, raising a hand as it dawned on him. "He wasn't in the room. He didn't even talk to Corstley."

"Correct," she said smugly. "He didn't even bother speaking with his 'client.' Just arranged for his release without looking into the details first. You heard him in the hallway—his job is to make sure they aren't *bothered* by anyone, so they can keep on-mission."

"A mission that Sergeant Harbison plans, directs, and executes," Ian said, finishing her thought.

Sergeant Torres gawped at her. "*You sly bitch!* You were looking for the ringleader!"

Levi smiled, rocking back and forth in her chair. "We had to see how high this goes. Now we know, the buck stops with Sergeant Harbison. I'm willing to bet the Major isn't even aware of the extent of the operation—he just clears the path so his superintendent keeps working."

"Just keeping the dance moving," Ian muttered, shaking his head.

"Exactly," Inspector Levi replied. "So now we've got the shipments tied to Sergeant Corstley and the lower Raiders, but we need hard evidence to tie Sergeant Harbison to this as well. He's too smart, he'll have covered his tracks well, so we'll need to catch him in the act."

She fixed her eyes on Sergeant Torres, still stroking his chin in amazement. "Can you work your magic with Customs and Immigration Cell again?"

"I suppose I'll try," he sighed.

"Great," she said, swiping to the line graph on her tablet, "because based on the data we have, they're going to bring in a new shipment in the next week."

"So we're set on the next move, good," said Ian. "Changing subjects though, anyone else notice something weird about their rooms?"

Levi and Torres looked at him confused.

Torres shrugged. "Like what?"

"I don't know," Ian said, scratching the back of his head. "Like things out of place? Every time I get home I swear my toothbrush has moved."

The two Sergeants shared a look.

Torres shrugged again. "You've seen my room, I'm lucky if I even find my toothbrush."

Levi shook her head. "And I live out of my bags. Everything I own is tucked away or strapped in. Nothing weird on my part."

"Sorry," Ian said, running a hand through his hair. "I guess I'm just being paranoid."

Chapter 16:

Barrett Harbison bounced against the nylon harness; the shadows cast by the dim red light flickering across his face. Surrounded by empty seats, he timed the descent of the cargo module plummeting through the upper atmosphere with soft taps of his boot. *Twenty-three...twenty-two...twenty-one...*he tapped, the metronomic cadence keeping the team abreast to their point of impact. He looked left and right as the cargo module hit another pocket of turbulence, surveying the five men lining the seats on the walls.

Huges and Kantz were on the right, swiping through pictures on a tablet and laughing about the girl Huges had hooked up with the night before. Zimmer was sprawled out in the corner, snoring softly as the module shook. Sergeant Harbison envied him; the enormous Special-Trooper possessed the innate knack of falling asleep anytime, anywhere. Buck-Sergeant Corstley sat by himself on the left, whistling under his breath as he cleaned the dirt from beneath his nails. With the investigation heating up, Sergeant Harbison had considered leaving him behind—no reason to draw attention with an undue absence. But no, he'd ultimately decided, this mission required both precision and finesse, it was better to bring him along.

The flinty grey eyes shifted again, landing on the final, and newest, member of the crew. A high-boned young man named Lindsey sat in the far corner by the door, a worn copy of the *King James Bible* open in his mahogany hands. Sergeant Harbison watched the murmuring of the Senior-Trooper's lips and frowned. He wasn't opposed to the belief in a higher power—quite the contrary, he'd seen enough of the universe in his twenty-five years of service to assume that there was at least a semblance of a grand design—but he strongly disapproved of prayer. It encouraged Troopers to put their trust in the assistance of something other than themselves, and that was something the Reed-Sergeant could not abide. He worshipped nothing higher than self-reliance.

Still, Sergeant Harbison thought, *he may be new, but he isn't green.* Lindsey had come to them almost two months ago, transferring in from the 7th Raider Group in orbit over Tamarin. He'd shown himself to be reserved, capable, and above all else discrete. He'd handled surveillance over the loadmasters without hesitation or question. It was time to feel him out for inclusion in 'the enterprise.'

His count reached ten, just as the repulsors began to fire on the underside of the module. The capsule shook violently as it slowed to impact speeds, rushing wind audible through the alloy walls. On another mission their descent would have been smoother, with high-altitude parachutes cushioning their fall as they landed. But New Wilstown wasn't a scene of active conflict, and so their entry required the utmost stealth of a low altitude repulsor approach. Sergeant Harbison looked around as his men put away their distractions and readied themselves for landing. Zimmer continued to snore in the far corner, broad chest rising and falling.

*Four...three...two...*he counted down, bracing against the nylon straps as the capsule slammed into the planet's surface. He was thrown against the harness when they hit, the usual twinge in his shoulder flaring up as he settled back down. The capsule was designed for hard falls, built to exacting specifications to land intact at high speeds and blast back into high orbit afterwards. *As usual,* thought Sergeant Harbison, rotating his shoulder back into place, *Trooper comfort was the smallest priority in the minds of the engineers.* He unclipped the straps and stood up, ignoring the pops and grinding as his back aligned itself. Landings were always hard, the Physician's Corps recommended limiting a Trooper's career to no more than fifty jumps to prevent undue wear on the soldier's body. Sergeant Harbison had cleared that number in his first ten years and had lost count ever since.

He walked the gangplank to the capsule's door, the men around him unclipping themselves and gathering their gear without a word. Even Zimmer was up by the time he reached the far end. The big Trooper had already pulled down his own gear and was reaching into the storage lockers for Sergeant Harbison's rucksack. The Reed-Sergeant accepted the gear in silence, slipping the straps over his shoulders and ensuring the magnetic connectors aligned with his vest. He tapped a dial near the shoulder of his vest, a small hum emitting as the polyreactive plates powered up. The hum vanished as the plates finished charging, the small field of ionic barriers activated beneath the hardened outer shell. The Reed-Sergeant nodded in approval— they'd field-tested *the* new plates during their scouting mission on UDR, but he still had his suspicions about the long-term power drain during storage. He set those aside for now, equipment doubts were helpful during mission planning or the after-actions report—not in between.

He squeezed a button on the inside of his jacket's wrist, watching as the mottled grey pattern of the ICF fatigues faded away and was replaced with a crisscross silver and black to match the metal floor. He moved to sync his vest as well but was pleasantly surprised when the striated green blinked once before changing to match. He'd been told when he ordered them that the poly-reactive plates would match the active camouflage of their uniform, but he'd assumed that meant they'd need to manually initiate the connection. *Glad they finally did something to make this easier.*

He looked back to the Raiders assembled behind him to confirm they'd gotten their vests initiated as well. Sergeant Corstley was well ahead of him, going down the line and inspecting the Troopers' gear. Sergeant Harbison felt the flicker of a smile cross his face. Corstley may lack the instincts for intrigue and finesse necessary to run a Raider group, but he was a damn good platoon sergeant. The Reed-Sergeant was glad he'd brought him along. Sergeant Harbison turned back to face the landing door, reaching out a hand to the large green button on the side. His hand paused over the molded plastic as he ran through the operation order in his mind.

Though New Wilstown lacked the declared hostilities of Karnassus or Ataxia, that wasn't the same as being at peace. Insurgent militias currently threatened the stability of the local government, waging a minor campaign of terrorism against the provincial Governor and engaging in skirmishes with the planetary guard. Several of the twenty different factions held wide support in the more rural areas of the planet, with some even gaining legitimacy with the backing of opposing political parties. It was a powder keg waiting to blow, but the Coalition Republic's primary stance had been one of benevolent neglect. So long as the Governor maintained his power through the continued successes of his planetary guard, there was no need for the Republic to get more involved and no need for the deployment of a full ICF pacification contingent. The mineral-rich planet was doing well enough on its own. The Republic officially maintained, and the Coalition respected the independent spirit demonstrated by the Governor's commitment to using his own forces to resolve the minor conflict—which is precisely why Sergeant Harbison and a small-strike force of Raiders had arrived on the rolling hills of New Wilstown.

There was a launch facility forty kilometers away, currently occupied by the forces of the planetary guard. They'd been using it as a staging platform in their campaign against the *Wilstown Liberation Army* operating near the town of Hamsbrook. The *WLA* was well-liked among the local populace, with the provincial government on the brink of losing control over the area entirely. The directive from the Republic's Small Council had been to assess the situation and find a way to tip the scales in favor of the *WLA*. Sergeant Harbison had sent a two-man team in over thirty days ago, embedding themselves with the

WLA to gain a better understanding of the area and opportunities open for exploitation.

Whang and Gorkey had reported back to him two weeks ago about the landing facility. It made an enticing target for the *WLA*. Not only would it afford them interstellar access for supply, but the planetary guard stockpiled the facility with both small and large arms, including at least seven light-attack vehicles. Bolstering the *WLA*'s armament and increasing their mobile firepower would put them on even keel with the greater guard forces in the area, further loosening the Governor's grip on the city. These reasons made it a simple call for the Small Council to approve his mission request.

Additionally, though he'd left this out of his report, the planetary guard had also been observed shuttling in crates of *Glib* seized from organized crime groups. With the investigation peering through every shipment coming through the Anian port, Sergeant Harbison had canceled their planned resupplies for the last month. He needed a new source for product to fund their enterprise, and with the amount Whang had told him was stored in the facility, they would be set for the next year.

Ride out, link up with Gorkey, Whang, and a contingent of WLA *fighters. Assault the facility, seize it while keeping the infrastructure intact. Load up the product, hand the keys to the building over to the* WLA, *and exfil back to the cargo module.* The steps were simple; he could picture each phaseline of the operation clearly in his mind. He let out a slow breath, hand still hovering over the green button.

"Good to go, Sarge," he heard Sergeant Corstley say from behind.

He pushed the button, lowering the hydraulic ramp onto the lush soil and revealing the glittering majesty of New Wilstown's night sky.

They rode south, weaving along the grassy hills that dotted the countryside. The wind whistled in his ears, the knobby handlebars gripped tight beneath his gloves. They tore across the verdant terrain, a small plume kicked up behind the three, black, four-wheelers. Specially constructed out of alloy and carbon nano-tubes, the all-terrain quadbikes were sturdy, light, and strong. Each had seating for three, and an additional cargo platform welded to the back. A gyroscopically mounted tempered-beam cannon was attached to the front, able to be operated by the driver or swung out on an articulated arm for a passenger to use.

Sergeant Harbison took a deep breath from the canned air flowing in his low-profile mask. The atmosphere on New Wilstown was only slightly higher in pressure than Earth's, but too rich in nitrogen. Breathe in too much, and you're liable to get the bends. Harbison blinked behind his goggles, reading the preprogrammed route along the heads-up display. There was a boulder up ahead, the landmark Whang had given them for their turn. He took a hand off the bike to direct them left, and the six Commandos cut west along the narrow switchback.

They rode to the edge of a narrow box canyon, killing their infrared headlights as they waited. Sergeant Harbison stood up in the vehicle's stirrups, looking around for the team's signal. A small infrared light invisible to the naked eye blinked twice from within a small inlet. Sergeant Harbison cut his hand sharply down and across, giving the signal for the team to fan out while he dismounted. He stepped off the bike and walked to the inlet, tapping the infrared illuminator on his goggles three times. Senior-Trooper Gorkey emerged from behind a small outcropping, coarse, curly hair just visible underneath his plaid flat cap.

"Whang?" Sergeant Harbison asked, looking around the outcropping.

Gorkey shook his head. "She's up on the ridgeline with De Soto—they've got eyes on the launch facility."

The Reed-Sergeant nodded, brushing his long hair back from his eyes. *Good, then we won't waste time getting her in place.* "Is there a good place to stash the quads?"

"There's an overhang that's got some decent cover just past those rocks," Gorkey said, pointing to the right. "We can cover them there, then we'll meet Whang on the ridge."

Sergeant Harbison nodded again, throwing his hand up and in a circle to grab his team's attention. He cut the hand down in the direction of the overhang. One by one the bikes followed suit, riding off along the craggy terrain. Sergeant Harbison turned back to the stocky Senior-Trooper.

"When's the last time you ate, son?" he asked, fishing a nutria-bar out of a vest pocket.

"Forty-nine hours ago," Gorkey shrugged. "But who's counting?"

The Reed-Sergeant smiled behind his mask. He held the bar out for Gorkey. "I hope banana's okay?"

"I hate banana," the Commando said, ripping into the bar's packaging. "But I'll make do."

Senior-Trooper Whang lay prone behind a rifle larger than herself, the long expanse of barrel of the LRS-7 stretching out between two chunks of sandstone. Like Gorkey, she was dressed in simple tans and plaids, the loose linen garments found fashionable by the Hamsbrook residents. She peered down the targeting scope, surveying the launch facility nestled in the bottom of the canyon. Two guards stood watch in the gate shack leading to the launch tower, while four more patrolled its parapets. She scanned the motorpool to the left, but there was no one guarding the light-attack vehicles nestled underneath its canopy. Whang panned her scope past the cemetery behind the compound, the small headstones jutting up from the rocky soil. She shifted again to watch the admin building to the right of the tower, but still no movement. From the last three days of observation, she knew there were ten more people working inside the launch facility's fenceline. She swung the scope over the six men outside, tagging each with the enhanced tracking reticle.

A tan-striped truck rumbled up the gravel road below her, the relief shift for the planetary guard. She shifted to follow the truck with her rifle, tagging each of the twelve men scrunched in the truck's bed.

"How many?" Sergeant Harbison asked behind her.

She was too well trained to jump, but a few curses stampeded their way through her mind. She'd served under Sergeant Harbison for three years now, and he was still the only one to get the drop on her.

"Six outside," she whispered back. "At least ten more inside. Shift change is in five mike, so double that number for the next hour."

The Reed-Sergeant nodded, grey eyes darting behind the spotting scope he'd borrowed from Gorkey.

"Armament?" he asked.

Whang kept her rifle trained on the truck. "Small arms, particle rifles, grenades. They've got two *slaws* mounted, one on the second balcony on a rail system and the other inside the gate shack."

Sergeant Harbison nodded again, factoring them into his plan for their assault. They'd need to move quietly, no gunfire until they're inside the compound and under the sighting range for the *Squad Laser Weapons*. "What about the heavy guns?"

Whang shifted behind the rifle, sweeping a jutting rock out from under her knee. "Locked up in the admin building. De Soto says there's a vault they're using as an armory."

Sergeant Harbison swept the spotting scope over the building, noting the number and placement of doors and windows. "And the product?"

"Kept separate in the launch tower," she said, still following the route of the tan-striped truck. "I saw them unload nine crates yesterday. There's at least two tons inside."

"Just enough then," Sergeant Harbison said, panning the scope over the tower. "How long until shift-change's complete?"

"They usually take an hour for change-over."

"Good," the Reed-Sergeant said, lowering the scope from his eyes. "Then we move in two."

They moved silently down the rocky embankment, winding their way to the canyon floor. They hugged the jagged edges of the terrain, using them as cover as they made their way closer to the compound's fence line. Sergeant Harbison wove along the broken ground, one eye glued to the glowing red reticle of the R-91 particle rifle. Up ahead, Huges took point, the bull-necked Senior-Trooper rolling his steps from rock to rock, GR-23 grenade launcher nestled under his armpit. Behind him was Lindsey, R-91 up and scanning ahead on the path. Then came Zimmer, the massive barrel of a SLW-18 cradled in his thick hands. It was modified variant, developed by ICF skunkworks just for use in the Raiders. It boasted a cut-down stock, additional cooling systems to sustain longer bursts of firing, and a toggle switch that flattened the beam, shortening the range but widening the path into a long triangle of destruction. Kantz was next, his rifle down as he worked the controls for their miniature ScanDrone flying overhead. The small, swept-wing craft relayed a continuous feed of the facility straight to Kantz's goggles, allowing him an overhead picture of the battlespace. Sergeant Harbison walked closely behind the Special-Trooper, team leads always positioned in close proximity to their communications support.

A pebble slid underneath the Reed-Sergeant's boot, kicked up from the men behind him. He stifled a curse as he turned around, glaring from behind his mask and goggles. De Soto and his three men stumbled over each other in the dark, the thin moonlight above doing little to illuminate the gravel strewn ground. Sergeant Harbison scowled, he'd just as easily have run the mission by himself, no outsiders or onlookers, but his directives were to include the WLA at every stage to ensure the Republic could maintain full deniability if things went south. De Soto had told him one of the men was a ticket receptionist at the facility before the planetary guard took over, and that he knew the buildings inside and out. Sergeant Harbison watched that man dig a finger in his nose, wiping it on his linen shirt as he walked. His scowl deepened. He couldn't stand slobs—it spoke to a disorganized mind. He ran through their odds of mission success if he just killed the three rebels right there, deciding against it only when he realized he'd have to justify his team going solo in the after-actions report. Behind the rebels, Sergeant Corstley brought up the rear, the burly Buck-Sergeant scanning the cliffs behind them with his rifle.

The nine men broke from the rock face as they neared the fence a hundred meters to the east of the guard shack. Huges approached the rough chain-link, slinging his grenade launcher and unsheathing a miniature plasma torch. He moved quickly, slicing a circle just large enough for them to crouch through. He pulled the section off to the side, ensuring it didn't rattle against the rest of the fence. One by one, the nine men slunk through, filing along as they crossed the compound.

"What's our count?" Sergeant Harbison asked, vocalizing into the microphone behind his mask.

"Two at the shack, three on the balcony," Whang answered, watching the movement of the guards tagged in her scope.

"Big picture?" the Reed-Sergeant asked as they fanned out against the back of the admin building.

"Five outside, ten inside," Kantz said, reading the thermal images from the ScanDrone's feed. "Three in the admin building by the vault and seven inside the tower."

Sergeant Harbison took a tactical pause, running through the permutations of their next action. The admin building was less fortified, boasted fewer men, but was structurally unimportant. The tower would be trickier to crack, it was a tight, vertical space consisting of an inner core of two offices on each floor surrounded by a wide, spiraling staircase. The elevator on the outside was an immediate no-go—they couldn't afford to be caught in a slow moving killbox. That meant ascending the stairs and clearing one floor at a time. Sergeant Harbison looked to De Soto. "The vault, how fortified is it?"

De Soto nudged his man forward, "Answer him, Parker."

"Iss a big door," Parker said, his voice tinny behind his loose-fitting mask. "Real thick."

The grey eyes narrowed behind the goggles. "How big? How thick?"

Parker shrugged, holding his arms about two feet apart.

"Fuck's sake, what color is it?" Sergeant Corstley snapped, shoving the pale-faced rebel.

Parker glared at him but did nothing in return. "Dark grey, yellow stripes on the front."

"That's Blast-Level II," Sergeant Corstley said quickly to Sergeant Harbison. "It won't take a breacher round, but it'll shrug off concussives."

Sergeant Harbison nodded. "Make it happen."

Sergeant Corstley tapped Huges, signaling him to follow as they peeled around on the right side of the building. Sergeant Harbison watched as the two Commandos made their way to the main door, crouching under windows and hugging the shadows as they went. They stopped at the side door, crouching in the shadows by the hinges. Huges tapped the controls on his GR-23, selecting the correct rounds and programming them for proximity detonation. He stepped out from the shadows, swinging the grenade launcher up to his shoulder. Sergeant Harbison heard the soft chuff as the launcher spat out two rounds, the concussion grenades adhering to the top corners of the door frame. Huges nodded, lowering the launcher and stepping back against the wall. Sergeant Harbison watched the two continue on their way, disappearing around the front of the building.

"Whang," he said into the mask. "Squelch in three."

"Rog, Sarge," came the reply

Sergeant Harbison cut his hand through the air, motioning for the remaining men to follow him as they crept around the left side of the building. *Two...one...*he counted, weaving his way around the patches of moonlight. He didn't hear the shots being fired, it was impossible this far from the suppressed rifle, but he saw their impact. He looked to the left, watching the two guards slump over in the gate shack. His eyes shifted up to the two balconies surrounding the tower. He watched as the head of one guard snapped up before he fell over, his horrified buddy joining him in the next second. Sergeant Harbison could almost make out the look of surprise on the third guard's face as the fin-guided kinetic smart-round sought him out and took his life. He dropped his gaze, focusing on the entrance to the tower ahead as the rest of his team followed behind.

Cortstley and Huges met them by the door, the last of the explosives primed along the front door of the admin building. Sergeant Harbison turned back to De Soto and his men. He didn't need any amateurs in there once the walls got tight and the blood was close.

"Wait here," he said. "Watch the door. Shoot anyone who leaves."

De Soto opened his mouth to protest but thought better of it. Better to let the Raiders die in there than waste his own men.

Sergeant Harbison fell in on the side of the door opposite of Huges and Corstley. The two groups stacked up on either side, with the two NCOs in the front. Sergeant Harbison watched as Huges slung the GR-23 and drew the P-3 sonic pistol from his side. In tight quarters, grenades were more liability than benefit. The Reed-Sergeant checked his own stack, observing Zimmer flipping the wide-angle toggle on the SLW-18.

He turned back to the front, locking eyes with Sergeant Corstley. He couldn't see behind the mask, but he knew the Buck-Sergeant was grinning. Sergeant Harbison nodded, and Sergeant Corstley swept in the door. The rest of the Commandos followed suit, alternating on either side as they fanned into the tower's narrow lobby. Sergeant Harbison spied the winding staircase on the right, next to a small office with a light in the window.

Options raced through his mind. He chose the quiet route, directing the rest of the Raiders to make their way to the stairs with Sergeant Corstley while he took care of the office. Sergeant Harbison slung his rifle as Sergeant Corstley and the others crept to the stairs. He made his way to the office door, the Commandos fanning out above him to cover every angle. Sergeant Harbison placed a hand on his belt, finding the leather-wrapped handle of his hatchet. One tug and it was free, rising in his hand as he pulled the door open.

He heard the muffled *whump* of explosions outside, the concussion grenades finding their mark as a guardsman opened the side door of the admin building. *So much for the quiet route*, he thought as the yanked the door suddenly. The pudgy guardsman inside had just started to rise from his desk, reacting too slowly to the distant sound of the grenades. Sergeant Harbison watched surprise sprint across the wide, flabby face, interpreting the threat before him a second too late. The Reed-Sergeant saw the jowly mouth flap open, accusation rising in the guardsman's throat before he brought his hand down and buried his hatchet in it.

Sergeant Harbison jerked the hatchet free, pausing to wipe it on the guardsman's tan uniform before sheathing it on his belt. From the stairs above he heard the dim *rat-a-tat* of suppressed particle rifles stitching their way through the offices on the second floor. He unslung the R-91 from his back, the knurled grip comfortable in his hands, and jogged his way up the stairs.

He met his men on the third floor, bypassing the bloodied offices of the second to join them as prepared to breach. He lined up with Zimmer and Lindsey, while Corstley, Huges, and Kantz stacked up on the second office. They moved as soon as they were in position, Lindsey slammed the door open, only to stop short as it smacked into a desk pushed against the other side. From the corner of his eye, Sergeant Harbison saw Corstley's crew disappear into their room, their shadows cast on the hallway behind them in the flashes of particle fire. Lindsey shoved against the door again, stymied by the makeshift barricade.

"Move!" barked Zimmer, rotating the barrel on his *slaw*. "Vert shot!"

"Vert shot!" they echoed back as he fired, the hallway lighting up red as the powerful, flat beam erupted out of the long barrel. *Brrrrrrrrrrrrrrrm*, went the cannon, the laser cutting a swathe stretching from floor to ceiling through the door and the desk behind it. Zimmer rotated the barrel, bringing it back to its horizontal position. He fired again, slicing the door in quarters. The giant Special-Trooper kicked the center of the door, the edges of the cuts still glowing molten red. It fell inwards on the shattered remains of the desk. Zimmer ran in, the room glowing red as he fired a third time. Sergeant Harbison and Lindsey followed close behind, clearing the corners to the left and right. He needn't have bothered, the flat blast of the laser cannon had sliced everything in the room in quarters, including the two guardsmen. Sergeant Harbison stepped over the severed remains, canting his rifle around the singed top of a crate pushed into the corner. The top layer of orange vials was a sheet of melted glass, but the rest of it survived. Sergeant Harbison nodded to the other two, and they stepped back to the threshold of the door.

"Clear!" Harbison snapped into the microphone in his mask.

"Clear!" Sergeant Corstley answered back.

The two teams stepped out into the hall, making their way up the stairs to the fourth level. They found the two offices there to be locked, but otherwise empty. The fifth and sixth floors were empty as well, occupied only by a small kitchenette with a pot of something acrid and burning on the stove. Sergeant Harbison switched the burner off, and the Commandos made their way to the last floor.

The landing control terminal was deserted. The room next to it was far more fruitful, a quick blast to the reinforced lock and they were in, surrounded by crates along each wall.

Sergeant Corstley let out a low whistle. "Gotta be at least three tons in here, Sarge."

"Enough to keep 'the enterprise' going well into the next year," Sergeant Harbison agreed, slinging his rifle as he stepped to the nearest crate. He motioned for Huges to come over, using his portable plasma torch to trim the lock on the crate's hinge. He hoisted the lid up, the glittering orange vials shining in the fluorescent light of the ceiling fixtures.

"What's that?" Lindsey asked, leaning in over the crate.

"That, son," Sergeant Harbison drawled slowly, "is what paid for your new armor."

It was a well-known facet of ICF life that all Troopers were paid the same base pay, each according to their rank. It was meant to be a unifying principle, to discourage the jockeying for raises and position that often accompanied civilian life. Every Trooper was treated and paid exactly the same, content in their equality.

As a young man this had galled Sergeant Harbison. How could it be that the ICF considered the men and women of the Commando Raiders to be equal to the slow-witted pukes of the Accounting Corps? It had frustrated him through the years, watching as the brave Troopers he served with, injured in the line of duty, were offered the same treatment and medical retirement as the common soldier. Those that died in service to the secret machinations of the Coalition Republic fared little better, their families received a holovid and the option for internment in the ICF *Arlington*, the orbital cemetery outside of Cerulia.

It took him many years until he understood the truth. The ICF was just too big—a vast, monolithic bureaucracy that projected power across a near infinite universe in service of an administration unparalleled in size and scope across the history of man. Of *course* it didn't care about the lives of a handful of Raiders lost to the making of its history. It couldn't. The system was just too large, the people that make it up too small, no matter how important they were to him or anyone else in his close-knit community of elite soldiers.

And so, he reasoned, if the ICF was too large to care for those dear to him, then he would do so himself. He promoted to Buck-Sergeant in the fall of 2314. By the next spring, he had started 'the enterprise.' It began small, as most things do, selling off a few war trophies here and there, distributing gold trinkets recovered from a warlord's palace. The big money had started nearly three years later, when he'd led a mission to destroy a purported cache of insurgent weapons, opening the bunker door to find crates of NorCan instead. He'd had the idea to expand the operation then, securing suppliers and selling their product to the lesser Troopers and local populations for the planets he served on. It took some time to get set up. He had to build a close inner-circle of trust to use as a base. But once he did, he'd watched the profits roll in, thousands upon thousands of credits each time.

He divided the profits from 'the enterprise' fairly and unequivocally. Twenty percent of the share went into a fund established to provide for those medically retired from the Raider unit, or the widows of those who died. Thirty percent was funneled into the purchase of equipment and supplies, ensuring his Commandos never lacked for the most advanced weaponry and protection money could buy, standard ICF issue and procurement processes be damned. The remaining fifty percent was divided evenly amongst those who participated. The smarter ones invested it on the galactic market, but he had watched plenty enough fritter it away on private ships, prostitutes, and luxury jewelry.

Sergeant Harbison had no desire for such things. He was a simple, thrifty man, squirreling away the vast majority of his career salary over the last twenty-five years. He had more than enough to buy a ranch on the outskirts of Tamarin, a lifetime supply of mass-market beer, a sturdy work truck, and a small pack of dogs to keep himself occupied in the twilight years of his life. He was partial to dogs. They loved their masters unconditionally, without expecting reciprocation.

Sergeant Harbison had no need for extra money, and so he donated his cut to the widow fund each time. He kept this contribution a secret, even from trusted men like Sergeant Corstley. He had no qualms about the others taking and using their fair share—they had earned it time and time again. And he knew that they looked to him as an example for guidance. So he kept his spending a secret, so the others wouldn't feel obligated to follow his lead.

A distant explosion pulled Sergeant Harbison from his musings. The room shook a little with the impact, but Sergeant Harbison and the others were already out the door, spreading out along the winding staircase.

"Big picture!" the Reed-Sergeant barked, brushing past Zimmer to find a window.

"Dialing it!" Kantz yelled back, syncing in with the live feed from the ScanDrone overhead. He'd cut the feed when they'd entered the tower, the visual overlay would've been a distraction as they cleared the tight corridors. The view from the drone flickered to life in his goggle. "Aw, *shit!*"

"What?" Sergeant Corstley called from the stairs above.

"It's a Striker 526!" the Special-Trooper stammered. "They've got a fuckin' *tank* out there!"

Impossible, thought Sergeant Harbison, as another explosion shook the tower. He reached a window midway between floors and looked out. There, on the ridgeline above, was the ICF's main battle tank, decked out in the tan-stripes of the planetary guard. He cursed the Coalition's reciprocal weapon-share agreements as he watched the massive turret shift left, training its mini-Ion Array on the last of the light-attack vehicles in the hangar to the west.

"How the fuck did they get that?" Zimmer shouted from the stairs above.

"Why the fuck did they come here?" Huges yelled from the floor below.

"You want me to call in an orbital strike?" Kantz asked from right beside him.

"No!" Sergeant Harbison snapped. "*We aren't here!*"

"Rog, Sarge," said Kantz, his eyes still on the footage from the orbiting drone.

"Plan?" Sergeant Corstley asked, meeting the Reed-Sergeant by the window.

Sergeant Harbison thought for a moment. With the tank on the ridgeline their primary route back up the cliff-face was cut off. That left their secondary egress through the cemetery in the back, but they'd never make it on foot.

"Whang! Gorkey!" he ordered into his mask. "I need you to grab the quad-bikes and meet us by the tower. We're using exfil Bravo."

"Roger, Sarge," the two Senior-Troopers replied in unison.

The bikes were made to carry three soldiers apiece, but he figured they could easily fit one more in the cargo basket mounted on the back. *We'll make do*, he thought bitterly, as another explosion rocked the tower. He turned back to Sergeant Corstley. "Grab the men, set up harassing fire with the *slaw* near the tower's base. That should buy us enough time to load up and beat feet out of here."

The bearded Buck-Sergeant nodded. "What about the crates?"

"Fuck 'em," Sergeant Harbison said, stepping away from the window as the tower rocked again. "We'll find another fix."

"What about the *WLA?*" asked Lindsey, crouching on the steps a few feet up.

"They can come if they hang on," the Reed-Sergeant snapped. "Now let's make like a herd and *move the fuck out!*"

The two NCOs barked orders as the rest of the Commandos filed down the stairs. The launch tower quivered as the Striker fire grew closer. They had just cleared the last stairs when the tower received its first hit, the landing control terminal disappearing in a flash of light and a boom like thunder. Sergeant Corstley martialed the forces outside, gathering Zimmer and Huges to set up a base of fire on each side of the tower. The two Commandos began plugging away, alternating shots to draw the tank's attention away from dismantling the structure above them.

Sergeant Harbison saw the flash of headlights in the distance. He tapped the infrared signal on his goggles, drawing them closer to their position. Whang and Gorkey pulled their quadbikes to the base of the tower, just as the Striker 526 began blasting away at the ground near Zimmer and Huges.

"Go! Go! Go!" Sergeant Harbison shouted, throwing his Raiders on the cramped bikes. He disengaged the locking mechanism and swung the mounted beam cannon out on its articulated arm, plugging away futilely at the poly-reactive armor of the tank. He looked over to see Sergeant Corstley loading the last man on the back of the bike, throwing him a thumbs up to signal it was time to leave.

Don't have to tell me twice. He pinched Whang's shoulder, holding on around her middle as the bike took off. He swung the cannon back around, narrowly avoiding clipping the side of De Soto's head as he maintained fire on the Striker.

"You still here?" He laughed as the hapless rebel clung to his perch on the side running board. "I thought you wanted the launch facility?"

They both looked back in time to see the tower shudder again under another hit from the tank's Ion Array, collapsing in on itself in slow motion.

De Soto locked eyes with the wiry Reed-Sergeant. "We'll get another one!" he shouted over the roaring wind.

They wove around tombstones, names blurring on the graves as they sped across the level ground. Sergeant Harbison felt the ping of rocks and gravel kicked up by the bike ahead of him on his helmet. He looked back just in time to lean away from an outcropping rising from the ground.

De Soto wasn't so lucky.

Sergeant Harbison watched the rebel tumble off the bike, carried back by the impact with the boulder. He took his hand off the gun long enough to offer a farewell salute to the young insurgent before tightening his grip on Whang with the other.

The two bikes sped along, over and around the hilly countryside, cutting a wide path back to the cargo module. They reached the lander just as day was breaking over the horizon, rolling the quad bikes up the ramp and into the capsule. Sergeant Harbison swung a leg off the bike, barking orders to secure the remaining gear and vehicles. He tapped a quick code into the terminal pin-pad mounted on the capsule wall, initiating the remote detonation of the quadbike they'd left behind in the canyon. He turned back to Parker, the *WLA* insurgent stepping down the ramp on shaking legs.

"Farewell, friend," he called out to him as the ramp door swung closed on hydraulic hinges. "Best of luck to your revolution!"

The door shut before him, cutting off Sergeant Harbison's last look at the shocked expression on Parker's face. He tapped another code on the pin-pad initializing the deep-space recovery signal and the module's launch sequence. The Reed-Sergeant walked slowly to his seat at the rear of the hold, passing by Troopers securing themselves and their gear. He sat down hard in the nylon jump-seat, ignoring the insolent pops of his knees as he did. Shutting his eyes, he felt for the nylon straps, clipping himself in place as the last of the Raiders did the same. Sergeant Harbison felt the rumble of the repulsors igniting be-low, counting down in his head as they lifted off.

The journey back to Anius was frustrating but uneventful. He gave the task of preparing the after-actions report to Sergeant Corstley. It was a good job for the burly Buck-Sergeant. It prepared him for the greater pain-in-the-ass of leading a Raider unit. Sergeant Harbison did his best to catch up on sleep over the twenty-four hours of spaceflight, drowning out his irritation at the failed mission and lost product with unconsciousness.

The cargo module shook and shuddered as they descended through the blistering atmosphere to the hot sands of Anius' surface. The capsule came to rest on the pneumatic buffers of their private launch pad, the rocking subsiding just enough for Sergeant Harbison to unclip his harness and stand up, stretching out the kink that had developed in his back. He strolled past the rows of men sorting out themselves and their gear to leave. Walking to the edge of the hold he slapped the big green button, resting for a moment as the heavy door unfolded. He knew there was a shelf-life for every Raider, a finite num-ber of missions any man could put himself through. Sergeant Harbison wasn't just any man, but in that moment, haunted by the failure of the last forty-eight hours, he began to feel his age.

The door ahead of him crept open, the ramp extending down and revealing the white concrete of the launch pad. Sergeant Harbison shut his eyes. *I just need another moment to rest...*

A voice called out to him from just outside the module. "Reed-Sergeant Harbison?"

The grey eyes snapped open, focusing for a moment on the cheery face of a thin Trooper standing on the ramp. 'Johnson' read the Trooper's nametape. Sergeant Harbison felt a scowl forming.

"Sergeant Harbison?" the Trooper repeated, extending a hand. "I'm here with the Customs and Immigration Cell here on Anius. I've got some officials from the Anian side of the house with me," he lisped, jerking a thumb behind him to two grim-face men in starched-white uniforms. "And, uh, they would like to look around your module here. If you don't mind."

Sergeant Harbison closed his eyes again slowly. This was that bitch Inspector's work; he just knew it. He opened his eyes just as the thin Buck-Sergeant looked ready to repeat himself. He cut him off with a sharp look, Sergeant Johnson's words dying in his throat. Sergeant Harbison's scowl deepened as he watched the Sergeant quailing before him.

"Get me the Major," the Reed-Sergeant said quietly as Sergeant Corstley walked up behind him. "Right. Fucking. *Now.*"

Chapter 17:

Sarah awoke that evening to the soft trilling of her tablet. Mr. Freeman's message was short and to the point, it read simply 'Girl come QUICK' followed by a series of exclamation points. A follow up message consisted only of the Raiders' insignia accompanied by pictograms of lightning bolts and yelling faces. *Guess the customs officials came through,* she thought as she pulled on her mottled grey uniform pants. *This should be fun.* She stopped just long enough to pull her curly hair into a respectable bun, checking her appearance in the scratched mirror in the bathroom. Then she was out the door.

Sarah strode brusquely through the scuffed halls of Command Central, past the blast door marked 'Classified Actions Only' and down the hallway to the glass doors with bold letters engraved above. The steel handles were cool under her hands as she pushed her way in. She could hear the muffled sounds of privileged indignation through the closed grey doors of the Colonel's office.

"Girl, I'm glad you're here," Mr. Freeman said, eyeing her from behind his bank of monitors. "Got a Major in there raising all kinds of fuss. Been throwin' your name around for a minute."

Sarah nodded as she crossed to the grey doors, flashing him a smile as she passed the SimuWood desk. She'd expected something like this to happen, involving the Anians in searching the Raiders' capsule was an act of aggression on her part, and she knew there'd be a clear escalation in response. *Customs must've caught them with something good if they were pissed off enough to go straight to the Baron.* She reached the grey doors, pausing for a moment as she gripped the handles. The shouting was clearer now, fragments of sentences about 'duty to office,' 'mission imperatives,' and 'impediments to command' drifting through. Scenes like this were nothing new, she'd weathered plenty of screaming matches from petulant unit commanders furious with the findings of her final report. She knew the drill, there was a rhythm to these sorts of things. She'd go in, then stand by patiently while they ranted and raged, letting them build in their red-faced anger as they blamed her for their unit's failings. Then, when they'd run out of steam, the installation commander would turn to her and ask if she had anything she'd like to add. She'd pause before answering, playing at being the unfortunate bearer of bad news, then softly deliver the *coup de grace* with her evidence of their unit's corruption. It had happened the same way time and time again, in dozens of cases across dozens of worlds.

But usually they wait until the report's complete, she thought, hesitating a second further at the door. And in this case she wasn't exactly sure what the evidence was for her knockout punch. Tendrils of doubt and unease began pushing their delicate roots through her mind. She'd checked her messages twice since she'd left. It was definitely odd that customs hadn't sent her their report yet. The shouting grew louder on the other side of the door, jarring her out of her thoughts. *Waiting on the sidelines is not an option.* Sarah shook her head, banishing her doubts as she pushed her way in. She knew she could handle whatever was waiting on the other side of the door for one simple reason; the commander that entitled Major was bitching to was Colonel John Schwarz Jr. And with Colonel Schwarz, it paid to be his favorite.

Lieutenant Colonel Brandon Pickelhaube had never been described as the type of man who enjoyed conflict. Some officers relished it, charging into every argument and debate with the sounds of guns ringing in their heads. Major Hudson, standing on the other side of the SimuWood desk with one hand raised to the sky in righteous anger, was clearly such an officer. But Lieutenant Colonel Pickelhaube, Vice-

Commander to the ICF contingent on Anius, three-time awardee of the ICF medal of Sustained Longevity, who was granted Delta-level clearance after he accidentally wandered into a classified in-brief and had been too quiet for anyone to notice until the mission-strategy briefing had ended, was not.

Lieutenant Colonel Pickelhaube was not the type of man that people described in general. He had a muted air and manner about him that caused his presence to fade from the memories of those that encountered him, almost as soon as he left the room. Those who worked with him on a daily basis as he floated in and out of the office, knew him to be polite, present, but otherwise utterly unremarkable. His twenty-year career formed a testament to the proud military tradition that prioritized keeping one's head down and nose clean as the primary tenets that begat a successful field-grade officer.

Those first meeting him could often describe him the clearest, their memories undulled by the passage of time. They would say that he had a stretched frame and distant look of panic in his eyes. Like a small child that had awoken that morning to find themselves magically transformed into the body of a grown man working desperately to keep anyone from noticing.

Lieutenant Colonel Pickelhaube was not the type of officer most people would expect to see presiding over the lives of ten-thousand ICF Troopers. And as he sat in the broad leather chair, pale blue eyes darting around the room while Major Hudson's complaints echoed loudly off the walls, it was readily apparent that he was both aware of the opinions of most people and shared them himself.

Major Hudson continued in his tirade, decrying the impertinence of a *safety* investigation that dared to infringe upon the noble operations of the Commando Raiders. Lieutenant Colonel Pickelhaube watched the Major pace the length of the office, his strong, purposeful steps carrying him in a loop around the battered paisley rug in its center. The Lieutenant Colonel sighed, ducking behind his steepled fingers. He looked up just in time to see a woman with kind eyes and curly brown hair slip in through the grey doors, saying nothing as she took up a spot against the wall. Her brown eyes widened a little as she saw him sitting behind the SimuWood desk. He nodded to her, as if to acknowledge that he shared in her confusion at his inclusion in the situation.

Major Hudson paused to take a breath, pivoting at the apex of his turn and finally noticing the latecomer to their meeting.

"Oh good, *Sergeant* Levi has joined us," he said, lip curling a little at the mention of her name. "Perhaps you would like to explain this *gross* overreach of your office? Or would you rather continue to jeopardize the lives of everyone present by impeding the critical missions *my* men carry out?"

The brown eyes hardened, losing their kindness.

"Perhaps you would like to explain why obeying the customs laws outlined in the charter agreement between the ICF and the Anian governorship is seen as a detriment to the mission of *your* men?" she said quietly.

"That capsule held classified intelligence files! Classified equipment!" he snapped, swept blond hair bouncing as he raised his voice.

Inspector Levi kept her voice level and calm. "Weren't the files and equipment appropriately marked and stowed in approved classified storage containers? I sincerely doubt the Anian customs officials inspected anything marked beyond their purview. They have no problems respecting the limits of their office."

"And what about the limits of *yours?*" Major Hudson barked, broad shoulders rising as his voice echoed off the walls. "I see you don't even deny your involvement in the whole affair."

"I am charged with conducting a *thorough* investigation into the injury of an ICF Trooper," the inspector said, quietly but firmly. "That investigation happens to involve equipment requested for, delivered to, and signed by, members of the Commando Raider unit here on Anius. *Your* men."

"An investigation that should be confined solely to the actions of the loadmasters responsible!" The Major's lip curled further, baring rows of perfectly straight, white teeth. "I have yet to see a scrap of evidence justifying this level of scrutiny into *our* unit."

"With all due respect, *sir*," she replied, an aggressive jut to her chin. "I have nothing to justify to *you*. My investigation is carried out under the orders of the installation commander."

And with that, they both turned and looked to the occupant of the SimuWood desk. Colonel Pickelhaube blanched as he realized the focus of the conversation had turned back to him. He had hoped during their exchange that the two might work it out amongst themselves, but now it appeared to fall on him to make some sort of decision. He swallowed hard, the wheels in his head turning but it appeared that the cog connecting 'input' to 'reaction' had failed to show for work that day. The pale blue eyes blinked slowly.

"Uhhhh," he stalled, slowly coming to grips with his presiding role in this dispute. "Colonel Schwarz didn't leave me instructions about any investigations when he took leave."

Major Hudson smirked triumphantly. "Clearly then, it was the top of his priority list."

Inspector Levi dug in stubbornly, crossing her arms as she leaned against the wall. "Why don't we wait then? Let him resolve this when he gets back."

"I, uh, don't know about that," the Lieutenant Colonel quavered, trepidation fluttering through his chest. "He's supposed to be gone for two months, for *Song Warjan*."

"*Wan Songkran*," Mr. Freeman corrected from the other room.

"Right, that," Colonel Pickelhaube murmured.

Inspector Levi's face fell, while Major Hudson seemed to positively swell with glee.

"Clearly," the Major remarked, square jaw parading as he spoke. "We cannot wait that long. I see no reason why my men should be burdened under the constraints of this investigation for *two months*. That is simply an unacceptable amount of time."

"It does seem quite a lot," Colonel Pickelhaube agreed softly, scratching the top of his head.

Major Hudson saw his opening, he pressed his advantage. "Every *minute* this inquiry stretches negatively impacts the Raiders, *sir*. Our most important missions, those handed down by the Small Council itself, require my men to have the freedom to operate with total focus and clarity. Two months is *far* too long to impact the objectives of the Small Council."

The Lieutenant Colonel felt himself pinned beneath the intensity of the Major's gaze. He had never before considered the objectives of the Small Council, or that he might ever be in the position to hold them up. The back of his throat was suddenly parched and coarse.

"Well. Of course," he mumbled, pale blue eyes darting frantically. "Two months. Too long."

"*Far* too long," the Major corrected, pouncing on the opportunity.

"Yes, far too long," Colonel Pickelhaube repeated numbly.

"Obviously, we want to be understanding to the demands of a *thorough* investigation," the Major continued, voice rising as he swept his hand to encompass the entirety of the room. "We value the tireless efforts of the ICF *Safety* Commission, and we want to make sure the good Sergeant has enough time to complete her investigation."

"For sure, for sure," Colonel Pickelhaube replied, avoiding the Inspector's eyes as she stood against the wall. "Thorough. Time."

"So perhaps we simply set a limit? Something fair to all parties involved?" the Major asked, flashing his perfect teeth. "Another fifty-four hours? To finalize her report?"

"What? No! That's ridiculous!" Inspector Levi protested, eyes sparking with anger as she rushed to the desk. "That's nowhere near enough time!"

"Fine, fine," the Major conceded, raising his hands in a show of placation. "Two days, then."

"Out of the question!" the Inspector snapped. She turned back to the Lieutenant Colonel. "Sir, you have to understand. This is a sensitive investigation, it requires adequate time. Colonel Schwarz—"

"Is not here now," the Major interrupted, holding up his hand to cut her off. "And you will forgive us if we do not concede to *your* understanding of the decisions *he* would have made. The decision now falls to Colonel Pickelhaube." He crossed around the desk, placing a patronizing hand on the Lieutenant Colonel's shoulder. "Sir? Two more days to conclude an investigation that's already going on a month?"

The Lieutenant Colonel looked from the contented Major to the Inspector, her jaw clenched in anger under eyes that pleaded with him for understanding. His mind raced, searching for the option that was least likely to end with the Small Council learning of him by name. A drop of sweat beaded and ran down the small of his back. After a moment of consideration, he looked back to the Major beside him.

"Yes," he said quietly, his tongue thick and dry. "I think two days is enough time to wrap this up."

Terrance sat cross-legged at the desk in Levi's dorm room, doodling idly on his tablet while they waited. They were supposed to meet her there, but she'd fired off a message earlier saying she'd be a little late, something about a meeting with the Baron. A high shriek sounded from the bathroom as a particularly brazen cockroach made its presence known to Bernard in an attempt to crawl up his leg and be his friend. Terrance rolled his eyes as the shriek was followed by a distant crash, then the thud of a body stumbling into a wall, then a separate thud of something thrown against another wall, then a polite flush, and then the sound of hands being fervently washed.

Terrance looked up as the bathroom door opened and Bernard staggered out. "Rough time in there?"

Bernard's eyes were haggard. "I jus—"

"Well, gents, we got *fucked!*" Levi shouted, throwing open the front door and storming into the tiny dorm. Bernard raced to shut the door behind her as she tore off her uniform jacket and threw it in the corner. She walked purposefully over to the neatly made bed, considered the two Buck-Sergeants with a sideways glance, and then flopped face first into the thick comforter.

"Tell me you have good news," she demanded, picking her head up to look Terrance in the eye. "Did they send you the inspection report?"

"Sure," he said dryly. "If by inspection report you mean a one page email from our ol' pal Sergeant Johnson apologizing and saying that he and the Anians found fuck-all when they searched the capsule."

Levi dropped her head back into the covers, conveying her frustration with a muffled full-body sigh that stretched out for an entire minute.

"Ah," Terrance said, turning back to his doodles. "I see your meeting went well."

"What did Colonel Schwarz say?" asked Bernard, making his way over from the door.

"Colonel Schwarz is on leave," Levi answered, picking her face up out of the covers again. "And I've been given two days to deliver my finalized report."

She dropped her head back down, sighing heavily again.

"So that's it then? It's over?" Bernard asked, folding his arms over his chest. "What about the stuff we've already found? The evidence on Sergeant Corstley?"

"Circumstantial," Levi mumbled around the thick comforter. "They'll deny most of the connections and any knowledge of what was in the crate when they signed for it. On its own it won't be enough to clear either of you."

"Should've beaten that confession out of him when we had the chance," Terrance mused, squiggling a few more lines on the tablet.

"So that's it then?" Bernard repeated, looking from the bed to the desk. "Just like that, we're through?"

"Not unless you can find evidence directly linking Sergeant Harbison to the drugs in the next hundred and eight hours," she said, picking her head up from the bed. "Or find a smoking gun big enough that I can make the case to stall for more time."

Bernard thought for a moment as she dropped back on the bed, running a hand through his short, black hair. He turned back to Terrance. "I got nothing, you?"

Terrance paused his doodling as he considered their options. They had the night off on account of the sandstorm rolling through around midnight. It was the start of the season, and they always shut down the port during a sandstorm to keep the shuttles' repulsors from glassing the landing pad. Terrance thought long and hard about the difficult times he had in tech school, about the various techniques he'd used to spark creativity and spurn his mind into greater comprehension of the problems before him.

"Well, after careful thought," he said gravely, drawing their attention as he broke the quiet of the room. "I think I may have the solution to our current dilemma."

He looked from Levi to Bernard, broaching his proposal with the dignity and solemnity it deserved.

"I propose we all get drunk."

The air in the PCCR bar was stale, redolent with the slight tang of salt and musk built from decades of soldiers gathering in a single space. The music was just loud enough to make conversation difficult, but quiet enough that it encouraged you to try. The lights flickered, always hovering on the diffused edges between warmly dim and outright darkness. The bar itself was a long stretch of elegantly molded Simu-Wood. It buckled and curled from years of spilled drinks, the initials and epitaphs of Troopers long gone gouged into its knurled surface. There were no bathrooms at the *Personnel Camaraderie Center for Recreation*, its designers felt their inclusion would only encourage mischief and casual hookups. As always though, Troopers made do with what they had, so the five dark corners were best avoided.

"Second round, coming in," Terrance said, expertly balancing the tray of drinks as he swung a leg over his stool at the round steel table. He set the tray on the tabletop, spinning it around to align the four glasses with their owners. "Bourbon for Levi, cider for Bernie, brown ale for Ishii..."

"Cheers, mate," Ishii said, downing the last of her previous pint.

"And gin for the win," he concluded, taking the last glass for himself. He took a sip of the tall-rimmed tumbler, savoring the piney freshness that washed over his tongue. It had taken him a long time to learn to like the taste of juniper—his father had always said gin was the 'drink of choice for the working-class gentleman.' He raised the glass to his father's spirit; it'd been nearly five years since the accident at the Hudson assembly plant. He took another sip before setting it back down, the bubbles from the tonic water fizzing gently on his tongue. Across the table, he noticed Bernard was still nursing his first bottle, the next two rounds stacked up in front of him like missiles on a launch pad.

"C'mon Bernie, catch up," said Terrance, reaching across the table to push the bottles closer. "I need you to embrace the process."

Bernard rolled his eyes but tipped the first bottle higher, finishing the last of the cider. He held the empty bottle over his head and put out his tongue, a few drops spilling onto his straight, black hair. "Better?"

"Much," grinned Terrance, swiping the empty bottle out of his hand and replacing it a full one. "There's four of us and we're allowed five drinks apiece. Republic school math says that comes out to just enough to get good and creative."

"We could've gone to a bar off-base," Levi suggested, chewing the ice cubes from her second glass of bourbon. "No limits with those."

"I'm not driving home thirty miles in a sandstorm," said Terrance, wagging his glass at the inspector. "And Ishii's got herself banned from the bars downtown after what happened last time."

"I was framed!" yelled Ishii, setting the empty pint glass down to join the other two. "'Ow was I suppose' to know she was the owner's wife?"

She let out a loud belch right in front of Bernard's face, patting her chest as he waved away the fetid cloud.

"Besides," Terrance said, ignoring as the burp wafted over him. "I've been stuck in this shithole for a year now, my tolerance is shot to hell. Five drinks is more than enough to get me goin.'"

"Lightweight," snickered Ishii, stepping up from the table to find a dark corner.

"Not all of us get drafted to the pro-leagues," Terrance called after her. He turned back to the other two. "Well, whatta we think? Any ideas yet?"

Levi and Bernard looked at each other before shaking their heads.

"Well, let's get a few more down then," Terrance said, shoving the third bottle into Bernard's other hand. "Do it for the sober Troopers on Karnassus!"

Bernard looked at the bottles in his hands with dismay before setting one back down. Terrance was crestfallen, it'd always worked in tech school.

"Fine," he said bitterly, scooping up his half-empty glass. "I guess *I'll* do all the heavy lifting."

Levi downed the last of her glass, ice cubes crunching thoughtfully as she looked around the bar. Her eyes settled on a table nestled in the back. Two Troopers sat around it, a reedy ginger and thick-necked blond, a palisade of empty bottles adorning the steel top.

"What's with them?" she asked, jerking a thumb behind her. "They the managers or something?"

Terrance and Bernard followed her thumb.

"Nah," said Terrance, turning back to his drink. "That's just Kantz and Huges."

Levi's focus sharpened. "Raiders?"

"Yup," Terrance answered, polishing off the gin-and-tonic. "They close the bar down almost every night."

"That's more than five," she said quietly, counting the bottles on the table.

"Sure is," carped Terrance, staring forlornly at the ice cubes tinkling at the bottom of his glass. "Must be nice to drink as much as you want, no limits."

"Excuse me," Levi said quickly, stepping up from the table. "I'll...I'll get the next round. It'll just be a bit before I get back."

He watched her stroll off to the bar, her eyes locked the whole time on the two Raiders in the back. Terrance turned back to Bernard, who was making a big show out of finishing his second bottle.

"Yeah, yeah," muttered Terrance, setting his own glass back down. "But your heart's not in it."

Sarah waited at the edge of the SimuWood bar, tapping her foot along with the music thumping out of the speakers suspended from the ceiling. A ruddy, heavy-set young Trooper was ahead of her in line, haggling with the bartender to get another drink.

"C'mon man," the Trooper whined, bracing himself up on the bar top. "Just one more round? We're headin' to Karnassus tomorrow night."

The bartended glared at him and shook his head, pushing the Trooper's hands off the bar as he wiped it with a dirty rag.

A broadly muscled Trooper with a shaved head and a crooked nose grabbed the young man by the shoulder and turned him around from the bar. "C'mon Reming, you had enough."

"This bar is bullshit," the Trooper muttered, allowing himself to be led away. Sarah could just make out a pink triangular scar on the back of the bigger Trooper's head, the tell-tale mark of recent micro-neurosurgery.

"ID, ma'am."

She turned back to the scowling barkeep.

"Hmm? Oh, right." She fished out her wallet, watching the bartender scan the back of her credentials to match the number of drinks left on her account.

"What'll it be?" he grumbled, handing the card back to her.

"Stepdad's Choice, double, on the rocks," she replied, looking over to the table in the rear. "And two more of whatever they're drinking."

She found Kantz and Huges deeply engrossed in a game of 'bloody knuckles' ignoring her as they pounded on each other's hands as she stood by the table. She cleared her throat to get the Commandos' attention.

"Join you, gents?" she asked, holding out two beer bottles as an offering. "I hate to drink alone."

"Sure, pretty lady," Kantz replied, graciously accepting the offered bottles. He passed one over to Huges, the bull-necked Trooper's mouth slightly agape. Attractive women rarely paraded themselves up to their table in the back.

"Thanks," Sarah said, pulling up a stool from a nearby table. "I hope I'm not intruding."

"Not as all," grinned Kantz, slurring a little as he tipped the fresh bottle to his lips. "We *like* to be intruded."

"Yeah," added Huges, raising his own bottle in cheers.

"Great," said Sarah, sipping at her bourbon. She flashed them both a warm smile. "I'm Sarah."

"Kantz, Huges," the reedy Trooper replied, jerking a shaky thumb between the two men. "Issa pleasure to meet you."

Sarah's smile widened. "So, what do you boys do?"

Huges opened his mouth to answer but hesitated. Kantz cut in ahead him.

"Raiders, ma'am," he said proudly, a dopey grin on his freckled face.

"*Really?*" Sarah purred, brown eyes sparkling in the dim light. "That sounds dangerous."

"Not really," Kantz shrugged, taking another swig from his beer. "Not when you're the best."

"Is that right?" she murmured back, keeping her face straight as she tipped up her glass. "It's not every day a girl meets *the best*. I guess I'm just lucky today."

Kantz just smiled wider, the dopey grin stretching ear to ear. Huges frowned from across the table, still unsure what to make of the newcomer.

"What brings you here?" he asked, heavy brow furrowing. "Passin' through?"

"Sure enough," Sarah said brightly. "I like meeting new people."

"Whatta coincidence?" Kantz exclaimed, clapping Huges on a meaty shoulder. "Uss too!"

The big Trooper merely grunted, suspicion deepening on his face. Sarah pretended not to notice.

"Anyway," she said, playfully swirling the ice in her drink. "Where are you boys from?"

Huges kept silent, staring her down over the lip of his bottle. Kantz showed no such restraint, gleefully jumping in again to answer for them both.

"Denver! Huges's from Tamarin," he announced proudly. "You?"

"Chicago," she lied quickly. No use wasting the truth on them.

"Chicago!" Kantz exclaimed, clapping a hand to his forehead. "Just like Wurley! God, I miss that guy. Now *there'ss* a man that could party."

Sarah watched Huges tense at the mention of the name.

"Him too?" she asked innocently enough, keeping her eyes focused nonchalantly on her glass. "Where at in Chicago?"

Kantz opened his mouth to answer, but the big Trooper cut him off.

"Nowhere," Huges grunted, the bottle held tight in his hands. "He doesn't know what he's saying."

Kantz shot him a look of glassy-eyed bewilderment. "Yess I do. Wurley, you 'member. Skinny guy? Took beers down like water?"

"No, I *don't*," growled Huges, veins standing out in the hand that gripped the bottle.

"Yess, you *do*," argued Kantz, coated in the obliviating cloud of cheap beer. "'E was with us for nine months!"

"No," Huges snapped, slamming a heavy fist on the table. "He *wasn't*. Now shut the fuck up!"

Kantz lapsed into stunned silence, blurry eyes blinking in confusion at his partner. The big Commando looked across the table to Sarah, who was making herself as inconspicuous as possible behind her glass.

"Now, I think we should go," Huges barked at Kantz, grabbing him by the arm and yanking him up from the table. "You've had enough."

Kantz looked down at his half-finished bottle. "But..."

"We're done here," snarled Huges. He tipped two fingers in Sarah's direction. "Thanks for the beer, ma'am. Ignore my friend, he doesn't know when to quit."

Sarah said nothing, watching the two men stumble for the door. She turned back to her previous table, catching the eyes of Bernard and Torres. Bernard raised an eyebrow in the direction of the receding Troopers while Torres mouthed 'What the fuck?' Sarah shrugged, gathering her glass as she headed back over. She wasn't sure who this Wurley guy was, but she had a feeling in her gut that finding him would be their next break.

Ernst Kantz awoke in his darkened room, the sounds of the sandstorm raging outside. He was about to settle back down to sleep when he thought he saw movement from a blurry shape in the corner of the room. He squinted through the darkness.

"Lights, on," he slurred, the lamp by his bedside flickering to life. He rubbed his bleary eyes, focusing his vision as the blurry shape resolved itself into the form of Sergeant Harbison. His thoughts turned slowly as he watched the Reed-Sergeant walk to the foot of the bed, resolving themselves in a flash as the pieces fit together.

"Shit, Sarge, I'm sorry," he stammered, pushing himself upright. "I fucked up. I didn't mean to talk 'bout him. I promise."

The Reed-Sergeant's face was grim and solemn, the drawn lines of his face deepening in the shadows cast by the small lamp.

"I know, son," he said quietly, approaching Kantz's side of the bed. "But you said too much. You put the unit at risk."

Kantz's eyes closed slowly, resolving himself to what was coming.

"Will it hurt?" he whispered, opening his eyes and focusing them on the stoic face of Sergeant Harbison.

"No, son, I'll make sure of that," the Reed-Sergeant said, looking down on him. A heaviness seemed to settle on the Sergeant's shoulders, and for the first time, Kantz saw the weight and wear that sixteen years of service had left on him. Kantz turned away towards to the foot of the bed, looking away from the grim NCO.

"Good," he mumbled, closing his eyes once again. "I never liked pain."

Chapter 18:

Three NCOs tapped away in the quiet hours before sunset, the soft whirrs and pops of their respective tablets echoing faintly in the dingy room. Each sat hunched over, their face a mask of concentration as they scanned and scrolled through databases, rosters, and personnel files. The soft hush of their busywork was broken only once, when Sergeant Torres stood up from his chair, twisted around, and cracked his back in three different places. He let out a satisfied groan, rolled his shoulders to stretch out the kinks, and then settled back down to continue his search. Another hour passed as they worked, the stiffness and aches setting in once more. This time, it was Levi who broke the silence, grumbling as she stood up from her articulated luggage stand.

"Alright, gents, status report," she barked, rubbing the strain out of her eyes. "Find anything yet?"

"Nothing in the unit rosters," Ian said, setting the tablet down on the desk. He looked over to Sergeant Torres. "You?"

Sergeant Torres shook his head. "Nada in the immigration orders."

"And nothing in the galactic network," Levi added, twisting her head to crack her neck. She frowned as she rolled her head from side to side. "Which means Wurley is either a ghost or he never existed the first place."

Ian shrugged. "Maybe he isn't ICF?"

"No," Levi said, brow furrowing as she picked up the tablet again. "Kantz said he was with them for nine months. They wouldn't have a non-Raider attached to their unit for that long. He has to be ICF, I just don't know why we can't find him."

"If Kantz knew him, why don't we ask him?" Torres said, rubbing his chin. "Go right to the source?"

"That's not a bad idea," Levi said, looked up from the tablet. She checked her watch, still plenty of time before their shift at the port. "Wait here, I'll run over and see what I can find."

She grabbed her jacket and her boots, throwing both on as she rushed to the door.

"We could come, too, you know," Torres offered, as a blast of heat rolled over them from the outside. "Might even be helpful?"

The door shut behind her, leaving the two Buck-Sergeants in silence once again. Sergeant Torres turned back to Ian.

"You know, I get the feeling she doesn't trust us talkin' to people."

It's not about trust, Sarah thought, as the LITCAT lurched along the gravel road. She knew that they were eager to help, but if she was to have any hope of clearing their name at the end of this, she needed every appearance of impartiality when she submitted her report. *I can't have them coming out to interview subjects with me, not this close to the deadline.* The LITCAT rumbled along the winding road to the Raiders' compound, the soft ting of gravel on its underside just loud enough to drown out the bagpipes burbling from the cabin speakers.

The corrugated tan walls of the compound rose in view before her. She slowed on the gas as she drifted forward, mentally rehearsing the arguments she'd need to get herself inside. She coasted up to the imposing black gate, surprised to find it already open. Cautiously, she crept through, half-expecting it to slam shut at any moment.

As she drove through to the tri-level dorms, she could just make out a flash of red and blue lights by the great rhombic structures. Her brow wrinkled as she put the truck in park, stepping out of the cab and onto the sandy soil. She walked over to the first dorm, spotting the tell-tale white and blue cruisers of the ICF Military Police. A thin line of yellow poly-synthetic tape stretched from the corners of the cruiser across the outer door of one of the rooms. A short, squat Trooper leaned on the hood of the cruiser, the tan gun belt and blue bandolier across his chest marking him as a patrol officer in the MP. She stepped quickly to the Trooper, flashing her credentials and introducing herself.

"What happened?" she asked, scanning around the taped off scene. The door to the room hung loosely on its hinges, a sandy boot-print on the spot where the responding officers had kicked it in.

"OD," the MP said, scratching at the stubble on his chin. "We got the call when he didn't show up for his mission brief."

Sarah's brow wrinkled further. "Overdose? On what?"

"*Glib*, what else?" the officer shrugged, taking a pull from a travel mug of SimuCaff. "Coroner is wrapping up the body, so we'll be able to pull out of here soon. They're searching for a note to rule out a suicide, but I guess this guy liked to party."

Sarah's mouth went dry. "What was the victim's name?"

"Uh, let me check," the officer said, setting down the mug to pull out his tablet. He scrolled back through his notes. "Ah, here it is, Kantz, Special-Trooper."

Fuck. Sarah turned back to the truck, trying to remember if she'd left her evidence bag in the second seat. *What are the odds he'd OD just after letting something slip?* She knew she needed to get access to that scene before Harbison or the other Raiders came in and mucked it up. She had just taken her first step back to the truck when she heard an arrogant, sanctimonious voice behind her.

"Absolutely not! Have you no *shame?!*" Major Hudson shouted, waving his hands as he strode out of the dorm room, Sergeant Harbison and the Medical Examiner following close behind. He glared at the MP leaning against the cruiser. "Who let her in here?"

The cop shrugged, returning his attention to the travel mug perched on the hood.

Sarah turned to face the Major as he ducked beneath the line of yellow tape. His swept-blond hair bounced in the dry breeze, square-cut jaw clenched in fury.

"The gate was open," she said coolly, looking around the furious officer to the dorm behind him. "I had a meeting with Special-Trooper Kantz."

"Clearly, it is canceled," the Major declared, jabbing an accusing finger at her chest. "As is your continued harassment of my men! There are limits to your office, *Sergeant*, limits you clearly need to be reminded of!"

"I have an investigation to conduct," she said stubbornly, planting her heels in the soft sand.

"For one more day!" he warned, storming off towards the command building. "And we'll see about *that* when I get off the phone with Colonel Pickelhaube!"

She watched him disappear around the corner of a dorm, shouts of 'duty' and 'upstart impertinence' ringing off the tan walls. Sarah sighed, turning back to her truck. As she climbed inside the cab, she paused for a moment on the running board, catching a last glimpse of the crime scene before her. Her eyes shifted down and she caught sight of Sergeant Harbison standing by the door to Kantz's room, staring at her. They locked eyes for a moment, a curious expression on his gaunt face, before he saluted her with two fingers to his temple. Then he stepped back through the doorway and disappeared inside the dorm.

Ian and Torres stared each other down from both sides of the neatly made bed, their tablets held like playing cards in front of their faces.

"Bolts," Torres hissed, swiping across the tablet, casting his card across the network onto Ian's tablet.

"Bust!" crowed Ian, swiping his own card in return. A pair of fireworks erupted on his screen while 'Taps' began to play from the speakers on Sergeant Torres' tablet.

"Fuckin-a," griped Torres, tossing it down on the bed. "Four in a row? You're cheating."

"Nice try," laughed Ian, standing up from his chair. "But you'll need evidence."

Ian ignored the jealous glare of the other Buck-Sergeant, bowing to him as he soaked in the glorious joy of victory.

They both looked over as the door swung open. Inspector Levi stormed into the room, slamming the door behind her as she walked straight past them and over to the articulated luggage rack. She ripped open the middle suitcase, ignoring them both as she pawed through its contents.

"Let me guess," Torres said dryly. "You didn't find Wurley."

"Noooope," Levi said, dropping the middle suitcase in favor of rummaging through the smallest one. "And Kantz is dead."

Ian's brows arched in concern. "Dead? How?"

"OD'd," she called behind her, bending over to dig further into the trunk. "Or maybe not. Probably murdered, probably by Harbison. But good luck sticking *that* to him."

She paused in her digging, looking back at them questioningly. "Shouldn't you be at work by now?"

"Sandstorm was heavier that we thought," Torres said picking his tablet off the bed. "Port's still shut down while they clean the sand off the launch pad."

"Ah," Sarah nodded, returning to her search. A few moments passed before she cried out 'Ah-ha!' and pulled the bottle of bourbon free from its constraints at the bottom of the suitcase. She fished around further, looking for her tumbler glass before giving up with a sigh of disgust. She pulled the cork out with her teeth, taking a long drag straight from the bottle. She strolled back to the neatly made bed, plopping down between the staring Buck-Sergeants.

"What?" she asked, finally lowering the bottle. "It's my reserve selection. I only break it out when I close a case." She took another long drink from the bottle, letting out a satisfied gasp when she was done. "Or when life kicks me right in the tits."

The shocked expression widened on Ian's face. Torres, in contrast, seemed to take it all in stride.

"Well, I hope you brought enough to share," he said, reaching a hand out for the bottle.

Levi grinned and passed it over. "Certainly, my good sir."

Sergeant Torres took an equally long swig, belching when he'd finished and offering it over to Ian. Ian shook his head. Torres shrugged, taking another drink before passing it back to Levi's eager hands.

"So, *now* we're done?" Ian asked, folding his arms as he watched the others drink. "No more leads? Nothing left to search through or dig up?"

"Nope, nothing left," Levi said, handing the bottle to Torres. "They fucked us good, gents. But at least we got fucked by the best."

"Cheers to that," Torres chuckled, raising the bottle to the others.

Ian remained unconvinced. *There has to be something else. Focus, Ian, find something small you can work with.* Just then, a chirp sounded from the tablet in his pocket.

"Oh!" he exclaimed, reading the message on the screen. "It's Sue. She translated the message from the crate."

Levi and Torres looked at each other, blinking for a moment before recognition set in.

"Oh, *fuck!*" Torres blurted. *"Call her!"*

"Get her on screen!" Levi cried.

"Alright, alright," Ian said, messaging Suzette to get ready for a vidchat. The three Sergeants scrambled over, anxiously connecting the tablet to the projection screen by the wall. A soft whirring filled the room as they waited for the call to connect. Then there was the sound of a bubble being popped, and Suzette's smiling, tired face filling the screen. Ian felt a smile creep over him.

"Sorry for the mess," Suzette said, gesturing to the toys scattered about the room behind her. "Taniel's been on a rampage all day." She was interrupted by the sound of furious barking from the other room. Suzette leaned away from the screen to yell down the hall. "Douglas, quiet! I'm on the phone!"

The barking continued undeterred. Suzette groaned, setting the tablet down as she stood up. "Sorry folks, I'll be right back."

Levi leaned in to whisper in Torres' ear.

"The kid's name is *Taniel?*"

"The *dog's* name is Douglas?" he whispered back.

Suzette appeared back on screen, her hair disheveled from wrangling toddler away from dog and dog away from window overlooking the mailbox.

"Sorry again," she said. "Didn't mean to keep you waiting."

Ian beamed at her through the screen. "No worries, Sue. What did you find?"

Suzette took in a deep breath, puffing out her cheeks as she blew an errant strand of hair back into place. "Well, I want to caveat this by saying that Indo-Aryan languages are not my specialty, but I had help from a colleague in the Archaeology department, and she was pretty sure we got the syntax correct."

The three NCOs nodded along, so far so good.

"I also want to say that the sample you sent me was a little irregular," she continued. "I'm not sure where you saw it, but my colleague and I both agree that it's not an original use of the language. The letters are a little shaky and the spacing is bunched where it shouldn't be. Based on the script style and the choppy wording, we definitely agree that it's a modern writer, maybe even a student. Someone who's learning Sanskrit, but definitely hasn't mastered it."

Ian smiled broadly, not quite sure how to use that information, but encouraging her to carry on. "But you were able to translate it okay?"

"Well, yes," she said, waffling a bit. "We were able to put together a translation. Again, I feel the need to point out that this is rough wording, but we think it closely matches the author's intent."

"Great," said Levi, anticipation naked on her face. "So what's it say?"

Suzette's face scrunched a little, head bobbling a bit as she weighed the best way to deliver the message. "It says—and again this is a *loose* translation. We believe it says, 'Chew penis, Pirates.'"

Levi's face fell. "What?"

Ian blinked in confusion. "Are you sure Sue? This is really important."

Suzette's face scrunched further as she nodded, she knew this wasn't what they wanted to hear. "I'm afraid so, the wording was imprecise, but distinct; 'Chew penis, Pirates.' We think there may be something lost in the idiomatic translation, it might more closely be described as saying—

"'Eat a dick, Raiders!'" Torres interrupted, speaking up from the far side of the screen.

"Well, yes," Suzette said lamely. "That's probably the intended message."

"Oh, that's *rich*," Torres said, breaking down into laughter as he walked away from the screen. "That's just too fuckin' *good*. That's the fuckin' cherry on the top of this shit sundae. 'Eat a dick, Raiders,' ha! Classic 'Dirt Star' bullshit."

They heard him cackling all the way to the bathroom, slamming the door behind him loud enough to make them jump.

"I'm sorry dear," Suzette apologized again. "I know you were hoping for something more."

"It's okay, Sue," Ian said, the smile fading a little on his face. "We appreciate the help anyway."

He looked back at Levi, but she had already shuffled off in disgust, snagging the whiskey bottle as she made her way to slump beside the bathroom door. Ian turned back to the screen, mustering up the best smile he could. "Thanks again. We...need to talk this over. I'll call you later when I'm in my room."

"Promise?"

"I promise," he said, tapping the screen to end the call. As Suzette's face faded to black, he groaned and stood up, dragging his feet as he joined Levi in her spot by the bathroom door. She held out the bottle of bourbon. He began to shake his head no but thought better of it. He raised the bottle to his lips, the smoky liquor burning his throat the whole way down. Handing back the bottle, he grimaced a little but succeeded in suppressing the urge to cough. Levi nodded approvingly, taking another sip from the bottle.

"You know," Ian said softly, choking down another drink. He wiped his mouth on the back of his hand. "I never thought it would end like this."

"Never thought your career would detonate in a fiery shitstorm because of a fuckstick and a fucking crate?" Torres said through the bathroom door.

"No," Ian said, shaking his head as he handed the bottle over to Levi. "I mean this case. When we started, all I wanted to do was get myself off the hook...and Torres too, I suppose."

"Thanks, buddy," Torres snarked through the door.

"Of course," Ian replied, a half smile creeping over his face. "But I mean it, all I was looking for at the start was to get us out of as much trouble as we could. But then...then we found the *Glib*, then the crate, then we talked to Bonsly, and then we tracked down the deep-jets. The more we went along, the bigger it all seemed. It all seemed so much more important. We weren't solving the case just to cover our asses; we were doing it because there's something seriously wrong inside the Raiders. Something ugly and corrupt—and it was our duty to find it and cut it out. It felt...*right*, working this case. Like it was a real calling for the three of us." He leaned his head back against the wall, staring straight ahead across the dingy dorm room. "That's why I didn't think it would end like this. I thought because we were right, we would win. No matter what."

The room lapsed into silence. A touched expression came over Levi's face as she handed him the bottle. He took a grateful swig and passed it back again, his face twisting as the fiery burn reached his stomach.

"I know that feeling," she said quietly, staring down at the bottle in her hands. "That's why I joined the ICF. It's why I became an investigator. To find out why bad things happen and stop them from happening again."

There was a flush from the other room. The bathroom door opened, and Torres strolled out, plopping down against the bed opposite the other two.

"That's nice, nobler than me, at any rate," Ian said, running a hand through his hair. "I was fresh out of high school. Young, scared, in love. ICF seemed like a sure thing, a career that would take care of me and the family." The half smile turned a little bitter on the ends. "Guess I should start looking at the job boards again."

"What about you?" Levi asked, handing the bottle to Sergeant Torres. "What got you to sign the dotted line?"

He took a long drink, holding his finger up to stall for time.

"Had to make some things right in my life," he said finally, passing the bottle back. He and Levi shared a knowing look. She nodded once and accepted the bottle from his outstretched hands.

"So how come you're not MP?" Torres asked, changing the subject from himself. "You seem halfway smart enough, why not be a real cop? Or OI?"

Levi blew a note on the rim of the bottle. "Never tried. Didn't have the right mentality, I guess."

This was not true. Reed-Sergeant Sarah Levi *had* tried out for the both the Military Police and the Office of Insight, spurred on by the encouragement of a commander ecstatic over the excellent work she'd put in for years in the ISC. She'd easily passed the written test, made short work of the panel interview, and ran circles around the physical aptitude battery. Her only failing had been in the background check, when it had been discovered that she had sought out and received treatment for depression. It didn't matter that she'd pursued the treatment years earlier, shortly after a messy divorce. Nor did it matter that she had only done so at the behest of her commander, the same one that would later encourage her to apply for a transfer. Both the MP and especially the OI had strict guidelines with respect to the mental stability of their officers—guidelines they amended for no one.

Levi took another long drink, the bottle now half empty between the efforts of the three Sergeants. She offered it back to Ian, who politely declined.

"No more," he said, shaking his head. "I don't know how you two do it. It's awful."

"The key is to hate yourself more than you hate the taste," Torres said, snagging the bottle from Levi's hands. He took a long draught before handing it back. "How did you get that in here anyway?"

"What do you mean?" asked Levi, corking the bottle and throwing on top of the nearest red suitcase.

"I was wondering that myself," Ian said, turning back to her. "Those customs officials were brutal."

Levi shrugged. "Guess they didn't look too closely. Seems to be a lot of that going around."

"I dunno," said Ian, leaning his head back against the wall. "They were thorough when *I* came in. Digging through everyone's bags, taking copies of everyone's orders. I saw them make a lady throw away her gaming dice."

"Gaming dice?" Torres grunted. "Like that nerd shit 'D-n-D'?"

"Yeah," Ian laughed. "They must have figured she'd use it for gambling."

The two Buck-Sergeants shared a laugh. Levi was strangely silent, her brow furrowed as she stared at Ian.

"What was that you said?" she asked quickly. "About taking people's orders?"

"Oh, yeah," Ian laughed. "They grabbed copies of everyone assigned here. I guess they didn't trust the ICF systems or something."

Levi blinked at him, the wheels in her head spinning furiously.

She whipped around to Sergeant Torres. "Hey, do you still have that friend in the Customs and Immigration Cell?"

Torres groaned. "Johnson? *Why?*"

"Because I have another favor I want to ask him."

Chapter 19:

The lobby to the Ministry of Anian Customs was an exercise in garish pomposity. Flourished white columns lined the center, with mosaic archways stretched between. The ceiling was painted in powder blue, with hexagonal accents of gold leaf. The floor was a promenade of polished, white granite tile that led along the path between the columns to an enormous front desk capped with a slab of white marble. The thought that white marble might clash with white granite had never occurred to the lobby's designer. Clashing was a concern for those whose funding *didn't* stem from vast reserves of valuable minerals. The lobby exuded the kind of wealth that firmly believed the confines of 'good taste' were made for those of lower status.

Three Sergeants stood on the path between the flourished columns, feeling very small before them. In this way the ostentatious design of the lobby had its intended effect. It made them feel shabby and grubby before its opulent majesty, acutely aware of both the trail of dusty bootprints that led behind them on the granite tile, and that they had come to such a place to ask a second favor from people fresh off the failure of their first.

Ian coughed nervously into his hand. Had he known their meeting with Sergeant Johnson would lead immediately to meeting with the Anian ministry, he would have worn a cleaner uniform. And showered at least one more time before coming. Maybe twice for good measure. Disheveled though he felt, he was still the most put together of the three bedraggled NCOs. *And at least I don't smell like cheap whiskey.* He watched Sergeant Torres scratch his armpit and then sniff his fingers. Ian shifted a little where he stood, discovering to his dismay that his actions had left a scuff on the perfectly polished floor. Panicking, he dropped to a knee, furiously scrubbing the rubber mark with the sleeve of his uniform jacket.

"What are you *doing?*" Torres whispered, leaning over the young Buck-Sergeant.

"I left a mark," Ian whispered back, scrubbing harder.

Torres looked around the palatial hall.

"Well, stop it!" he hissed. "You're making a scene."

"Shut up!" Ian hissed back. "I'm fixing it!"

Torres caught the eye of the security guard by the entrance. He bent down to Ian's ear. "You're embarrassing us!"

Ian kept scrubbing. "*You're* embarrassing us!"

"Hopeless neurotic!"

"Screw you!"

"Screw *me?* Fuck *you!*"

"Both of you, *shut the fuck up!*" Levi interrupted, smacking each of them on the arm. "We don't have time for this!"

"Proceed!" announced the official from behind the great marble desk, his voice echoing across the hall. Ian got up quickly from the floor, straightening out his pants while the other two left him behind. They approached the wide lobby desk, each trying to recall the cultural details Sergeant Johnson had impressed upon them in the five-minute conversation they shared. *Appear humble, don't offer your hand to shake, and was it look them in the eye when they speak or DON'T look them in the eye?* Ian tripped a little over his own feet, bumping into Sergeant Torres' back. The ministry official frowned down on them from his tall chair behind the desk, the waxed ends of his thick mustache drooping to accentuate his low appraisal of his guests. His starched shoulder boards stood out from his gleaming white uniform, the gold braiding around his elbow telling the story of a career spanning years of leaning over desks and frowning at visitors.

"What is it you require?" the man asked obsequiously, mustache drooping further.

Ian's mouth dried to match the sands outside. He struggled to swallow humbly while both making and avoiding eye contact.

"We need to pull some records," Levi said quickly, remembering Sergeant Johnson's advice on answering questions as directly as possible. "A Trooper's immigration orders. Sometime in the last three years."

The official fixed his judicious eye on Sergeant Torres.

"You," he said, his voice rolling accusation and recognition into one convenient package. "You are the one that sent us to search the Raiders' ship."

Sergeant Torres nodded. "Yeah, that was me."

The official's mouth was a hard line. "They were very angry about that."

Torres crossed his arms across his chest. "Yeah, I heard they were."

The official stared him down. "They did not want us to search their ship. They yelled very much. Even to *me*."

His intonation of the last word made it very clear that those in his positions of his stature and importance were not accustomed to voices being raised in their vicinity, let alone their direction.

Sergeant Torres scratched the underside of his chin. "I heard they did that too."

The official's eyes narrowed, bearing down on the stocky Buck-Sergeant. "They were *very* angry about that."

Sergeant Torres stared straight back, lifting his chin. "I *heard*."

The ministry official's beady eyes shifted left and right, encompassing Levi and Ian in their indictment.

"Are these two, with *you?*"

Sergeant Torres nodded, veins standing out in his arms as he crossed them over his chest.

The ministry official returned his gaze to Torres. A few seconds of silence crawled by as they stared each other down before the official spoke again.

"Good," he said curtly, mustache curling up at the end. "You may follow me."

And with that he stepped down from the tall chair, winding his way around the marble desk and over to a door in the wall behind them.

"Come, come," the official said, opening the door and waving them on. "Records are this way."

Ian and Levi stared opened mouthed at Sergeant Torres, presently engaged in examining his fingernails. Inspector Levi shook her head, a small smile as she walked away to the door.

"How? Huh? *Why?*" Ian asked, agape as the Torres strolled past him.

"It's easy, little buddy," he said, brushing some dust off his shoulders. "You just have to remember who they hate more."

The Anian records room was surprisingly precise. A neat bank of storage towers lined the walls from floor to ceiling in the narrow room, red and blue lights glittering in their reflection on the granite floor. Sarah approached the nearest bank, reading the label stamped in metal on the wall. 'Seized Items' it read in block letters, '2215-Present.' The plaque on the next bank had a similar inscription for the previous twenty years. Sarah looked back at the ministry official, waiting with one hand still on the door.

"Immigration orders?" she asked, sweeping her hand around the room.

The official pointed to a row of banks in the far-right corner. Sarah walked over, followed by Bernard and Torres. The towers in these banks were arranged in yearly increments, in order to store the vast amount of records for every person traveling to and from Anius.

"We want immigration records from the last three years," she said quickly, pointing out the stack of towers. "I'll take 2332, Bernard, you take 2331, and Torres, you take 2330. We're looking for someone with a last name Wurley, there might be a few, so try to see what unit they were assigned to."

The two men nodded, sidling up the towers and plugging their tablets into the terminal. Sarah plugged hers in as well, syncing the tablet with the storage retrieval subsystems. She typed 'Wurley' into the search parameters. The device whirred and chirped in her hands, circuits flaring as it pored through millions of records. A loading bar appeared on screen, counting down the minutes as it made its slow journey to the right.

Five minutes passed in silence, the three Troopers bent over their tablets, the Anian minister maintaining his watch by the door.

The table in Torres' hand chimed. "Nothing."

Another chime from Sarah's tablet. "Me neither."

They both turned and looked at Sergeant Bernard, chewing on his lower lip as he watched the agonizing slowness of the bar's path across the screen. There was a chime, and then a small whoop from the young Sergeant.

"I got one!" he said, excitedly turning the screen for both of them to see. "Private Dobbins Wurley, assigned to Anius on 21 November 2331 as a member of the 4th Raider Group." He looked down and read the details on the screen. "It's funny, no emigration date. As far as this record shows, he's still assigned."

Sergeant Torres rubbed his chin. "Alright, so what's the catch? We found the record for some guy? So what? Are we gonna track him down in the next thirty-six hours?"

"No, we can't," said Sarah, taking the tablet from Bernard's hands. "Because according to the ICF, he doesn't exist."

Torres' brow furrowed. "Of course he does, we got his record right here."

"Harbison," Bernard said quietly, drawing their attention back to him. "He's the only one with the authority to do something like this. To erase someone entirely."

Sarah nodded. "Exactly, we needed something to show this case went beyond Sergeant Corstley, beyond a single delivery of *Glib*." She waved the tablet in the air. "This Private Wurley is our smoking gun. According to these orders, he was stationed on Anius less than a year ago, but now he's a ghost. Gone. Vanished. No Buck-Sergeant could do that by themselves. That takes someone bigger, with a lot more pull and connections. This is our link to Sergeant Harbison, to someone with the motivation and the means to make an ICF Trooper—a Raider no less—utterly disappear. We can take this to the MPs or OI, someone with the resources to pursue this deeper than we can and dig further into this whole tangled mess. *This*, gentlemen, is everything we needed."

"Big enough to pump the brakes on *our* case?" asked Torres.

"Trust me, gents," Sarah said, staring down at the record on the screen. "Your crate is the last of anyone's worries now."

Sarah was riding high all the way back to her dorm. Their trip to the Ministry had been quick, almost painless, and finding Private Wurley's record had been the final key to unlocking this winding and frustrated case. This incident was shaping up to be the second longest running investigation of her career, and easily the most frustrating. They needed this break; *she* needed this break. Sarah bounced a little in her steps as she made her way to the dented front door. She swiped her fob against the doorknob, listening for the grinding click as the door unlocked.

The lights were on as she pushed her way inside. Sarah stopped, frowning. She never left the lights on. She looked around the empty room and shook her head, *must've been Torres*. Stripping off her jacket as she walked in, she threw her keys on top of the alloy desk. She made it about three steps further in, fingers reaching behind her to close the door, when she felt it shut of its own accord. Sarah whipped around, heart thudding in her chest.

"You're back early," Sergeant Corstley said quietly.

Sarah sprinted for the door, throwing an elbow out as she passed him. Fingertips brushed the smooth metal of the knob, just curling around the handle, when he grabbed her by the waist. She felt her feet leave the ground.

He threw her.

Sarah twisted as she sailed through the air, bouncing off the far edge of the bed before the faded carpet rushed up to meet her. Her head snapped against the bedside table, a thunderclap erupting in her skull. The yellowed ceiling tilted over her, threatening to engulf her in a wall of black. She rolled over on her hands, tasting blood in her mouth where she'd bit the inside of her cheek.

But then he was on top of her.

Strong hands pushed her down, grinding her face against the carpet. She pushed back hard, tucking her knees underneath to give her leverage. *Get off the ground!* She pushed, the scuffed carpeting receding by inches. She pushed, until a meaty fist acquainted itself with her jaw.

Fireworks exploded in her head. Sarah tumbled to the right, rolling further from the bed. Her left eye was clouded. She blinked to clear it. She kipped up, crouching on the balls of her feet.

But then he was on her again.

His knee was in her chest, knocking her back. She hit the ground with a shallow '*whumph,*' the air vanishing from her lungs. She sucked and wheezed, fighting against the iron grips around her wrists. They struggled, as he leaned his full weight on her, forcing her deeper into the floor. She felt the hands release her wrists, only to reappear on her shoulders. He slammed her head against the ground. Once. Twice. And then her whole world was black.

No!

Sarah gasped as she came to, just moments after fading out. Corstley was still sitting on her chest, his knees shifted higher up, pinning her arms to the floor. She heard fabric ripping, then the pressure lifted off one arm. She tried to pull it back but he caught it with one hand, the other winding a strip torn from the bedsheet around her wrist. She twisted and wriggled, but he held her fast. Sarah watched as he tied a knot in the sheet around her right wrist, dragging it over and binding it to the other. He shifted his weight, the knee back on her chest. She watched a drop of sweat run off his nose and splatter on her cheek.

More ripping. More tying. He seemed to be making something, crafting while she fought underneath him. Sarah saw a length of sheet, coiled around and tied in a loop. The loop came down, he fumbled a bit as it caught around her ponytail. Sarah bucked her hips, trying to throw him off balance. She felt the noose tighten around her neck.

And then he was off her chest. Her hands were bound, but she pulled anyway, feeling a little give in the ripped fabric. She watched him push a ceiling tile up, throwing the other end of the bedsheet around the crossbeam. She wedged her fingers under the loop around her neck, working for inches. He pulled down on the other end of the bedsheet, and the noose tightened further as she was lifted into the air.

She fought against the makeshift rope, kicking out with her feet as she dangled. A strong hand caught her by the middle, the firm grip on her belt holding her in place. She kicked out again, connecting with something before he stepped off to the side. Another strong hand grabbed the cord around her wrist, pulling her hands down and fastening the knot to her beltloop.

"Easy, easy," Sergeant Corstley said.

She heard something drag across the carpet, then felt a chair being thrust beneath her feet. Sarah sucked in a breath as the noose loosened. Corstley pulled again on the length of bedsheet, raising her to the edges of her tiptoes as she fought to keep her perch on the chair.

"It wasn't supposed to be like this," Sergeant Corstley muttered, crouching as he tied the rope to the foot of the bed. "You were supposed to be left alone."

He sat back from the knot, tugging twice to check the tension on the line. Satisfied, he stood back up, facing Sarah as she stood on the chair.

"You just came back too early," he shrugged, then returned to the knot by the foot of the bed.

Sarah felt the rope pull higher, her toes just grazing the chair as she spun lazily at the end of the rope.

"Saw your chart there, by the way," he said, jerking a thumb back to the hierarchy outlined in cards and red string. "Real cute."

She saw him rifle through her luggage as she continued to spin. He pulled something out on her second time around, holding the bottle of *Stepdad's Choice* up to the light.

"Good taste," he said, sniffing the bottle. He set the bottle back down on top of the luggage, turning to continue his search of the room. He caught sight of something folded on the bedside table, seizing it in his stubby fingers and lifting it to the light. Sarah wriggled against the bedsheet around her neck, but that only made her spin quicker. He waved the letter for her to see.

"A 'Dear John' letter, huh? Didn't think women got those." Sergeant Corstley shrugged. "Guess that'll seem like reason enough."

He set the letter back down on the nightstand, unfolding it carefully so it would be in plain sight. She caught sight of him walking over again as she spun.

"Well, ma'am," he said with a sigh. "I suppose it's that time."

And he kicked the chair out from under her.

Sarah tensed as soon as the slack left the rope, the ripped sheet digging into her neck and choking her as she spun. *This can't be it!* But as the rope cut deeper, the edges of her vision began to tunnel. She bucked and kicked again, spinning around faster as she swung from the ceiling. *This CAN'T be it!* She kicked out one last time, despair clawing at her chest. Then, as she spun back and forth, she felt the tiniest shake in the crossbeam above.

"Hey, Levi, sorry to barge in like this," Torres called out, throwing open the scuffed door and walking inside. "But Bernard thinks he lost his tablet, is it okay if we check in here?"

Torres' mind adjusted to the scene before him. The bed a mess, covered in scraps of torn bedsheet. Sarah swinging in her noose, brown eyes wide as her face turned red. Sergeant Corstley by the alloy desk, rifling through its drawers.

"Oh, fuck," he said.

Corstley moved with a speed that belied his size. Torres ducked the right hook, tipping his shoulder and rolling to the side.

Bernard wasn't so lucky. Coming in right behind Torres, he stepped directly in the path of Sergeant Corstley's fist. He tasted blood and plaster as he spun around and hit the wall.

"Oh, *shit!*" Torres yelped, dancing back as Corstley turned to him. He retreated further, dodging jabs as the distance grew between the two Sergeants. He was just thinking he'd gotten the hang of it when a spinning back-kick sent him sprawling.

Sarah continued to kick out as she swung, floundering at the end of the rope. The jiggle in the crossbeam grew. She snaked her body up and down, fighting with her last ounce of breath.

Torres had just picked himself off the floor, rising up on shaking knees. A line of blood ran down from his split lip, his chin up and out.

"Try that again, motherfucker," he growled, raising his fists in front of his face. "I'll fuckin' *shave* you."

Sergeant Corstley smiled behind his beard. His front foot began to pivot while his back foot lifted off the ground. He had just begun to turn when Bernard's knee collided with his side. Bernard wrapped his arms around Corstley's head, carried higher than expected by the momentum from his jump. He jabbed a thumb in the Commando's eye, loosing a primal cry from the depths of his chest.

Sergeant Corstley cried out, yanking the thumb out of his eye. Torres heard the snap as it bent back, Bernard's shouting arcing higher into pain. Corstley shook him off, sending the young man careening into the side of the bed. The Raider turned back, just in time to see Torres' cross connecting with his good eye.

"Stay down, bitch," the Buck-Sergeant spat. He pulled Bernard to his feet with a free hand.

"Thanks, buddy," said Bernard, shaking the static out of his head.

"Of course."

There was a thunderous crack from across the room. They watched Sarah tumble to the ground as the crossbeam split by the moldy spot on the bathroom wall. A second sound drew their attention behind them, just as the chair swung into their backs.

Bernard hit the ground. Torres hit Bernard. The two men tried rolling in opposite directions, tangling themselves in a jumble of limbs. Sergeant Corstley stood over them, spinning a splintered chair leg in his hands. One eye was swollen and bloodshot, the other filled with pure hate. Bernard shut his eyes, expecting his world to end with the sound of alloy hitting bone.

He opened them to the sound of crashing glass.

Sergeant Corstley dropped to his knees, his eyes rolling back as he fell forward. Blood rushed from the cuts spiderwebbing the back of his head. Bernard looked up to see Sarah standing over him, the jagged neck of a bourbon bottle clenched in her bound hands. She looked down at the three Buck-Sergeants, then back to the bottle.

"Shame," she said, and tossed it aside.

Chapter 20:

Ian watched Sergeant Corstley attempt to scratch his nose, his hands cuffed at the wrists to the high-backed chair in the interrogation room. The chain linking his cuffs to the chair stopped short, forcing the Buck-Sergeant to lean forward. It felt odd, seeing him struggle to reach his own face. It was too human a moment for someone who'd tried killing him only hours before.

Ian crossed his arms, careful of his thumb cemented under layers of StimWrap. The nanotech embedded in the cloth worked wonders to speed up the healing process, knitting bones in a few days, but the itch was nearly unbearable. Ian resisted the urge to scratch, shifting his attention to the one-way poly-plex separating the two men. He'd been told by the MPs that he was invisible to the other side, the plastiform window textured and painted to blend in seamlessly with the grey walls of the interrogation room. Ian watched the Raider shifting in his seat, searching for a comfortable spot on the bare metal.

Ian heard the click of the door opening behind him. Levi joined him in the dark viewing room, looking decidedly fresher than when he'd seen her at the hospital. As usual, her hair was pulled straight back, a layer of light concealer obscuring the mottled bruising under her left eye. There was more concealer on her collar, rubbed off in patches from the layers covering her neck. Her wrists were red and raw, a few stitches on her hands from the broken glass.

"How's your neck?" he asked, eyes full of concern.

"Fine," she lied, forcing a smile. "How's the thumb?"

"Itches," he shrugged, looking down at his hand. "But the wrap comes off Friday."

Her smile a little less forced. "Good."

"I saw Bradshaw at the hospital."

"You did? How is he?"

"Better, recovering, but there's still a long way to go." Ian's voice sank to match his gaze. "They're saying he'll need a permanent Stim-Brace for his back, so he'll be on light duties only from here on out."

"There's far worse things than light duty." Levi tried a comforting smile. "Not getting medically discharged is good. At least he gets to stay in."

Ian nodded. "He's still in the ICF. For now."

A quiet pause stretched between them, broken by the click of the door.

"Sorry I'm late," Torres said, sweating a little, his undershirt hanging out from beneath his wrinkled uniform jacket. "I lost half my body-weight taking a shit."

Ian rolled his eyes. *What do you expect from slapping on three Stips at once?*

"How's our boy?" Torres asked, tucking the edges of his undershirt in with one hand. "He pullin' the lawyer card yet?"

"He did," Levi answered, turning back to the poly-plex window. "But it won't matter. Between the attempted murder and the drugs, he's looking at thirty years to life, Republic Max Prison."

"What about Harbison and the others?" Ian asked, watching Sergeant Corstley tap against the arms of the chair.

"I took Private Wurley's file straight to Colonel Pickelhaube this morning," Levi said, recalling the look of shock on the Lieutenant Colonel's face when she barged into his office. "It took me a bit, but I explained what we found and walked him through what it meant."

Levi smiled a little at the thought. She'd purposefully gone in straight from the hospital, bruises fresh and vivid against her pale skin. Colonel Pickelhaube had been shaken by both her appearance and the file. She'd seen him pale as she spoke to its significance, growing even whiter when she added that the investigation into Wurley's disappearance might even necessitate a trial before the Small Council. Their finding, she explained, had the potential to impact the entire Raider mission on Anius. The Lieutenant Colonel had sat silent for a few minutes when she'd finished. When he spoke again, he thanked her for the diligence and effort she'd put forth in discovering the file. He'd smiled at her as he praised her discretion. He then requested all documentation of the evidence she'd found related to Private Wurley, citing concerns over its possible leak if she kept it on an unclassified system. He thanked her again for the bravery she'd shown in bringing this to his attention and assured her that he would speak with OI that evening to pursue the investigation further.

"So, *this* is it then?" Ian asked, accidentally bumping his thumb as he re-crossed his arms. "We've finally got them?"

Levi nodded. "It'll take a few years to get through Corstley's trial, and I have no idea how long OI will take with the investigation into Harbison and the other Raiders, but yeah, we got them."

They watched an MP enter the interrogation room, advising the Buck-Sergeant that his counsel was in the building.

"Be nice if he just confessed," Torres grunted, stroking his chin. "Speed this whole thing up. Just like the vidplays."

"Major Hudson would never allow it," Levi said, raising her hand unconsciously to rub her neck. She stopped half-way when she caught herself, clearing her throat to cover the movement. "Knowing him, they're going to drag this out as long as they can."

The MP left, leaving Corstley alone on the other side of the glass. There was a knock at the door, the three Sergeants turning as the MP poked his head in the dark observation room.

"Sorry folks, but I can't have you listening in when he talks to counsel." The young officer fixed an eye on Levi. "I'll grab you, ma'am, when we're ready to confer charges."

Ian shifted where he stood. "Where does that leave us?"

The MP looked back at Levi. "They with you?"

The inspector nodded, a small smile on her face.

"Alright then," the MP shrugged. "I'll grab you too."

The waiting room to the Military Police Precinct was sparsely furnished, just a half-dozen chairs surrounded by three green walls and a half-painted fourth. Sergeant Torres spun idly in his chair, kicking around from edge to edge with one foot. Sergeant Bernard stood in the corner, too anxious to sit. Sarah watched him cross and re-cross his arms, rocking back and forth on the balls of his feet. Minutes stretched by in the empty room, the quiet broken occasionally by the exaggerated yawns of Sergeant Torres.

A knock at the door drew their attention as the young MP from before poked his head in.

"Inspector, and, uh, assistants," he said, locking eyes with Sarah before remembering the others in the room. "He just finished up with counsel. They're ready for you."

Sarah nodded, following the MP down the hall to the observation room. She and the two Buck-Sergeants took up their spots in the small dark room, angling themselves to get the best view of the proceedings on the other side of the window. The interrogation room looked smaller than before. A burnished table and three more chairs had been brought in, filling the edges of the space. Two MPs sat on one side, fiddling with the camera mount on their tablet. On the other sat Major Hudson and Sergeant Corstley, the latter's hands still cuffed to the edges of the bare seat. Behind him stood Sergeant Harbison, utterly still save for the constant darting of his grey eyes.

"Are we ready?" asked Major Hudson, blond curl bouncing a little as he spoke. "My client is ready to respond to the charges."

The MPs finished checking the feed on their screen, turning back to the Major and nodding.

"Alright," the first MP said to Sergeant Corstley. "State your name, occupation, and unit for the camera."

Sarah watched Corstley hesitate, fingers flexing as he gripped the edge of the burnished table. Sergeant Harbison placed a hand on the Buck-Sergeant's shoulder, giving the bearded man a reassuring squeeze. Corstley nodded, and the hand released, the Reed-Sergeant turning then to head out the door. Sarah heard the click of the door through the poly-plex window, her eyes fixated on the man in chains. She saw him suck in a deep breath, leaning forward over the table.

"Buck-Sergeant Hermes Corstley, Platoon Sergeant, 4th Commando Raider Group," he said, looking directly into the camera. "And I wish to confess to all charges."

Sarah's jaw dropped through the floor.

"I organized the delivery and sales of a banned substance," the Buck-Sergeant continued, beard shaking a little as he spoke. "I conspired to smuggle illicit substances through ICF shipping ports. I coordinated with local dealers to distribute said products. I contributed to the delinquency of ICF personnel and knowingly created a criminal enterprise for self-enrichment."

"*What the fuck?*" Torres muttered behind her.

"Why's he talking like that?" Bernard whispered back. "That doesn't sound like Corstley at all."

Sarah opened her mouth to answer, but no words came out. She was too engrossed in the scene on the other side of the window.

"After becoming aware of an investigation into said enterprise," Sergeant added, "I conspired to interfere with the actions of that investigation. I gained unlawful access to another's residence, assaulted an investigating officer and two others..."

"Assaulted?" grumbled Torres. "He tried to fuckin' *murder* us."

Sarah shushed him. Back in the interrogation room, Sergeant Corstley was finishing his speech, renouncing his right to trial in exchange for the acceptance of his guilt in all charges. Sarah watched numbly as the Major spoke, hashing out the terms of the plea agreement: forfeiture of ICF rank and benefits, surrendering of monetary assets gained in the course of the illicit enterprise, and twenty-two years of service in Republic Max Prison.

"What the fuck?" Torres muttered again. He turned to face Sarah. "I thought you said he wouldn't confess."

"That's because he didn't," Sarah snapped, running out the door and down the hall. "Those aren't *his* words."

She caught Sergeant Harbison walking down the stairs to the first floor. Her knuckles were white as she gripped the railing, staring down at him from the top of the landing. The Reed-Sergeant stopped, alerted to her presence by the scuff of boots on the tile.

"Inspector Levi," he said quietly, turning back to face her. "So good to finally meet you."

Enough fucking games.

"Do you honestly expect that farce in there to hold up?" she demanded, leveling an accusing finger at him. "An entire smuggling and distribution operation consisting of *one* man?"

Sergeant Harbison's face was impassive, the lines around his mouth were drawn and still. He studied her in silence, grey eyes boring into hers.

"You're used to winning," he said after a moment. "I can appreciate that. But you need to learn to accept the victories you have."

And with that he turned away, heading back down the stairs. Sarah stood stiff on the landing, her shoulders shaking with rage.

"This isn't over!" she called down to him. "I'm going to keep digging."

He paused on the last step. She couldn't see his expression, but she thought she heard a soft sigh.

"Of course, inspector," he said, continuing on his way. "I'd expect nothing less."

Colonel Schwarz loomed over the young Buck-Sergeant, frowning down at him with his thumbs hooked in his belt. He was halfway to Earth when the got the call, during a layover on Tamarin. He liked to think he'd heard just about everything in his eighteen years of service, but the call that came through the LinkNet on his tablet was beyond the pale. It had taken every ounce of the discipline instilled in him over his decade in command not to just leave, abandoning the proceedings to his second in command. Instead, he ordered a deep-jet run back to Anius. He didn't say a word to anyone as he boarded, taking his seat and strapping into the nylon harnesses in complete silence, a fresh tablet in his pocket after he'd smashed the first against a wall.

Raiders, smuggling, and an assault on one of *his* investigators; it was almost beyond the imagination. Colonel Schwarz stared down at the Buck-Sergeant before him, the corners of his mouth drawing lower the longer he stared. He was used to wielding discipline, bestowing it on hundreds of Troopers over the years. He had never seen a case like this. And so he frowned.

"So," the Colonel began, his voice soft and low. "An investigation disclosed that while performing your duties, you ignored the guidelines in ICFOI 2397-42B directing your use of safety cables during mechlift operations."

Sergeant Bernard did his best to hold absolutely still, staring straight ahead past the Colonel to the painting in the wall. He resisted the urge to scratch his thumb. It'd been almost a week since the cast came off, but it still itched with the phantom sensation of knitting bones.

"Yes, sir."

"The investigation further disclosed that you directed an unlicensed driver to utilize a mechlift during cargo retrieval operations, ultimately resulting in the severe injury of a subordinate Trooper when an unsecured crate slipped out of the grasp of the mechlift operated by the unlicensed Trooper."

"Yes, sir."

"Do you understand that under the circumstances, you face punishment under the military judicial system for failure to obey a lawful instruction and for negligence in executing leadership duties? The consequences for which may include reduction in rank, forfeiture of pay, and dishonorable discharge?"

"Yes, sir."

"Do you understand that your negligence jeopardized the safety of Troopers under my command, and the effectiveness of the supply mission conducted at my port?"

"Yes, sir."

"Did I not explain to you on your very first day, the criticality of the port's mission and the potential consequences for failing to maintain its operational capabilities to the fullest possible extent?"

"Yes, sir."

"What did I say the consequences would be?"

Sergeant Bernard's voice was quiet, but firm. "That you would burn me, sir. Worse than Private Silman."

Colonel Schwarz looked over the slim young man. The Colonel's brow wrinkled under the thick black hair, steeped under the weight of what was to come. Sergeant Bernard kept his eyes leveled on the painting ahead. Lieutenant Ligen and Reed-Sergeant Gherwiz stood behind him, silent against the back wall.

"Additionally," the Colonel continued, "it was disclosed that the investigation that began as a result of your negligence discovered evidence of a criminal conspiracy perpetrated by members of the 4th Commando Raiders Group. It was further disclosed in the report, that the evidence unearthed in this subsequent investigation could *not* have been found without the efforts of yourself and Buck-Sergeant Torres—that your actions in assisting this investigation were instrumental in the uncovering of a criminal smuggling conspiracy surrounding a trusted member of the Raider unit, and that your actions saved the life of the inspector involved in your own investigation as she was assaulted by that same member."

Sarah smiled from her spot along the back wall. She'd been playing to the Baron's soft spot with that last one.

Colonel Scharwz unhooked his thumbs from his belt, balancing the scales of justice in his outstretched hands.

"It therefore falls to me to weigh the actions you conducted on behalf of the investigation against the knowledge that the investigation was only necessary due to your negligence."

Sergeant Bernard stood in stoic silence, awaiting his punishment.

"Buck-Sergeant Bernard," the Colonel said, his voice a little louder as he rendered his judgement. "Effective immediately, I am reducing your pay by half for a duration of one year. I am documenting your incident within a formal letter of reprimand, to be included in your Primary Career File. Additionally, I am assigning you to serve an additional one hundred and eighty days in your position on Anius, to ensure that you have fully embraced the lessons of your mistakes and do not repeat them."

"Buck-Sergeant Torres," the Colonel pronounced, turning to the other Sergeant standing at attention by Bernard. "Though your actions in sustaining an operational culture of negligence did not cause injury, they very well could have. Based on the findings of this investigation, I see no reason you should not share in this punishment. I am assigning you an additional one hundred and eighty days of service as well. May you use them to reflect on the responsibilities of your position as loadmaster."

Colonel Schwarz bent down, eye level with the two Buck-Sergeants. "Do you understand?"

"Yes, sir!" Torres and Bernard said with one voice.

"Dismissed."

The two Sergeants snapped a quick salute, marching out the door with Sergeant Gherwiz and the Lieutenant behind them. Sarah made a move to follow them as well.

"Not so fast, inspector."

Sarah froze mid-step, pivoting back to face the Colonel.

"Yes, sir?" she asked, clasping her hands behind her back.

Colonel Schwarz frowned, disapproval dripping off his shoulders like rain off a roof. He had a soft spot for those in whom he saw reflections of himself. But good graces only carried someone so far, when they broke your trust.

"I asked you if your extenuating circumstances were criminal in nature, and I was assured that there was nothing occurring outside the jurisdiction of a *safety* investigation."

Sarah pursed her lips, thinking through her next words carefully.

"At the time, sir, that was an honest assessment of the case," she said slowly, her hands gripped tight behind her back.

"Do you mean to tell me," the Colonel asked, eyeing her carefully. "That you had no way of knowing the extent of this case when you asked me for an extension two weeks ago? Not a single, solitary clue?"

Sarah kept her face passive, mulling over her response. *If there was ever a time to press my luck, it's now.* She straightened, looking the Colonel in the eye as she answered. "Sir, two weeks ago I had no way of knowing I was about to solve the mystery of the persistent drug issues in your command *and* uncover the biggest scandal in Anian history."

"*Get it, girl! You tell him!*" interrupted Mr. Freeman, cheering from the room.

Colonel Schwarz's sigh flowed from the very core of his being, erupting forth with the slow-moving inevitability of magma cascading down a mountainside. It followed him as he walked back behind the great SimuWood desk, continuing as he slumped into his chair and through until his head thumped softly on the top of the desk.

"Good work, inspector," he announced without lifting his face from the desk. He waved her away with a sweep of his hand. "You may go now."

Sarah suppressed a smile. Now was not the time to get cheeky.

"Yes, sir," she said, spinning on her heel and heading for the door.

"It appears I was wrong about you," he remarked drolly from his spot on the desk. "There appears to be no limit to your talents."

Sarah paused as she drew open the door.

"Oh, they exist, sir," she said, a smile stretching across her face. "I just haven't reached them yet."

She caught up with Ian in the garage of Command Central.

"Wait!" she called out, rushing through the swinging doors and into the cool darkness of the garage.

Ian stopped halfway to a LITCAT parked haphazardly over the double yellow lines. Terrance was just ahead, standing on the running board with one hand on the door to the truck's cab.

"I'm sorry," she said as she ran over to meet them. "I did what I could to bid for clemency. I thought it would carry a lot further than it did." She stopped just before them, her head and shoulders drooping as she spoke. "I'm sorry I couldn't do more to help."

"Don't be," Ian said, reaching a hand out to her shoulder. "You heard the Baron, I was looking at a dishonorable discharge without your help. Besides, Sue's due for tenure soon, so we won't hurt too bad for money, and I can plea my case for the letter's removal from my record in two years." He smiled at her as she lifted her head. "We did it though, right? Solved the case, keep this from happening to anyone else?"

"Right," Sarah nodded. "We put a bad guy behind bars, sometimes that's enough." A half-smile crept over her face. "And if you need a character letter when you plea your case..."

"I know just who to call," Ian finished for her.

"I just wanna know why nobody talked about *my* contributions to the case," Terrance called out from the step of the truck. He jabbed a thumb into his chest. "Instead everyone's acting like I'm some kinda terrible fuckin' influence or something."

Sarah laughed while Ian shook his head.

"You know, Bernard," she said, getting serious once again. "You make a damn good detective. When you rotate home from your tour here, I hope you'll consider a job in the ISC. I might know someone that can fast-track your application."

"Don't do me any favors," Ian said with a smile. "But I'd like that."

"C'mon, *number two*," Terrance shouted from the truck. "We're already late for work."

Ian shrugged. "In the meantime though, I guess I've got to keep the dance moving."

Sarah put her hand out for him to shake. "Goodbye, Buck-Sergeant. I hope to see you again."

He took her hand in his. "Goodbye, inspector. I know you will."

And with that she watched him go, shuffling over to the light work truck. As she turned back to the swinging doors, she saw him elbow Terrance out of the way as he climbed up the running board.

"Move over," she heard him say. "*I'm* driving."

Epilogue:

The suns set low on the Cerulian farm, the twin stars turning the clear skies amber behind the silvery treetops. Sergeant Harbison sat in a wrought-iron deck chair, savoring the crisp, cool air.

"How're you settling into the new house?" he asked, watching the suns sink behind the grove of trees.

"Good," Bella Corstley said, reaching over to refill his glass from her pitcher of sweet tea. "Tommy and Renee still miss the house on Tamarin, but this place is much bigger." She sighed a little at the memory of their old farmhouse, nestled at the crook of two rivers. She shook her head, banishing the rude memory away. "But anyway, you just can't beat a Cerulian sunset."

"No, ma'am," Sergeant Harbison agreed, taking a sip from his glass. "You sure can't."

He turned his head away from the ochre skies, flinty grey eyes shifting to Mrs. Corstley. "Did they unpack everything for you? Get everything where you wanted it?"

"Oh... yes," Bella said, hesitating a little before she spoke.

The Reed-Sergeant watched the shake in the young woman's hands. He reached out his own to comfort her, folding his leathery hands over hers.

"It's just so hard," she sniffed, the trembling in her hands moving up to her chin. "They came in and took the house, took the truck, and they were saying such horrible things about Hermes."

"There, there," he soothed, holding her hands tight in his own. "Don't listen to them. Corstley did a good thing. A noble thing. He sacrificed himself to take care of his unit."

He drew a kerchief from his pocket, drying her eyes as he lifted her chin to look at him.

"They gave him twenty-two years," he said, speaking with calming authority. "That means he'll be eligible for parole review in ten, out in eleven with good behavior. And we'll see to that." He folded the kerchief gently, tucking it back into his pocket. "In the meantime, though, we'll take care of you. Corstley did right by us, I'll make sure we do right by him."

Bella nodded, mustering up a smile. She dabbed her eyes with the corner of her apron.

"What about the kids?" Sergeant Harbison asked. "How are they liking Cooley Academy?"

"It's great," Bella said with a laugh, a fresh tear rolling down her cheek. "More than we could hope for. We can't thank you enough, the waiting list was so long when we got here—

The Reed-Sergeant cut her off with a wave of his hand. "We take care of our own. That includes their own too."

Bella nodded, getting up to refill his glass one more time.

Sergeant Harbison took another drink, downing half the glass with a satisfied gasp. "That's the best sweet tea I've had in far too long."

Mrs. Corstley blushed. "Thanks, it's the last of the crop we had on Tamarin. I'm hoping to get the hydroponics set up again next month."

"Well, if you need any help," Sergeant Harbison offered, setting the glass back down on the table, "you know who to ask."

Bella reached for the pitcher, but he waved her off.

"This was lovely, ma'am, but I'm afraid I must be going." He stood up from the table, grabbing his hat and coat. "I'll stop in again from time to time, but for now I need to be in orbit in the next two hours. I have a ship to catch."

Bella nodded, swallowing hard as she cleaned up the glasses on the table. She watched the Reed-Sergeant leave down the road to the shuttle parked in the middle of the field. She found herself choking up a little as she watched him walk away, silhouetted against the fading suns. The last few weeks had been so hard, but the Raiders had been so kind, so thoughtful, so generous.

"God bless you, Barrett," she blurted out after him.

She saw him stop mid-step, turning back to her and tipping his cap. She wiped away another tear with the back of her hand, then busied herself with clearing the table.

Sergeant Harbison walked up the green-lit ramp of the DC-229, climbing aboard the narrow shuttle and finding his seat along the far wall. He sat down and buckled the nylon straps, ignoring the creak and protest of his aging joints. He had a lot on his mind as he headed for his new assignment with the 2nd Raiders Group. Anius was done. He'd liquidated their operation as soon as the investigation had wrapped up. It was too hot there, too many eyes scrutinizing him and his men. He'd applied for transfer the day after Sergeant Corstley confessed, organizing similar arrangements for everyone involved in their mission there. He spaced out their orders over eight months, covering his tracks just in case anyone was still watching their movements. He was sure they weren't, but still, it paid to be paranoid.

He was heading to the 2nd Raiders, in high orbit around Pyontun aboard the ICF *Olivier*. It was going to be a long trip, no deep-jet runs this time. But that was fine—he had plenty of stops to make along the way. He had to re-establish contact with his suppliers, suss out new distributors, and plan out a half-dozen missions in between. He had an enterprise to run.

Sergeant Harbison tapped his foot as the shuttle door closed, counting down the seconds until they launched.

A Raiders' work is never done.

**ENJOY OTHER STORIES FROM THE
INTER-STELLAR COALITION
FORCE!**

For the troopers of AZH-01, life is an exercise in routines.

Wake up, respond to alarms, stand in formation—slack off in between. Get your gear, don't break scram-time, and stay out of Sergeant's crosshairs. Securing the edges of populated space isn't the glory and excitement they were promised, but these aren't the Inter-Stellar Coalition Force's best and brightest.

Rania doesn't mind routines. Routines give her something to hold on to, they guide her as she finds her niche in the sweaty locker room of military life. Just like the other troopers, all she wants is to do her job, stay out of trouble, and get one day closer to getting out. That routine is shattered when something claws its way through the station's doors. Something swift. Vicious. *Hungry.* With the chain of command shredded and the power knocked out, it's a race against time for Rania and the other troopers of AZH-01.

They were just trying to get through the day, now they're fighting to survive the night.